PAMELA MORSI

Mr. Right Goes Wrong

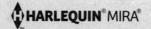

HARLEQUIN® MIRA®

Recycling programs
for this product may
not exist in your area.

ISBN-13: 978-0-7783-1649-7

MR. RIGHT GOES WRONG

Printed in U.S.A.

www.Harlequin.com

For my niece, Kerry, who knows how to pick 'em.

And my nephew, Steven, who is somebody's Mr. Right.

Mr. Right Goes Wrong

1

For her seventh birthday, Mazy Gulliver got a Play Bride set that included a white veil, a plastic bouquet and a rhinestone ring. She immediately organized a wedding celebration under the basketball goal where she married Termy Latham, the boy next door. An argument could be made that the incident was merely the first in a long series of hasty, ill-conceived and unwise decisions about men.

For the most part she'd managed to live over her mistakes. Or at least live with them. But this latest was more than boneheaded heartbreak, it was life-altering.

Which was exactly why she found herself moving back into her mother's tiny home in Brandt Mountain, North Carolina. It was a life alteration not particularly welcome.

Brandt Mountain in early October was already showing some autumn color, which couldn't quite overcome the steel-gray sky overhead. It was a sharp contrast to the balmy temperatures she'd left in Wilmington. She'd walked on the beach that morning at dawn, just to say goodbye. The place had some very bad memories for her now, but the roar of the ocean wasn't one of them. There was something about the way the tide could obliterate the footprints in the sand that gave her hope in a new beginning even if it was far from that shore.

Beside her in this relocation, both literally and figuratively, was her fourteen-year-old son. Tru sat silently, watching Main Street go by through the passenger's window. He was tall for his age. Tall for the compact rental car. By necessity his knees were folded up and pressing against the glove box. He was undoubtedly uncomfortable. But he said nothing. Mazy tried to kid herself that he was becoming the strong-and-silent type. But she knew more likely it was an aversion to her conversation.

Maybe there was simply nothing left to say.

She turned left on Sawmill Road. The narrow street, with its vintage cracked and overgrown sidewalk, was as familiar to her as the memories it evoked. Skipping off to school. Rushing home after a basketball game. Sneaking out in the middle of the night.

Two long blocks down the hill, set back from the street, was the house she'd grown up in. The paint on the clapboards was faded and peeling, one of the porch posts listed slightly to the right, but otherwise it was the same home of her childhood. The place her parents had called their "little love nest."

Mazy hardly pulled into the driveway before spotting her mother. Giddy with excitement, Beth Ann—as Mazy had called her for more than a decade—hurried down from the front porch to greet them.

"Hello! Hello! Hello!" she called out as she eagerly waved the pressed hanky that she always carried. Mazy thought it might easily have been mistaken as a flag of surrender.

"You're here. You're finally here. It's been too long since I've hugged my boy," she declared. "Way too long!"

Whether the boy in question actually heard her words was uncertain. He had not removed his earbuds since Greensboro. But by the time Mazy had gotten out and walked around the car, Tru had unfolded his long legs out of the vehicle and enfolded his arms around his grand-mother.

"Hey, Gram," he said, smiling at the older woman as if he were actually glad to see her. It was a stark contrast from the angry silent treatment he'd been giving his mother for the past three days. Mazy took a bright spot wherever she could get one.

"You are so tall," Beth Ann told him. "It almost hurts my neck to look up at you."

He shrugged and smiled. "I'm only six-one," he assured her.

Next to the tiny woman, he did look gigantic. Mazy was a very medium five-seven, but taller than both her parents. Her son's height obviously had not come from their side of the family.

"You need some meat on those long limbs," Beth Ann told him. "What do you like to eat?"

"Anything," Tru replied. "Everything."

"That's exactly what I've got," his grandmother promised him.

Beth Ann offered a weary, long-suffering smile as she came to hug her daughter, as well.

"You could use a little meat on your bones, too," she said. "It's good to have you home."

The first statement was probably true. Mazy had lost some weight during the past few stressful months. But there was nothing good about having her home. Her mother was eking through her senior years on a cheerful smile and a pittance of a social security check. Two more mouths to feed would be more than a struggle. It could be a disaster.

"I should be able to get a job," Mazy told her.

Her mother nodded. "There's always a job for a smart girl who's willing to work hard."

The words had been her father's. Having her mother quote them now was her attempt to be reassuring, but Mazy feared that the fallacy of the statement was the conviction that she was a "smart girl." Bright and intelligent did not, apparently, always add up to that definition.

She opened the car's trunk and began unloading their pitiful suitcases and cardboard boxes. Apparently their entire lives could be crammed into the measly storage space of a tiny rental car, which didn't say much for what she'd accomplished over the years. But it wasn't wise to contemplate all that right now. Mazy had things to do, tasks to perform. Keeping busy wasn't merely a good idea. It was essential if she were going to shovel her son and herself out of the dirty, dumb ditch she'd managed to dig.

"Where's the rest of your things?" her mother asked, coming up behind her.

"She sold it all," Tru answered before Mazy had a chance to explain. There was no resentment in his voice, only fatalism. That worried her more than his anger.

"We owed everybody," Mazy said by way of explanation. "I couldn't…I couldn't just walk away from that."

Her mother smiled bravely. "Of course not," she agreed. "Come on in the house, it's too chilly to stand out here in your shirtsleeves."

With Tru's help, it only took a couple of trips to carry their belongings inside. Beth Ann's home was welcomingly warm in the chill of the autumn air. And the smell of her mother's marinara sauce simmering on the stove brought back memories that were, for Mazy, mostly good. Once upon a time she had been happy here. *They* had been happy here. Her father had been a lineman for Rural Electric. Her mother did Prayer Partners and Ladies Aid at the church. They had laughed and loved and cherished their only child, a pretty, healthy, clever little girl. They'd held dreams for her that included state college, a promising career and a happy family all her own.

Mazy had not been able to pull off any of those dreams. But she was determined that she would change. She was determined that Tru would learn to feel safe and settled as she once had. He deserved that.

She gave her son the back bedroom that had been her own. If he noticed the girlie white bedroom furniture or the frilly edges to the pink-and-lavender bedspread, he made no comment. But then, he wasn't really speaking to her. He threw himself diagonally across the bed, his giant sneaker-covered feet hanging off the side. His hair, a sandy blond, was a little too long. And his typical summer freckles had yet to fade. His earbuds were in again and he was looking at the device in his hands.

"You should probably unpack," she told him.

He mumbled something unintelligible. Mazy supposed that was an improvement over complete stonewalling. She tried to be annoyed, but she couldn't manage it. All she wanted was to wrap him in her arms again and tell him that she was sorry. But she'd already done that. She'd done it too many times. After a while she knew it was more for her comfort than for his.

In her mom's room Mazy hung her meager collection of business suits in the closet. If she got a job—*no,* she corrected herself, *when* she got a job—she'd need clothes.

"Why do you always wear such drab colors?" her mother asked from the doorway.

Mazy shrugged. "I'm an accounting clerk," she answered. "We're supposed to look boring."

"Wearing something brighter always makes me feel more cheerful."

Beth Ann's color wheel was a serious mix of hot pinks and bright yellows.

"In my last job I wore neon-orange every day—it didn't cheer me up a bit."

Her mother didn't find anything funny in the joke. "Dinner should be ready in fifteen minutes. I'm sure you must be hungry."

In truth, Mazy had no interest in food at all. "Tru will be," she assured her. "He eats constantly. But I don't want you to think you have to cook for us."

The older woman waved away her objection. "I'm happy to do it. It's easier to cook for a family than it is for myself."

Mazy was pretty sure that wasn't true, but she didn't say so.

"It will be such fun having you home," her mother added. "Much better than rattling around on my own."

The tiny two-bedroom cottage had very little "rattling around" room. With two adult women and a teenager with feet the size of Kentucky, the place was going to be bulging at the seams.

"I don't know how long I'll need to be here," Mazy admitted. "But Tru and I are determined to cause you as little trouble as we can."

"You are no trouble," Beth Ann replied. "I have missed you so much. And now it will be like our own slumber party."

"I'm not going to sleep in here," Mazy told her, indicating the four-poster double bed that her parents had once shared. "You know how restless I am. I'll be fine out on the couch."

"Are you sure? That thing is awfully old and lumpy."

"I love that couch," Mazy said. "I think Tru was conceived on that couch."

"He certainly was not!" she responded with a gasp.

Mazy laughed lightly. She was teasing, of course, and she thought a bit of humor might be welcome in the situation.

Her mother shook her head, but couldn't resist a chuckle as she wagged a threatening finger at her daughter.

"You are not so grown up, young lady, that I won't stand you in the corner for a time-out."

"Mom, if I thought it would do me any good, I'd volunteer."

2

Eli Latham ran his hand lovingly along a long piece of prime poplar. Then he raised it to eye level and looked down the length of its grain. Poplar was a very undervalued wood. Straight grained, sturdy and lightweight, it was easy to work and could always do the job it was asked to do. But no matter how long you aged it, it always looked kind of green. It didn't take a stain well, it was almost impossible to pretty it up. The best thing was to paint it or hide it under a veneer.

That was Eli's plan. He'd use the poplar for its best qualities and then cover it up with a thin layer of fancier wood. Typically his customers didn't want veneers, the style had gotten a bad reputation from shoddy work. But the music department at the museum was more interested in the function of their sheet music cabinet and had left the aesthetics to him. The sheer size of it would have made the cost prohibitive in solid wood and the weight would have been impractical. He had come up with a unique design that was both beautiful and serviceable. Both the curator and her patrons would be very satisfied. He was always harder to please than his customers were.

He stacked the board with the others he'd chosen on a rack shelf that lined the west side of the building. Bringing the wood inside a few days before he began a project allowed it to acclimate to less variable temperatures of being indoors. Cut lumber was no longer living, in the accepted sense of that term, but it continued to expand and contract with heating and cooling. It was one of the earth's most efficient systems for carbon storage. It was also beautiful. And Eli had a gift for making it even more so.

"Do you want me to plane that?"

The question came from his brother, Clark.

"Nah, let's let it sit here a couple of days," he answered.

Clark should have known that, of course. He was almost four years older than Eli and had been a hand at Latham Furniture longer than he had. But Clark had never had the interest. He'd never had the vision. It was Eli who was the company now and his older brother worked for him.

"Why don't you sand the Windsors," he suggested.

The six chairs taking up way too much space on the floor were already looking very good covered with the combination of tung and linseed oil. But by using superfine grit to rough them up, the color would penetrate deeper and they could take more coats.

The eleven-hundred-square-foot building boasted both an abundance of natural light and plenty of overhead electricity. The workshop's back corner, mostly used as an office now, was built of hewn logs by his great-grandfather, the original Elias Latham. The rest of the building had been raised by his dad and granddad in the 1970s when the company had contracted with a national furniture chain for nice profits and a line of Shaker-style tables. But the chain now bought their Shaker-style from Asia, and Latham Furniture had gone back to handmade custom pieces and a modest living for the craftsmen's current generation. That suited Eli better, anyway. He didn't mind making the same piece over and over, if he could strive for perfection or improve it slightly every time. But he could never have been happy with assembly-line production.

"Man, I'm getting hungry," Clark commented. "I hate it when we have sandwiches for lunch. It doesn't stay with me."

The paunch around his brother's midsection said differently, but Eli didn't bother to say so. Happily married and a victim of his wife's great cooking, Clark had put on a lot of pounds in the past few years. Woodworking was good exercise for shoulder and biceps, even legs and thighs. But it was no help for his brother's beer gut. And allowing his hair and beard to grow down to his waist did not serve to disguise it.

"The customers expect us to look like hillbilly hayseeds," he often said. "We could probably raise prices if I'd knock my front teeth out to complete the picture."

Eli didn't agree. Or at least he didn't agree completely. Marketing certainly sold furniture. But he wanted to fashion the kind of pieces that sold themselves.

And he preferred to look ordinary.

That's how people thought of him. That was how he thought of himself. He was medium build, not tall but not short, with a face that was, to his mind, fairly average. His hair and eyes both unmemorably brown. His demeanor was calm and his opinions carefully considered. He'd always been soft-spoken and unassuming. So much so that it had startled his high school classmates when he'd been named valedictorian. Even today, if most were asked to list the most successful businessmen in town, Eli's name would not have come up. He didn't mind. Fading into the wallpaper was a plus for anyone engaged in a solitary vocation. Not being noticed had never bothered him. Or rather, it almost never bothered him.

"I guess you heard that Mazy Gulliver is home," his brother said with such studied nonchalance that it had to be faked.

Eli was eyeing another piece of poplar that momentarily trembled in his hands.

"I heard."

"Sheila says she knew we'd see her again as soon as Tad and Genna split the sheet."

Eli gave a dismissive huff. "Not likely. Your wife must be getting really bored, Clark, if she's dredging up gossip that old. Mazy and Tad were fifteen years ago. Can't see that starting up again."

"Probably not," he agreed. "I just don't want anybody else getting ideas about her."

The silence within the building was not lengthy, but it was intense.

"I don't know what you're talking about," Eli replied.

Clark made a clicking sound and shook his head. "This is me you're talking to, Termite," he said. "I know you always get your hopes up. I can't stand to see you get your heart broken."

Eli shook his head. "Don't worry about me," he told him. "And don't call me Termite. I'm not three anymore."

"Hey, you'll always be my kid brother no matter how old you get," Clark told him. "And I know, just as sure as I'm alive, that she'll come crawling over here, looking at you with those big brown eyes. Don't fall for her again. That woman is not for you."

Eli gave a huff of dismissal. "Trust me, I know that," he said. "Mazy's been out of my league since middle school."

"Out of your league? That crazy psychochick would

need an extension ladder and a hot-air balloon to even get close to your league."

"She's not a psychochick. She's…she's just kind of mixed up."

"Mixed up is what people are in high school," Clark said. "When you get past thirty, that definition slides into crazy."

Eli waved off his words. "Neither of us have talked to her in years. For all we know, she's a staid, solid citizen these days."

"Not likely," Clark said. "Mazy is one of these people that no matter what the options are, she's going to choose wrong."

"Ah, come on, Clark. That's not fair."

"Maybe. Maybe not," his brother said. "But I do know that she is never going to give you a second look."

"Isn't that what I just said? She's out of my league."

"Not that," Clark answered, stopping his work to stand thoughtfully. "It's that you're too decent a guy."

"What?"

"She's one of those women who wants a jerk."

Eli tossed another board onto the rack.

"That's nuts."

"You're right. It is. But some women are just that way. For some reason they're just attracted to the creeps of this world. The only men they fall for are the ones who are going to treat them like dirt. They can't stop themselves. Gangsters, outlaws, cheaters and beaters—they are always surrounded by women. It's nice guys like you that never get noticed."

Eli shook his head. "Obviously there are men who treat women badly, but it's not like the women want it that way."

"You could sure fool me," Clark said. "Given a choice, some women always choose the son of a bitch."

Eli knew it was true, but he didn't like to imagine it. He really didn't like to imagine it about Mazy.

"From what I've seen of her," Clark continued, "she must love the drama. Roller coaster relationships can be a thrill. And thrill is something people get addicted to."

Eli shook his head. "How 'thrilling' can it be to have a guy walk all over you?"

"Hey, if he's tough, confident, domineering—that can be mistaken for being a *real* man. Especially when a woman has daddy issues."

"Mazy doesn't have daddy issues," Eli said. "She loved her dad. He was a great guy."

Clark nodded. "A great guy killed in a freak accident. One day he's there, the next day he's not. Perfect recipe for screwed-up psychochick."

Eli rolled his eyes. His brother meant well, he knew, but Clark had always been the sort of guy who was quick to judge. Eli tried to give people the benefit of the doubt. "Mazy is not a psychochick. Anyway, that's just a stereotype. She's made some mistakes in the past, but that's the past. People change, Clark."

His brother looked skeptical. "I guess we'll see," he said. "I do believe that all of us get smarter about stuff, get more mature. But our basic personality is the same as it always was. If she wanted a jerk in high school, she wants one now. I mean, why do you think she picked someone like Tad over you?"

Eli chuckled. "Oh, wow, I dunno," he said facetiously. "Taking a stab at it, I'm thinking it could be that he was the high school hero, captain of the basketball team, class president, tall, good-looking and rich. I'm just guessing, of course."

Clark shook a finger at him. "But he was also going steady with somebody else. He was totally unavailable to her. And he didn't even try to pretend otherwise. He never dated Mazy, never took her any place, never acknowledged her in public. As far as I know, he didn't so much as buy her a burger."

Eli couldn't dispute that.

"So what does Mazy do?" Clark asked rhetorically. "She gives it up for him. He honks his car horn at the top of the hill and she sneaks out of her house to show him a good time. While you're right here next door, her best friend, the nice guy, practically falling on your face to worship her, and you can't get the time of day."

Eli shrugged. "I was a year behind her. That's an incredible age gap in high school."

"Yeah, well, it wasn't quite so big after you graduated and she got bored with diapering her baby," Clark pointed out. "You two weren't exactly secretive. Humping like rabbits every chance you got."

"Teenagers are like that."

"Okay, that accounts for round one," Clark said. "What about when she turns up like a bad penny a few years later? You were all into curing her heartache and getting her back on her feet. You were all starry-eyed, thinking happily-ever-after, and she goes running off with the first creep that crooks his finger at her."

"We weren't *really* a couple," Eli defended. "It was a friends-with-benefits thing, and when it was over, it was over."

Clark gave a huff of disbelief. "Yeah, right. It meant nothing to you. The hangdog look and black mood that went on for months, it was a coincidence."

Eli could hardly argue with that. He'd been devastated when she'd dropped him. She'd been positively gushing about the vacuum cleaner salesman from Charlotte. He'd felt like he'd been kicked in the gut.

"Okay, so maybe I got in over my head," he admitted. "But that was my fault, not hers. She was clear from the first that we were just best friends."

"Yeah, well, I'm more than your best friend, I'm your brother," Clark said. "And I'm warning you right now. She's never going to want more from you than a temporary distraction."

His brother was probably right. Mazy had never been able to see him as anybody but her childhood playmate. Eli didn't think he could bear to be put through the ringer again. It was never going to work out between them, despite how drawn to her he was. Steering clear was good advice. He might have taken it, too, if his brother hadn't added one more thought.

"The only way you could ever get Mazy Gulliver interested is if you start walking all over her like bubble gum on a shoe."

3

Everything was different and nothing had changed. Cliché and contradictory, but it summed up Mazy's first day back in Brandt Mountain.

This morning she would be going with Tru to enroll him in school. She had done this chore many times and openly speculated about that number over breakfast.

"So this will be your fourth new school."

"Fifth," Tru corrected. He was eating the pancakes that Beth Ann had fixed him. He didn't even look up. "Freshman year and I'm already in my second high school."

"But you spent all of middle school at Roland-Grise."

"Yeah," he agreed, looking up at her finally. "All my friends were there. Now all my friends are at Hoggard and I'm…here."

It was not a new subject of discussion for them. Mazy wasn't about to get into it again this morning.

"You'll make new friends," she told him.

He rolled his eyes, but she left the room pretending that she didn't notice. Making an issue of some justified insubordination seemed like a stupid thing to do. He had apparently given up the silent treatment. Mazy was going to take her victories wherever she could find them.

They were not in her mirror, however. In the tiny bathroom featuring the same bad lighting that had bugged her in high school, she eyed herself with dissatisfaction. The blond highlights that she'd worn for a decade had disappeared in an overgrowth of brunette, which might have been okay if she wasn't still using the makeup from the lighter era. There was no money to waste on self-adornment—she'd even discovered that she could cut her own hair using her jawline for a guide. It was certainly not the best she'd ever looked, and she hated to give the homefolks the satisfaction of being able to say so, but it couldn't be helped. And it was the very least of her problems. Gamely, she brushed her teeth, put on her lipstick and held her head high.

Still driving her rental car, she and Tru pulled up in front of the high school at 8:02 a.m. Nobody had to tell her that it was better to show up late than to walk through the social gauntlet of students waiting for the bell to ring.

Her son looked deliberately nonchalant. Not smiling, not curious, totally teen. His jeans hung only slightly lower than God had intended and his hoodie featured a digital game that was both geeky and gory.

He'll do fine, Mazy reassured herself for the millionth time.

Tru was smart, likable and resilient. He would definitely find a place for himself.

On the glass front door of the school, someone had painted a fierce-looking insect in black and gold.

"They're bees?" Tru asked, incredulous. "The mascot is a bee?"

"That's Buzz," Mazy told him. "Bees can be very dangerous. Fatal if you're allergic."

"I think I'm allergic," her son said.

She shot him a look and got the first smile aimed in her direction for weeks.

Having been there on many occasions, Mazy walked

directly to the admin office. The furniture was newer and the puke-green paint she remembered from her youth had been replaced with a more Zenlike blue, but it was exactly the same atmosphere.

She walked up to the counter where a slightly plump woman with a curly perm grinned at her excitedly.

"Hello, I'm here to enroll my son in school."

"Mazy! Mazy! It's me. Don't you recognize me? Karly Wilkins, Karly Farris now. You haven't changed a bit."

Mazy tried a half smile, her brain scrambling through a million dusty memory files to try to recall the person in front of her. She would have testified in court that she'd never seen the woman before.

"Karly Wilkins," she repeated eagerly. "Remember, we were home-ec partners for Breads and Pastries."

Mazy did remember. The shy girl with the bad clothes that nobody wanted to befriend. She and Mazy had been paired together as class pariahs.

"Oh, sure, I remember," Mazy said. "You literally pulled my biscuits out of the oven."

The woman laughed. "I still bake those little sailor knots for my kids from time to time," she told her. "So, is this your boy?"

Tru was slouching, looked uncomfortable.

"Yes," Mazy answered, setting his transcript and old class schedule on the counter. "Truman Gulliver."

"Coach Keene is going to want to get a look at you," Karly told him, her smile friendly and enthusiastic.

"Me?"

"I bet you play basketball, don't ya."

"Basketball? Uh, no."

Karly looked genuinely surprised, but then glanced guiltily at Mazy.

"Are you sure?"

Tru kind of snorted at the question. "Well, yeah, I can play basketball. But I'm on the swim team in my school. I mean, my last school."

"Oh, we don't have a pool," Karly said. "And I guess we all thought you'd play basketball."

It was like a secret code and Mazy wasn't ready for her son to be in on it. She intervened.

"As his mom, I'm more interested in his algebra than his athletics."

"Oh, oh, of course," Karly said, a bit more brightly than necessary. "Let's see what your class schedule looks like."

It took less than twenty minutes to get it all settled. Freshmen everywhere tended to take the same courses, and with no credits to match up, Tru was almost a high school blank slate.

As she watched him walk down the hall, being shown to his classroom by a fellow student, she had to resist the impulse to run after him and drag him out of the building. She had never kept secrets from her son. She was not a keeping-secrets kind of gal, and her son had always been told the truth. But knowing something was quite different from having everyone around you know it, too.

It couldn't be helped. She kept thinking that there had to be a statute of limitations on screwing up your life, but apparently not. Especially since she managed to do it again and again.

She returned her car to the rental place on the highway where it Y-ed off to Main Street. The walk to the town center was more than a mile and she hadn't worn her most sensible shoes, but in her experience a gutsy gambit required the highest, most uncomfortable nonsensible heels. And hitting up your ex for a job was about as gutsy as it gets. With her chin up, her outlook determined, she made her way along the cracked, uneven sidewalks. It was hard to imagine a course of action more humiliating than her current one, and she refused to anticipate the outcome. If the past months had taught her anything, it was to allow the chips to fall. Nothing could fit into place until they did.

Brandt Mountain was wide-awake. There were people coming and going. Mazy tried not to make eye contact. She didn't want to have to make polite conversation. A place where everybody knows your name is not always a good thing.

The town's tiny commercial hub was only a few blocks long. The buildings were mostly early twentieth century, with an occasional throwback to eras perhaps a hundred years earlier. A line of cars fronted the diner and the shops were beginning to open. The store windows featured antiques and flower displays and vintage clothing. A plumbing shop showed off several toilet models. The bookstore boasted a sale of used paperbacks for fifty cents.

Mazy walked past each one as she headed up the hill to where Main Street crossed Depot Road. On that corner, in a four-story building trimmed in gray granite and white marble, was the Farmers and Tradesmen State Bank.

Mazy hesitated for an instant and then, as if she might lose her nerve completely, she jerked the door open and stepped inside. The cool, quiet foyer revealed a line of old-fashioned tellers' windows with their bars still in place. Only one was occupied and the woman standing there looked familiar. But in her hometown, almost everybody did.

"I'd like to speak to Mr. Driscoll, please."

The woman literally looked down her nose at her. "Honey, he's kind of busy. Do you have an appointment?"

Mazy stood at her full height and smiled the biggest, fakest sugar smile ever. "No, honey, I don't. But you run and tell him Mazy Gulliver is here. All right?"

The teller didn't run, she actually used her phone before suggesting that Mazy have a seat in the waiting area.

Perching on the edge of a too-cushy sofa, she silently went through her practiced spiel. She would have to confess everything. But she would not cower.

She heard the footfall of someone approaching across the marble floor, but she did not turn her head until he was standing beside her.

"Mazy?"

"Tad."

The years had not been unkind to him. He still had that athletic build, though perhaps a bit softer than in his youth. He was tall, with the same sandy-brown hair she remembered. It had started to gray, but even that leaned to his rather attractive, sophisticated appeal. He was wearing glasses, which was totally new, but she could still see the pale blue eyes that were so familiar.

"Step into my office, please."

His words were crisp and cold. Despite the polite verbiage, it was not a request. It was an order.

She followed him to the front corner office. He went in first and held the door for her. Once she was inside he closed it sharply behind her.

"What the hell are you doing here?"

"I need to talk to you."

"I've got nothing to say to you, Mazy. And if I did, this would not be the place to say it. This is my place of business."

"I know that," she told him, willing her voice not to

tremble. "I'm here on a matter of business. May I sit down?"

He glared at her for a long moment and then, without answering, walked behind his desk and seated himself.

Mazy accepted that as a *yes* and took the chair across from him. She opened her briefcase and retrieved a three-page item stapled together. She set it upon the desk in front of him.

"What's this?" he asked without bothering to look at it.

"My résumé."

"Your résumé?"

"I'm back in town and I'm looking for a job," she told him. "I have an associate degree in accounting from King's College and another thirty-four hours at UNC Wilmington toward a bachelor's. I have six years of increasing experience, moving from accounts receivable to bookkeeper to head of accounting at a small independent company."

She had the satisfaction of seeing his eyebrows go up.

"I am very good at what I do," Mazy continued. "I can be an asset to any organization that hires me. I'm here today to give you that opportunity."

Tad continued to look at her for a long moment and then chuckled. "Well, you've really developed some balls, Mazy. I'll say that for you."

"Fourteen years is a long time," she pointed out.

He nodded. "It is," he conceded. "But it's not. Not long enough in Brandt Mountain. If your résumé is as good as you say, you're sure to be able to find a job somewhere. But not working for me. It wouldn't look right. I don't even know why you would want it."

"I don't," Mazy answered. "But I'm not sure I have any other choice."

His brow furrowed at that.

"There was some trouble at my last job," she said evenly.

"Trouble?"

It was a euphemistic term.

"The company was a family business, privately held. The CEO was the son-in-law of the founder, but wanted to leave his wife. He began stashing money off the books for his getaway. I discovered it and I covered for him."

Tad's jaw dropped.

"We were caught, of course. And I was compelled to testify against him in court. I pled guilty to conspiracy. I did four hundred hours of community service. And I owe fifteen thousand dollars in restitution."

"My God, Mazy! Talk about screwing up your life. What were you thinking?"

She didn't answer that. There was some nakedness that even she could not bear.

"I'm trusting you with these facts," she continued, "because, as my employer, it will not be in your best interest to spread the story around."

"Your employer?" Tad gave a humorless chuckle. "Mazy, I can't possibly hire you. Even if it wasn't awkward on a personal level, I'm a banker. We don't hire felons."

"Technically, the charge was lowered to misdemeanor. I know that I'll never be a CPA now, but I can work at what I know. I simply need to get another job on my résumé. One with no trouble and a good recommendation. I just need a few years to reestablish myself and I can move on from this. The problem, of course, is that no one wants to be the employer that took that chance."

"I'm sure they don't. I certainly don't."

"But you see, Tad, you're going to have to."

"Excuse me?"

Pamela Morsi

"I have to have a job. I wouldn't be asking if I weren't desperate. Desperate enough to utilize other measures to convince you to help me."

"I'm not sure I know what you mean," Tad told her. "I hope you're not offering me sexual favors, 'cause trust me, babe, I can get all that I want without having the headache of hiring somebody for it."

Mazy felt redness streaking her neck. She wished she could punch the guy in the nose, but she couldn't give herself the satisfaction. She needed him.

"I am not offering to sleep with you," she said. "Been there. Done that. I am offering you the opportunity, quietly and without any open embarrassment, to help me support your son."

Tad made a huff of disbelief and sat back in his oversize leather chair.

"I should have known you'd get back to that old story," he said. "Like I told you fourteen years ago, that kid could be anybody's."

Mazy held on to her temper.

"Tad, I've got three letters for you. D.N.A. I am not the slightest bit worried about having such a test done. But you know how things like that get around town. It could be really embarrassing for you and Genna."

"Oh, so you think you can threaten me into this? Well, too bad for you. Genna and I are divorced. She and the girls have moved to Boone and she doesn't give a damn about what kind of gossip goes down in Brandt Mountain."

Mazy was surprised. Somehow she always imagined Tad as living happily-ever-after. Still, it meant nothing to her.

"Well, then," she said, giving him a very wide smile. "You must be very familiar with the concept of child support. I'm sure the state of North Carolina will be happy to grant me a stipend similar to the one you pay for your other children. That's the way these things are done, you know. Then, of course, there is the issue of fourteen years of nonsupport. Judges don't usually look kindly upon that. The whole deadbeat-dad thing. I'll take mine in a lump sum, please. Perhaps you can sell your house to get the cash together."

Tad's eyes were wide, his cheeks puffed out and his face so red it looked as if it might explode.

"Look," Mazy said more kindly. "I'm not here to punish you. It's all water under the bridge to me. My only interest is in the future. I need a way to support my son. I'm only going to be able to do that with a chance to start over. How much more convenient and inexpensive would it be for you to put me on the payroll instead of the hassle of court dates and child support payments? I'm not asking to be made vice president. All I need is an entry-level job, something to pay the bills and clean up my reputation."

Tad sat there looking at her. She was sure that if he were going to refuse, he would have done so immediately. The time ticked by. She refused to turn back the clock to that time so long ago when she loved him. She was determined to stay in the here and now. Tru's future was dependent upon that.

Finally he sighed. "Will you sign an agreement never to pursue me for child support?"

She nodded. "As long as I get to sign up on the payroll."

"I'll come up with something, then. Show up here tomorrow morning."

4

The celebratory mood over dinner at her mother's house was deliberate and slightly deceptive. Beth Ann had looked horrified at the news that Mazy was going to work for Tad. But she'd said nothing. Instead, she made a casserole and presented it with as much fanfare as could be managed with canned tuna and noodles.

At least Tru should be pleased, Mazy thought. But he was quiet and almost distracted over dinner. When his grandmother plied him with questions such as "How was school?" and "Did you make any friends?" his responses were polite, if noncommittal. But while she and her mother nervously picked at the meal, he managed to eat everything left on the table so Mazy knew that at least he wasn't ill.

After dinner he went to his room, and Mazy shooed her mother to her seat in front of the TV while she cleaned up. The encounter with Tad had taken a lot out of her. Dr. Reese, the psychologist she'd seen for her mandated court counseling, would have been proud of her for standing up to him. She was rather proud, herself.

But she was also exhausted by it and slightly deflated.

Once the last pan was dried and put away, the counters scrubbed down and the floor swept, Mazy lingered alone in the kitchen. She thought about her son. Her mom.

Her life. She wished she had somebody to talk to. She needed a friend.

As if by force of habit, her gaze turned to the window. There were lights on in the house next door. Did Eli still live there? They'd been buddies since childhood. They'd had that little fling before she left home. And then he'd been her rebound guy after another brush-off a few years later. But they could still be friends, couldn't they?

She'd found friendship to be a lot more durable than sex. And a lot harder to come by. A woman would be crazy to waste it.

She walked into the living room. And waited for a commercial to pose her question. "Termy Latham? I suppose he still lives next door with his parents."

Beth Ann looked up. "I don't know why you'd suppose that," she said. "That young man is quite a catch. Steady, trustworthy, hardworking—a lot of women find that very attractive."

"Yes, Beth Ann, we're all aware of your high regard for the boy next door," Mazy responded, tongue-in-cheek. "So he's living elsewhere with some lucky woman?"

"No, no," her mother answered. "He lives next door, but not with Jonah and Ida. He has his own apartment in the basement."

"Oh, wow," Mazy said. "So he's really come up in the world. Living in his parents' basement."

Her words were facetious, but they puffed her mother into defensive mode. Mazy waved away her indignation with a smile. "He's my best friend. I'm going over to say hi."

Night was already falling as she stepped outside. The brisk bite of autumn in the air was joined by a faint scent of wood smoke. It conjured up a warmth of nostalgia that was unexpected. The shrink had asked Mazy about her hometown. She remembered telling her that she hated the place, declaring that nothing good had ever happened to her there. But in a moment of honest self-reflection, she knew that wasn't so. There had been a lot of positive things in her life here. It was only when she'd let men get the best of her that things in Brandt Mountain had gone downhill.

The well-worn path between the back of the two houses was no longer in evidence, but Mazy could still see it in memory and followed it as if it was still tamped down by the constant back and forth of two busy children.

The workshop was locked and dark. As she came around the corner of the house, it was her intention to knock on the basement door. That proved to be unnecessary. Eli stepped out onto the little back porch, still shrugging into his jacket. His expression pensive, his gaze on the steps in front of him, he did not immediately notice her. Mazy had one long moment to observe him, unguarded. She was surprised at what she saw. He was a tall, well-built, attractive man. He had that look that always caught her attention. A man who exuded confidence and power was always so desirable. If she had not known him, she would have wanted to be introduced. She would have given him a flirty glance. Urged him to buy her a drink. She would have listened with apt interest to every word he said. Laughed at all his jokes. And made sure that he got a good look at her legs.

But she did know him. He was her Eli. And in that moment, he caught sight of her and his mouth curved into a familiar, welcoming smile. Here was the person who was supportive and safe and always on her side. She had to resist the temptation to run into his arms.

"Look at you," she said. "Still so cute, but all grown up."

His smile faltered, but only for an instant. "Hi, Mazy. Gosh, you look great. It's been a long time."

"It has. Too long," she said, feeling that truth. She hurried up the steps and gave him a sisterly smooch on the cheek. "How are you?"

"Great."

She couldn't resist wrapping her arms around his waist and hugging him tightly to her. She had missed him. It was nine years since she'd last seen him. Nine years since they had spoken. Why had she not bothered to keep up with him, to let him know where she was or who she was with? It wasn't lack of interest exactly. It was complicated. She had made their friendship complicated.

They stood together, looking at each other, basking in the familiarity and taking in the changes.

"I like your hair that color," he told her.

"Thanks, I decided to go natural," she answered.

"Natural suits you."

"So, Beth Ann says you're living in the basement now."

Eli nodded. "I was here checking on my dad."

"How's he doing?"

"You know he had a stroke?"

Mazy nodded. "Yeah, I'm so sorry, Termy. That's so tough for such an active guy."

"It is," he agreed. "Life is like that. Nothing stays the same."

"Well, at least you haven't changed," she said.

Eli's brow furrowed, but he managed a smile. "I've changed a lot."

"I don't believe it."

She said the words with laughter in her voice. He *had* changed, she could see that, but it felt good to tease him.

"I was barely legal last time you saw me," he said. "I'm thirty now. You can't expect me to be that guy you left."

The phrase *that guy you left* momentarily tugged at Mazy. She didn't remember exactly how it was between them when she'd broken it off. She hoped she'd been polite, at least. But she might not have been. Eli had always worn his heart on his sleeve. And he'd had a crush on her basically his whole life. Their affair probably meant more to him than it had to her.

But then she'd run into Marty Ellis. She was single-mindedly obtuse when she was in love. It was one of the many things about herself that she hoped to change. But back then she'd fallen totally, was in love desperately and behaving crazily. It had barely lasted two months. But it had gotten her to Charlotte. And put Eli back on the market.

"I didn't expect to come back and find you still single," Mazy said. "What the heck is wrong with the women in this town?"

Eli managed a wry smile and shrugged. "I guess I haven't met the right one," he said.

"You let me know if you need a reference," she teased. "I speak from experience. Most guys are heartbreakers. But you, you're a heart mender."

Mazy had been grateful for that. Eli had been the perfect rebound guy. Sympathetic. Easygoing. Always understanding. He had made her feel good about herself. And he'd made her feel great in the sack. But they had never let that get in the way of the real genuine feelings that they had for each other. She'd needed a friend and she knew him to be a great one.

How lucky was that?

Mazy seated herself on the second step and smiled up at him as she patted the space beside her. "Sit down,

Termy. I don't like having to strain my neck looking up at you."

His expression was a little strange. She couldn't quite read it. And instead of seating himself, he stepped down to the bottom of the steps and leaned against the railing. She could look straight at him, but somehow it wasn't the same.

Their conversation was casual.

He asked politely about Beth Ann and her drive up from Wilmington.

She reciprocated with questions about his dad and Ida.

He talked about owning the wood shop on his own.

She talked about Tru and being a mom.

"It's been so much fun watching him grow up," she told him. "In some ways it's like revisiting our own childhood. Of course, Tru has always been such a good boy, so it's probably more like your childhood than mine."

She laughed.

Eli didn't seem to find it as funny as she did.

"So how long are you going to be in town?" he asked her. "Are you between moves or are you back?"

Mazy hesitated. She had come over here to talk. Eli had always been a friend and it would feel wonderful to blurt out the whole sordid story. But in close proximity it was impossible not to notice how attractively masculine Eli was. She'd always thought he was nice-looking. He had wonderful, penetrating brown eyes. Nice body. Nice smile. But he'd been schoolboy sweet rather than hot. Now he was different. His movements were easy, graceful. He seemed bigger and more solid. She hadn't remembered the square jawline and the afternoon shadow. Listening to him talk, she found herself watching the movement of his lips.

There was something about those changes, that attraction, that caused her to hold back. He had always been her best friend, but tonight he appeared to be very much a man. And she was trying to learn not to be so eager to trust herself with the opposite gender.

"I think I'm here for a while," she said. "It's like I'm the bad penny that continually shows up."

"I wouldn't describe you as the bad penny," he said.

She smiled at him. "That's because you are kinder than the rest of us."

Eli's brow furrowed at the compliment. "No, I'm not any kinder than anyone else."

"Don't be silly," she said. "You're the sweetest guy ever. And you know me—I've sampled plenty of guys."

He didn't laugh at her self-disparagement.

"I just accepted a job this morning," she said, awkwardly trying to change the subject. "So I'm sort of celebrating being gainfully employed."

"Oh, Mazy, that's great," he said. "Where are you going to work?"

"At the bank."

"The bank?"

"Farmers and Tradesmen."

"Tad Driscoll's bank?"

People were going to wonder about that. People were going to gossip about that. Mazy knew it. Mazy expected it. She'd practiced a pat explanation, which she rolled out for Eli.

"Accounting is my field," she said. "I've been taking night classes for several years. It's the kind of work I like and that I'm good at. So banking is really a natural."

"But working for Driscoll?"

Mazy waved the question off as if it were trivial. "Tad and I get along fine," she lied. "All of that was a very long time ago."

Even to her own ears the excuse sounded fake.

Eli was looking very serious as he gathered his words.

"Are you hoping to get back with him?" The question was almost too quiet.

"Of course not," she assured him. "When I'm done with a man, I'm done. I never make the same mistake twice."

Eli's left eyebrow raised slightly. "The way I remember it, you and I were together twice."

Mazy almost answered, *But that wasn't a mistake!* Eli had never used her, never lied to her or betrayed her. It probably hadn't been smart to sleep with him, but she had a hard time regretting it. Even when she'd talked to the shrink, she'd never lumped Eli in with all the creeps and losers that made up her romantic history.

Unfortunately, the words that came out of her mouth weren't exactly how she meant them.

"Oh, Termy, you don't count."

5

——◆——

At exactly 10:00 a.m., Eli's phone alarm went off and he allowed himself to finish the measurements that he was working on and mark the cuts with a pencil. But then he wiped his hands and offered only an absent wave to Clark as he left the shop.

He walked up the path toward the house. It was wide and worn and packed down nearly as hard as concrete. The family home, a two-story "foursquare," had been built in the late 1880s. Keeping it in good repair was a labor of love for Eli. It was more than just a residence or a nice piece of American architecture, it was a symbol of the life that was important to him, the life that he wanted for himself.

At the back there were two doors. One where he could walk directly into the basement apartment where he lived, the other up three steps and across a small porch to his father's kitchen. He didn't even glance toward his place as he took the steps.

He knocked twice on the door, but went inside without waiting for a response. In the mudroom, he wiped his feet and hung up his jacket.

"It's me!" he called out.

"Morning, Eli," was the response.

Sunlight flooded the east side of the kitchen that was

clean enough, he suspected, to perform surgery. Sitting at the table peeling apples was his stepmother, Ida, formerly Miss Ida Jakes, local spinster.

When his mother had died ten years ago, after a long-suffering struggle with a debilitating disease, her sons had not been pleased at their father's hasty remarriage. Neither had been particularly welcoming to a woman who seemed to be a fussy and fastidious old maid. What could their father have seen in her?

It was no longer quite a mystery. The two had spent nearly a decade square dancing twice a week and flea marketing on the weekends. They were happy together, enjoying each other's company and making the most of their time, so it was hard for Clark or Eli to hold a grudge.

"How's Dad today?"

"His eyes are very bright this morning," she answered. "The man must have been up to no good in his dreams."

Eli smiled back, although it felt bittersweet.

"I'm going to fry up a batch of these apples for dinner. Do you want me to set some aside for you?"

Eli and Clark were agreed that Miss Ida was, unquestioningly, the worst cook in western North Carolina, but sometimes the taste of food was the least important aspect of an offer.

"I'd love that, Ida," he answered. "And I'm sure Clark would, too."

She tutted her head disapprovingly. "If your brother can't be bothered to walk up to the house to visit his father," she said, "then he can fix his own apples. Clark is just plain wrong leaving all his father's care to you."

Eli didn't dispute her assessment of the situation, but he wasn't about to be drawn into it, either.

"I won't tell him you said so," he assured her, teasing.

He'd heard it before. The inequitable share of responsibility bothered other people a lot more than it did Eli.

He went through the house to his mother's sewing parlor, which had been turned into a downstairs bedroom. His father lay on the bed looking very much like himself, only older, paler and quieter than the active man he'd once been.

"Hey, Dad," Eli said. "How are you doing today?" He gave his father a big, optimistic smile. "I've been working on a pretty piece of red oak this morning. You should see it. Looks real old-growth. Are you interested in getting cleaned up? Nothing more relaxing than a nice hot shower, right?"

Eli didn't wait for answers to his questions. He knew there wouldn't be any. His father's first stroke had made speaking difficult for him. With the second stroke a few months later it had disappeared completely.

The doorway to the nearby bathroom had been re-routed to open directly into the room. Eli quickly stepped inside and gathered up the towels, soaps and shaving gear that he needed before returning to his dad. He pulled his father up into a sitting position and knelt down to slide his house shoes onto his feet.

"I'm using the red oak for the top of a lowboy I've designed. You're going to love it. It's as if Stickley had an illegitimate oak son from Wales." Eli chuckled as his own little joke.

Squatting next to the bed, he draped his father's arms around his neck. Only one arm really worked well enough to give anything like a grasp, and it was weak. Eli clasped his dad around his pajama-clad waist and raised him into a standing position. Jonah Latham had once strode through his life with powerful grace. Now he could not even hobble to the bathroom on his own.

Eli kept up a steady stream of words as he partially led but mostly carried his dad into the shower.

"The color is nicely pinkish. I'm going to try to finish the grain as clear as it will varnish."

His father weighed so little these days that it would have been easier for Eli to simply hoist him up into his arms like a child. Eli didn't do that. Even if he couldn't say so, Eli knew Jonah would prefer to be treated like a man.

He seated his father in the plastic shower chair and buckled him in before going back to shut the door. Then he undressed him piece by piece. Slippers, socks, shirt, trousers. Then Eli stripped down to his own boxers. With the help of the handheld shower and a basin of warm soapy water, he lovingly washed his father. The procedure was many faceted, including a couple of unbuckle-and-stand followed by sit-and-rebuckle. It took physical prowess to do it. But it took tenderness, as well.

As soon as his father's body was rinsed and dried, Eli swathed him in more towels and brought out the shaving gear.

"Clark's still finishing up those Windsors," Eli told him. "You know how I hate doing chairs, but they're looking really fine. The finish on them is so good, I'm afraid it'll be mistaken for poly."

He mixed his father's favorite shaving soap in the ancient mug that he'd used for years and then applied the messy white foam to his dad's face. With practiced precision, he drew the old-fashioned safety razor across the one-day growth of beard, scraping it neatly clean. All the while, he kept up the one-sided conversation about anything and everything except the crippling disability that was now front and center in his father's everyday life.

"Mazy Gulliver came to see me last night," he said.

"Wow. Years have been good to her. She looked so beautiful, I thought my heart might actually explode out of my chest."

Eli wasn't sure if his father knew as much about his ill-fated relationship as Clark did. But he had confessed to being in love with her years ago.

"I am seriously going to have to watch my step," he admitted. "Clark was so right about her. She doesn't really see me as a man."

Eli stepped back and spread his arms. "Imagine how I feel. All my functional parts in good working order and in the prime of my life, and the only woman I care about thinks we're best girlfriends."

He was incredulous.

"I should invite her over to spend the night. She'd probably think it was a slumber party. We could paint each other's toenails."

He sighed heavily.

"You should have heard her, Dad. She totally infantilized me. I'm so sweet. I'm so cute. I'm the nicest guy she knows." Eli shook his head. "All this time, deep inside, I kind of held out hope. What a waste. She said I was a 'heart mender' not a 'heartbreaker.' Can you believe that? It's so…it's so demeaning, right?"

Eli wiped the residue of soap from his father's face. "Now you're looking good," he told his dad.

He dressed his father, brushed his teeth and combed his hair.

"The very worst thing," Eli continued. "Ugh. I hate even remembering it. We were standing on the back porch. Mazy sat down on the step and patted the space beside her, like I was a trained puppy. Here, Eli. Jump, Eli. Fetch the stick."

He made a growling sound reminiscent of a much-larger canine.

The whole daily ritual with his father took three-quarters of an hour. By the time Jonah Latham was spiffed up and seated in his recliner in the living room, his dad looked exhausted.

"Why don't you take yourself a little catnap here in front of the television," Eli suggested. "Rest up a bit before Ida brings you some lunch."

His father looked up at him and made a sound. It was guttural and indecipherable. Along with it, however, his father used his good hand to clasp Eli's and brought it up to his heart.

"You're welcome," Eli told him. "I love you, too."

His dad heaved a sigh of relief, as if the effort to make himself understood was the most difficult one of all. He relaxed back into his chair and closed his eyes.

Eli looked at his dad for a long moment and then quietly walked out of the room.

In the warmth of the kitchen, the sweet smell of cooking apples permeated the atmosphere. Ida looked up at him.

"I've got some nice bean soup if you want some."

"Thanks, but the apples will be enough for me," he told her, picking up the two heavily filled plastic containers on the table.

"The big one is for you," she told him.

Eli smiled at her. "Good. If you need me for anything, holler. I'll be back before bedtime."

He retrieved his jacket and let himself out the back door. Walking down the slope he allowed himself one nosy glance toward the house next door. The car that had brought Mazy home yesterday was gone now. There was no activity visible and no evidence that Mrs. Gulliver wasn't alone as usual.

Mazy was probably at her new job. Making lovesick calf eyes at Tad Driscoll.

That thought had him growling again.

6

Tad was waiting at the door when Mazy arrived at the bank. For a moment she feared that he'd had second thoughts about their agreement, but in fact, he was there to unlock the door and let her in.

"Good morning, Tad," she said politely.

"The employees address me as Mr. Driscoll," he replied, setting the tone for their new relationship as crisply professional.

"Then, good morning, Mr. Driscoll," she corrected.

In the lobby he called an impromptu meeting of bank personnel. She couldn't miss the wary looks from the other people in attendance.

"I want you all to meet Mazy Gulliver," Tad said, though it was completely unnecessary to introduce her. She was fairly certain that everyone in the room already knew who she was. "We are very fortunate to be able to add her to our staff. I've decided to consolidate all of our collection duties under one job description, and Miss Gulliver has a good deal of experience in getting past-due accounts to pay up." He shot her a phony smile that had meaning only for the two of them. "So if each of you girls could take a few moments to meet with her this morning and turn over the delinquent loans that you currently manage, we'll allow her to utilize her skills at asset recovery."

Mazy was pretty certain that, unlike Tad, most supervisors did not refer to female employees as *girls* unless they were running a lemonade stand on the sidewalk. She let that go. Taking on the bank's delinquent accounts was enough for her to get her head around.

If Mazy had expected any better, she quickly realized that she shouldn't have. Credit collection and asset recovery were the two most difficult and depressing jobs in banking. Hounding people for money they owed and then seizing their cars, homes and businesses when they couldn't pay was probably no one's dream job.

She was to set up her "office" in the small windowless room that also housed the printers and copy machine. She was given a phone, a desktop computer and a couple of file boxes. The rest of the staff, who'd been sharing the onerous collection duties, stacked the evidence of their efforts on her desk.

Tad made it clear that Mazy was not to work the teller's window, interact with patrons coming into the bank or even to be seen in the front lobby. She was to stay in her place and out of everyone's way.

She knew what Tad was up to. He couldn't risk going back on his end of the bargain, so he wanted to make the situation so miserable for her that she would voluntarily quit. He really had no idea how unlikely that would be. Mazy needed this job. She needed it for herself and for her son.

She could have told him that picking up trash by the side of the highway through a hot, humid Carolina summer can make a cramped, windowless office look like a bit of heaven. It was an opportunity. Meager as it was, Mazy was determined to make the best of it. She knuckled down immediately to get acquainted with the accounts.

Her interaction with the other employees was limited. No one went out of her way to make Mazy welcome. But she had to admit there was no particular hostility, either. In that, she decided, Tad had accidentally done her a favor. He probably assumed that the other workers would be predisposed not to like her. She was new. She seemed to be getting special treatment. And in a small town, gossip never died—it only slept lightly through other scandals. What he had apparently not recognized was how grateful each of them would be to turn over their delinquent accounts. She heard actual sighs of relief from the other women. If Tad had made her a loan officer, she would have been roundly hated. But credit collections everyone was happy to allow her to do.

The day passed more quickly than she would have expected. At noon she sat alone in the break room eating the sandwich that she'd brought. From the cleanliness of the place and the emptiness of the refrigerator, it seemed that most of the staff went out for lunch.

In the afternoon she wrote a letter introducing herself as the new collections officer. It was a cheerful, friendly and deliberately disguised dun notice, warning the bank's past-due debtors that there was a new sheriff in town, so to speak, and they would be hearing from her.

It was after four-thirty when she finally got them all into their printed envelopes and franked through the postage meter. She dropped them into the outgoing mail as she signed out for the day.

"Good night," she told Deandra, the teller on the ten-to-six shift.

The woman gave her a vague nod of acknowledgment. Not so bad for the first day of work, Mazy assured herself. Not so bad at all. She would walk home. Find out how school went for Tru. Eat whatever cheap, carbohydrate-heavy meal her mother had cooked, read herself to sleep and get up tomorrow to do it all over again. It was a life. A very controlled, noncrazy life. She could use one of those.

Out on the sidewalk, she was startled to hear her name called.

"Mazy! Oh, Mazy, hi. I was hoping I'd run into you again."

She looked up to see Karly, former home-ec partner, now school secretary.

"Oh, hi."

"Did you just get off work? I heard you got on at the bank."

Karly said it innocently, as if there wasn't anything strange about a woman walking back into town and immediately getting hired by the father of her illegitimate child.

"Yes, my first day," Mazy answered. "I'm doing collections."

Karly grimaced. "Wow, tough job. But somebody's got to do it, right?"

"Right."

"I was headed over to Local Grind. Come get a coffee with me. We'll toast your first day."

The last thing Mazy wanted to do was waste any of her last few remaining coins on overpriced coffee shared with a woman she hardly remembered.

"No, I want to get home. I want to find out how Tru's day was at school."

"Well, there's no rush on that," Karly said. "You know teenagers. They need at least an hour after class for decompression before they can even be expected to behave like normal human beings."

Mazy had never considered that, but in retrospect it did seem that her son always gave her the silent treatment in the afternoons.

"Please come with me," Karly continued. "I need adult conversation and I'm totally addicted to café macchiatos. I always let myself have one on my way home. Some days it's the only thing that gets me through fifth and sixth periods without screaming and tearing my hair out."

The woman was so open, so friendly, so very different from the shy silent person Mazy knew in high school. It was hard to say no to her, but Mazy had no choice. She'd moved here to make changes, to be smarter than she had been. And if that meant admitting the truth in order to avoid spending money she didn't have, then so be it.

"I, uh, I haven't gotten paid yet."

"Oh, good grief, it's on me," Karly said. "As far as that goes, Charlie would probably let you run a tab. Come on. If lack of cash was an excuse in this town, you wouldn't have a job, would you?"

The coffee shop was just across the street, the corner storefront in the two-story brick building that Mazy remembered as a place to buy hardware. The café was now furnished in dull earth tones, with dark wood paneling on the walls and work surfaces done in stainless steel. The alluring scent that permeated the place could wake you up before you even got a sip.

"So you brought a friend with you today," the man behind the counter stated.

"Do you know who she is?" Karly asked, teasing.

"Of course I do," he answered. "I never forget a pretty face. And you, Mazy Gulliver, have always had one."

Karly laughed delightedly. "Don't worry, he's harmless," she told her. "Charlie's very married, but a big old flirt. Do you remember him? Charlie McDee? He was a few years ahead of us in school."

The name did ring a bell, but not from some long-ago playground memory. She'd looked at his delinquent loan account that very morning.

"Hello," she said as evenly as possible. She didn't offer a hand or a smile. He wasn't going to want her to be his friend. And she could not afford to have him as one.

The women ordered their drinks and Karly led Mazy to the two-person table next to the front window. She would have preferred a less public spot, but it wasn't worth making a big deal. She would be friendly, drink her coffee and go on her way.

And yet, Mazy was quickly surprised to find she was enjoying herself. Karly was funny and personable. Not at all like the vague impression of her that was in Mazy's memory.

"So your last name is Farris?" she asked.

"Yes, I married Walter Farris."

"I don't think I know him."

"Oh, sure you do," Karly insisted. "He was older than us, but he used to ride around town on his motorcycle all the time."

Mazy had an immediate recollection of a mysterious loner guy roaring through town on a vintage Indian two-tone chopper.

"You don't mean...*Apache* Farris?"

Karly laughed. "Nobody calls him that much these days," she answered. "It's Che among family and friends, but mostly he's Walt, the Little League dad."

"He was so hot," Mazy pointed out. "And so unavailable."

Karly nodded. "Right. Women still ask me, 'How did *you* get him?'"

"They do not," Mazy said.

She laughed again. "Oh, they do. Seriously, I wonder about it myself sometimes."

Mazy's imagination immediately conjured up a fabulous fantasy of the two of them. It was such a romantic idea—the quiet loner in black leather and the shy, friendless hill girl. A man, a woman and a motorcycle. She could picture it so perfectly she almost sighed.

"So tell me everything," Mazy said. "There is nothing I love better than a great love story."

Karly shook her head. "I'll tell you all about it one of these days. It's a love story, but it's also a *long* story and I want to hear about you."

"Me?"

"Of course! The whole town is buzzing. Are you back for good this time? Are you just passing through?"

"Probably the latter," Mazy answered. "I'm sort of rebooting my life. Coming back to get a fresh start."

She thought her answer was innocuous enough, but it raised one of Karly's eyebrows.

Her next question seemed very deliberately casual.

"So are you and Tad getting back together?"

"No." Mazy's answer was simple. She punctuated it with a sip of hot, foamy coffee.

"You *are* both single now," Karly continued. "I mean, there was a spark there, once. That kind of thing can smolder for decades and then reignite. It happens every day."

Mazy shook her head. "It's not happening this time," she said. "*Mr. Driscoll* is my boss. Period. I have no interest in that direction."

"Sure?"

"Absolutely."

Karly let out a gush of breath as if she'd been holding it. "Thank God," she said. "I was really worried."

"Why?"

"I've always really liked you," she said. "And I don't like him."

That was surprising. "Tad was the most popular guy in town," she pointed out.

"Blah," Karly said, sticking her tongue out as if the thought made her sick. "What he did to you was totally crappy. Not everyone took his side, you know."

Mazy shrugged. "They probably should have. What happened was more my fault than his."

"You'll never convince me of that," she said. "And anyway, I have my own reasons for disliking the creep. He was a jerk to me in school."

Mazy was a bit shocked at that. Not that Tad was incapable of meanness, but that he'd even noticed Karly.

"What happened?"

"Don't you remember the clothespins?"

"Clothespins?"

"I guess I remember it so vividly, I expect everyone else to, as well. It was in sixth grade."

Mazy shook her head. Sixth grade was when her father died, she was hazy on any other memories from that year.

"Maybe I wasn't there," Mazy said.

"Everybody was there," Karly assured her. "It was General Assembly, grades six through twelve."

Mazy shook her head.

"It was the middle of winter and we were in the auditorium with all the windows closed. I always sat by myself near the aisle at the back of the room," she said. "When I came in that day all the seats around mine were filled with Tad and his friends. I didn't know why. I was so naive I actually smiled at them."

Mazy nodded.

"I was always so hopeful in those days," Karly said. "Every morning as I waited on the bus I'd think, 'Today is the day that I'll make a friend.' Crazy, huh? I never did make one, aside from you. It's hard for me to even believe it now, but that day I thought, 'Oh, look, the coolest guy in school is being nice to me.'"

Karly laughed and shook her head.

"So what was he up to?"

"He'd brought a bag of clothespins and passed them out to the other guys. A minute after I sat down they all pinched them on their noses, in unison. Once the other kids noticed, the whole building cracked up at how funny it was that they thought I smelled bad."

Karly's tone was matter-of-fact, but there was a slight tremor in her hand as she brought the cup to her lips.

"Even Principal Berger laughed, though he tried to cover his up with a cough."

It was clearly a humiliation that still stung.

"Oh, wow, Karly. I'm sorry."

She shrugged. "It was a long time ago. And it was a very different place. I wasn't the most spick-and-span girl in school. I probably did smell bad."

"I don't remember that," Mazy replied honestly.

"If I did, it wasn't because Tad and his friends were better than me. It was easy for them to be clean. I was growing up in my grandpa's cabin with no running water. Tad's house had, like, three bathrooms or something. Washing up with pan of warm water was the best I could do before school. I managed a whole bath and a shampoo when I did laundry on Saturdays."

Mazy recalled with clarity the sound of Tad's laugh

when he was humiliating somebody. He wore haughty condescension and snarky superiority like a badge of honor. But Mazy had assumed that behavior had been mostly reserved for herself. And that she'd earned it. That she deserved it. Certainly Karly did not.

"I'm so sorry that he did that to you. He was a real shit."

"Yes, he was," Karly agreed. "I think he probably still is. But for me, that was like a million years ago. Now I'm all grown up, living happily-ever-after in a split-level ranch with all the amenities of modern life."

Karly laughed and Mazy managed to chuckle with her.

"Still, if you were to decide that you wanted to give bad old Tad another shot, I wouldn't judge you."

Mazy shook her head. "No way. I seriously don't want him."

"Good. You can do so much better."

"Well, I don't know about that," Mazy said. "My track record's not very impressive."

"Because you've been chasing the wrong ones," Karly said. "You need a better kind of fellow."

"I keep telling myself that the smart thing is to swear off men entirely."

"That'll never work," Karly told her.

Mazy nodded. "I know. I am such a romance addict. I'm in love with love. I can tell myself to steer clear, but I'll be falling for somebody before I know it. And, knowing me, he'll be just as big a jerk as Tad."

"Well, maybe this time, instead of falling you should jump."

"Huh?"

"Don't wait to stumble into Mr. Wrong," she said. "Find a really nice guy. One who could actually *deserve* all the love that you have to give."

Inexplicably, her words conjured up the image of Eli looking long and lean and sexy standing on the Lathams' back porch.

7

The story was on everyone's lips. Mazy Gulliver had not only sought out Tad Driscoll on her first morning back in town, Tad had hired her to work at the bank. Eli had overheard more than a few jokes about the banker so thrifty that he put his mistress on the payroll.

The community barely had time to recover from that tidbit before a new one appeared in their daily mail. An unpleasant buzz began filling the phone lines.

Eli paid no attention, deliberately focusing on the tenons that he was carefully shaping from cherry. Clark, however, had taken two back-to-back gossip calls, but before he'd had a moment to share what he'd heard, Sheila arrived brimming with news.

Eli's sister-in-law was short and, thanks to her own great cooking, tending toward extra curvy. Her hair was bleached a blond so platinum that it was actually white. The color didn't do anything good for her complexion, but she was still an attractive woman when she smiled. Today she was smiling with what seemed malicious glee.

"Guess what she's done," she said to Eli in a manner he could only describe as accusatory.

"She who?"

"Mazy Gulliver," Sheila answered. "Some women go

out of their way to make trouble for themselves and everybody else."

Clark was frantically trying to listen to the phone and his wife at the same time.

"The be-yatch is back in town to do Driscoll's dirty work," his sister-in-law announced. "Apparently Tad has hired her to put the squeeze on folks. It's why she moved home. She's probably been plotting for years how to get back at us."

"What are you talking about, Sheila?"

"She sent out a letter yesterday saying she is now in charge of collecting debt for the bank. She's threatening people's families and their livelihood—and she's only been here a few days."

Clark managed to free himself from his caller.

"Are you sure about that?" Eli asked her as Clark made his way over to them. "It sounds like a tale somebody made up."

"It absolutely is not!" Sheila said. "Sandra Peavy got the letter and so did Lacey Wallender. Big as brass she says that she's the new 'collections officer' and that she'll be contacting everyone individually."

"So, these are people who owe the bank money," Eli clarified. "That doesn't sound like she's 'threatening' anybody. It sounds like contacting them might be her job."

"Well, people feel threatened. And what's *she* doing sending out letters?"

Clark nodded. "The whole town is in an uproar," he said. "That was Jimmy Ray Esher on the phone. He wanted to see if we'd let him hide his bass boat in our garage."

Sheila huffed in disgust. "It would almost be worth it to keep it out of her hands. Wouldn't you know that she'd have some scheme to move back here and get revenge on the whole town."

"That's not why she's here," Eli argued. "She probably moved back to take care of her mother."

Sheila looked skeptical. "Beth Ann is as healthy as a horse," she said. "Mazy had some other motive for moving back. And if it wasn't revenge, then it has to be a man."

Eli swallowed hard and deliberately turned his concentration back to the work at hand.

"She's trying to get back with Tad Driscoll. I'd bet anything on it," Sheila said. "But you'd think she'd have the decency to see him openly, not restart a nasty little affair."

"Maybe she's not," Eli suggested. "Maybe she's just working there."

Both Sheila and Clark raised their eyebrows.

"The man got her pregnant, didn't marry her, wouldn't even acknowledge the child and did everything he could to paint her as a scarlet woman and make her a public joke in this town. Is that where you would go looking for a job?"

It was a question Eli had already asked himself.

"I doubt it's where she'd be looking for romance, then, either. Anyway, all that is ancient history," he said. "She's probably put it behind her."

Sheila snorted. "Well, I haven't."

To be honest, neither had Eli. He deliberately did his banking in Boone so he wouldn't have to offer more than an absent nod to Tad Driscoll. Imagining Mazy forgiving him, picturing her back in his arms, bothered Eli more than he was willing to admit.

He couldn't even pretend to himself that he'd gotten over her. Over the years, he'd dated a number of nice women. His sister-in-law was always trying to fix him up with some sweet gal from her bowling league or PTA. And he met women curators and interior designers who were as interested in him as they were in his furniture. He'd even kept up a year-long relationship with a bright and beautiful woman from Johnson City. But not even she could capture his heart. He'd given it to Mazy a long time ago, and although she obviously didn't want it, he couldn't seem to get it back.

The gossip-fest was forced to a halt with the arrival of some new customers. They were retirees from Connecticut, recently relocated to Asheville. They were furnishing their new home and the wife had heard about Eli's furniture.

Typically Eli let Clark handle client visits. But on this day, he found the distraction welcome. He showed them around, priming them with coffee and then slathering them with Southern hospitality.

Word of mouth was the best kind of promotion for his business, and typically he was grateful for any new interest coming his way. But it wasn't long before he was regretting taking the lead over Clark.

The wife was nice. She appeared to have a keen eye for design and an interest in craftsmanship. Her husband, however, was far less pleasant. In fact, in the vernacular that had been Eli's dad's, the man was a "gen-u-wine horse's patoot."

"I know how this stuff works," the man told him. "There's a couple of you guys here at this site for show. But once we order the furniture you get a crew of Mexicans to do the work and charge us like it was handmade."

Eli didn't even allow himself to make the obvious point that even a "crew of Mexicans" could do handmade work. He tried to politely stick to the facts.

"All our pieces are made right here. And the work is all done by either my brother or myself."

The husband continued to look skeptical.

"I don't know how you ever expect to sell anything. You don't even have a decent showroom."

"A lot of our pieces are built to your specifications," Eli explained. "If you want to buy something that we have on hand, you can look through our photobook or check out the finished pieces on our website."

The "patoot" insisted on seeing the finished pieces that were for sale. Unfortunately, they were stacked up in a nearby shed that was packed in solid. Even when Eli tried to show him around, the guy seemed to prefer spouting off and making complaints. Clark kept his head down, appearing to ignore the guy. However, Eli was pretty sure that his brother was likely to plane the board he was working on into a toothpick.

"So, I guess a lot of fellows up here in the hills go into this line of work. What's the deal? Did you get laid off from some textile plant and decide to open a carpenter shop?"

Eli ignored both the misnomer of carpenter as well as the implied insult to their business origins. "Our family has been woodworking here since 1878."

"Oh, so you boys just don't know anything else."

"No, I guess we don't," Eli replied.

In the end, the wife picked out a very lovely entry table and asked to email measurements for another piece she wanted Eli to design. She had a good eye and excellent taste. She was also polite and still attractive for a woman of her age. And she seemed clever and capable. Enough so that Eli wondered what she'd ever seen in the loudmouth patoot she'd married.

When they got around to prices, the husband bad-mouthed and disparaged so thoroughly that when Eli caught the wife's eye she mouthed, *Sorry,* behind her husband's back. The guy was equally unhappy about the waiting list. But he eventually figured out that it was a waste of time to try to negotiate the nonnegotiable. The wife had the patience to wait for the exact piece she wanted. Eli was sure that she would be glad that she did.

After they left, Eli reflected on the mismatch. Was what he'd seen a good example of the wife's life? Did she spend her days quietly apologizing for the behavior of the man she married? Eli figured it was likely. Could she be another one of those women inexplicably attracted to assholes? And was she happy with her choice, or did she wish she'd married the boring nice guy?

Eli imagined that it was the latter. It was really too bad that her friends or family or someone hadn't warned her. Maybe they had. Maybe warning was not enough. Perhaps it was like a kind of addiction. Compulsively choosing the bad guy. If that was true, her family and friends could only watch in despair.

Or maybe a friend could take action.

8

━ ◆ ━

Mazy was seated in the tiny noisy excuse for an office. Behind her the folding machine was loudly doing its best to get bank statements ready to send out. She was lucky to hear the phone on her desk when it rang.

"FTSB. Collections. This is Ms. Gulliver. May I help you?"

"I want to see you in my office. Now!"

Tad didn't bother to identify himself. He didn't have to. And he was obviously angry. Mazy quickly ran a list of possibilities through her head. Had she said something to Karly over coffee? They had talked about Tad, but she was pretty sure that she hadn't offered any new information, except to say that she wasn't there to restart their old romance.

As she walked through the lobby between her work area and his office, she noticed that the glances this morning were more hostile than they'd been the first day she'd arrived. She couldn't imagine what that was about.

She tapped on Tad's door.

"Come in!"

The response was gruff. Forcing a pleasant smile to her face, she stepped inside. Tad was sitting behind his desk. His face so puffed and red it looked like it might explode.

"Shut the door."

She did.

"What the hell do you think you're doing?"

Mazy was pretty sure that wasn't the typical language that Mr. Driscoll used with his subordinates.

"What am I doing about what?"

"Did you send a letter from this bank on our letterhead without my authorization?"

The tone of his accusation far exceeded the supposed crime she'd committed.

"It was just a letter of introduction," she explained. "I wanted the people with past-due accounts to know that I'd be contacting them and to give them the opportunity to contact me first."

"I know exactly what it said," Tad answered, holding up a sheet of paper that had the appearance of having been wadded up and then smoothed out. "Kite Bagby was by here and chewed my head off about it. What do you think you're doing contacting these people?"

Mazy was confused.

"I don't understand," she admitted. "Isn't it my job to pursue the bank's debtors?"

"There are debtors and then there are people that we *invest* in," Tad answered. "You can harass all the bankrupt bass players and mobile home buyers in the hills you want. But don't you even *suggest* to our local businessmen or the guys I play golf with that we don't think they are going to pay off their loans."

Mazy raised an eyebrow. She had a sudden, unpleasant memory of the in-crowd at Brandt Mountain High when Tad was the center of it.

"I don't know how they do things in Wilmington," he said with an emphasis so derogatory that anyone unknowing might have pictured that beautiful coastal city as an urban hellhole. "But in our community, every customer is unique."

To Mazy's ears it sounded like favoritism. She did not, however, use that term. "So, all uncollected bank loans are not created equal."

"Certainly not," Tad told her. "There are always people who have chronic money trouble. There's actually very little we can do for them. If they put up their house or their car as collateral, well, we might as well make the loan because somebody else will." Tad raised his hands and shrugged. "When those people stop making payments, we carry them for four to six months, then we sell the loan to an agency. We get our money back, but the agency handles the messy business of repossessing the collateral."

"So no harm, no foul," Mazy interpreted.

"Pretty much," he agreed.

"But your friends are treated differently."

"They are not simply my friends," he pointed out. "They are the basic fabric of this community. The people who make money and spend money."

"And owe money."

"It's not the same to owe money when you are making money as it is to owe money when you're living hand-to-mouth," Tad explained. "On Wall Street they don't even call it lending, they call it 'buying on margin.' And it's certainly more akin to that than it is to the guy who has to borrow against his car to pay doctor bills."

"But they're both using the bank's money," Mazy pointed out. "And the bank's money belongs to the depositors."

"Precisely," Tad said. "When we lend, we must be responsible about it. We must represent the best interest of the depositors."

"But aren't 'the depositors' a lot of the people that are borrowing to pay off the medical bills?"

Tad shrugged again. "There are lots of customers with tiny accounts and some customers with much bigger ones. I have found that those with larger accounts are better risks."

Mazy didn't agree. "If they have 'larger accounts,' then why aren't they paying off their loans?" she asked.

"They will. They are," he insisted. "That's the way I encourage our staff to approach this. If someone more… more valuable has missed a few payments, the bank calls with concerns that their accounting clerk or their secretary or their wife has made some horrible snafu and they certainly want to get it cleared up. But for you to suggest that these prominent people are behind on their payments and that the bank wants to help them with a plan toward solvency? That's just insulting, Mazy. I will not have it."

"All right," Mazy said with all of the polite mollification she could manage. "But the accounts themselves look very similar. How am I going to know these 'more valuable people' from the less valuable ones?"

There was more than a little sarcasm in her statement, but Tad didn't pick up on it.

"You're not a stranger," he reminded her. "Most of the cream of the crop when you left town are still on top today."

"I didn't pay that much attention even back then," she admitted. "People were either nice to me or they weren't."

"Well, that's one way to sort out the world," he said. "Not that it will be particularly helpful here at the bank." He held up the crumpled letter that he'd showed her earlier. "Kite is not very nice to anyone, but he holds enough strings that we all have to be nice to him."

Mazy hated this, the sorting of people based on their

family name, their occupation, the origins of their grand-parents. There were a number of things about her small town that she didn't like. She considered the petty class consciousness one of its least attractive features.

"So what do you want me to do?" she asked him.

"I think the other girls have simply erred on the side of treating everybody with kid gloves," Tad said.

Mazy nodded slowly. "I'll bet that when the lesser folks discover that their loans have been sold to collection, it comes as quite a shock."

Tad nodded as he thought about that. "I suppose so."

"Why don't I try to work with them," she suggested. "I could see if maybe I could get them to pay up. I'm sure that would help our reported stats and make our bundles more attractive to loan purchasers."

"We can't let anything go unpaid for six months," Tad reminded her. "You can't sell loans that are already in default."

"I understand that," Mazy said. "I won't let anything go that long."

"And you keep your distance from the…the VIPs. If you're not sure about any one, then I want you to run the name by me before you contact them."

Mazy nodded agreement.

She had seriously not imagined that "introducing" herself would cause such a reaction. But throughout the afternoon, in her little cubbyhole of an office, call after call came in. Some spoke with shaky voices. Others with giant chips solidly on shoulders. Mazy waded through all of them with deliberate calmness and caring. She was clearly typecast as the villain. She was trying not to resent that. There was no use attempting to explain that she was going to be the one to help them, that her plan for their troubles was to see that they were not foisted off on the highest bidder.

By the end of the workday, she felt exhausted.

Which was undoubtedly why, sitting across the table from Tru and Beth Ann, she was a little snappish.

When her son had pointed out, quite accurately, that his sneakers were getting too small again, she was quick to attack.

"You'll have to make do until I get paid," she told him. "Even then it'll be a bare-bones paycheck. Don't be thinking that we can suddenly buy anything you want."

The words were unfair. Tru had been stoic about the money situation and never made complaints about their forced frugality. Mazy's words had been fueled by her own frustrations and she wished she could call them back or maybe just cut her tongue out altogether.

"Maybe Tru can get his own little job," Beth Ann suggested sweetly. "Then he'd have his own cash to do whatever he wanted."

Tru nodded. "Yeah, I think I'd like that," he said.

Mazy frowned. "You're going to be busy at school," she told him.

"He could get something after school," Beth Ann said.

Mazy shook her head. "He's too young to get a job."

"Fourteen is legal age to work in North Carolina," Tru pointed out. "So the state must think I'm old enough."

"I don't care what the state says about it," Mazy barked. "What I say is that you need to concentrate on schoolwork and making friends, not selling fries at McDonald's."

"Of course he won't do that," Beth Ann agreed. "We don't even have a McDonald's."

"I could probably rake leaves or do chores for people," Tru suggested.

"You can rake leaves and do chores for your grand-mother," Mazy said. "That should be enough to keep you busy."

"That doesn't give him any walking-around money," Beth Ann pointed out. "Teenagers can get pretty hungry at most any time of day."

Mazy gave her mother a look. "Why don't you fix him a nice cardboard sign—Will Work for Food—and we can let him stand out on the intersection by the highway."

Beth Ann wagged her finger at her daughter. "Don't make this about you," she said sternly. "If the boy finds something he wants to do, you owe it to him to get out of the way."

Mazy knew her mother was right, but she didn't like it one bit. She looked at her son, so long-limbed and gawky and, to her, totally adorable.

"I…I don't want to see you giving up your childhood because…because of mistakes I've made."

Tru shrugged and a wry grin turned up one side of his face as he winked at Beth Ann. "Most kids have to give up childhood because of their own mistakes. I'm going to be really lucky to always have somebody else to blame."

The two of them thought that was funny and Mazy had no choice but to lighten up. Her son's humor, offbeat as it might be, was an improvement over the silent intro-spection he sometimes fell into. And she was determined that her new job was going to open a door for them, even though she felt that she'd practically had to kick it in.

Once the meal was finished, Mazy took on the cleanup chores. After some serious shooing, her mother settled into the living room to watch her favorite reality televi-sion.

To her surprise, Tru began clearing the table without being asked.

"You wash, I'll dry," he said.

That surely meant something. She hoped it wasn't a reemergence of their earlier discussion. They did need money. And she knew how tempting the idea of a job could be. But she wanted ordinary teenage life to be his first priority. The classes, the activities, the friends—she wanted those things to fill his thoughts, not the hours on a time clock.

The pep rallies and weekend parties would have been more important to him back in Wilmington, back among his friends. But he could make new friends here, she was sure of that. New friends, new memories, a whole new life. Maybe even a better life.

"So school's going okay?" she asked. "Remember high school isn't forever. Before you know it, you'll graduate and go off to live some adventure wherever you want."

"I've pretty much had all the adventure I need," Tru answered. "And four years is almost a third of my life so far."

"I'm sor—"

He raised a dishcloth-covered hand to halt another apology.

"I can do the time," he said. "Don't worry about me. Just watch your own self. Don't hook up with another jerk."

"I'm done with that," Mazy promised.

Tru shook his head in a way that was far too world-weary for his age. "Mom, there is always going to be someone. I get it. For you, being alone is always going to be just a lull between…adventures. I'm okay with it."

"Oh, Tru, I really hate that I'm like that."

"I don't," he said. "You're really good when you're in love. You're happy and carefree and, well…fun. You deserve some fun, Mom. But please, no more thieves, cheaters, megalomaniacs or assholes."

"I don't believe that *asshole* is on the vocabulary list for appropriate conversation with your mother."

"'A rose by any other name,'" he quoted with a teasing smile. "And you'll find a reason to date it."

She flicked dishwater in his face and he dodged.

They both laughed.

"Seriously, Mom," her son continued. "This time could you try falling for someone who can actually love you back?"

"I think it's time for you to stop worrying about *my* love life and start concentrating on your own," she said. "Nothing defines being a teenager like high school romance. Have you seen any likely candidates for your affections?"

Tru shook his head. "I'm afraid to look at the girls," he said.

Mazy was surprised. Her son had never been one of those boys who got tongue-tied at the sight of a pretty face.

"Why?"

"We're pretty far back in the mountains, Mom. I don't want to go giving *the look* to somebody who might turn out to be my cousin or, worse yet, my sibling. Eww, yuk. Incest is so uncool these days."

She threw the dishrag at him. He caught it.

"You have no cousins," she told him. "And no siblings in this school or in this town."

Tru raised his eyebrows and nodded thoughtfully. "So the sperm donor has other kids."

"He was not a 'sperm donor,' Tru. He's your birth father," Mazy answered. "And, yes, he does have a couple of daughters, but they are much younger than you and they live someplace else."

"So you were, like, the only person he got pregnant in high school?"

"Well, of course."

"Why *of course?* I mean, for all I know he was like a Johnny Appleseed character spreading his genetic material far and wide."

"He was not Johnny Appleseed."

"Yeah, the name's all wrong. Maybe something like Ivan Impregnator."

Mazy deliberately did not laugh.

"That was not his name," she said. After a moment's hesitation she asked, "Do you want to know his name?"

"No. Well, yes. Wait, does he know my name? He does know about me?"

"Of course he knows about you. I told you how it was. He decided he couldn't be a part of your life, so it was easier not to see you at all. It's like the women who give birth and then allow the child to be adopted without ever holding them. They don't get attached and it allows the child to bond to someone else."

Tru was nodding as he dried the casserole dish. Mazy had been explaining his lack of father to him this way since he got old enough to ask.

"Except I didn't have any other man to bond with," Tru pointed out. "All I had was a series of assholes moving in and out of my mom's bedroom."

"Hey!"

"Sorry. I guess…I would have liked to have a dad."

Mazy would have liked that for him, too. She had *tried* to have that for him. Her memories of her own father were some of the most precious she held. Tru would never have a connection like that. It was the kind of thing a person couldn't beg, borrow or steal. It just was. Or it wasn't.

There had been a few guys along the way that she'd thought had the potential to be dad material. Her last ex was number one on that list. But then he *was* a dad, and a husband, and a crook. And turned out not to be particularly good at any of those.

"Tru, if you want to know your birth father's name, I will tell you," she said. "If you want to meet him, that could be arranged."

Tru's eyes widened, then his brow furrowed. She could see that he was tempted. Fourteen years of curious imaginings could be answered in one fell swoop. He could stand eyeball to eyeball with the one person on earth who shared his Y chromosome. But after a half minute of consideration, Tru shook his head. "No. If he didn't want me then, why would he want me now? If he doesn't want me, why would I want him?"

Mazy managed not to sigh with relief. She already knew that Tad did not want her son. And after the deal she'd made with him, he might have considered having to meet Tru to be reneging on the agreement.

Still, her son's disappointment was palpable. It could have been so good for Tru to have someone else to call family. Someone more together than herself or Beth Ann.

Mazy stood on tiptoes to give him a hug. "It's an undisputed fact that I'm a mess of a parent," she told him. "But you can trust that no mother, no father, no nobody anywhere, loves her kid more than I love you."

He nodded. "Hey, I got it, Mom. That's the only way you know how to love. Pedal to the metal and all in."

9

——•——

The veneered music cabinet had tremendous potential. Eli found two sheets of the thin, sixteenth-inch ocotea. The wood, commonly called Brazilian walnut, was easily confused with actual Brazilian walnut, the ipê. Ocotea was an evergreen from the higher elevations of the tropics. It was prized for its essential oils and it was used in flavorings. But it was also beautiful and durable lumber for furniture. Fifty years earlier it had been a common flooring material in many parts of the world. With the clear-cutting in the Amazon, it had become scarcer and more expensive. The pieces Eli had were pricey, but they had gorgeous graining, even a rare whorl that he wanted to use on the face of the center drawer.

With a square and a pencil, he measured out and drew the sections that he wanted and carefully noted the locations he had planned. Then, like an artist with a canvas, he would step back to survey, seeing in his mind the finished product.

It was, in some ways, the most important work that he did. A lot of men and women could successfully and superbly fashion furniture from a plan. The ability to vision a plan was an innate gift. He was born with the aptitude for it. He worked hard and pushed himself to excel, but like a professional athlete or a virtuoso musician, he understood that he had advantages others simply did not have.

He had not intended to frame out the veneers today. There was a lot of more lackluster work to be done fashioning the poplar. But he found this task very distracting. And he needed to be distracted. A tiny seed of an idea had planted itself in his brain a mere three days ago. Although he had tried to ignore it, the weed was growing like kudzu through Georgia.

It was a crazy idea. It would never work. Eli was determined to ignore it. But he couldn't quite let it go.

He stood back again, forcing himself to concentrate on the work in front of him as he tapped his pencil on his thumbnail.

He could never pull it off. She would never believe it.

There was a knock on the shop door.

He and Clark exchanged a glance. No one ever knocked on the door. Visitors were relatively rare. And the place was a business. People simply walked right in.

"It's open!" Clark hollered.

A tall, gangly teenager stepped through the doorway.

Eli recognized him immediately. It was difficult not to. He'd played summer league with Tad Driscoll when he'd looked just like that. Then the kid's shoulders sagged slightly as he shoved his hands in his jean pockets. That didn't look like Tad. Tad's chin had always been held high and he wore confidence to the point of arrogance. This open awkwardness and uncertainty showed him as Mazy's boy.

"Uh, hi," he said. "I, uh…my grandma told me that I should come talk to Termite."

Clark chuckled.

Eli walked across the room to stand in front of the teenager. Arms crossed he looked the kid straight in the eye.

"I'm Eli Latham," he said. "Nobody calls me Termite unless they're looking to get punched in the face."

"Sorry," he said. His apology, while seeming sincere, was immediately followed by a slight quirk of a grin from the right corner of his mouth. "You're not going to punch my grandma in the face, are you?"

Eli couldn't quite maintain the tough-guy demeanor. With a chuckle, he shook his head. "No, probably not. But you can call me Eli."

"Yes, sir," the kid replied.

Eli liked the respectful manners. At least Mazy had done that right.

"This is my brother, Clark."

The teenager gave him a slight smile and nod.

"I'm Tru Gulliver," he said. "I just moved in next door with my grandma."

Eli nodded. "What can I do for you, Tru Gulliver?"

"Well, I'm looking for some after-school work, and Gram thought you might have something that I could do."

Eli thought about that.

"What do you know how to do?"

Tru paused, considering.

"Basically nothing, I guess," he answered. His eyes were Driscoll blue, but the honesty in them was all Gulliver. "But I'm not afraid to learn and I'm not opposed to hard work."

The shop didn't need any help. And taking on a minimum-wage worker, even on after-school hours, could cost at least one hundred and fifty dollars a month. Somebody who didn't know anything was definitely not worth the price. Still, Eli found himself eager to take Tru on.

"I'll think about it," Eli told him. "Hang up your coat and grab that broom. See if you can make yourself useful."

The teen looked as happy as a kid at Christmas. His brother, who caught his eye as he headed back to his worktable, not so much.

As Tru began diligently sweeping up the sawdust and shavings on the shop floor, Eli considered his options. Unfortunately, he was not going to be able to consider them in private.

"Eli, I need to show you something in the shed," Clark announced.

He managed to keep his sigh inaudible as he slid on his jacket and followed his brother outside. The day had turned sunny, but in the wide expanse of land behind the shop, the wind that whistled through was crisp and cold.

Clark waited to speak until they were safely out of earshot. "What the heck do you think you're doing?"

"I haven't said that I will take him on," Eli answered. "But it might be helpful to have someone to clean up."

"We don't need anybody to do that."

"Well, you don't, because you go home at the end of the day and leave it for me," Eli answered.

"If you're tired of doing it yourself, then we'll trade off."

"Doesn't Sheila insist you get home to play with the girls?" Eli reminded him. "You don't have time to do it. You shouldn't object if I find somebody who will."

"I'm your brother and you're doing something boneheaded. I have an obligation to object."

"It's not boneheaded," Eli insisted. "It might be a good idea for us to get used to having some help around here. We're going to be bringing your oldest into the business sooner than you think."

"Ashley's eight and she's a girl."

"Latham is Latham, I don't think we ought to show any gender bias."

"Don't try to change the subject," Clark said. "The only reason that you're considering hiring this kid is because he's Mazy's son."

"Okay, I'll admit that. I'd like to help her out."

"Well, it's a pretty nice favor," Clark said. "But I hope you know that it won't do you any good. She's not going to fall for you because you give her kid a job."

"Jeez, do you think I'm completely stupid? It's not about her. Or it's not entirely. It's about…well, it's about the kid. His mom's fallen on hard times. He needs a job. There's no reason we can't try him out. If he turns out to be a nuisance, I'll let him go."

Clark was shaking his head.

Eli brought in the big guns. "It's what Dad would do," he said. "You know how much he liked Mazy, how much he and Mom tried to help out Mrs. Gulliver. Dad would have hired him immediately and you know it."

It was the truth—inconvenient as it might be that Eli was still hung up on Mazy, his father *would* have taken the boy on. And not just to sweep up. Dad would have tried to teach him skills.

Clark threw up his hands in defeat. "Whatever," he said. "But don't expect me to put up with any crap from the kid just because you're trying to score with his mom."

"Understood," Eli replied.

Clark kept his word and was a gruff old bear for the rest of the afternoon. If Tru noticed, it didn't seem to bother him. He kept his head down and kept busy. He swept and put up equipment, he even scrubbed the toilet, which Eli was pretty sure hadn't been done in three months at least.

While Tru got a lot accomplished, Eli did not. He found himself unable to concentrate on the veneer and unwilling to get busy with anything else. The kid was not a big talker. Typically Eli was the same. Today, however, he couldn't quite shut up.

"You know, your mom and I were playmates practically from the time we could walk," he said. "And in the winter, when it was too cold to be outside, we were often underfoot in here."

"Oh, yeah?"

"Those shavings from the plane," he said, indicating the thin loops of wood peeled off the lumber. "We once glued about a thousand of them into her hair so she could have blond ringlets."

Tru laughed.

"You grandmother screamed when she saw what we'd done. I thought she was going to kill us."

"Did you get into a lot of trouble?"

"No, not too much," he said. "But that was the year that Mazy got her summer haircut in the winter."

Eli was surprised at all the stories that he remembered and allowed himself a nostalgic trip down memory lane, careful to keep to their pre-middle-school era. Tru seemed to enjoy this new version of his mother.

"My mom never talks about being a kid," he said. "I mean, she tells me the factual stuff. But not a lot of funny stuff."

"I guess that's the way I remember it," Eli said. "There was a lot of fun stuff."

Even Clark got into the act, complaining about the two of them running wild.

"It's bad enough to have a little brother," he told Tru. "But it's twice the trouble when the pest has a sidekick."

"Mazy was never a sidekick," Eli protested.

"Of course not," Clark agreed. "Eli was her sidekick."

Tru laughed aloud at that.

It was almost five when Eli sent the boy outside with

the trash for the compost pile. Clark gathered up his lunch box and retrieved his jacket.

"I'm off," he told Eli. "Do what you want about the kid. He's okay, really. And someone to sweep up at the end of the day could be a help. I just hate to see you getting mixed up with Mazy again. I'd feel better if you'd tell me that it's not going to happen."

"Don't worry about me," Eli answered. "I can take care of myself."

He was careful not to make any promises about Mazy. The plan that was hatching in his mind, the one that he was valiantly trying to ignore, continued to gnaw at him.

Don't go there, he admonished himself. There was simply way too much wrong with the whole idea.

When Tru came back inside, Eli motioned him over. There was no trepidation in the teenager's step. The boy had clearly relaxed within the atmosphere of the shop.

"Well, you did pretty good today," Eli told him.

"Thanks."

"This is the kind of work you'd be doing," Eli said. "Cleanup and carrying. Are you still interested in that?"

He nodded enthusiastically. "It's pretty cool here," he said.

Eli thought so, too.

"I'll pay you minimum wage. We'll keep your hours on a tally sheet. If you're not going to be here, you'll have to let me know. I don't want to be guessing whether or not you're showing up."

"Yes, sir. I mean, no, sir. I mean, I wouldn't not show up."

"Good," Eli said. "There is absolutely no smoking anywhere on this entire lot. Fire is a real hazard for us. If I so much as see you with a lit match, you're out of here."

"Yes, sir."

"Oily rags, any cloth with solvent of any kind, has to be put in the metal container outside the minute you're not using it."

"Okay.

"How many afternoons can you give me? Two or three a week?"

"I can work every day, if you want me to," Tru assured him. "I get out of school at three-thirty. By the time I get home and grab something to eat, I can be here by four."

"What about basketball practice?"

The kid's jaw dropped slightly and he took a step back. "I don't play basketball," he said.

"Oh, uh, my mistake. Well, never mind. Every afternoon will be great."

Tru was nodding, but he no longer looked so pleased. He folded his arms across his chest and eyed Eli critically.

"You know, people keep asking me about this basketball thing," he said.

Eli shrugged. "We play a lot of basketball in this town," he said. "You're tall. That's probably what it's all about."

"Maybe," Tru said. "But I'm beginning to think the sperm donor must have been some basketball jock."

Eli choked. "The sperm donor?"

"That's what I call my birth father," Tru said. "The term *baby daddy* just doesn't fit. If you're such great friends with my mother, then you must know that she had me on her own."

"Well, yeah. I know that."

Tru's eyes narrowed. "You aren't the sperm donor, are you?"

It was an unexpected question. There had been a time when this tall, skinny kid had been a chubby toddler. Back then, Eli had totally taken on the idea of being his father. He'd convinced himself that being a dad was about love, not shared hereditary traits. He had stoked himself up for the challenge. But Mazy hadn't given him the chance to take it on.

"No," he answered simply.

The teenager nodded. "I didn't think so," he said. "You're not the type that my mom usually goes for."

10

Mazy thought she'd made it crystal clear that she didn't want Tru to work. The fact that her son, in cahoots with Beth Ann, had paid no attention to that was a little galling. But it was made a little less so by the identity of his employer.

"I can't believe you went behind my back to talk to Termy."

"Don't call him Termite, Mom," Tru corrected her. "He goes by Eli."

"Does he?" Mazy found herself amused at that.

Eli was a grown man's name. It did seem that he finally fit the bill. Maybe because they had been kids together she had continued to think of him that way. He'd only been one year younger, but she always felt more mature by decades.

"The guy is nice, okay?" he said. "And he said nice things about you."

"I'm not making fun of him. I like him. He was my best friend when I was a kid. And although I don't like the idea of you having a job, I'm glad you're going to work with him. Maybe you'll learn something useful, like how to nail stuff together."

Her son gave her a long-suffering look. "Mom, I've

only been around there two hours and I already know they don't 'nail stuff together.'"

Mazy shrugged.

After dinner she rushed through the cleanup. She'd decided to go visit Termy. She wanted to thank him for hiring Tru, but she also wanted simply to see him, to talk to him. Their short chat together earlier in the week had been pleasant, friendly. Once upon a time he'd been her friend. She needed all the friends that she could get right now. And if some startlingly pleasurable flashbacks assailed her, she didn't have to allow that to complicate things.

So she fixed her hair, repaired her makeup, walked across the back lawns and knocked on the basement door.

Eli opened it hurriedly, but the look of surprise turned to pleasure at the sight of her.

"Hello," he said.

"My son says I can't call you Termite anymore."

Her abrupt statement was answered with a grin. "*He* can't call me Termite. You never did. But Termy is actually worse."

"So it's Eli now?"

"It is Eli," he said. "And this is Eli's place. Would you like to come in?"

"I would."

She did.

Eli held the door open for her and helped her with her coat. Mazy couldn't remember the last time a man had done that for her. She tried to think of herself as a no-nonsense person, but she really liked that feeling of being treated so politely. She made a mental note to double-check Tru on gentlemanly manners. They were undoubtedly not a priority in high school, but she wanted him to have them, anyway.

"I've got beer in the fridge if you'd like one. Or I can fix margaritas. Is that still your drink?"

"Margaritas? I used to drink margaritas?"

"On the rocks, no salt."

She laughed. "Well, I'm a vodka-tonic gal these days," she told him. "And I mostly leave that for a special occasion."

"Having you here in my home is certainly special to me," he said.

Mazy glanced around his living space. His was well past the age of mattresses on the floor and flags for curtains. Still, she was expecting Spartan decor. In truth, the more accurate description would have been comfy or cozy. The living room/kitchen combo was painted butter yellow. The color both warmed the room and kept it from having the dungeonlike feel of most basements. The decor was masculine, but without the saddle-soap appeal that so many bachelor pads go for. Of course, Mazy thought, it made sense that a guy who builds furniture for a living would have an eye for design.

After some clinking of ice and glassware, he handed her a drink.

"To Mazy in Brandt Mountain," he said, by way of a toast. They clinked glasses and she took a taste.

"Very good," she told him. "I like your place." She heard the incredulity in her own voice and hoped he hadn't noticed.

"Thanks."

He showed her to the gray chenille couch. There was a big overstuffed armchair nearby that she knew must be his favorite, but Eli hesitated only for an instant before taking a seat beside her and lolling his arm casually along the back.

"I came over to thank you for hiring Tru," she said.

Eli shrugged. "He seems like a nice kid, Mazy. Smart, polite, willing to work—you must be doing something right. That doesn't happen by accident."

She laughed. "Oh, sometimes I think it does. Tru is a great kid, *despite* having me for a mother."

"I'm sure that's an exaggeration."

"Well, I still appreciate that you're taking him on," she said.

"I was happy to do it," he said. "I knew Dad would have done the same. If he has any aptitude, we'll be able to teach him a few things that he can use."

She expected that. It was interesting to think that Tru would be hanging out in the wood shop after school, just as she once had. A close association with the Lathams would be nice for him. They were regular people, salt-of-the-earth guys, not the kind of screwed-up variety that her son had seen so often. If Tru could grow up to have the lifestyle and values that seemed to come so naturally to other people, then he might end up happier than Mazy had been. And happier was definitely something she wanted for her son.

But in that particular moment, with Eli so close beside her, it was difficult to keep her mind on her son.

"And I promise to keep a close eye on him," Eli said. "We're very big on safety and I'll make sure that he is, too."

The scent of him enveloped her. It was an intoxicating mix of sawdust, shellac and…sexual male. She was definitely enjoying this close encounter with masculine pheromones.

Mazy sipped her drink and tried to keep her gaze on his face and their conversation light, but she allowed herself some worthwhile glances. Denim jeans covered thighs that were heavily muscled. And his loose long-sleeve tee couldn't quite disguise the cut, working-man biceps that a million reps in the gym couldn't duplicate.

Who knew that Termy would turn out to look like this? An enormous feeling of regret welled up in her. This man had once been hers for the taking. If she had been smarter, less romantically dysfunctional, she could have been nicely settled down with security and safety and a man who was gorgeous, crazy about her and, if she remembered right, very competent in the sack.

Mazy pushed back against the thought. It probably wouldn't have worked that way. The very private surroundings and the fact that she hadn't had sex in months was probably making him look better than he was. And without lessons learned and the recent calamity, she'd had nothing beneficial to offer this very good, very decent man.

Eli interrupted her thoughts. "He doesn't know about Driscoll."

It was a statement more than a question. "He knows what he needs to know," Mazy said. "I haven't tried to keep anything from him. But I have tried to keep…well, my own anger and bitterness to myself. Every person deserves to believe that they were conceived in love, even if it was only love of the moment."

"You're a good human being, Mazy Gulliver."

She laughed out loud. "Only *you* would believe that, Eli Latham," she replied.

He was thoughtful for a long moment before he gave her a look. "He asked me today if I was 'the sperm donor.'"

"What? Oh, my God! I'll kill him. Termy, I'm so sorry."

"No problem," he assured her. "It probably made sense

to ask. I'd told him that we were friends. I'm the right age. It reasonably could have been me."

"As if!" Mazy responded, shaking her head. In memory she recalled the youthful face of the man beside her, gritting his teeth amid his teenage passion as he dutifully stopped to pull on a condom. Eli was far too responsible to get a girl pregnant. And if contraceptives had failed her, he would not have.

"Have you forgotten that we used to go at it like rabbits?"

She had not forgotten. In fact, at that particular moment she could hardly keep at bay the memories of sex with Eli.

Her eyes strayed to his crotch. Was that a bulge? No. Her imagination. It was wishful thinking. Mazy crossed her legs and cleared her throat.

"Your…your home here is very nice," she told him before she remembered that she'd already said so.

"Thanks," he said, apparently accepting her abrupt change of subject. "I did all this work myself." There was genuine pride in his voice as he glanced around the room. "Do you remember what it was like down here? All spiderwebs and old mason jars."

"Vividly," she replied. "It bears no resemblance to that scary place. I think I still have nightmares. I hated hide-and-seek in here."

He glanced at her with surprise. "You're kidding. You always *suggested* it as the best place to play."

She nodded. "You know how I am. I go straight at the things that scare me the most."

The psychologist had called that part of her nature "flailing for control." Mazy didn't share that estimation with Eli.

"Then I guess you're the person I should have con-

tacted to help me fix it up," Eli told her. "I tried to get
Clark down here, but he always had some excuse to avoid
the place."

Mazy nodded. "I would have gone straight at those
spiderwebs, but I probably would have tried to talk you
out of all this effort. Two words—*apartment complex*."

He laughed. "I'm not sure I could find happiness in a
place built with one-by-twos and stuccoed chicken wire."

"Still, most people do leave home."

"And sometimes they come back."

Mazy thought he was referring to her, until he continued. "I actually rented a condo out near Keeper's Wood
for a couple of years. But when Dad got sick I knew I
needed to be closer, so I fixed this place up. It's perfect
for me, really. I have all the privacy I want and I'm only
a shout-out away from being there to help."

"That's a really good thing," Mazy said. "I used to
worry that if something happened to my mom or she got
sick, nobody would be there."

"But now you are," Eli pointed out.

"I am," she concurred.

"I'm glad," he said. "And I was hoping…"

"What?

"I was hoping that now that you're back home, you
and I could maybe pick up where we left off."

Mazy's mouth inexplicably went dry. She felt an in-
escapable *zizz* of electricity in the air.

"Where exactly did we leave off?" she asked him.

"I believe it was somewhere near the bedroom. Although it may have been a couch much like this one."

He was making a joke. She could see that. He was trying to get past the awkwardness of being together again
by putting it all in the past and making it a punch line.

That was the right thing to do. She should be laughing about it, as well. Strangely, she didn't want to be.

Mazy recrossed her legs and deliberately looked around the room again.

"It seems like you're still single."

"Don't remind my sister-in-law. She thinks it's her life's calling to fix me up."

"Ah, Sheila. Once a cheerleader, always a cheerleader. She never really liked me. I bet she's got some really special, perfect girl lined up for you."

He shrugged. "More like a long line of perfectly lovely, ordinary girls that I'm not interested in."

"What kind of girls are you interested in?"

"No girls, just women."

"Right. Any particular kind of woman?"

He shrugged. "I'm not real picky," he assured her. "She should be, I'd say, about thirty-one years old. Five-seven. Brunette with brown eyes. Slim figure, shapely legs and a great backside. Her breasts are not too big, but nicely perky. And…she'd have to be a vodka-tonic kind of gal."

At that, Mazy laughed.

"Well, I did hear that there was a woman back in town who is very much like that and seems to be pretty much available," she told him.

"How available?" he asked.

She should tell him that she was taking some time. She should tell him she wasn't ready to be involved. She should tell him that she'd given up sleeping with guys just for sex.

"How fast can you get your clothes off?"

She didn't need to ask twice. Eli laid a large, calloused hand upon her jaw and raised her face just slightly before he brought his lips down to hers. She felt enveloped in the scent of him, the warmth of him. Her body remembered him in ways that her frontal lobe had discounted. A little moan of delight escaped her. They had been very good at this. And it had been such a long time.

When the kiss ended she opened her eyes. He was only inches away.

"I wanted to do that since the minute I saw you," he told her.

"I wanted to do it before I even walked over here," she replied.

She slid into his embrace and heard a sigh of pleasure escape him. They had a history. The last time the two had been alone together, they had been like this. Male and female fitting together so perfectly.

His mouth explored hers. Not with undue pressure or thrusting tongue, but slowly, unhurried, searching the experience. Their lips parted hesitantly and she looked into the depths of his eyes, her heart plummeting and then flying to her throat like a roller coaster.

She disguised her reaction with a joke. "Hey, bud, don't you know you're supposed to ply me with strong drink and make promises that you don't mean?"

"I can do that," Eli answered. "But I'd rather do this."

He tilted his head slightly and kissed her again. This time he kept his hands on the couch. Not one finger touched her skin. Only his lips caressed her. But his lips were enough. Her nipples hardened uncomfortably against the fabric of her bra. And an ache began to pulse between her thighs. She squeezed tightly against it, which did not alleviate it in the slightest.

"I'd rather do this, too," she told him.

She began tugging at her shirt and managed to get it up over her head. She reached behind her for the hooks on her bra, but he pushed her hands away. Instead of taking it off her himself, he leaned down and bit her nipple through the fabric. The tease got more response than it should have. She pressed against him, despising the barrier.

"Take it off. Take it off," she pleaded.

"I think that's supposed to be my line," Eli told her before lowering his mouth to the other breast.

It had been so long. And it felt so good. It felt so good she could barely stand it. Mazy threw her head back and moaned aloud.

Finally he released the hooks on that cursed binder and she was able to feel his flesh against hers. She slid her arms around his neck and he enfolded her into his lap.

Mazy straddled him on the couch to press against him. No doubt about that bulge now. It was big and it was hard and she wanted it. She kept her knees as wide apart as the cushions would allow, hoping his hands would take the invitation.

Eli's mouth moved over hers, tugging and tasting. It was hot, but without any sense of hurry. He kissed her as if kissing was the only thing he wanted and as if they had all the time in the world.

She did not have his sense of leisure. Her love-starved body reacted to him with desire in full throttle. She craved sexual release. She didn't simply want it, she needed it.

Futilely she tried to caution herself. She admonished herself to hold back. Her better judgment screamed out warnings about ill-considered intimacy. But her body had never paid any attention to the rational being inside her head. And today was not the day she would start. She always wanted what she wanted. And, at this moment, she wanted Eli.

She broke off the embrace, but not to beg apologies

and run to the door. Instead, she unbuttoned her jeans and tried peeling them down her hips.

"Slow down, Mazy," he whispered to her.

"I don't want to slow down," she answered. "I want to do it before we both come to our senses and talk ourselves out of it."

He chuckled as he ran his thumb down the length of her torso, slipped his hand inside that scrap of nylon that covered her throbbing place and made the ache wonderfully worse.

"Why would we talk ourselves out of it?" he asked.

"Because… Oh… Oh… Because I was a shit to you nine years ago." The words came out in a rush as he unerringly found that perfect place on her body and caressed it with exactly the pressure that she liked. "I was a shit and I'll probably be like that again. I don't want to hurt you, Termy. You're a nice guy."

For an instant his hand stopped. "A nice guy," he repeated.

She pressed her hand atop his own. "Don't stop," she pleaded. "Please don't stop. Do me and we'll talk about it later."

For one heart-sickening moment, she was afraid that he wouldn't. But they were alone, she was naked from the waist up and he was a man with his hand down her panties as she was literally begging for it.

They skimmed the remainder of her clothes down her legs. She didn't give him time to discard his own. She unzipped him and climbed aboard. She was too ready, too eager. She came practically the moment he was inside her. It had been so long and it felt so good. She was like warm jelly in his arms as she collapsed against his chest.

"Wow, oh, wow," she breathed against his neck.

"I know," he answered. "For me, too."

But he was too much the good guy to finish on his own. He laid her out beneath him on the plush couch where he savored her and favored her until he brought her there again before they were done.

He woke her a couple of hours later and carried her from where they'd fallen asleep on the floor to the bedroom. It was slow and sweet this time, almost achingly sweet. *He's such a good lover,* Mazy thought through the haze of pleasure. *He's going to make some lucky woman a great husband.*

11

—◂ ▸—

The scent of coffee filled her nostrils and Mazy opened her eyes. Eli was sitting on the bed beside her, mug in hand. From the tiny basement window next to the ceiling, a gray light was seeping in. He was smiling.

"Good morning, Mazy," he said. "My wonderful, amazing Mazy."

He planted a tender kiss on her forehead.

"Morning."

She sat up in the bed and pushed the hair out of her face. Her body felt great. The release of tension and the surge of hormones was exactly what the doctor ordered. Her conscience, however, was not quite as pleased. Mornings after were always dicey. She feared this one might be more so than usual.

"Have you got some of that for me?" she asked, indicating the cup.

"This is yours," he said. "One sugar, no milk, right?"

"You remember how I take my coffee?"

"I remember everything."

The phrase scared her. She suddenly felt trapped. She had warned him last night that she had been a shit and she would probably be a shit. But she'd also begged him to do her. She should never have jumped back into bed with him. He deserved better. He always had. He knew her too well and he cared too much. Now there would be expectations. And she didn't know what she felt yet.

She knocked back a hot swig of coffee. "What time is it?"

"About six," he answered. "I don't think anybody next door is up yet. You can probably sneak back inside with no one being the wiser."

"Whose reputation am I saving? Mine or yours? Trust me, nobody in my family will be surprised that I've crawled in bed with somebody."

It wasn't quite the truth. Beth Ann and Tru might not be surprised, but they might be worried. She was worried herself. What was she doing here? Did she want a relationship with Eli? This should be familiar territory, but it wasn't. Her new self, the woman she was trying to be, was more thoughtful, more deliberate. What if this was more of her old self creeping back? What if she couldn't overcome her psychology? What if her compulsion to seek out rejection overrode her conscious desire for a more healthy, loving relationship? What would happen to Eli then? Would she use him like she had before?

She couldn't see his eyes in the darkness, but she could hear the confusion in his voice.

"If you want to stay, of course you can stay."

"No, no. I've got to get home."

She threw back the covers. Ignoring her own nudity, she hurried through the basement retrieving her clothes, putting them on as if all the demons in hell were after her.

Of course, these particular demons were strictly her own. Once more she'd allowed her physical desires, her love of love, her longing for connection, to override all her rational brain cells.

What she'd said last night when she saw him was typically true. She tried to never make the same mistake twice. Or rather, she made the same mistake over and over again, but she always tried making it with somebody new.

But this was a worse mistake than simply sleeping with a jerk. Rebounding with the rebound guy. She didn't want to do that again. Hadn't good old Eli, the sweetest guy in town, been on the wrong end of her bad behavior enough already? She needed to get out of here fast. They'd never be able to pretend it hadn't happened. But she had to get away before she did any more damage.

"What's wrong?"

Eli had followed her into the living room.

"Nothing."

"Something," he countered with conviction.

"Look I…" Mazy didn't know what to say. "I…I had a great time. You and I, well, we're good together in the sack. We already knew that. I just…I just don't want to rush into being more than that."

"I'm not in any rush," Eli told her. "Remember, you're the one who was in such a hurry last night."

He was smiling at her. More than smiling, he was glowing at her, heart in his eyes. She recognized that look for what it was. Eli was totally hooked. Damn! Why couldn't she learn to keep her pants zipped?

"I know," she answered. "You know how I am. *I* know how I am. I'm not saying that I didn't know what I was doing. And I'm not suggesting that you pushed things. You wouldn't. You're way too decent. Far more decent that I deserve."

"You've got to quit talking about yourself like that," he told her. "You are not anyone's opinion of you. You are whoever you choose to be."

She chuckled humorlessly. "And we both know what spectacularly bad choices I've made."

"They weren't that bad," he said. "And whatever they were, they're in the past now."

She hopped a couple of times to get on her left shoe. Fully dressed, she walked over to him. But when he would have embraced her, she clasped his hands.

"Eli. Sweetie." She stood on tiptoes to kiss him on the cheek. "I…I need to think about whether we really should get involved. You're just such a nice guy."

His eyes narrowed slightly.

"I'm not that nice," he insisted.

Mazy shook her head. "Yes, you are," she answered. "I've known you all my life. Trust me, you are as sweet and kind and good as any man I've known."

"And that's a reason not to be involved with me?"

"I already hurt you once, Termy. I'm not sure that your heart can be trusted with me."

12

━ ➤ ━

Eli's coffee sat on the counter getting cold as he paced the living-room floor. He was agitated. He was confused. He was furious. But he wasn't sure who he was mad at—Mazy, for being the kind of woman who was only attracted to assholes, or himself, for not being the kind of asshole she was attracted to.

Eli went over the past twelve hours in his head until he was nearly crazy.

He'd imagined being with her again a million times over the years. She'd walk straight into his workshop. Or maybe it would be a surprise encounter in another city. Their eyes would meet across a crowded dance floor. Or he'd walk up to her mom's porch and knock on the door. In all of those scenes, he was cool and clever. And she was always his gorgeous Mazy. But not even in the very best of those fantasies had she walked into his apartment and practically ripped her clothes off, begging to screw his brains out.

For that moment, the bottom had fallen out of the universe and he was walking on air. She was more beautiful now than she had been as a young girl. She had one of those faces that didn't get stuck in girlish prettiness, but aged into a woman's beauty. Her body, too, was curvier and more voluptuous. But it was that smile, that unchanged smile, that almost tugged his heart right out of his chest. And those sounds, those wonderful sounds from the back of her throat. They were mostly incoherent cries of pleasure, but among them he was sure he'd heard her say she loved him. And for a blissful few hours of sex and sleep, he'd believed it.

What an idiot!

Mazy didn't love him. She thought he *looked cute*.

You're so sweet.

So kind.

So good.

I don't want to hurt you, she'd said, as if she held all the power and he had none.

Why did a statement like "You're the nicest guy I know" feel like utter disrespect?

He felt like slamming his fist into the wall. Remembering that he would have to work with his hands, he angrily kicked the mopboard instead. He regretted that as he hobbled to a seat at the bar stool.

"Maybe I *am* her trained puppy," he declared aloud. "I've been faithfully following at her heels all my life, grateful for the slightest pat on the head."

Clark had been right. He hated to admit it, but his brother was one hundred percent correct. Mazy would never fall for him. She'd never see him as her type. He was too "Boy Scout" to capture her interest. Oh, she was fine with having sex with him. But their relationship would be for recreational use only. If and when it was convenient for her. She'd made that crystal.

"Damn!" he said aloud.

Eli took a swig of coffee, but the taste in his mouth was already bitter enough.

He was cursed. Unlucky enough to spend most of his life in love with a woman like her. He would never be the kind of man she would want. Well, at least not until it was too late. Good guys finish last. Everybody said so. He needed to accept that or change.

Could he change?

Taking a few deep breaths, he got a handle on his anger. He needed to think this through rationally. Could *he* be the bad boy that she wanted?

In the back of his mind he'd been kicking around the idea for days.

How tough was it to be a hard-ass? Some of the stupidest guys he knew managed it nearly every day of their life.

And it wouldn't have to be forever for him. He'd only need to play the role until she was hooked. Completely hooked. No chance of backing out. He'd have to keep it up until…until she married him.

Married. If he was going to trick her into a happily-ever-after, he would need to lock it down tight.

And wasn't marriage what he'd always wanted? It's what he'd been working toward all those long years ago. He'd been eager to shoulder the responsibility of husband and father even way back then. Now he was older and wiser. More financially stable. The future he could offer her today was even brighter than what she'd been so willing to reject before.

Not that he could just offer it up. Marriage would have to be the brass ring pulled out of her grasp time and time again. That's the only way he would ever get it on her finger.

Mazy had never managed to tie the knot with anyone. All the fish she'd gone after seemed to wiggle off the hook. But to make his plan work, Eli couldn't settle for anything else.

The way he understood it, and truth to tell it didn't

make a lot of sense, women wanted to marry the bad boy. But once they said, "I do," they became committed to changing him from the jerk they fell for into the good guy they would never have given the time of day.

Eli chugged the rest of the contents of his cup and set it decisively on the counter.

Beginning today, he was going to be the crappiest SOB that Brandt Mountain had ever seen—and the competition for that honor was tremendous. He'd treat Mazy like she was worse than nothing. He would be insolent and dismissive. He'd use her for sex and take her for granted. He would be rude, crude and always in the mood. And she'd fall passionately, desperately in love with him. She'd work, plot, scheme, to win him.

He wouldn't make it easy for her. There would have to be hurdles. There would have to be heartache. There would be tears. But somehow, some way, she would finally win him.

And, oh, how great Mazy was going to feel about her ability to turn her bad-boy husband into Mr. Nice Guy!

There was some weird flaw in her personality that made her seek out guys that were all wrong for her. Eli could pretend to be one of those guys and thereby help her to accidentally find the loving, attentive husband that she'd always deserved.

It was the perfection of that plan that got him out of the morning's rejection and back to the satisfaction of the night before. Sex with Mazy. The plan required an abundance of it. And from his perspective, there was no way to get too much.

He didn't share that part of his strategy with the one person he felt safe to talk it over with, his dad.

"It's not like I've completely invented a whole new thing," he explained. "When people start dating, nobody is being completely honest. Both women and guys try to show their best side to the other person. I'll just be going the other way. Instead of pretending to be better than I am, I'm pretending to be worse."

His father could not respond.

"Just so we're clear," Eli added. "This has nothing to do with revenge. It's not in any way trying to get back at her because of the way she treated me. No, that's not it. I'm going to be a jerk because she *likes* jerks."

Eli considered that and hoped that his father understood, as well.

"Seriously, I'm doing her a favor," he insisted. "Mazy is going to hook up with someone, some lousy no-good someone. Better to be lousy no-good me, than lousy no-good someone else. People have money bet all over town on Tad Driscoll. I cannot and will not let that happen again. You can trust me on that."

As he buttoned his father's shirt, his brow furrowed.

"Mazy came back to town for some reason. And showing up at the bank to get a job is a fairly broad hint about what that might be," Eli said. "If being the bad guy can save her from him this time…well, it's the least that I can do. As long as she's with me, she won't be with him. That's for certain. Mazy has a lot of faults, but she is never dishonest," he said. "I guess that leaves all the lying to me."

Eli broke the news to his brother over lunch. Clark's jaw dropped open and he looked at Eli disapprovingly. "Oh, come on. You're kidding, right?"

"I am not kidding," Eli told him. "Mazy and I are an item."

"Well, I hope you know what you're doing," he said.

"I do," Eli answered. He hoped he sounded more certain than he felt.

Clark made a sound that was pure exasperation. "Sheila's tried to fix you up with some of the sweetest, nicest girls in the county. Women who could really care about you. It makes me nearly crazy to think that you prefer someone like Mazy Gulliver."

Eli had a sudden flash of insight that perhaps he and Mazy weren't so different in their choices. But the idea ran so counter to his image of the man he was that he disregarded it.

13

⬤—◀—⬤

Mazy had had a lot of experience sneaking into her mother's house at dawn. This morning, however, she had the advantage of a key to the back door. She was not quite as pleased to see Beth Ann standing at the counter next to the coffeepot. In contrast to the bright pink bathrobe with turquoise flowers, her mother's mood seemed grim.

"Don't start," Mazy said firmly.

Beth Ann responded with raised eyebrows. "Why would I start?" she asked. "He's the one I've been rooting for since you were children."

Mazy shook her head before reaching for a coffee cup. "You just wanted me to live next door."

"That would have been a nice bonus," she admitted. "But what I wanted was for you to find a good man who would love you."

Mazy shrugged and gave her mother a little smile before taking a sip of the hot, brown brew. "That's what I want, too," she admitted. "But I'm not sure I can jump from scrumbag to saint in one leap. I might be better off to work up to it with somebody who's good for right now."

"Humph," Beth Ann responded. "Seems to me you've had enough practice that it's time to go for the gold. That would be Eli."

"Mother," Mazy said firmly. "Don't push."

As the day went along, however, she was thinking that her mother might be right. Eli might be just exactly the man she needed. The freak-out that morning had simply been a weird reaction to his tenderness. Even the crappiest guys were nice on the first morning after. Naturally a sweetheart like Eli would seem…loving.

That would be a fabulous improvement, she decided. To be with somebody who could be loving, even if it was just sex. That could work for her. And the "just sex" had been pretty spectacular. Maybe it was the results of her drought, but it had been so good. He'd obviously acquired some moves since his younger days. He also smelled really great and was muscular but not beefy. And he seemed to take genuine enjoyment in making her come. Not in a look-what-a-lover-I-am kind of way, but as if experiencing her pleasure was as sweet as getting his own.

At work, she sat at her desk having to remind herself to wipe the goofy grin off her face. It was important to keep her mind on her work. Her debtor clients were still defensive and distrustful. The interactions weren't going that well. Every bank employee got the occasional angry phone call, but all of Mazy's were hopping mad.

Yet by midafternoon she was imagining a long evening with a glass of wine and her feet up as she poured out her troubles to…Termy.

Eli. She wanted to remember to call him Eli.

Yes, she thought. This was actually going to work out perfectly. Eli was a good friend and a good listener and a good lover. Any woman could live through crappy days when the expectation for evenings was so nice.

She'd checked her cell phone, but there were no messages. That wasn't too big of a surprise. She felt a self-satisfied grin cross her face. Last night they'd had better things to do than exchange phone numbers.

Tonight, after the wine and the whine, there would be more of the same. That thought had her smiling as she walked home from the bank.

When she arrived, her mother was in the kitchen. A big pot emitting the enticing smell of goulash simmered on the stove.

"You don't have to cook for us every night," Mazy reminded her.

"Should I let you cook for me, after you've put in a full day at work?" Beth Ann asked. "I wasn't raised that way. Besides, I was thinking you might need some comfort food tonight."

"Well, you're probably right about that," Mazy admitted. "Any calls for me?"

"All we've had are calls," Beth Ann answered. "Every friend I have and every favor I've ever gotten is trying to call in their chit to save them from my daughter, the big, bad banker."

"Seriously?"

Beth Ann nodded as she pointed to a list that she'd attached to the refrigerator with a magnet.

Mazy glanced through the names and shook her head. "Some of these people aren't even delinquent," she said.

Beth Ann shrugged.

"You know that I'm not going to hurt anybody," Mazy told her mother. "I'm actually trying to help."

"I know that's what you want to do," Beth Ann said. "But things don't always work out the way we plan. I mean, think about your boss in Wilmington. I'm sure you were only trying to help him out."

"Totally different," Mazy said. "I was sleeping with my boss. I thought he was leaving his wife for me."

Beth Ann pursed her lips but kept her silence.

"So I should be safe, since I'm not sleeping with the whole town."

"Well, not yet, anyway," Beth Ann quipped.

Mazy laughed.

"So did Eli call?"

"Eli? No. He's still working."

Mazy didn't bother to point out that a man who owns his own business can make phone calls whenever he likes. He was probably waiting until he knew she was home from work.

She went to her mother's room and changed out of her work clothes. Most of her really attractive casual clothes, all her cute tops, had gone for a buck a piece at her yard sale. She pulled a ratty tee on over her jeans and then tied a knot in the hem to make it a little more fitted and show off her bustline a bit better. Fortunately, Termy wouldn't care what she had on. He liked her for who she was, not for how she looked.

She recalled with a smile the "day after" from the beginning of their previous hook-ups.

As a teenager he'd tried to give her his class ring. She'd laughed at that one.

"Grown-up women with babies don't go steady," she'd teased.

When she'd fallen in bed with him again four years later he'd shown up with a dozen red roses. It was a romantic gesture and she'd liked it. But it had made her feel weird, too. It had made the other guys, the guys that she'd truly loved, sort of look bad.

Probably because they really were bad, she realized.

She wondered if there would be roses again. Maybe not red this time. Red was corny. She liked the lavender-colored ones. And those that were sort of peachy looking. After the day she'd had, flowers would be nice.

How would she explain roses to Tru?

Eli and I are dating.

We're great friends.

There was a sale at the florist shop.

Mazy shook away her concern. Tru wouldn't need an explanation. He was fourteen going on forty. He knew all about Mom and her men.

By dinnertime Eli still hadn't called. She listened idly to the casual conversation of her mother and son and wondered why.

"How was work?" she asked Tru.

"Okay," he answered. "I'm mostly sweeping up and learning where everything is. Did you know he has twenty-seven different kinds of wood planes? And every one of them has to be put back in the same place every time."

"Hmm," Mazy said. "Maybe this is a system you can try to adapt to all the junk in your room."

Tru chuckled. "As if."

"So nothing out of the ordinary going on?"

Tru looked at her as if she'd lost her mind. "How would I know, Mom?" he asked. "It's my second day on the job."

Mazy shook her head. "Of course it is, sorry."

She changed the subject to school. The last thing she wanted to do was interrogate her son over goulash. Eli was probably with a customer or checking on his dad or simply running late.

All through the meal and during the cleanup, she expected the phone to ring. She even checked it once to make sure it had a dial tone.

With the kitchen spick-and-span and Tru in his room, she joined Beth Ann in front of the TV. The silly chick flick from the '90s kept her mother laughing, but Mazy's humor seemed to have temporarily deserted her.

There were two calls that evening. The first was a sales pitch. The second a giggly girl calling Tru with a question about homework.

How annoying.

Mazy really wanted to talk with Eli, be with Eli. She wanted to tell him about her crappy day. She wanted him to hold her in his arms and make her feel safe and warm.

Suddenly she was gobsmacked with the stupidity of waiting by the phone. Being back home was apparently throwing her into some retro time loop. She would simply call him.

Of course, she didn't really have his number. The ancient phone directory in Beth Ann's kitchen listed only his parents' phone. Mazy really couldn't call there and disturb Ida and poor old Mr. Latham.

The internet search for Eli's business brought up a pretty fancy webpage with lots of photographs of beautiful furniture. There was no name under the contacts, just an email address and a telephone for the shop. Since it was the only number she had, she called it. No answer. Maybe she'd misdialed. She called again. Perhaps he was in the shower. She waited fifteen minutes and called again.

Obviously it was the business phone and the business was closed.

When both her mother and son were in bed and she was sampling the offerings of the late-night networks, she gave up the expectation that he was going to call. As she dressed down to her pajamas and stretched out on the lumpy couch, she began to postulate the reasons why he hadn't.

Had he said anything about going out of town? Mazy

didn't remember him mentioning that. Maybe he had had a dinner with a client. Small-business people did that often, she imagined. Or it might be that his dad was having a bad night and he needed to stay at the bedside.

Eli could be sick himself. He sure seemed healthy enough the night before. Maybe that was it. Maybe he'd overdone it and sacked out early. She shook her head at that. No, even the nicest guys didn't get incapacitated from too much sex.

She fell asleep counting excuses instead of sheep.

14

——▸◂——

Eli had thought about her all day. Her smile, her laugh. The taste of her lips filled the back of his thoughts with the same frequency that oxygen filled his lungs. In day-dreamy moments, the scent of her seemed to surround him with well-being and contentment. In flashes of lust he'd recall her body clenching greedily as she made that sound at the back of her throat.

Discussion of her as the bank's new "enforcer" was on everyone's lips. And that widespread anger and sus-picion made him want to enfold her in his arms and tell her that he was on her side, reassure her that everything would be all right.

He was convinced, however, that that was exactly the wrong thing to do. That's the kind of thing he would have done in the past. It's the kind of thing she'd expect from her sweet friend Termy. Eli was determined not to let her see him that way again.

So he resisted the impulse to call her. He dismissed the idea of taking her out to lunch. He tamped down all thoughts of a heartfelt gift as a remembrance of their night together. He was pretty sure that Lesson One in the Basics of Being a Jerk was that you have sex and you don't call. Eli figured if he couldn't manage that, his whole plan was doomed to failure.

He spent much of the afternoon concentrating on the pieces of poplar that he was going to use for the music cabinet and reminding himself that their long-term happiness together was seriously worth the sacrifice of no sex tonight. He would not call her. And, eventually, she would call him. It might take a week. It might take ten days. He tried to hold on to the certainty that she would. Because the minute that she did, their relationship would be forever changed. She would be the pursuer. He would be the pursued. She was going to chase after him until he caught her.

At least that was how he explained it to his father.

He'd gone over for his usual after-work visit, but had stayed to help get his dad through supper. He knew Ida welcomed the break and he needed someone to talk to. It was a bonus that the someone he chose was in no position to try to talk him out of it.

"You know I'm no misogynist. I've never wanted to be the big-man-of-the-house type," he said as he spooned finely diced-up bits of beef roast into his dad's mouth. "I don't like giving orders at work, and I sure don't want a life of giving them at home. I need a woman to love, not a doormat to walk on. I want the kind of relationship you and Mom had or like the one with you and Ida. A marriage of equals."

Eli scraped the last bit of mash potatoes from the side of the bowl and fed it to his dad.

"Somehow she and I got off on the wrong foot," he said. "Maybe it was just because I was younger. Or because she was used to Tad and his type. But, whatever it was, she's never really respected me. If she doesn't respect me, she can't love me. That's all there is to it."

He set the empty bowl on the tray and used the napkin to wipe his father's mouth.

"I really love her. You probably already know that. Maybe you knew it before I did." Eli sighed. "It might not work," he continued. "I'm going into it understanding that. It may be that Mazy is incapable of returning my feelings. That wouldn't be her fault. It would just be… what it is. If that's how it turns out, then at least I'll know I gave it my best shot. Every weapon in my arsenal. And then…then I'll move on. I promise us both that, Dad. I know Clark and Sheila are sick of me mooning after her. I'll bet you and Ida are, too. You two just aren't busybody enough to say so. If I get burned this time, I'm done. I'll give her a nice kiss on the cheek and send her off into the horizon with whoever it is she really wants to be with." He raised his hand as if giving the Boy Scout pledge.

His father's eyes were bright as he looked at his son with concern.

"I'm pretty hopeful, really," Eli reassured him. "Third time's a charm and all that. And you're going to love having her as a daughter-in-law. She's always been sweeter to you than Sheila has."

Later, after his dad was in bed, he paced the basement floor. This morning it had all seemed easy enough. Even after talking to his father, the plan seemed doable. But now, being alone and knowing that, after all these years, Mazy was only a phone call away… That didn't make it easy. He also knew about all the outcry her letters to the bank's debtors had caused, and that she could probably use a friendly face right about now. And arms to hold her and lips to whisper that it would be okay—those things would be useful, too.

He tried to stay strong. If he couldn't manage not to call her, he would never be able to follow through on anything worse. And he had to do some jerking around. He had to appeal to the side of her that wanted to fall for the bad boy. It would be difficult but, after the lying was over and they were happy together, everything would be worth it.

When the phone rang, he almost picked it up before catching sight of the caller ID.

She'd called him! He glanced at his watch—8:20 p.m. and she'd already called him. But he couldn't answer it. Too soon. Too fast. Wasn't the whole purpose of not calling being hard to get? If he simply picked up the phone, that made him too easy.

He continued to let it ring, and when it stopped he let out a long breath that he hadn't realized he'd be holding.

Almost immediately it started ringing again. This time he had enough strength to walk away. If she kept this up, it was not going to be easy to stay disciplined. And he was going to need some advice.

He sat down at the kitchen counter and opened his laptop. He typed the term *bad boyfriend* into the search engine and a plethora of blogs and articles popped up. They had titles like 7 Signs Your Boyfriend Is Bad News or No, It's Not You, It's Him and Lose That Loser You Think You Love.

Eli pulled out the little notebook he kept in his shirt pocket to jot down measurements and began writing notes. Some of the bad-boyfriend revelations were completely out of the question. Under no circumstances would he make a secret sex tape of them and post it on the internet. He would not be stealing money from her purse or running up charges on her credit card. He would never make a public scene so that everyone would know who was the boss. And even if Mazy had a sister, Eli would not sleep with her.

However, there were some less monumental but easily irritating complaints that he thought he'd be able to pull off. The next time the phone rang, he was able to give it a slant-eyed glare. He wasn't going to be had with a phone call.

15

— ◄ ►—

Mazy decided the next night that she would simply wander over to his place after dinner, like she had before. It could be very casual. She might have given the impression that she wasn't interested on that awkward morning after. In truth, that was exactly what she'd done. She distinctly remembered calling it a mistake and expressing regret. So Eli was undoubtedly holed up nursing some hurt feelings.

She would have to learn to be *gentle* with him. She joked to herself that she'd messed up because she hadn't been with many *gentle*men.

She'd left the dinner dishes for Tru and freshened her makeup. She had just made it to the back door when she saw his truck pull out into the street. He turned right and headed up Sawmill Road. Disappointed, she had fallen asleep that night still dressed as she watched TV in the living room waiting for him to come home.

The next day, with a crick in her neck, she decided to take more decisive action. She called from work.

It rang three times before a voice answered.

"Latham Furniture."

"Eli?"

"No, this is Clark."

"Oh, hi, Clark. This is Mazy Gulliver. Do you remember me?"

"Of course. The pesky brat next door who always dragged my brother into trouble."

She laughed. "Is Eli around?"

"Well, uh, Mazy, you…you just missed him."

"Oh."

"He…he had to go see about…something."

"Do you know when he'll be back?"

"Not sure. Later, maybe."

"Oh. Okay. Well, if you could tell him I called."

"That I will do," Clark assured her.

"Let me give you my cell phone number. I'm not sure he has it."

"Sure."

Mazy recited it and Clark read it back to her.

"I'll give it to him the minute I see him," he assured her.

"Thanks."

The interaction was singularly unsatisfying. But she assured herself that now he could call her directly and not have to call her mother or the bank, that it would be exactly what he would do.

When she still hadn't heard from him by late afternoon, she decided that Clark was unreliable and had forgotten to give him the number.

She called the shop again.

This time the voice on the end of the line was more familiar, too familiar.

"Tru? Hi."

"Mom? Is something wrong?"

"No, no."

"Are you checking up on me?"

"No, not at all. I was actually calling to talk to Eli."

"Eli? Oh, okay. Hang on."

Tru laid the receiver down, but Mazy heard her son's voice clearly. "It's my mom. She wants to talk to you."

The reply from across the room was less clear. Then Tru picked up the phone again.

"Mom, he's right in the middle of cutting a dado. He says he'll talk to you later."

"Oh, sure. That's fine. I, uh, I'll see you at home."

"Okay."

Mazy didn't know what a dado was, but she was fairly certain it wasn't brain surgery. He could have taken the call. But maybe he didn't want to talk to her in front of Tru. He said he would talk to her later. That obviously meant that he expected to see her tonight. She would go to his place as soon as she got home. If he was still in the shop or upstairs with his parents, she'd wait on him.

That was her plan as she stepped out of the bank at four o'clock. What she had not planned was for Karly to be waiting for her.

"Hi, hi, hi. I'm sorry I didn't make it up here for coffee the past couple of days."

"Oh? I didn't think we had a regular meet-up planned," Mazy told her.

"No, we don't. But as soon as I heard all the stew being stirred up in town, I knew that you'd need somebody to cheer you up. I'm your friend, remember? I'm supposed to be around when you need to talk. And I'm pretty sure you need to talk."

Mazy was not so sure that she needed to talk. And if she did, she wasn't sure that Karly was the person she'd choose. Then she reminded herself that she was not a particularly good judge of character. If Karly wanted to be her friend, with no apparent motive other than friendship, it would be silly to turn down the opportunity.

"Let's go get a coffee," Karly insisted.

"I'm not sure if I should," Mazy answered. "Some of the banks clients are—"

"Oh, I know. Charlie McDee's coffee shop has an overdue loan," Karly said. "He already told me. He feels bad about it. But he doesn't blame you. It's not like you held a gun to his head and said, 'Take the money.'"

"Still, I was going to go home and—"

"Don't even think about it," Karly interrupted. "If you seem to hide out, it makes all their distrust of you seem reasonable. Sit with me and we'll show them that you are not wounded and dangerous and back in town to make people pay."

"What? That's crazy. Make people pay for what?"

"I told you. A lot of us know that you got a raw deal in this town. He was a basketball hero and you were a nobody. There should have been somebody—his parents, his coach, the townsfolk—to make him do right by you and his child."

"That is so yesterday's news," Mazy said.

"But it's back on the front page again," Karly replied. "Come on. Coffee."

Mazy followed her as they crossed the street and entered Local Grind. They sat in the same seat in the window where they could be seen by the entire world. Charlie McDee took their order without making eye contact with her.

Karly settled in with her macchiato and Mazy was expecting an adult version of Twenty Questions. But Karly was more conversational. She talked about Che and their kids. The crazy everyday life of the working mom. The goings-on at school. Upcoming first game of the season. And the current spat between the social studies teacher and the janitor that had spiraled to a point where the teacher was having to stash her trash next door in the chemistry lab.

Mazy found herself laughing, relaxing, even. Maybe having a friend should be a first order of business for her.

"I think Tru is settling into school very nicely," she told Mazy.

She was pleased to hear it. "He's had a lot of experience at being the new kid. I've dragged him around too much. This is his fifth new school."

Karly waved away her concern. "I've seen kids that have been in twice that many. We had one kid for a few months that had been in three different sixth grades."

"And they struggle," Mazy said.

"Some do, some don't. Challenges are not always bad for kids. Look at us and what we had to deal with. We turned out to be better people for it."

"You turned out to be a better person. Remember— I'm the bad penny turning up again to collect people's loans."

Karly tutted and shook her head. "Well, Tru doesn't seem at all the worse for all the places he's been. He seems to know exactly how to get along with new people. The girls all want to get friendly because he's so good-looking. He's nice enough, but never singles anyone out, that keeps the boys from getting their noses out of joint. His decision not to play basketball could go either way. There are some who think we need him competing. And others who worry that he might take their position on the team."

"I don't think he's going to change his mind about basketball," Mazy told her. "He's taken an after-school job that would keep him from practice."

"Really? Where's he working?"

"Latham Furniture."

Karly dropped her jaw dramatically. "Half the men in this town want to get their sons in there as apprentices. But you just walk in there and he takes Tru on?"

"Actually, Tru did it on his own," Mazy said. "I told him I didn't want him to work. But my mother told him to ask Eli and he did."

"That's great. I want my kids to go to college, but it would be fabulous if they could learn a trade and have that option, as well."

Mazy nodded agreement.

"Of course, the people who always think the worst of you are going to say something like you slept with Eli to get your son the job."

Mazy didn't reply and stared intently at her coffee mug.

"Whoa, what was that?"

"What?"

"The weird look on your face. And you're blushing." Karly leaned forward, her brow furrowed with concern and whispered, "*Did* you have sex with Eli to get Tru the job?"

There was more amazement than censure in her question.

"I did sleep with him," Mazy admitted, suddenly realizing how much she needed someone to talk to about everything. "But not for that. It…it didn't have anything to do with that. Eli and I, well, we have a history."

"Really?" Karly sounded genuinely surprised.

"He's been…well, he's been my rebound guy a couple of times already. And it felt kind of natural to be back in town and getting it on with him. Do you know what I mean?" She felt her blush deepen, but it had been so long since she'd been able to have another woman to chat with, and it felt so good to finally open up without worrying about judgment.

Karly nodded. "Sure. Well, actually, I don't. I've never had to rebound. But I can tell you that if I had been wanting to set you up with somebody who could be really good for you, Eli Latham would definitely be high on the list."

"Yeah, he's a tremendously nice guy," Mazy agreed. "That's the problem."

"Being a nice guy is a problem?"

Mazy nodded. "I…I did some therapy before I left Wilmington. Twelve weeks actually. We talked a lot about why I'm always attracted to the wrong guys."

"Did you get an answer to that?"

"Sort of," Mazy told her. "I can't explain it as well as the doctor did, but it seems to be about deliberately picking the men who are going to ultimately reject me."

"Why would you want to do that?"

"It's not that I *want* to do it. It's more that I feel compelled to repeat a pattern."

"What does that mean?"

"You know my father died when I was eleven."

"Of course, I remember that," Karly said. "Our class got permission to attend the funeral. But I didn't have a dress to wear and it seemed disrespectful to show up in jeans."

Mazy shrugged. "I wouldn't have even known that you were there. It was such a strange day. My mom was just wilted and all these relatives that I didn't really know were taking over everything and telling everybody what to do. It was all so emotional and overwhelming."

"I'm so sorry."

"Thanks," Mazy replied. "Daddy and I were very close. Then suddenly he was gone. Our life was never the same after that. I was never the same after that."

Karly was nodding.

"Anyway, according to the shrink in Wilmington, when he died I was 'on the cusp of womanhood' or something, and the pattern imprinted on me in my relationships with men."

"What does that mean?"

"I loved him and he left me," Mazy explained. "So now I subconsciously choose to fall in love with the men who will leave me."

"That's crazy."

"By definition."

"Your father didn't mean to leave you. Now my dad, he hightailed it out of town on purpose. But yours didn't mean to die."

"Apparently it doesn't matter. The subconscious mind is not a rational mind. Even if you intellectually know something, emotionally you may react as if you don't."

"Wow."

"Exactly," Mazy said. "It was a real eye-opener for me. I'd begun to think that either all the interesting men in the world were jerks or that I was completely unlovable. Either option was pretty depressing."

"Sounds that way. So, is there hope? Can you cure this? Take Prozac or Xanex or something? One of the teachers at school swears by Xanex."

Mazy laughed. "I wish I could take a pill. More therapy would help, I guess. I can't really afford that right now. Mostly I'm trying to follow the therapist's advice. Live day to day and look at my decisions about men a little deeper than the surface. Hopefully I'll be able to change up my behaviors. I want the next serious relationship I have to create a new pattern. A pattern that values me."

Karly nodded. "I'd say you've got a good start. Eli Latham is not going to do anybody wrong."

Mazy smiled. "That's what I've been thinking," she said. "I was a little freaked out by falling into the sack with him in the heat of the moment. That's never a good idea and my shrink would definitely not have approved. But the past couple of days, as I've been thinking about it, I'm feeling better. I'm not any good at celibacy, that's just a fact. Eli is so safe, so good. And if I can learn a new pattern, learn to appreciate a man that won't leave me, maybe I can finally heal the old wounds. Wouldn't that be something?"

"It would be something worth shooting for."

16

—▶ ◀—

Eli made it through the afternoon feeling by turns self-satisfied and skittish. There was a tremendous feeling of accomplishment at having put Mazy off for three long days. But there was always the niggling fear that she might give up. If she didn't continue to chase him, what would his next move be? There was no use in being a jerk if the woman you wanted didn't fall for it.

But concerns about a plan B scenario vanished into thin air when she showed up at his door that night. He'd thought her beautiful, desirable and sexy when she was in her baggy sweater and mom jeans. Tonight the sweater was tight enough to show off her gorgeous breasts and the skirt was short enough to show a long expanse of shapely legs in high heels. With an excess of eye makeup and red, pouty lips, clearly this was a have-sex-first, ask-questions-later situation.

Which was exactly what they did.

Without so much as a "Hello, how was your day?" he pulled her into the apartment, led her to the bedroom. Normally he would have been welcoming, offered food and drink, and they would have politely sat through a conversation before he made any moves. But he was not being normal, he reminded himself, finding surprising pleasure in that fact.

He tossed her on the bed, scooted up her skirt and went for it, both of them fully dressed, except for the panties that he discarded on the floor. Eli had never had sex with high heels rhythmically jabbing him in the back. He decided he kind of liked it. She apparently liked it, as well, as she began making those wonderful moaning sounds and her body clenched him again and again.

Afterward they both lay sideways on his bed, staring at the ceiling as they caught their breath. Straightforward sex—satisfying and efficient. He hadn't actually meant for it to happen like that. He had meant to make her sort of beg for it. She needed to struggle to get him. Too late for that now.

Then, as if a lightbulb had appeared, Eli recalled one of the letters the bad-boyfriend advice columnist had posted.

He acts like I just came over for sex, and after that's over, he's not very interested in me.

That was the way forward from this.

Eli sat up. He turned to look at Mazy. She was glowing and gorgeous. Smiling up at him with eyes shrouded by satisfaction. She was everything that he'd ever wanted. Everything that he'd ever dreamed of. He wanted to make love to her again, this time slowly, tenderly, tasting every inch of flesh on her body.

He resisted.

Instead, he gave her a couple of congenial pats on her bare thigh. Something akin to a teammate in an athletic event.

"Thanks, babe," he said. "That was great."

He stood, zipped up and walked out of the room.

In the kitchen he got a beer from the refrigerator and deliberately began whistling. He felt good. Sex had a way of doing that. But he was also back to being worried. What was Mazy going to do? How was she going to react? At the very least she would probably come in and ask him what was going on. And she had a perfect right to be pissed off when she did. Honestly, what she ought to do is walk out of the place in a huff and slam the door behind her, never to return.

She did none of those.

He heard her running water in the bathroom. He decided that he shouldn't drink beer on an empty stomach, so he heated up last night's leftovers in the microwave.

By the time Mazy joined him in the kitchen, he was sitting at the counter eating dinner. She was wearing one of his shirts and her high heels.

She smiled broadly at him. "Is there some of that for me?"

"Nope, sorry. I figured you'd already eaten."

"Oh, okay."

She sat down on the bar stool next to him and effectively crossed her legs. One of her shoes dangled perilously from her foot.

Eli concentrated on his plate. Without bothering to look at her he said, "There's another beer in the fridge. Help yourself."

"No, thank you."

After another minute of watching him eat, however, she did get up and fix herself a glass of ice water. As she was returning to her seat, he slid his empty plate in her direction.

"Put this in the sink for me, while you're up," he said. "And could you run some water in it?"

"Sure."

While she had her back turned he moved to the living room. He grabbed the remote control from an end table, seated himself in his favorite overstuffed chair and

turned on the TV. He flipped through the channels looking for something that was all testosterone. He finally
settled on a reality program with two fat, redneck guys
noodling giant catfish. It was not his kind of thing. But
he pretended apt interest as Mazy sat down on the sofa
across from him and got him wondering if she was naked
beneath that shirt.

"Eli?" she asked eventually. "Are you mad at me?"

"No, babe. Why would I be mad?" He said the words
without turning to look at her.

"No reason, I just thought…well, never mind. I came
over here because, well, there's something I need to talk
to you about."

"Sure, I'm listening."

She hesitated. "Could you turn off the TV?"

For an instant he debated with himself. He couldn't
go too far, she'd know something was up. He clicked the
screen into silence and turned to look at her directly. She
looked beautiful. Wide-eyed and solemn, her skin was
still rosy from sexual satisfaction, as she bit her lower
lip pensively.

"What's up?" he asked.

"I may owe you an apology."

He didn't expect that. For the way he'd been acting
tonight, she was the one with the apology owed. Then
he realized what she must mean and the bottom fell out
of his stomach. She wasn't going to fall for the jerk routine, she was still going to dump him and do it nicely.

"An apology?"

Mazy nodded. Those high heels were flat on the
ground now and her knees were chastely together.

"It's very late to say this," she began. "Years late, really.
But I want to apologize for what happened between us in
the months before I left home."

That was a pretty good start, he thought. She waited a minute for Eli to comment. When he remained silent, she continued. "I think I probably took advantage of you back then. You were so young and sweet and I…I used you and I dumped you. I am sorry."

For a moment the words she said didn't quite compute. Then he realized that she was being genuine. The words *young* and *sweet* were especially painful to hear from her lips.

"Nine years ago was a fun little romp, which I think you took more seriously than I did. I'm sorry for that. And I feel especially bad about that summer when you were right out of high school," she said. "I was more than just a year older. As a young mom on the rebound, I was a lifetime older. And I took advantage."

The taste of bitterness in his mouth was not imagined. He had been in love with her, willing to sacrifice anything for her, eager to commit his entire future to her and she'd interpreted that as naïveté.

Eli looked at her intently. He felt almost insulted. Mentally, he scrambled for words to express himself. His feelings, his desires, his love, counted for nothing with her. For a moment he thought he should throw her out of his house and tell her never to come back. He deserved better than a woman who valued his devotion so cheaply.

Insight forestalled him. Had she behaved with Tad this way? Or the dozen other guys she'd run after? No. She had treated him shabbily because he had allowed her to do so. He had uncomplainingly accepted junior partner status in their relationship and he'd shown gratitude for whatever crumbs of affection she'd been willing to throw. If there was ever to be a chance for the two of them to be equal partners, he was going to have to even up the score.

Deliberately he made a humorless chuckle.

"So, let me understand this. Are you apologizing for corrupting me or are you just sorry that we had sex?" he asked. "Because if it's the former, let me reassure you that, like most guys, I don't see a bit of learner sex with a more experienced woman as particularly regrettable."

"Good, I'm glad," she said. "I thought maybe...maybe I had hurt you."

He laughed again. "Oh, I was devastated!" he assured her. "Truth to tell, you really know how to put the crush in crush. On behalf of my eighteen-year-old broken-hearted self, I accept your apology. But I'm thirty now and remember it as a great time. Hey, everybody has somebody as their first."

He knew that the words, supposedly meant to reassure her, really implied that she was simply another vaguely memorable shag in a long, busy sex life.

Her brow was furrowed. She looked uncomfortable.

"So, is that it?" he asked.

"Uh, yes."

"Then should I turn the TV back on, or would you like to use that gorgeous mouth of yours for something other than apologies?"

17

A full week after her letter went out, Mazy was disappointed that not one person had tried to meet with her to reevaluate a payment plan. She had the distinct feeling that the group consensus was that if they just ignored her she would go away.

She wasn't going anywhere. This was her job and she was determined to do it. So at exactly 11:00 a.m., when the morning rush was clearly over and people were just beginning to think about lunch, Mazy grabbed her purse and her briefcase and crossed the street to see Charlie McDee.

Initially she assumed that Charlie would have made the list of Tad's untouchable local businessmen. But, no, McDee apparently didn't make the cut, so he was fair game for Mazy to try to help.

One lone customer was leaving as she made her way through the door. Charlie's wife usually helped him in the mornings, but he was alone in Local Grind and he visibly paled at the sight of Mazy walking into his shop.

"Hi, Charlie," she said.

"Hello, Mazy." He was loading stacks of foam cups into the dispenser next to the work area. He wiped his hands unnecessarily on his apron. "Can I get you something? Is it too early for a macchiato?"

"Yeah, I think it probably is," she answered. "I actually came over here to talk to you."

"I hope the subject is who we knew in high school."

Mazy's heart went out to the guy. He already looked defeated and she hadn't mentioned the word *money*.

"How'd you get interested in the coffee business?" she asked.

He paused before answering, as if he wasn't sure the purpose of the question.

"I always liked coffee," he said. "I can drink it all day. Caffeine never bothers me. Alice, my wife—if she so much as has a sip after noon she'll be sitting awake all night. But I can take a cup to bed with me on a cold night."

"So this place is a labor of love," Mazy said.

"Yeah, I guess you could say that," he replied. "I got interested in different kinds of coffee. Then I started roasting my own beans. Getting my buddies to try out my efforts. One day I got it in my head that I could make a living doing something I love. I've been dreaming about it ever since."

He sighed with a fatalism that aged his face twenty years. "I guess you could say my dream has turned into a nightmare." Charlie squared his jaw and looked Mazy in the eye for the first time. "I don't know how this works," he said. "Do you put a sign on the door? Seize my coffeemaker? What?"

"Oh, no, Charlie, I wouldn't do that," she assured him. "The bank would never do that."

"They wouldn't?"

"No, we would actually do something worse," she said. "We would sell your loan to a collection company. Those people will be nameless, faceless strangers who will hound you night and day for months on end. They *will* get their money back. Only bankruptcy will stop them, and even then they'll be first in line to pilfer through whatever you have left."

"Oh, jeez," Charlie said, running a hand down his weary face. "I never thought my life would end this way. Broke and a failure. I had this nest egg that I put away to invest in my little retirement business. I was going to start slow. But Paul Brakeman—you remember Paul—he was selling this building and he told me that it was a great deal. The rents from the tenant business alone would pay the mortgage. And if I started too small my place would never catch on. He talked to Tad and Tad was willing to loan me the money. It all seemed like the perfect opportunity." Charlie sounded defeated. "I don't know what I was thinking. If it was that good of a deal, Paul would have saved it for one of his friends."

Mazy remembered Paul from high school—he was one of Tad's crew. She wouldn't have been surprised if they'd planned the whole thing for their own benefit.

"So what happened?"

Charlie shrugged. "Basically nothing. We got the shop open. People come. We've got regulars every day. They'll pay two bucks for a coffee, but the old guys expect free refills, like in the old days, so I'm never making a dime on them. The other folks keep the lights on and milk in the fridge, but it's a small town and I'm never gonna get rich here."

Mazy didn't need him to get rich, only to do better.

"What about the building tenants?"

"There aren't any. That's why the building was available at such a good price. Nobody wants a business on Main Street anymore. Everybody has moved out to the highway. The structures are newer, parking's not a problem and there's all that visibility from the traffic passing through."

Mazy nodded thoughtfully.

"You know where the Jiffy Dog used to be?" Charlie asked.

She knew exactly.

"I could have rented that building and started up without borrowing a red cent. But, no, I've got to have this old monstrosity."

"I always loved this building," Mazy told him.

"Well, I'm thinking you'll be able to buy it for a cutrate price when the bank takes it, or the people that you sell the loan to take it, or the devil takes it. It's going to go cheap."

"Charlie, we're not letting anybody take this away from you," she said. "I think I speak for myself and the bank and the folks in this town when I say that as long as you still have your heart in this business, we're going to try really hard to keep it open."

"How are *we* going to do that?"

She couldn't blame him for being skeptical, but she was determined to prove that she was here to help. "Well, first we're going to get you out of default," she said. "Let's try to figure out what you can pay. Then we can restructure the loan to give you some breathing room to try to build the business and attract some tenants."

It was almost two o'clock when Mazy returned to the bank. She'd gone over Charlie's books and they weren't as dismal as she'd feared. He did have some options. She was going to be able to get him some space, but she was also going to have to build business and cut corners. There was no magic bullet, but she was hopeful.

She thought about calling Eli. She couldn't really talk about bank business, but she wanted to share her upbeat mood, her sense of making a small positive difference in one life.

Mazy smiled as she thought about Eli. He was so… so not how she remembered. He'd always been good in bed, but he'd also been kind and considerate and sweet. He was still those things, she assured herself. But now he was something else, too. He was demanding and kind of bossy and…and like a guy.

That thought caught her up short. *Like a guy?* What he'd always been was a guy. There had never been anything wussy about him. He was always strong and tough. He'd always been her defender.

No, he wasn't really changed, she assured herself. They were simply getting reacquainted as true adults. And of course, there would be some new things that would be different. They were different. Mazy hoped that the lessons she'd learned had made her a smarter, better person. Eli had already been that, but maybe his years had matured him in other ways. He was a truly nice guy and this time she was determined to value that.

The phone on her desk rang.

"In my office. Now."

Tad never bothered to identify himself and it was not necessary to ask.

"Yes, sir," she replied.

What had she done now? She quickly gathered up the files in front of her and carried them with her as she walked down the hallway and across the foyer under the watchful eyes of the rest of the staff.

She knocked on his door and was immediately given entry.

The gray fall day was visible from two directions in his corner windows. Tad sat behind his immaculately clean desk. There was not so much as a Post-it note to hide the finish.

Dressed in a dove-gray suit with a pale blue shirt and Windsor tie, Tad looked especially attractive today. Mazy might have said that he was handsome, except that his mouth was one thin line of disapproval and his eyes cold with dislike.

She shut the door behind her and walked toward the chair opposite him.

"I did not ask you to take a seat," he said sharply.

Mazy stood.

He leaned back and silently glared at her.

The moment stretched on. It was all Mazy could do not to roll her eyes. What on earth was this about? This was not how people in business conducted themselves. Maybe the young women in this town thought they had to put up with this kind of crap, but she'd worked a lot of places and she knew better.

"You wanted to speak with me?" she asked, determined to end his little force of wills.

His words were slow, dripping venom. "I don't *want* to speak to you," he answered. "I would like to never even get another glimpse of you for the rest of your life, but unfortunately your behavior has forced me to *have* to speak to you."

From his tone she would have thought that Tad was the school principal and she was a recess ruffian sent to the office.

"My behavior? What behavior is that?" she asked.

"I know that you believe that you've got the upper hand here, forcing me to give you a job."

Mazy opened her mouth to deny it.

"Don't interrupt me!" he snapped. "Women like you always think you can lead a man around by the nose. That you can manipulate everything to get what you want. You think that you've got it made here and can do what you please, but believe me, I don't get bullied. I don't allow anybody to bully me. You'd be smart to remember that. I could throw you out that door today and take my chances with the judge. And I just might have to, because I will not allow you to make a mockery out of me or thwart my authority in this building."

Mazy was incredulous. "I have not, and would not, do that," she assured him.

If anything, that statement seemed to make him angrier. "Do you think that I don't know what's going on with my staff?" he asked. "Do you think that I simply sit in this office all day and do nothing?"

From the look of his desk, Mazy might have thought exactly that, but she didn't say so.

"I don't know what you think I've done," she told him. "I've not been talking about you to the staff. Honestly, I've not even been talking to the staff. I'm not sure I know what I'm being cautioned about."

"Don't you?"

"No, I really don't."

"Did you think you could simply waltz out of here, like you own the place, and take a three-hour lunch and nobody would notice?"

"What?"

"Don't even try to pretend it didn't happen. Every woman on my staff saw you leave and return, most of them noted the time and more than half of them made a point to tell me about it."

Mazy wanted to sigh in frustration. At any new job there was always a certain amount of new-employee distrust. But it felt excessive.

"Perhaps the bank would be better served if the women

on your staff spent more time concentrating on their own work than second-guessing what other people are doing."

"Oh, so they're all lying?"

"No, they're all misinterpreting," Mazy answered. "I did leave here at eleven, but it was for a meeting with Charlie McDee."

"Charlie McDee? Isn't he a bit old for you, or are you scraping the bottom of the barrel these days?"

"Charlie is a client of the bank," Mazy answered. "He's one of my accounts and I spent three hours going over his financials."

"What a waste of time," Tad said. "That old building is an albatross. He was an idiot to buy it."

"Was he? And who advised him that it was a great deal? I believe it was this bank. And if he goes into foreclosure, who's going to end up with that albatross? This bank will."

Tad shifted in his seat uncomfortably. "I'll sell his loan off before it gets that far."

"No, that won't be necessary. I've found a way to give him some time, so we're going to keep his loan out of default and his building from becoming another abandoned downtown property. That's what you hired me to do, and that's what I intend to 'manipulate' into happening. And as for lunch, I haven't even had any. But now that you mention it, I'm starved. Is there anything else, Mr. Driscoll?"

18

> ➤ ◄

All day Eli fantasized about calling Mazy. She might not be able to pick up, but he could leave a message. He could say something sexy about last night. Or tease her—that was probably better, nothing seriously sexy, but more like dirty joking. Or he could simply ask her out on a date with him. Take her out someplace for a romantic dinner— No, he couldn't do that. It was way too dangerous. He could see himself getting starry-eyed and confessing how much he was totally back in love with her.

No, he was definitely not going to be that kind of guy. He was going to be the one who never called, even if that meant he didn't get to see her.

Strangely, having his mind on Mazy was somehow conducive to his labor. Woodworking typically required focus and concentration. Each piece of wood had its unique characteristics affecting how it could and should be used. And the joinery was exacting. Spacing too tight didn't allow for natural expansion and the piece could crack. Spacing too loose didn't allow for contraction and the piece would be rickety. Mistakes in wood were expensive. So he couldn't allow his thoughts to wander. But he found that keeping Mazy in the back of his head didn't distract him, it seemed almost to help. Having her

in his life again, in his bed again, settled over him like
a warm, healing salve.

What didn't sit as well was the constant comings and
goings at the front of the shop.

Eli set up the workspace deliberately with Clark in
the front. His brother was more gregarious than he was.
He enjoyed having people come in and out. He preferred
talking over working. That was simply the way that it
was and Eli tried to be okay with it. Some days were
easier than others. The Windsors were finally ready
to be shipped. Eli had already mentioned it twice, but
Clark hadn't made a move to package them, to contact
the freight company or even to phone the customers. He'd
spent most of yesterday piddling around doing nothing.
And today he was deeply involved in setting up the PTA
concession booth for the first game of the season. He
took call after call about it. Sheila was chair of the com-
mittee, but apparently needed to consult her husband on
every possible question.

Eli finally mentioned it.

"Are you going to get those Windsors ready to ship?"

Clark looked up, glanced over at the chairs taking
up valuable space on the far side of the room. "No, not
today."

Eli was annoyed, but pushed back against it. "I guess
you wouldn't really have time, with that big load of wood
coming this afternoon."

"Damn!"

Eli looked up.

"I forgot about the wood delivery," Clark said. "I'm
not going to be here this afternoon."

"What?"

"Ashley's class is going out on a field trip to the pump-
kin patch. Sheila's too busy to take her, so I said I would."

"Just come back afterward," Eli suggested. "Dale and I can get it off the trailer. But it's likely to rain overnight—I don't want it sitting outside until morning."

Clark shook his head. "Not happening," he said. "You know Sheila wants me home with the kids in the evening."

"This is our business," Eli pointed out. "Not an eight-to-five job."

Clark chuckled. "For me, that's exactly what it is."

In a family business, Eli believed it was often better to say nothing than to blurt out what he was thinking. Eli owned the business, not because it was given to him, but because he had saved his money and bought out Clark's share. It was that cash that had financed the nice family home that he and Sheila lived in. Still, Clark had a good paycheck, stable employment, excellent benefits and a boss that he treated like a kid brother.

"Sorry, Termite," Clark told him casually. "I'll make it up to you."

That was doubtful.

Clark didn't even wait until noon. In fact, he left while Eli was at the house giving Dad his morning bath. With his brother gone, all the noise and commotion that circled around him disappeared, as well. Eli was able to knuckle down on the rasping. He worked straight through lunch and managed to chisel the hinge impressions on several of the music cabinet's fifteen doors.

Dale Krakalovich arrived a little after three. Eli inspected his order while it was still on the trailer. Then they off-loaded the wood near the storage shed. Once the hauler was paid and on his way, Eli faced the task of getting everything inside and out of the weather on his own. Sorting, measuring, marking, stacking, up and down on the ladder—the process was time-consuming.

About an hour later, he heard the buzzer on the shop entrance. He walked up there to find Tru quietly and industriously engaged in sweeping up. When he opened the door, the boy looked up.

"Hey, glad you're here," Eli said. "Come down to the woodshed."

Tru put his broom up. "Taking me to the woodshed? Isn't that the way you say 'getting in trouble' around here?"

Eli shook his head. "Different kind of woodshed. I need your help."

The building that housed the raw lumber was set apart from both the shop and the house. The front was double sliding doors. Windows in the eaves on both the east and west side allowed enough natural light to negate the necessity of electricity. There was no heat source or wiring.

"We got a wood delivery today. It's mostly ash and maple, but there are some beautifully grained pieces of white oak, as well."

The doors were open wide, the afternoon sun dappling though the remainder of autumn leaves to illuminate the inside. A grid framework twelve feet high was divided into labeled square yard sections.

"Let's start with the ash, since it's up top. Are you pretty steady on a ladder, you think?"

"Sure," Tru answered.

Eli rolled the outsize stepladder into position and locked it down securely.

"Okay, you see where the ash is? Stand maybe three steps up."

The teenager got into place. He ran his hand over the placard indicating the lumber type.

"This is like wood burning, right?"

Eli glanced up. "Uh-huh."

"I was in a Boy Scout troop once, we were going to learn how to do that."

"Oh, yeah? What happened?"

Tru shrugged. "We moved. Did you do these?" he asked, indicating all the wood nameplates.

"No. I think it was my dad," Eli answered.

"Your dad used to work here?"

Eli chuckled. "Yep. My dad and his dad and his dad's dad. Lathams have been whittlin' on this hill for a might spell, the old-timers would say."

Tru laughed. "So your dad's, like, retired or something?"

"Something," Eli answered. "He's not feeling very well these days. He still lives up in the house."

"Oh."

"Okay, so this is what we do," Eli said, handing Tru a bucket filled with small scraps of wood. "Hang this on the ladder hook."

Tru complied.

"I'm going to measure the length of each board," he explained. "And I'm going to write the length on the end. Then I'm going to hand it up to you."

"Okay."

"You lay it on the pile and then you wedge in a couple of those shims to raise it off the board beneath it."

"Okay."

"The lumber needs to get air underneath it so that it dries at the same rate on both sides."

Tru had a little bit of trouble at first managing the shimming of the long, unwieldy boards. But Eli was glad to see that he had the patience and the determination to get it done right. Within a few minutes, they were doing the job fairly efficiently. The snapping sound of the measuring tape and the clunk of boards fitting into place filled the air.

"So did you start here working for your dad?" Tru asked.

"I did," Eli answered. "I spent my days in the shop when Clark started kindergarten. And then, after school and summers all my life. Not as a job, really. Dad let me hang around and help until I learned enough to actually be a help. He didn't officially hire me until I was in high school."

"How was that? Working for your dad?"

"It was fine. Great, actually."

"Really?" Tru sounded genuinely surprised. "My buddies always complain about how their dads yell at them and never like anything they do."

"Well, I guess some dads are like that," Eli said. "Or maybe guys remember getting yelled at more clearly than when somebody says, 'Hey, nice job.'"

"Yeah, maybe."

When they moved on to the white oak, Eli traded places with Tru, giving him the responsibility of measuring and marking. That slowed the process a little as he picked up his new task. But Tru also asked questions, which occasionally had Eli stopping to show him the answers. The kid seemed to have a genuine interest. And curiosity could be worthwhile when focused in such a purposeful direction.

"See how these two fit together," Eli said, sidling up the board Tru had just handed him with the one he was now holding. "See the grain in these.

"They're called sister boards or sometimes brother boards, something to let you know that they are siblings. They came from the same place on the same tree. They're part of a family. When you put them together, the look is not only really nice, it's really strong."

Eli heard something behind him and turned to see Mazy standing silhouetted in the doorway.

"Hi, Mom."

"What are you guys up to?"

"We got a lumber shipment and we're sorting and storing it," Tru answered.

Mazy smiled at her son.

Eli had never seen her dressed for work. He thought her business suit was sexy somehow. The skirt was not short and the cut did not show off her curves, but it was almost as if the concealment itself was sexy. Or maybe it was to Eli, because he knew what was beneath that drab gray tweed.

Tru explained to her how the storage system worked and why it was so important to stack the wood properly.

"I'm impressed," Mazy told him finally. "And I thought all you did was sweep sawdust."

His reply was long-suffering and just superior enough to be typical teen. "Mom, I sweep up shavings and chips. Sawdust is captured in the dust collection system. I only empty that."

"Oh, okay. I stand corrected," Mazy answered. She glanced up at Eli on the ladder. "I'd better get to the house. I thought…I thought I might come by tonight. Would that be okay?"

"Yeah, sure," Eli answered, before remembering that he was supposed to be harder to get. "I, uh, I don't think I've got anything going on."

"I'll wait until after you've seen your dad," Mazy said. "And I'll bring over some dinner. Beth Ann has been cooking like a fiend every day. I'm sure there'll be enough to share."

"Okay."

Mazy shot a glance toward Tru and then continued with unneeded explanations. "I've had a pretty crappy day. I got chewed out for something I didn't do. I guess I need to vent."

"You have my permission to rant incessantly so long as you'll bring me some of Beth Ann's cooking," he said.

She laughed, as he'd intended her to.

19

Beth Ann had baked a casserole and was delighted to share it with Eli.

"It's the least we can do for all he's done."

Mazy raised an eyebrow. "What *all* has he done?"

"Oh, in the summer he mows my grass when he does his own. He's the one I call if there's a problem with the plumbing or the furnace. He trapped that raccoon that got in our attic. Whatever I need, I call him first."

"Why would you do that?"

"You know Jonah and your dad were great friends. From the day I was widowed, Jonah always looked after us. He told me at the funeral that he knew if the positions were reversed, he would have counted on Truman to look after his wife and boys."

"But that's Jonah. How did Eli get involved?"

Beth Ann shrugged. "When Jonah's health failed, Eli simply took over. That's the kind of man he is, Mazy. Solid and dependable. The kind a smart woman would build a life with."

Mazy was beginning to see the advantage of that. She'd been so eager to get to talk with him, be with him, that she'd gone straight to his workshop after work. And she certainly couldn't deny the thrill of excitement that swept through her at the sight of him.

Was she falling for Termy?

It was hard to imagine, but it would be great if she was finally beginning to wise up.

When she arrived at Eli's, the basement was unlocked, so she let herself in. She heard the shower running, so she went ahead with getting dinner ready for them. She had loved how neat and comfortable he kept his place. She was even more grateful for his sense of organization as she set the table and made the salad.

If he were surprised to find her puttering in his kitchen, he didn't say so.

"Wow, a real sit-down dinner. And I thought you would be standing beside me at the sink."

She laughed as she sat at the table.

"You know, a guy could really get used to this," he told her.

Mazy thought she could get used to this, too.

It was comfortable but also intimate, eating together, chatting about nothing, talking about their day.

"This is great…great whatever it is."

"I think Beth Ann calls it Swiss chicken, though I doubt it had its origins in any place more far away than Durham."

"Are you as good a cook as your mom?" he asked her.

"Not even close," Mazy answered. "I use exactly the same recipes, with the same ingredients in the same amounts, but somehow her food is always better."

"It's probably the pleasure of having somebody else cook," he suggested.

"Could be. Beth Ann says that she puts love into every bite."

"And you don't?"

"I think I do," Mazy said. "I certainly try to. I love cooking for Tru, knowing that what I feed him not only fills him up, but helps him grow. But I think the taste of my love must have a bitter quality to it."

It was a joke. But it wasn't.

Eli looked at her for an instant and then half stood to lean across the table and kiss her lips.

"Everything I taste is sweet."

She laughed it off and changed the subject.

"So you and Tru spent the day stacking lumber?"

He explained Clark's afternoon off to attend his daughter's field trip. "Tru turned out to be a real help to me, getting all that wood inside. Without him, I'd probably still be out there trying to get it done in the dark."

"Couldn't Clark come back and help you?"

"He should have," Eli admitted. "But it's actually my business. Dad and Ida signed over equal shares to both of us, but I bought Clark out. He needed cash to buy a house and I'd been sticking money away in savings since I was a kid."

"So Clark works for you."

"Yeah. Which is the good news and the bad news. When he wants time off or to fool around all day getting nothing done, he acts like it's still a family business and we're equal partners and nobody tells him what to do. But when something has to get done, to meet a deadline or fulfill an order, then he's all 'I just work here. I'm off the clock.'"

"Why do you put up with that?"

"He's my brother," Eli answered. "He's got a family and needs to make a living. It's not like this town is swimming in job opportunities for a guy with his skills."

"Couldn't he do construction or cabinetry?"

"Of course he could," Eli agreed. "He's a pretty good woodworker. He's never had the patience or the vision that's really required for quality furniture. But he does know a lot about what we do and how it's done. I mostly leave the sales to him, talking to the customers. He's good at that."

"Doesn't that leave the actual furniture building to you? Like a one-man show?"

Eli nodded. "That's pretty much the way it is. He does some things to help me. It's not that he's afraid to work. And he even enjoys it. But sometimes his priorities are all screwed up." Eli shook his head almost apologetically. "If I was a regular boss, I'd straighten him out or send him on his way. But I'm not a regular boss. I'm his kid brother. Neither of us ever seem to forget that."

As they got up from the table, Eli was stacking the plates to carry to the sink. Suddenly, as if he'd forgotten something, he set them back down on the table.

"Why don't you take care of this," he said. "I've got... I've got something I need to do. Rinse 'em off and put them in the dishwasher. That'll be a treat for you. Beth Ann doesn't have a dishwasher, right?"

"Ah, right."

Eli walked into his bedroom and shut the door.

Mazy looked down at the dishes and mentally shrugged. No big deal. She did the dishes every night. And he was right, it was a novelty to use a dishwasher again.

The machine was running and she was wiping down the counter when he returned to the room. His expression was sheepish, guilty.

"I, uh, I had to make some phone calls," he said by way of explanation.

"No big deal," she said.

He smiled at her and took her hand, leading her to the couch where they snuggled up together.

"I believe you said you'd had a crap day," Eli pointed

out. "I've been talking all about myself and haven't let you get any venting done."

Mazy let out a groan and laid her head against his shoulder. "It was a frustrating ending to the week," she said. "But it's getting better hanging out with you."

"Tell me what happened."

"Well, I can't really tell you much," Mazy said. "Client confidentiality."

He murmured understanding. "You don't really have the job where the clients are going to like you."

"No, the client was okay," she said. "I expect them to be defensive and angry and scared. It's standard for financial troubles. We just have to work through that until they can learn to trust me. But with my history in this town, it may take longer than usual."

"Your history is now ancient history. You have to treat it that way so that everybody else will."

"Thanks. I'm trying," she said. "Actually, the problem was with Tad. And, as you know, we *share* some of that history."

"What's got Driscoll teed off?"

"I left to do this client meeting," Mazy told him. "The meeting went really well. I think the client believes I genuinely want to help and he offered to let me look over his books. So I stayed to do that, right then and there. I got a clearer picture of where things are. Hopefully, I'll come up with some ideas to make things better. That's all good."

"Yeah, it sounds like it."

"When I got back to the bank, apparently my colleagues had all been to tattletale to Tad that I'd taken a three-hour lunch. He called me into his office and, without even giving me a chance to defend myself, tore into me."

Beside her, she saw Eli's jaw tighten.

"It was the whole ball of wax," she said. "Sarcasm, shouting, threats. And all without letting me get a word in edgewise."

"He's a bully, Mazy," Eli said. "He always was."

She nodded. "I know. You'd think that after all these years, so much water under the bridge, his own personal tragedies like the deaths of his parents and his divorce from Genna, you'd think those things would have mellowed him, made him more thoughtful."

"I don't think that people really change," Eli said. "The way we are, that's the way we'll always be."

That statement caught Mazy up short. If it were true, she knew she was doomed. The shrink had assured her that people could change. More specifically that *she* could change. She was counting on that, for herself, for her son. If Eli was right, that meant that she'd continue screwing up her life over and over again. Always making the wrong choice, always heading down the wrong road. She shuddered against the possibility.

"You shouldn't work for him," Eli said. "He's had a reputation as a bad boss for some time."

She nodded. "I can really see that. The staff doesn't seem like 'mean girls,' but they are all suspicious and secretive. That's what you get in a workplace where stabbing your coworker in the back gets you farther than quietly doing your job."

"You should quit," Eli said.

"I need a job."

"Working for Driscoll isn't the only job," he insisted. "I know people at the bank in Boone. I'm sure I could get you an interview there."

Mazy chuckled. "And how would I get there?" she

asked. "Beth Ann's old Ford will barely get us to the su-permarket and back. I can't take up commuting in it."

Eli barely hesitated. "You can take my truck until you can afford to buy your own vehicle."

"Don't be silly," Mazy answered, laughing. "I am not mooching a car to drive fifty miles a day to a job when I already have one I can walk to."

"Okay, the job doesn't have to be banking, does it? Give me some copies of your résumé. Companies are always needing bookkeepers and accounting clerks. I can talk to some people, see what I can come up with."

Mazy had no intention of doing that. Anybody who hired her would have the right to know about her con-viction and her probation. And as soon as they saw her record, abetting theft, they'd not only pass on her job prospects, the story would be all over town. Her plan to clean up her reputation would only work if she stayed on the job and didn't get into trouble. Plus, after today's meeting, she was starting to feel as though she might actually be doing something worthwhile—and that she was pretty good at it.

"I'm not quitting," she said. "I...I like my job."

"You *like* foreclosing on people?"

"I'm not foreclosing. I'm trying to keep folks out of foreclosure. Seriously, I like working up there. I want to make a go of it."

"You can make a go of it somewhere else."

"No. It has to be there. It has to be at Farmers and Tradesmen."

Eli was sitting forward looking directly in her eyes. She couldn't quite meet his gaze. He knew something wasn't quite right. She had never been able to lie to him. And she knew she shouldn't. The right thing to do would be to tell him about her arrest. She should confess the whole sordid, crappy, stupid story and let the chips fall where they may. But she simply couldn't. He'd always thought so well of her, he'd always believed the best of her. If he knew what a terrible person she truly was, he would be disgusted. And his disgust was more than she could bear.

Deliberately she pasted a big smile on her face. "No solutions needed, please. Only an ear so I can whine about all my daily job gripes. Now, what do you say, mister?" She ran her hand up his thigh. "It's Friday night. Have you got something big tucked in these blue jeans that can take my mind off my workweek and get my weekend rated X?"

20

▬◄◄▬

An hour later, the two lay naked, snuggled up together in the middle of Eli's bed. He was relaxed, sated, exhausted. Beside him, his beautiful Mazy made the very tiniest of breathing sounds. It was too gentle to be called a snore, but more than simply inhale/exhale. He decided that he loved the sound. He wanted to never sleep without it. He should record it, so the nights when she couldn't be here, he could play it back to lull him to sleep. His eyelids were so heavy. He loved the weight of her against his chest. The scent of her, mixed with the smell of sex. Everything was warm and sticky, but in such a good way. Like melting caramel or hot fudge. He eased her closer, laying his hand on her bare bottom. Her skin was so soft. His eyes closed again. He was drifting on a cloud. Picturing her face smiling at him. Teasing him. Laughing with him. Picturing her face flushed and taut as orgasm pulsed through her. And then afterward, all loose-limbed and satisfied as she looked into his eyes with something that felt close, so very close, to love.

The sweetest sleep enveloped him and he almost slid contently into it when suddenly another image interfered.

Her face when she had lied to him.

His eyes came open. He held his body rigid.

When Mazy had told him about her day, he had

wanted to drive over to Driscoll's house and piss on his lawn. But of course, he couldn't really do that. Even if Mazy was his wife, which she still was not, a man didn't have the luxury of avenging every guy that deserved it.

The best that could be done was to deprive the creep of the opportunity to insult her further. That's what he wanted to do. He'd immediately thought of the bank in Boone. It was where he banked. She was right about the commuting, it probably wouldn't have worked. And it was true that a little town like Brandt Mountain wasn't awash in good job openings.

But when she said that she "liked" working at the bank—when she wouldn't consider looking for something else—there was a deception behind her eyes, something that was not being told. Eli saw it as clear as a billboard. He could only wonder what it said.

He'd asked her point-blank the first day he'd seen her if she wanted to get back with Tad. She'd said definitely not. She hadn't been lying then. He was sure of it.

But there was something different now. What had happened? Had being around Driscoll rekindled the old fires? What fires? Good grief, he'd burned her to a sexual cinder just minutes ago. He'd keep her so satisfied she wouldn't be able to think about another man.

Maybe it wasn't sex, though. Maybe it was never sex. Tad was a seriously selfish guy. Too selfish to ever be much of a lover. And the two of them had been teenagers when they were together—an era much more about quantity than quality. No, it was something else.

It was the whole ball of wax, she'd said. *Sarcasm, shouting, threats.*

He had berated her. He had bullied her. And as the obvious explanation dawned on Eli, he moaned aloud.

She had liked it.

He was being beaten at his own game. Driscoll, the natural a-hole, was besting him on the being-a-jerk front. Competition meant he'd have to dial it up. And he was already failing from time to time. At dinner, he was having such a good time he'd completely forgotten to treat her badly at all. He'd almost cleaned up the dishes like a perfectly good guy would. He'd been clumsy about dumping the work on her. Then even after hiding out for fifteen minutes in his bedroom, the excuse he'd intended to use was, "I told this gal I'd call her." After days of not calling Mazy, his eagerness to share that would be pretty crappy. And allowing Mazy to clean his kitchen while he flirted-up somebody else—that would be a serious sleezeball move. But he hadn't been up to the challenge. His mumbling about "had to make a phone call" didn't really convey that he was talking to some other woman. And she'd obviously not taken it that way.

If Driscoll had the luxury of screaming at her at work five days a week, he was going to really have to get a lot meaner.

Under the covers, he found her naked behind again. This time he didn't bother to caress the soft skin, instead he gave it a vigorous swat.

She startled awake. "Huh?"

"Okay, babe. Time to go home."

"Huh," she asked again, groggily.

"Time to go home."

"What?"

"You fell asleep."

She sat up groggily, the sheet falling down to her waist. Even in the darkness he could see the enticing curve of her breasts. He clicked on the bedside lamp for a better view.

She made a moan of protest and covered her eyes.

"See, you shouldn't have fallen asleep. It'll be harder for you to go home."

In the yellow glow of the light, her bare flesh looked creamy and her mussed hair was more sexy than simply disarrayed.

He'd thought his body was as done as a doornail, but he stirred at the sight of her.

"Babe, you have to get going now," he said firmly.

She slowly peeled her hands from her eyes, still squinting against the light. "No, no. It's Friday," she reminded him. "I don't have work tomorrow."

"Well, I do," he said. "And I need a good sleep."

"You work on Saturdays?"

"Some Saturdays," he hedged.

"That doesn't mean I have to leave," she said. "I can have coffee with you in the morning and leave after that."

"No…I don't think so. Mazy, I sleep alone," he offered finally. "It's my policy. I don't let women sleep over."

"Your policy?"

Hearing it on her lips, it did sound ridiculous.

"Truth is, I can't sleep with anybody else," he said. "I don't get any rest unless I'm alone in the bed. So, no, I don't allow women to stay the night."

She was squinting again, but it wasn't about the light, her brow was furrowed in disbelief.

"You let me stay here the other night," she said. "Our first night I stayed."

He'd forgotten about that.

"I didn't sleep a wink, though," he declared adamantly. "I lay wide-awake all night."

"Then why'd you let me stay?"

His first choice for answer was *I was trying to be nice.* But he quickly rejected that. Jerks didn't really try to be nice. They just tried to please themselves.

"Well, I…I thought I might do you again in the morning. I'd let you spend the night and maybe I'd get a b.j. with my breakfast."

Her eyes widened at that. She was certainly awake now.

"O-oh, well…" she stammered. "I'm…I'm okay with that. You hadn't asked, but if that's what you want I—"

"Rain check," he answered. "It's not worth the lost sleep tonight. But I'll tell you what…" Eli grasped the covers and threw them off the end of the bed, revealing both of them in their nakedness and his newly risen erection in evidence. "I'll give you a quick doggy poke as a send-off."

"A what?"

"Hands and knees, babe. I promise you'll like it."

In fact, he didn't intend for her to like it. He entered her without so much as a whistle to foreplay. He'd decided that he was going to be totally sexually selfish. This was, after all, his favorite position; and this was not about what was good for her, it was about being all for him. He knew he wasn't going to be able to maintain very long. Which was also in his favor. It would be all him. That was something that he was sure that Driscoll, and the guys like him, would have no problem with.

After little more than a minute, however, Eli did have a problem with it. Her body felt wonderful. The angle was perfect. The sound of flesh against flesh was erotic. But where was his Mazy? He knew she made noise, but her silence was even louder. He might as well have been masturbating. He couldn't stand it.

He reached around her body to caress her intimately. He heard that wonderful catch in her voice as soon as he touched her. He wanted to make it good for her and he loved that he could. He used the depth of her response like a game of Hotter/Colder to find the perfect place, pressure and approach to please her. He had to grit his teeth to hold off until she caught up. But she did. She made that wonderful sound as he felt her body clenching his. It wasn't the best of the night, but it was still great.

She collapsed on her stomach and he on top of her for long enough to catch his breath and roll over. He pulled her onto his chest and planted a kiss against her hair. He needed her with him. He could never let her go.

"I love you," he whispered before he could catch himself.

Horrified that he'd let the words slip, he immediately rolled her off him and hopped out of bed. He went into the bathroom and shut the door.

He gazed at himself in the mirror. He was more than naked and sweaty. He was weak. He had wanted to be the kind of man his father was. A good man. A dependable, responsible man. A generous man. Somehow his father managed to be those things without knuckling under, without giving in. Eli gave in.

Mazy couldn't love him if she couldn't respect him. He was going to end up losing the woman that he loved if he didn't learn to be made of sterner stuff.

He turned on the cold water tap and splashed two handfuls on his face. He dried off with a towel and looked himself in the mirror one more time. He raised his chin and hardened his jaw. This time, he was not giving in.

He opened the bathroom door.

"That felt great. I'll sleep like a baby," he said as he gathered her clothes and handed them to her pointedly. As soon as she was dressed, he ushered her toward the door. "I'll call you," he said. "I mean, I really will. I've still got to cash in on that b.j., right?"

21

—➤ ◄—

Mazy woke up on her mother's lumpy living room couch. She groaned a little as she rolled over and stretched her legs out over the armrest. For sleeping, this piece of furniture was about three inches too short. Or maybe Mazy was three inches too long. She thought of Eli's big wide bed with longing. That would have been nice to wake up in. And there would have been the added bonus of Eli. She'd gotten plenty of sex last night, but she felt a little short on her cuddling quota. *But that's how men are,* she reminded herself. All the men she'd known were that way. Somehow she'd remembered Eli as being different. But that was a long time ago.

Her mother and Tru were both still sleeping. The gray light of dawn in early fall meant it was probably around seven-thirty in the morning. She'd had fantasies all week of sleeping until noon on Saturday. She would have been very pleased with nine o'clock. But seven-thirty was going to have to do.

She made her way to the bathroom and decided to get her shower while the rest of the house was still in bed.

As the hot water rolled down her body, she lathered up and allowed her thoughts to wander to the night before. It had felt so good being with Eli. They could have conversations about anything, everything and nothing and they both enjoyed them. So many men she'd been with got a little bored when the conversation wasn't about them. Oh, at first they'd seemed interested in what she had to say. But it didn't take very long before they'd be texting or gaming or tapping a foot on the floor with every word. Gable Sherland certainly had been that way. Her former boss had so little time for her, anyway, so most of that was spent in bed. If they were talking and it wasn't about him or about money, he'd quickly make an excuse to leave. Mazy had learned not to converse so much as entertain.

She pushed her face into the water as if she could rinse those memories right out of her brain. She was never going to be that woman again. As God was her witness, she vowed never to be a pawn, a trophy or a fool for love.

She had wasted so much of her life chasing after men. And not a one of them could hold a candle to the great guy who lived right next door. She was so glad she'd finally realized that.

And she was proud of the way she'd stood up to Tad at the office yesterday. In the bad, old days—basically a year ago—she would have cowered in the face of a man's anger. She would have cried and pleaded for him to understand. She would have believed, even if she knew better, that somehow she was in the wrong.

She was determined never to be that woman again. And she knew how lucky she was to escape her former self. If Sherland hadn't been caught, if she hadn't been implicated, if she hadn't pled guilty on a deal with the D.A., then the judge would never have added counseling to her probation sentence. And without the doctor helping her lay it out all out, how much longer would she have lived like that?

Still, it was like being an alcoholic or a drug addict or a cigarette smoker. She had to be very careful to completely avoid those bad-news boyfriends. She had to watch for the signs of inequitable relationship and guard herself against involvement, because she was pretty sure that if she let herself get a taste of it, she'd end up right back where she'd started.

She felt optimistic as she got out of the shower and toweled off. It was a lot easier to avoid the bad guy when the good guy was so wonderful.

She smiled to herself as she thought of Eli, her Eli, working congenially with Tru. This could actually work out better than she'd imagined for everyone.

And he'd said he loved her.

The memory of that brought a delighted blush to her cheeks. Of course, she was experienced enough to know that postcoital declarations weren't exactly currency you could take to the bank. Some guys actually felt that way when they said it, but it was only one fleeting moment. Others said it because they thought it was what a woman wanted to hear. For some it was simply more polite than voicing, "I'm a stud and I totally nailed you!"

Eli, though, she thought, *Eli probably does love me. He always has.*

The fanciful romantic that still lingered inside her, no matter how hard she tried to dampen that enthusiasm, soared into a blissful imagining of the two of them. Finally she was beginning to overcome her demons, gird her self-esteem and be able to care for a good, decent man who could love her back. It was such a breakthrough, such a blessing, such an achievement. It was wonderful. It was perfect.

She sighed with sweet contentment.

Of course, there was that sleeping thing.

Mazy caught sight of her furrowed brow in the mirror. Eli had been downright grumpy about getting her out of his bed last night. Sleeping alone must be a new thing. She certainly didn't remember that about him. But then, they'd had no options before. She was living with her mom and he was living with his parents.

It was a surprise. And a disappointment. She liked the idea of lying in his arms through the night. But nobody was perfect. Humans have issues. And she'd known other guys who didn't like women to stay over. Those guys were probably just jerks. Undoubtedly Eli has some kind of little phobia. He was a loner kind of guy. An introvert. He was never going to be the life of the party. And he was apparently never going to sleep with Mazy in his arms.

"Okay. You can deal," she told her image in the mirror.

It was probably for the best, she decided.

At least that's what she told her mother as the two of them walked through the Walmart in West Jefferson that afternoon.

"I think it will be a good thing for Tru," Mazy said. "He probably suspects that we're more than friends, but if I come home to the couch every night, that's plenty of deniability."

"So, you don't want him to know," Beth Ann clarified. "I'll need to be careful not to let something slip."

Mazy shook her head. "It's not so much that I don't want him to know. I mean, the poor kid already knows way more about my personal life than I ever did of yours. It's more like I don't want him to worry."

"Worry?"

"About how and when it's going to affect him."

Beth Ann was trying to retrieve a giant container of generic detergent from the bottom shelf. Mazy squatted down and shooed her away.

"Let me do this," she told her. "That's why I'm here. To do the heavy lifting."

Beth Ann didn't argue.

"Do you think Tru wouldn't want you to get involved with Eli?"

"No. Yes. I don't know. Tru likes Eli. At least for now. I think he's the kind of man Tru would want me to get involved with. But I don't have a good track record, you know? And every time I start up with a new man, Tru's life gets turned upside down."

"I'm sure that's not so," Beth Ann said. "Maybe when you were younger and more…more flighty. But he was a baby then and didn't care where he was or why, as long as he had his mommy with him."

"That's nice of you to say," Mazy told her soberly. "But we both know that it was worse than that. I'd move in with some guy. We'd pretend that we were a family. Then one night we were just out, moving on. It's hard enough for kids who go through one family breakup. Tru went through one about every other year."

"Nonsense. You're exaggerating. Remember, I've known you your whole life. By my tally, there've been only five men you've broken up with."

"You didn't know about Sherland."

"I counted him in the five."

"Did you count Eli?"

"You haven't broken up with him yet."

"I've already broken up with him twice," Mazy corrected. "And you know there were guys between those guys."

"Well, I'm thinking of the ones that you lived with," Beth Ann said.

"I quit moving in with them after Coby Dax," Mazy said. "He got mad at Tru and slapped him. I couldn't believe it. I was incensed. Coby said an openhanded slap was no big deal. That it was his house, where he paid the rent, so he had a right to enforce the rules."

Beth Ann made tutting sounds. "I never really liked him. He seemed very common."

Mazy gave a humorless chuckle. "Well, he certainly was the kind of guy who became a common choice for me."

"But you left him," Beth Ann pointed out. "And that was a good thing. And very brave, too. Moving from Charlotte to Wilmington where you didn't have any friends or family and starting night school. Not every woman has the gumption to do that."

"Not every woman gets her life in such a mess that she needs to do that," Mazy said. "Anyway, I made a pact with myself not to move Tru in with any man who wasn't officially a legal stepdad."

"Very sensible of you. You always try to be a good mother."

"I do try," Mazy admitted. "But I also fail."

"Honey, we all fail."

"You didn't fail," Mazy said quickly. Then she stopped short. "Oh, wow. I'm your screwed-up kid, so I guess you did fail."

Beth Ann stopped and grabbed Mazy by the arm. "You are my smart, beautiful, generous and giving daughter. You are so full of love, it just pours out of you. I couldn't be prouder of you. And don't you forget that. Now grab one of those bags of noodles. No, the really big one. Winter is coming and we have a giant teenager to try to feed."

Once they'd gathered the big bulk groceries they intended to buy, the two women wandered through the rest of the store. *Touristing,* her mother called it. When she was a girl, Mazy remembered going window-shopping with Beth Ann. It was the same kind of activity. Looking at things that were available to buy, knowing with certainty that they were not buying any of them. They did not seem to be the only people with this pursuit. The store aisles were crowded with whole families for whom a day at Walmart was inexpensive entertainment.

Amid the bustle and the noise, Mazy didn't find touristing as fun as she had at age fifteen, but she knew that her mother did. For Beth Ann, the monthly trip to Walmart was the only time she got out of town. In Brandt Mountain she saw very few people. Her outings there were to the church, the grocery store and the doctor. She rarely met anyone new or had conversations with strangers, and she liked getting the opportunity to do that.

Mazy deliberately chose not to rush Beth Ann. If her mother wanted to spend five minutes telling a harried parent she'd never met that her child had the prettiest brown eyes and coaxing a smile from the cranky tot in question, then it was little enough for the roof that Beth Ann provided for Mazy and Tru.

Anyway, all she had waiting for her at home were loads of laundry. Eli had said that he would call. And she'd hoped that maybe, for Saturday night, he'd ask for an actual date. It had been so long since she'd gone out to dinner or to a movie. That would have made it feel like a real weekend.

Beth Ann was now sharing stories of falling down with an older woman who was trying to find the least slippery nonskid bathroom rug.

Mazy was, more or less, trapped in the aisle. A huge set of temporary shelves had been set up with a big red Close Out sign attached. She casually glanced in that direction and spotted something that brought back a sweet memory to make her smile.

She reached down to the bottom shelf and pickcd up

a heavy white ceramic mug. It was very ordinary, yet similar to one her father had used for shaving. Daddy's had a line crack in one side and a big chip on the lip, but it was exactly the same style. Mazy remembered watching him as he stood in front of the bathroom mirror in his undershirt, whisking up the lather of shaving soap. As he spread it on his cheeks and neck and chin, she asked him a question.

"Do you like shaving?"

"It's okay," he told her. "It's like washing your face and brushing your teeth. It's something you gotta do."

"It looks like fun."

He smiled at her, creasing the white suds on the lower part of his face. And his tone turned teasing. "You know, when I was a little girl, just like you, I thought exactly the same thing."

"Daddy! You were never a little girl."

"I wasn't?" His expression feigned astonishment. "Oh, you know you're right! I never *got* to be a little girl. I am so lucky to have my own little girl to let me know what it is like."

"I'll tell you anything you want to know."

"I'm counting on that," he answered. "I want you to know that you can always talk to me. Whether you're four or fourteen or forty."

"Forty? Isn't that really old?"

Her father laughed and used the shaving brush to press a dollop of soap on the end of her nose. "When I get to forty, I'll let you know."

He hadn't made it to forty, of course. Mazy and Beth Ann had buried him at only thirty-eight.

"Oh, that looks like the old coffee cups they used to have at Schmeltz's Diner," Beth Ann said beside her. "I miss that old place. Coffee always tasted better there.

Maybe it was those cups." She laughed. "Do you remember?"

Mazy did not. She stared at the cup as an idea took shape. She turned the mug over to view the price.

"The sign says thirty percent what it's marked," Beth Ann told her.

"I'm going to take this," Mazy said. "Wait, how many are left there?"

"Three."

"I want all of them," she said. "And we need to visit the art supplies."

22

— ⚫ —

Eli spent the early-morning hours lurking on internet forums where women were venting about the lousy men in their lives. If Tad the Cad was now in the competition, he was going to have to crank his behavior up a notch. Picking his favorite sex position was not in the same league with actual yelling.

He took more notes from the furious and frustrated strangers online. He discovered the need to write his strategy in code. Going through their boyfriends' pockets looking for scraps of paper with clues to the men's behavior seemed a major pastime for some women.

At the usual time he went upstairs for his father's shower, but he didn't linger. This was Clark's day. He and Sheila would bring the children for a visit and he didn't want to get in the way of that. He didn't want either of them to hang on to the idea that "Dad wasn't lonely because Eli was there." His father's world had become very, very small. He needed both his sons. He needed his granddaughters. It was crazy that Clark couldn't see that. It felt like a willful blindness, but Eli determinedly chalked it up to competing priorities.

He went down to his shop and tried to get some work done, though he didn't typically work on the weekends. He thought it was important to do something else, think about something else, in order to keep his life in balance. But he'd been spending most of his brain cells on his strategy for winning Mazy. It was a salve to his spirit to concentrate on the music cabinet that was taking shape on his worktable. Even in its ordinary poplar, it had a delicate form that belied its strength. He wished he could show it to Mazy. He wished that she could appreciate it the way he did. But, of course, she wouldn't. It was only a raw wood piece. It wouldn't catch the eye of a non-woodworker until he'd applied the lacquer finish to the veneer. People always oohed and aahed at the final product. But for Eli, the process of making something beautiful and functional from the remains of forest vegetation was equally as amazing.

It was a little after one when he retrieved his sandwich from the shop's minifridge and took a lunch break. It was a kind of "working lunch" as he made notes on the cabinet's process. Keeping records on every piece he made was one of the few things he did differently than his father.

He'd learned so much from working alongside his dad that he had been way ahead of most of the students at the North Bennet School. He hadn't actually considered taking classes. Doing the work was the best teacher, he'd thought. But after that first summer and the bad breakup with Mazy, his father had insisted.

Under virtual protest, Dad had packed him onto a train for Boston. The two-year program with some of the premier furniture craft faculty in the world had honed his skills and altered his style. It had also allowed him to grow up and get over his loss.

He'd returned to Brandt Mountain as a more mature man, eager to work and heartbreak completely healed. That lasted until Mazy was back in town and the two of them started up once more. Until she'd dumped him for another man…again.

The sound of a car caught his attention and Eli glanced through the window to see Clark, driving Sheila's mini-van, pull up in the driveway of the shop, near the back door to the house. The whole family got out. The girls were in matching sweaters. He could see Sheila's mouth moving as she talked a mile a minute. Clark glanced down toward the shop as if considering that direction instead of the house.

"Don't do it," Eli whispered aloud. "Go see him!"

As if his words were transmitted telepathically, Clark sighed heavily and turned to follow his wife and girls into the home he'd grown up in.

Finished with his notes and his sandwich, Eli got back to work feeling more optimistic about his dad and his brother. Those two needed time to get over the past and forge a new relationship together, before there was no time left to do that.

Eli laid the pieces of the constructed cabinet down on the workbench. He'd chosen the wood for the doors very carefully. He planned to do the veneer in a cracked ice pattern. To make such a complex surface attach properly and remain solidly in place for a hundred years, the graining of the base wood was important. No amount of adhesive, hot irons or pressure could make up for a sketchy substrate. Eli had personally hand-planed the pieces, wanting to fully familiarize himself with the unique characteristics and spot any flaws in the board that might need to be taken in consideration. Understanding the positives and negatives of each poplar rectangle, he laid out the doors across the cabinet in the order that seemed most likely to enhance the structural foundation.

In some ways, it was like a big puzzle. He set all

parts of the door out. Then stood back and surveyed. He made a couple of changes and surveyed again. When he was completely satisfied with his choices, he grabbed the pencil that he'd tucked above his ear and began labeling. To his way of thinking, it was a waste of brain space to keep anything in your head that was easy enough to write down.

Outside, he heard the chatter of children and looked out the front window. Clark and Sheila were leaving. Eli glanced at the clock. Thirty minutes exactly. He sighed aloud.

Not already.

Sheila must have their weekly visitation on a timer, he thought unkindly.

It was not Sheila's fault, he reminded himself. Somehow it felt easier to blame his brother's failings on his sister-in-law. But Clark was responsible for his own shortcomings. It was just too bad that his wife was amenable to aiding and abetting the least generous of his tendencies.

He worked until after four and then made his way back to his place, where he puttered around. He turned the TV on, but only half watched the Tar Heels versus NC State. He kept imagining what he might be doing if he and Mazy were more like he wished they could be.

They could have spent the whole day together. Maybe they would have driven down to Blowing Rock for some fresh air and great views. And then he would have taken her to the Best Cellar for a candlelight dinner with crab cakes and roast duckling. Between bites they would gaze at each other across the table. He wouldn't even have to say that he was in love with her. She'd be able to read it in his eyes. But he would say it. He would say it and he wouldn't have to cover it up with some pseudojerk behavior.

Loser!

If he did something like that now, he'd be more than a loser, he would *lose her.* Tad the Cad was just waiting in the wings to sweep her out of Eli's life.

"Stay strong," he admonished himself.

On that night, staying strong included eating leftovers alone and over the sink.

His phone rang twice. He ignored it both times.

In case she popped over, he shrugged into his coat and went upstairs to hang out with his dad and Ida.

They were glad to see him. Ida even fed him a slice of sweet potato pie that she'd baked. The crust was kind of doughy, but it wasn't completely bad.

The three of them sat in the living room. Dad in his recliner. Ida in her chair. And Eli on the sofa. His stepmother kept up a steady stream of conversation, filling him in on virtually every word that was spoken by either Clark or Sheila on their visit, which weren't many, and relating every cute and adorable thing that Ashley or Ava had said or done. Ida clearly adored the girls. And even if Sheila had explained that "grandma" was her own mother and that Ida was simply Ida, Ashley had taken to calling her Grandma Ida and little Ava was now doing the same.

As Ida talked about the children, Eli shot a glance toward his father. He couldn't really smile anymore. His expression always remained almost frozen in a grimace. But he could see somehow in his more relaxed countenance that he'd enjoyed the visit and was relishing Ida's recounting of it.

The conversation waned as the two seniors paid attention to their favorite TV program. Chatter was relegated to commercial breaks. Fortunately for Eli, there weren't that many on public television.

"So I hear that you and Mazy are keeping company again," Ida said.

Eli shot a glance toward his father, who was eyeing him with interest.

"Did Dad tell you that?" he joked.

"Sheila did," Ida answered. "Truthfully, your sister-in-law didn't have much good to say about your choices in female companionship."

Eli shrugged. "She's dating me, not Sheila."

Ida nodded slowly. "So you two are dating?"

"Yes."

"Interesting."

"What do you mean?"

"Well, I don't know much about that sort of thing," Ida said. "I had a few fellows call on me when I was in my teens. But for most of the little dating I did in my life, I was older and stepping out with Jonah."

"Yeah."

"Seems to me," she continued, "that on a nice Saturday night like this one, with a big harvest moon in the sky, Jonah would have had me dancing my feet off until midnight and then we'd move to a cheek-to-cheek hug and sway until they closed the joint down."

His father make a sound that to Eli seemed pretty close to a chortle.

"Ida, I could never in a million years be the dancer my father is."

"A woman doesn't really care how well you dance, she's enjoying being held in your arms. Do that to music or do it to a baseball game. But on a Saturday night, you'd better be doing it. Not sitting with a pair of old-timers watching thirty-year-old reruns of *The Lawrence Welk Show*."

Eli shrugged. "I'm playing hard to get."

"Are you now?" Ida's reply included a raised eyebrow.

The middle-aged band leader returned to the small screen and announced a number with Bobby and Cissy. They all watched the ever-twirling, ever-smiling couple, Eli believing the discussion on his dating life done.

However, at the very next break, Ida returned to her commentary.

"You may be right about not making things so easy for her," his stepmother said. "It's human nature to value those things that we have to struggle for and take for granted those things that seem to fall naturally into our hands. You've been pretty easy pickings in the past."

"Too easy," Eli agreed. "This time around, if Mazy wants me, she's going to have to make an effort."

Ida nodded sagely. "Well, as I said, I'm no expert. But I think it's worth pointing out that *people* are not things. When couples come together, it's for big reasons. Sometimes more than they believe. And the person who is right for you is exactly the one that makes you become who heaven intended you to be."

Eli considered that. With a quick glance toward his father he replied, "That's what I'm counting on. And I'm hoping she'll be a quick learner."

Ida turned back to the television, as if she had said all that she intended. But Eli heard her murmur, "You might have a thing or two to learn, as well."

He stayed long enough to get his dad into bed. Ida packed up a piece of leftover pie as a thank-you.

Outside on the back porch, the night was crisp and cool. He could see the lights on at Beth Ann's house, but the shades were down, concealing the activities of the inhabitants. Was she sitting by the phone? Puttering in the kitchen? Surfing the internet? He wanted to share her every moment. He wanted to know her every thought.

Maybe someday they could do that. But tonight, as Ida had put it, he needed to teach her how to be the woman that she was meant to be, the woman that could love him.

With a determined sigh, he took an unnecessary walk down to the shop and around the sheds. Bright moonlight bathed the area away from the trees with a silvery gleam. He checked the doors, which, of course, were all secured, and wasted as much time as possible dawdling around the storage. If they were going to keep unsold pieces in there, it really should be climate controlled. Last year he'd brought what he had down to his apartment. But that was really no solution. This year he'd need to rent storage and he needed to do it soon. There wasn't anything local. Maybe he could get Clark to check out what was the best, closest choice.

When Eli had wasted all the time he could outside, he went into his apartment and walked the floor. He checked his watch every two minutes.

It was still too early. It had to be later to be obvious.

He decided that this must be what it was like to be a smoker trying to cut back. Anxious, pacing, watching the clock. He didn't like it.

Finally at one minute after ten, he decided it was time. Then he waited five more minutes, just to be sure.

Taking a deep breath, and steeling his determination, he walked to the phone. He dialed her cell number.

"Hul-lo." She sounded groggy.

"Are you asleep?"

"Oh, hi. Hi! No, no, I'm awake. I guess I drifted off in front of the TV. But I'm awake now. What…what time is it?"

"I don't know," he lied. "It's maybe ten, ten-thirty."

"Oh, okay."

"You want to come over?"

She hesitated. "Now?"

"Yeah."

"Uh, well, okay."

"Great, I'll leave the door open."

He hung up before another word could be said. He let out a deep breath, as if he'd been holding it, and shook his head. It was easier than he'd thought. He walked over and unlocked his door. Then he walked through the basement turning out all the lights until it was completely dark, except for the lamp on his bedside table.

In a quick trip to the bathroom, he brushed his teeth. But he mussed, rather than combed, his hair. He stripped himself naked and climbed into the bed and pulled the covers up to his waist.

With a little sigh of satisfaction, he congratulated himself. "Eli Latham, you are now stud enough to booty call with the worst of the bad boys."

23

Mazy had gotten home from Eli's place at three in the morning. She'd left him satisfied and sleepy in that big wonderfully warm bed as she'd braved the dark night and the cold air to return to her mother's house. Once again she lured herself to dreamland on the lumpy couch by promising to loll about in slumber until noon. Unfortunately, by seven-thirty that morning's preparations for church attendance were in progress.

"I can't make you go," Beth Ann said, her tone scolding. "Although you should. But I insist that Tru will accompany me and I won't accept any arguments on that."

Her son was giving her his this-is-all-your-fault glare. So she returned a big, incongruous smile.

"I wouldn't miss it for the world," she told them both. "I've been looking forward to it all week."

In truth, it wasn't too bad. Her memory of the congregation looking down their collective noses at her and insisting that she exhibit shame was apparently now out of fashion. Person after person welcomed her as if she were a long-lost friend. Maybe that's what they thought she was.

She'd kept her head down in Sunday school class where the discussion about first century gender politics was worthy of a number of eye rolls.

Pastor Blick's sermon, on the other hand, was cerebral and academic. Though the man had been with the church for over a year, he was still being referred to as "the new preacher." His kinder, less strident message was a stark contrast to the fire and brimstone of his predecessor during her teen years.

On the whole, everything had gone rather smoothly. As they filed out, a tiny, mouselike person timidly buttonholed her in the vestibule.

"So sorry to bother," she said. "But if I could talk to you for just a second. I know it's Sunday, but I…I don't know what to do."

The woman bit her lip as her eyes welled up.

Mazy quickly motioned for Beth Ann and Tru to go ahead of her and she led the younger woman into the relative privacy of the deacon's coatroom.

"I thought you might be here, because your mama always comes," she said. "But I wasn't sure."

The woman was gaunt and pale. Lines of worry marred a face that couldn't have been much more than twenty. Her clothes, while clean and neat, were bordering on threadbare.

"I'm sorry," Mazy said. "I don't really remember you. I'm sure you were still a kid when I was here last."

The young woman dabbed at her eyes with a tissue. "I'm Nina Garvey. I used to be Nina Pryor. I was in third grade when you…when you had your boy. Of course, I remember you better than you remember me."

That was undoubtedly true. Her name was slightly familiar but her face was not.

"I…I got knocked up in high school, too. So I always thought we had something in common. Maybe not something good, but something."

Mazy's eyebrows went up. Perhaps she should suggest

they start their own special interest group, High School Knock-Ups of Faith Presbyterian. It had a certain ring to it. Or maybe it was a discordant clang. Vaguely she wondered if the congregation had treated Nina differently than they had her. She wouldn't have been surprised. Nina seemed so small and vulnerable. Mazy always pretended she could take care of herself.

"Being a mom is totally worth it, right?"

It was a platitude, but a good one. Nina nodded agreement and looked as if she felt a little better.

"Jeremy is five. He thinks he's a big boy now that he's started off to kindergarten."

Mazy hoped her expression didn't betray her astonishment. This petite little person looked way too young to have a child that age. She supposed that was how she appeared once herself.

"Time goes fast," Mazy said. "Did you see my son? One day you can cover him with a dishtowel and the next time you look up he's six feet tall."

The chatty conversation had allowed Nina to regain her composure.

"What did you want to talk to me about?" Mazy asked.

"I…I got that letter from you. And then my mom got a phone call and…Mom says it's all on me and it's time I learn to fend for myself, but I don't know what to do."

Like a lightbulb appearing over a cartoon figure, Mazy immediately realized why the name was familiar. Garvey. New car loan. Seventeen thousand dollars, plus change.

"You owe money to the bank," she stated for verification.

"My husband does…did. My husband did. He…he passed away."

"I'm so sorry," Mazy told her soberly.

The young woman accepted her consolation with a nod.

"Everybody says that you're here to get back at us," Nina said. "But I didn't do nothing to you. I'm like you. Please don't…don't do whatever you're going to do."

"I'm not here to get back at anyone," Mazy assured her. "I'm only trying to collect the bank's money."

"The payments are almost five hundred a month. How am I going to pay that? I don't really have no job," Nina said. "Well, I do, sort of. I work at Brandt Burger when I can get hours. Mostly the Rands have their daughter for extra help. They use me when they can. But I rarely get more than eight or ten shifts a month. That can barely pay our rent."

"I'm very sorry."

"I've tried not to think about it," she said. "But it weighs down on me till…till I can't sleep at night. I don't know what I'm going to do."

"Sometimes," Mazy said quietly. "Sometimes it's simply better to let the car go. I know it was your husband's, but perhaps someone else will enjoy driving it and you won't have to worry about the payments."

"There's no car."

"What?"

"It was totaled," she answered. "That's how he died. He was drunk and ran it up along the guardrail. Cut the Mustang clean in half and him with it."

The words, spoken so matter-of-fact, belied the bleakness in her expression and magnified the horror of the mental image.

"I am so sorry," Mazy said before she could stop herself from repeating it. Deliberately, she forced herself into business mode. "Have you not heard from the insurance carrier? That's why we pay for that, so that money is available in case of a tragedy."

"He didn't have no insurance on the car."

Mazy frowned. "You're required to carry insurance on vehicles that have auto loans."

"And he did, when he bought it," she answered. "But he got a DUI last winter. And when the policy came up for renewal, they'd raised the rate on him way high. He got real stubborn and wouldn't pay. It lapsed two months before the accident."

Mazy almost groaned aloud. When the insurance lapsed, the carrier was required to notify the lien holder. The bank should have immediately repossessed the car until the situation was rectified. Why that hadn't happened was anybody's guess. But for Nina, it didn't matter anymore. The loan still had to be paid.

"Have you to spoken to anyone at the bank about this?"

Nina nodded. "I talked to Mr. Driscoll a few times. He…he showed up at my house the day of the funeral. Folks in town took up a collection to pay for Wesley's burial. He told me that instead of putting money in the kitty, he was giving me two months grace period on the loan payments. Two months came and went and I didn't win the lottery or marry a millionaire. I can't imagine any other way that I'd be able to pay five hundred a month for a car I don't have."

Mazy closed her eyes and took a deep breath so she wouldn't say *I'm sorry* again. This was truly what was terrible about this job. She was not a social worker. She was an accounting clerk. All her training was about numbers and cash strategy. There was never any course work on dealing with the plight of desperate people.

"I've been scared to go to the bank," she said. "My mama says you all will send the loan to collection and we'll be ruined. I'll never get credit or rent a place or even pass a job screening."

"Never is a very long time," Mazy told her. "It takes patience and hard work to get out of a tough spot, but it can be done."

The woman looked up at her, clear blue eyes with hardly a glimmer of hope. "I don't even know where to start."

"I'm sure we can figure something out," Mazy told her as she dug a business card out of her purse. "Call me at the bank tomorrow and we'll set up a time for you to come in."

The woman took the card and pressed it against her heart as if it were a talisman. "I will. I promise," she said. "And thank you for talking to me and not yelling at me and I'm so glad that it's you handling my loan and…and nobody else."

"Bankers don't yell," Mazy told her, and then wondered if yelling was something that Tad had done.

She caught up with Beth Ann and Tru at the car. Her mother was seated in the passenger's seat, apparently resigned to letting Mazy do the driving. Tru was lounging longwise in the backseat with his earbuds in.

Mazy backed out of their parking place and turned onto Maple Street.

"Bank business?" Beth Ann asked.

Mazy nodded.

"I was afraid of that," Beth Ann said with a sigh. "Shame on Vergene Pryor for not being more of a help to her girl. I have my share of faults, but I'd never turn my back on my flesh and blood."

"No, you didn't," Mazy said. "And I want you to know I'm grateful."

Beth Ann waved off the thanks. "I've got no regrets,"

she said. "It's part of being a parent. You teach your child to be kind to others by being kind to them."

Mazy thought there might be some truth to that.

"And what's the value of continuing to punish the girl long after there is any possibility of changing the situation?" Beth Ann continued. "Nina was only sixteen and he was a grown man. Vergene should have had him arrested. Instead, she pushed Nina to marry the fellow. And then she never failed to point out what a lousy husband he turned out to be."

Beth Ann tutted disapprovingly. "Vergene was always too prideful by half. Nina was a sweet, hardworking teenager who stumped her toe on some sweet-talking galoot. Her family should step up and help her instead of wasting time judging her."

Mazy appreciated her mother's point. But sometimes, in some things, nobody could stand up for you except yourself.

"I'm sorry that the guy is dead," she told Beth Ann. "But he doesn't seem like a prize husband."

"Wes Garvey? Good Lord, he was completely worthless. And a no-account, bad-tempered drunk to boot. Nobody in their right mind would have gotten tangled up with Wesley Garvey. Even *you* would have known better than that."

A little snicker from the backseat alerted them that their conversation wasn't completely private.

In the afternoon, she and Tru were raking leaves in the front yard when Eli pulled his truck into his driveway next door. He stopped and Mazy felt a thrill of expectation. He was undoubtedly going to get out and talk to her. Maybe help them rake. She imagined the three of them doing yard work as a team, sort of like a family, and she really liked the idea of that.

The Silverado's horn beeped twice.

She looked over and the driver's side window eased down.

"Come here," he called out to her.

Mazy walked across the space toward him. As she got close enough to see him plainly, she noticed some wariness in his eyes. She smiled at him and it immediately vanished.

"Hi," she said, hearing a bit of breathlessness in her own voice.

"You know you'll have to rake again when all the rest of the leaves drop."

She nodded. "I know, but there will be fewer and it will be colder. I thought this might be a good day to get started with it."

"Maybe so," he agreed. "Look, how about we have dinner together tonight. Would you like that?"

She liked it a lot. Finally a real date. They'd been having sex for two weeks already. It was past time for them to make a public debut as a couple.

"It sounds wonderful, Eli. What time do you want to pick me up?"

"Oh, come on over to my place about seven."

"Okay. What should I wear?"

He smiled at her. "You always look good, babe. My favorite is naked, of course. But a short skirt could be very appealing."

She laughed.

"See you at seven."

He put the truck into gear and pulled away, leaving her standing there.

Mazy started after him for a moment. She was happy, but something felt not quite right.

She began raking again. Mentally she was inventorying the contents of her closet. It was still two more weeks before her first paycheck. But even if it had been yesterday, not a dime of that could go for clothes. She would wear what she had, and she'd be grateful that she had it. Eli didn't give a hint of the restaurant. But in Brandt Mountain, a skirt was about as fancy as it got. The pink chiffon blouse she'd bought her mother a couple of years ago still hung on a hanger and looked barely worn. If she borrowed it and wore it with the skirt to her black suit, that would dress it up, a lot. It was too bad the black suit was so knee-length professional. If she could shorten it by, say, two inches, it would really show off her legs.

You always look good, babe.

It was a lovely compliment. Still, why was he always calling her *babe?* It didn't sound like Eli at all. It sounded like some jerk who couldn't remember her name.

She pushed away the useless negativity. She was going on a real date with a genuinely nice guy. In a town as small as this one, that was tantamount to a commitment.

Mazy decided to tell Tru before he heard it from somebody else.

24

Eli was edgy. More than he'd expected to be. It all seemed pretty straightforward when he'd planned it, but now, ten minutes before seven, he was losing his nerve.

"Buck up, wimp!" he admonished himself. "If you start treating her like a queen, she'll have as much interest in you as last week's fish."

He had gotten her hooked. He could see that in her eyes, hear it in her voice, her every gesture. That hadn't happened because he declared undying love. It had happened because he acted like he could take her or leave her.

He was reminded of his father's advice when Eli had gone to negotiate his first deal.

"You can only have one mind-set. I care, but not that much."

For the past few days, he'd really warmed up to the role-playing. He was getting all the sex he wanted, the way he wanted and when he wanted. Fortunately, he really liked it when she liked it, so she was enjoying it, too. And they did talk and laugh and share stories and insights. Mazy had always had a quick mind and a kind of fearlessness in following through when others might have cut their losses. And she was empathetic, which con-

tributed both to her generosity and her romanticism. Both
of which made her easy prey for the wrong kind of guy.

The kind that Eli was currently portraying.

Outside the sack, he was doing absolutely nothing—
zip, zero, nada—to show any consideration for her.

He'd not given her even one tiny gift. Not even so
much as a beer or a pizza to share. That wasn't easy.

When he'd caught sight of her raking leaves with Tru,
he didn't simply think he *should* help. He'd wanted to
help. They had done that job together as kids. They'd
figured out early that since both yards had to be raked,
it was faster and more fun to do it together. And if, occasionally, one or the other went crashing and bouncing
into a pile of leaves, so much the better. He'd wanted to
do that with her again. He'd wanted to share the gloves
and giggling and red noses. Instead, he had not deigned
to get out of the truck. That was no fun at all, for either
of them.

And he hated sending her out to walk home alone in
the middle of the night. But he rudely and insistently
did it, anyway—and she would never know that as soon
as she was out the door, he crept out of bed and secretly
watched from the narrow window in the living room to
make sure she got home safe.

He let her bring him dinner and clean up without the
slightest hint of thanks. And she continued to be sweet,
biddable and available. Also grateful and respectful.

None of these things had been at all in evidence during their teenage wasteland romance. And he recalled no
great improvement in those virtues in what he thought
of as their Second Coming nine years ago.

But now, now she was being nice. Maybe it was that
she'd finally grown up. Finally matured enough to ap-

preciate him. Or maybe she was being nice because he wasn't. Knowing her history, the latter made more sense.

He heard the sound of her footsteps approaching the door. Eli grabbed the remote, turned on the TV and ripped open the bag of chips that sat in his lap.

The crisp sound of a familiar knock could barely be heard over televised play-by-play.

"It's open!"

Deliberately he kept his eyes glued to the set in front of him and stuffed a handful of empty calories in his mouth.

In his peripheral vision he saw her walk up to the end of the couch.

"Hi. What—"

Without looking he held up his hand in her direction. "Fourth and five," he announced with his mouth full.

The defense held and he made a sound as if he cared.

He turned to look at her then. It was all he could do to keep his jaw from dropping. The pretty pink top was a filmy thin material that wasn't exactly see-through but kind of gave the impression that it might be, so you couldn't stop looking at it. The simple black skirt covered her only down to midthigh, leaving a long expanse of shapely bare flesh to draw the eye in either direction. Down to distinctly doable high heels or up to soft secrets that he already knew he liked.

God, Mazy, you're gorgeous! came to his lips, but he caught himself before he spoke it.

"Damn, Mazy, not bad. I could totally hump that."

She laughed. "Thanks," she said. "But maybe we should postpone the humping until after dinner."

"Sure," he answered. "And I'm hoping to cash in my rain check tonight."

She blushed a little, but also raised an eyebrow flirtatiously. "I'm a woman who keeps her promises and honors her obligations," she told him.

He gave her a wink. "Then I'd be honored to oblige you."

Eli could have wrapped her in his arms that very moment. He deliberately did not. Instead, he turned back to the screen.

"Oh, no, they're going to kick a field goal. *Block it, you numbskulls!*"

They didn't, of course. And Eli cursed vividly, using the type of words that his dad would have washed his mouth out for. Men did not need to swear in order to make a point, he'd been taught. And under no circumstances did a decent man use rough language in the company of women.

Eli knew that caliber of politeness was passé, although he still held himself to it. But the kind of men that Mazy admired would never show such compunction.

"Is this an important game?" she asked.

"Babe, they're all important."

She was still standing there by the coffee table, apparently waiting to be asked to sit down. He could do that.

Eli patted the place beside him on the couch. "Plant your big butt right here, honey, and I'll put you to work at halftime."

"Halftime?" she asked, surprised for a second before the rest of his statement sunk in. "I don't have a big butt."

Eli laughed as if she were making a joke. "I have to admit, it doesn't look quite as gigantic in that black skirt." He gave her bottom a friendly pat. "Still, it's a good-size target. Sit down, babe. You're distracting me and it's third down."

She sat.

He focused his eyes on the TV and didn't even glance

in her direction. From the corner of his eye he could detect a furrow in her brow. He hated that. He hated hurting her feelings. But it was like taking a bitter medicine. It didn't matter how it tasted if it worked.

As far as Eli was concerned, Mazy was incredibly sexy. Her body was better than it had been at nineteen, and he was pretty sure he was in a very small group able to make that comparison. But the internet had made it crystal clear. Bad boyfriends weren't into compliments, they were into critique. Not that they could be mean all the time. There had to be enough sweetness to keep the seesaw going. It was the constant waffling between naughty and nice that kept the women off balance and vulnerable. Never knowing what to expect added tension that often was mistaken for excitement.

Eli turned to her, offering the open bag of chips. She shook her head.

"Come on, you're not going to sulk up into a snit about it, are you?"

"Of course not," she answered. "But my bottom is not big. I wear size eight jeans!"

"In your dreams! And mine, too, come to think of it. Look, babe, it's fine," he told her. "You've had a kid and that jump-sizes a woman every time. It's for sure not as big as it could be. Anyway, I didn't expect anything else. When you date an older woman, you get an older body."

He stuffed another handful of chips in his mouth and turned back to the game.

They sat there together, mostly silent for the next several minutes as the huge men in pads and helmets pushed up the field and back down again. Miami scored. Eli moaned dramatically. In truth, he really couldn't have cared less. He did watch football from time to time, but mostly college. He didn't follow any professional team.

And more often than not, the first NFL game of the season that he'd watch would be the Super Bowl.

Time-out was called as the Ravens had an injured player on the field.

"So when are we leaving?" Mazy asked.

"Leaving? Leaving for what?"

"Aren't we going out to dinner?"

"Going out to dinner?" He feigned surprise and pointed toward the TV. "It's the Ravens versus Miami. I can't miss that."

Her expression was incredulous. "You invited me for dinner."

"Right," he said. "There's some barbecue wings in the freezer. They heat up in the oven. And grab me another beer, would ya, hon? Get one for yourself, too."

25

—▶ ◀—

Any disappointment that Mazy felt about her Sunday night nondate had been rationalized away by Monday morning. She had misunderstood Eli when he'd asked her over. Of course he'd want to stay home and watch the game if he was a Ravens fan. And then there was the whole big deal about going out in public. The minute people saw them together, they would start to speculate. She was pretty sure that Eli hadn't kept his reputation clean all these years by encouraging speculation. Added to that was, of course, the expense of an evening out. She recalled how generous he had been to her in their past relationships. Nearly every day he'd surprised her with some little gift. Sometimes it was candy or flowers, but more often it was a more practical choice for her or her mother or the baby.

This time there had been no gifts. Beth Ann had made it clear that Eli had bought both the house and the business. That couldn't have been cheap. And how much money could a person make building one piece of furniture at a time? The poor guy was likely cash strapped. And now he was paying extra to employ her son.

Mazy firmly declared to herself that she would not be a grasping, selfish girlfriend. Under no circumstances would she demand expensive evenings out or have expectations for gifts. The tenderness of his kiss and the shelter of his arms made her feel valued. So many men had offered so much less.

With that small speed bump ironed out in her mind, she faced her workday with a smile on her face and a burst of enthusiasm.

She was excited about her new idea and wanted to get over to Charlie's coffee shop to pitch it to him. She wanted to show him what she'd done. She couldn't race over in the morning, of course. That's when he'd be most busy with customers. She wanted his undivided attention when she talked with him.

So she spent the first part of her day looking through the Garvey file and attempting to make direct contact with some of her clients. The latter was not going so well.

"Hello, this is Mazy Gulliver from Farmers and Tradesmen State Bank. Could I speak with Ronald Peavy, please."

The voice on the other end of the line, she was pretty sure, *was* Ron Peavy.

"No, uh, no, ma'am. We haven't seen him in…months, I guess. This ain't even his phone number no more."

Mazy wasn't about to call out the bank's clients as liars.

Even less promising were the responses from those like Mitzi Gassman.

"Me and my man done split the sheet. If you're wanting to take this mobile home and throw my young'uns out in the woods, you just come 'head. But bring a dadgum army with you when you do!"

Mazy wasn't intimidated. And she didn't lose her temper. She felt a kinship with these people. If it were not for her mother, she and Tru might very likely be homeless themselves. And she would have lied or threatened or whatever it took to try to keep that from happening.

What it was going to take for these people was some commitment to change, some creative thinking and some good luck. She tried to offer what help they would let her.

As the noon hour approached, her intent was to cross the street to talk with Charlie. But a pair of unexpected visitors showed up. Travis and Lacey Wallender were both in their early twenties. Nice looking, well-dressed and well-spoken, both had jobs and a combined good income. Shame-faced and nervous, they had come on their lunch hour to lay out their financial chaos on Mazy's desk. It was breathtaking.

"We were making payments on the bank loan with the credit cards," Lacey explained. "But these are all maxed out. I've applied for a couple more that I haven't heard back from."

Mazy lined up the plastic cards, a sinking feeling in her stomach.

"Okay, you've got the home mortgage and the second equity loan. Two car notes. And nine maxed-out credit cards."

They were nodding.

"And the hospital," Travis said as an afterthought. "We still owe fifteen hundred to the hospital from when the baby was born."

"I guess the good news is that nobody can repossess the baby," she said, offering what little levity the situation provided.

There were always going to be people that she just couldn't help. She seriously feared that this couple might be one of them. But she was willing to try.

It was after two-thirty before she finally left for the coffee shop. She made a point of announcing her destination to the tellers, to save them the trouble of needing to speculate.

She carried the examples of her new idea in a brightly colored beach tote, hoping the sunny optimism that it represented was a portent of the future.

The little bell over the door tinkled as she walked in. Charlie was not alone, but the man sitting at the counter abruptly cut his long story short and headed to the door.

"Who was that?" Mazy asked after the man made his escape.

"Jimmy Ray Esher," Charlie responded.

"Ah," Mazy said, nodding.

Charlie cleaned off the foam cup and napkin that the man had left and wiped down the area with a rag.

"So what can I get for you?" he asked.

She pulled the retro mug from the tote and set it on the counter in front of her. Emblazoned across one side of the white cup was the name *Mazy*.

"May I have a cup of regular coffee, please?"

He picked up the mug and nodded. "Sure." He filled it from the thermos carafe before setting it back in front of her. "This mug reminds me of the ones they had at Schmeltz's Diner."

"Yeah, my mom thought so, too," Mazy said. "That place was before my time. But my father had a chipped one that he used for a shaving mug."

"I like that you had your name put on it," Charlie said.

"I didn't have it put there," she told him. "*I* put it there."

From within the tote she brought out what looked like markers.

"Oh, you just wrote it on there."

Mazy nodded. "I wrote it on there with a porcelain marker. You have all these colors, and you can put what-

ever you want on it. And then you bake it in the oven and
it becomes permanent."

"That's pretty neat," he said.

"Yes, it is. And I think your customers will think so,
too."

"My customers?"

Mazy unloaded the other two cups that she'd bought.
"I got these at Walmart," she said. "But I checked on
the internet. They're available for almost nothing from
several restaurant supply places. Of course, you have
to buy a case of them. But one case ought to be a pretty
good trial."

"You want me to start using dishware?" He shook
his head. "That's what the cafés use. This is a coffee
shop—our role model isn't Denny's, it's Starbucks, and
they use foam."

"I'm not thinking that you change your coffee," Mazy
said. "Just add a twist to your presentation. And don't
give up foam, cut down on it."

"Cut down on it?"

"For the regulars," she said. "How much does this
stuff cost?"

Charlie thought for a moment. "Honestly, it's about
seventy bucks a case."

"So that's seventy dollars that you throw in the trash."

A groan escaped him, but he shook his head. "That's
what we use. Not just us—Starbucks, Dunkin' Donuts,
Seattle's Best, they all use foam cups."

"And why do you think they do that?"

"It's clean. It's convenient. People are on the go. They
can carry it out and get into their cars."

"But here in your place, most people aren't rushing
into traffic. They're sitting down for coffee and conversation."

"True."

"And a lot of people, like the guy just here, would probably prefer to sip every day from a nice clean china mug than from an eco-unfriendly and God-only-knows how potentially carcinogenic polystyrene container that cost you way too much."

"Maybe," Charlie agreed.

"Starbucks gives their customers the option. If they're going to be staying a while, they can get a mug instead of a disposable cup. Why not give that option to your customers?" Mazy said. "Those who choose can opt for a foamless cup."

"I'm listening."

"You sell these mugs to the customers. Just enough to get your money back. You have them write their name on the side, or you write it for them. Then you display them in plain sight, maybe on hooks or a shelf or something. When Joe Blow comes in, you pull his mug down, fill it with his choice of coffee. If he drinks just one or if he refills five times, there is no cost to you but the coffee and the labor, probably your own, to wash them out."

Charlie nodded slowly. "It would save money," he admitted. "Legally, I can't refill a disposable cup. Sometimes I do, but I shouldn't."

"With this you'd have no worries."

"It might change the feel of the place, though."

Mazy shrugged. "It might change it for the better. Make it feel friendlier."

He gave a thoughtful moue. "It might," he agreed. "I do like that they look like Schmeltz's Diner. There were lots of good vibes in that place. Those that remember it recall it with a smile."

"Not a bad legacy to evoke," Mazy said.

The bell chimed over the door. Before Mazy even

had a chance to glance in that direction, she was being greeted.

"I was just wishing that I could sneak you out of the bank and here you are!" Karly declared with delighted enthusiasm.

"Hi. You're here early. Did the high school go out of business?"

She laughed. "Not as long as there are fertile young minds that we can fill with more than manure." Karly glanced over at Charlie. "The usual, please. I'm desperate." She turned back to Mazy. "Early dismissal today. You didn't get the note?"

She had not. "Maybe he gave it to Beth Ann," Mazy theorized. "Although he's not good on that kind of thing. He mostly thinks he can handle his own life without my help."

"I think that's in the definition of *teenager*," Karly told her as she took the seat beside her at the counter. "What's this? You brought your own cup?"

Mazy gave an abbreviated version of her presentation to Charlie, who offered his own addendum.

"It won't save me enough money to put a dent in my debt," he told her. "But Mazy is right that every little bit helps."

Karly agreed. "I think it's a great idea," she said. "It's what this place needs. I always thought the interior looks a whole lot more hipster than hillbilly. And we have a real shortage of hipsters in this town."

That statement made them laugh.

"Are those the pens?" Karly asked, motioning Mazy to hand them over. "You know, I could do a lot with these. Charlie, sell me these other mugs and I'll decorate them for me and Che. Mazy's done hers very minimalist. I'll do one really artistic and the other one…" She pondered for a half minute. "The other one I'll let the kids decorate for their dad. That will show people what they can do, maybe spark some interest."

"That's a great idea," Mazy said.

"You really think this will work?" Charlie asked her.

Karly nodded. "I do. I think it will work great. Of course, people will need to be able to see them."

All three of them gazed at the wall across from the counter. Except for the blackboard listing Coffee Flavor of the Week it was completely blank. The dark wainscot paneling was ten feet high and topped by a narrow ledge.

"You could stack them there," Mazy suggested.

Charlie was doubtful. "As long as there are a half dozen or less," he said. "Beyond that, it would be a hassle getting to them and we'd have more breakage."

"What about hooks?" Mazy suggested. "You could arrange them in some kind of pattern and add more as you needed them."

"No, hooks would look cheesy," Karly said. "It needs to be a shelf. A shelf that you can add other shelves to."

"Where can we get a shelf? I saw some of those wire ones at Walmart the other day."

"No," Charlie said. "It would need to match the place better than that."

"Can you build something?" Karly asked him.

Charlie chuckled. "I got a C in shop class forty years ago. And I'm not much improved."

Karly turned to Mazy. "Could we get Eli to do it? I was going to ask how that girlfriend/boyfriend thing was working out for you two."

Charlie's jaw actually dropped. "You're dating the Termite?"

"Well, we're, uh, we're seeing each other...some," Mazy hedged.

"Could you get him to volunteer to do that for us?" Karly asked.

Mazy immediately thought about the money thing. Eli would do it if she asked him. But if cash was tight, he should be working on things he could sell.

"I hate to ask anybody to use the labor that they live on to do things for free," she said.

"I'd trade him all the coffee he could ever drink," Charlie vowed.

Two new customers arrived and he went to wait on them.

Mazy turned to Karly. "I don't want to ask it of him," she said. "I don't feel like...like we're close enough for me to beg a favor."

"If you can't, you can't," Karly said, patting her on the arm. "I'd ask Che, but he's working out of Johnson City this week. And the weekend, he's got two Fall League teams to coach. How about that boy of yours? A mom can certainly ask a favor. It would probably be a good project for him."

"Tru? Build a shelf?"

"He's working at Latham's shop," Karly pointed out. "He must be learning to do something. Ask him."

Mazy had grave doubts about her son's capabilities. "Well, I can ask Tru about it, anyway."

26

Eli was yawning all through Tuesday. He'd had a "booty call" again on Monday night, and this time he'd waited until well after ten o'clock. Mazy had hurried right over. She hadn't mentioned the time or that he was going to send her home as soon as he was done with her.

She did, clearly, want to talk to him. She was enthusiastic about a project she was working on for Charlie McDee's coffee shop. So much so that he literally had to take her breath away to keep her from conversation. She brought it up again during the afterglow.

Eli changed the subject abruptly and definitively.

He gave her behind a hard smack.

"Ouch!"

"Don't bring another man's name into my bed," he growled. "When you're in my house, with your bare ass on my sheets, it'd better be all about me."

She was stunned, her eyes wide with disbelief. "I…I…"

For one shiny, hopeful moment, he thought she might tell him where he could go and how he could get there.

But she didn't.

"Sorry," she managed to choke out.

Eli moaned aloud at the memory. It was like slapping a puppy.

He didn't know how long he could keep this up.

"What are you groaning about?" Clark asked him. "Don't tell me you're getting too much sex these days. There's no such thing as too much."

"My sex life is my own business," Eli answered. "What are you working on today?" He hadn't seen his brother stir from his workbench all day.

"Nothing much," he admitted, holding up a tool catalog from Lie-Nielsen. "My back is hurting a little. I decided to give myself a light duty day."

To Eli's mind, thumbing through a catalog wasn't "light duty," it was no duty.

"Would you like to find us some winter storage?"

"Sure, sounds great," Clark replied. He got up from his spot and walked to the rack to get his coat.

"You're leaving?"

Clark looked at him as if he were an idiot. "You want me to find storage, I'm going out to look at storage."

"I thought you'd call around first, get some prices or whatever."

Clark shook his head. "Best thing is to see what's out there, then worry about whether we can afford it."

Eli didn't agree, but he let him go. It was a safe bet that Clark was, in fact, going straight home and he'd make his phone calls from the comfort of his couch.

His brother was becoming less and less of a help to him. He could do the work, but it was rarely up to Eli's standards. And things that he found tedious, like sharpening tools and grain filling lumber, he simply wouldn't do. Those chores were always left for Eli. He didn't mind doing them, he didn't mind doing anything. But he did mind doing everything.

At least with Clark gone, he could bevel the door

fronts of the music cabinet in peace. He actually got quite a bit accomplished for the day, more than he'd expected.

And he was able to restrategize on his bad-enough-for-her-to-fall-for-me plan. After the past few days of some very doltish behavior, it was time for a kinder, gentler Eli. He recalled in the self-help blogs how the women kept saying that aside from all the crap, their boyfriends weren't truly horrible. For sure the yo-yoing was more difficult to deal with than constant bad dude. He needed to spend time being nice to Mazy so that when he wasn't, it would be more startling.

He was eager to be good to her. He loved the sound of her voice, her laughter. He loved the excitement in her eyes when she talked, the enthusiasm for life that even the crappiest of circumstances couldn't dampen for long.

Yes, maybe he would take her on a real date in her short skirt. Show her off to the world and gaze at her in candlelight.

By the time Tru showed up in the afternoon, Eli was in a happy mood.

Mazy's son was actually working out pretty well. He came in every day with no fanfare. He seemed to understand that concentration was required. He would hang up his coat, put on an apron and start cleaning up. He didn't talk, whistle or sing. And his phone didn't go off with text notices every other minute.

Today, however, he did have something he wanted to say.

"I wanted to kind of ask you a favor."

"Kind of ask? Or kind of a favor?" Eli clarified.

"It's a favor. For sure, it's a favor."

"Okay."

"My mom needs me to build a shelf," he said. "I told

her that I would try. But you know I don't know exactly where to start. Do I get a board and some brackets?"

"What type of shelf is it?"

Tru looked uncertain about the question. "The type that goes on a wall?"

Eli bit his lip to keep a grin at bay. "Kitchen shelf? Bathroom shelf? Books? Knickknacks?"

"Oh, it's for coffee cups."

"Coffee cups?"

"Yeah, Mom is helping the guy at Local Grind get his business in order. I guess he probably owes money. Mom came up with this idea to have personal coffee cups so he wouldn't need to buy so much Styrofoam stuff."

"Oh."

"Yeah, she and Mrs. Farris, from my school, they are doing these cups, but people coming in need to see them," he said. "So Mom asked me if I can make a shelf."

"Of course you can," Eli told him. "It's not rocket science. It's carpentry."

"I probably know as much about one as the other."

Eli smiled at him. He liked that the kid was willing to do whatever was needed, but not puffed up with fantasies of his own abilities.

"Have you got a pencil and paper?"

"Uh…" He glanced toward the coat hooks. "No, I dropped my book bag off at home. Gram always makes a snack for me, so I go by there first."

Eli walked back into the office area and retrieved a blank notepad from the bottom desk drawer. It was the kind he always used. He grabbed a pencil and carried both back to his workbench.

"Pull up a stool," he told Tru as he handed off the items.

The teenager sat down, opened up the pad, poised the pencil and looked at Eli expectantly.

He remembered thinking Tru was a ringer for Driscoll. But now, now that he knew him better, he saw that all that similarity was on the surface. Same facial features, same color hair, same color eyes, but the intensity and intelligence in those eyes was very different from the scheming, cynical gaze that was such a big part of Tad. Whether it was his upbringing or a harkening back to generations gone by, Tru Gulliver was not a Driscoll.

"Okay," Eli said. "I want you to go to the coffee shop after school tomorrow. You need to see the space where they want the shelf. You should talk to Charlie McDee about what his expectations for the shelf are."

Tru was writing Eli's words in the notepad.

"I'm sure Mazy told you what she thinks. And maybe even what Karly Farris thinks. But every person will have a unique vision of what they want. All of those visions are valid, although ultimately you'll have to do it the way that you think is best."

Tru's eyes widened. "You'll help me figure that out, won't you?"

"Sure."

He let out a breath as if relieved.

"Take a tape measure with you. Do you have one?"

"No."

Eli rooted around in his worktable drawer for a moment before coming up with one that he handed to Tru.

"You'll need all the dimensions," he said. "How high and wide the space is. And how deep it needs to be for the cups to fit in easily."

Tru was nodding as his pencil scratched across the paper.

"Find out what kind of numbers we're talking about. A

shelf to hold a dozen cups will be different from a shelf
that needs to hold forty."

Eli thought about that for a moment.

"But then, you don't want to have a bunch of empty
space," Eli said. "We'll rough out plans to add another
shelf if it becomes necessary."

"Okay."

"There are questions to ask about the surface, as well."

"Surface," Tru mumbled as he wrote down the word.

"I haven't been inside the place since I was a kid," Eli
told him. "I don't know what Charlie had to do to rehab
the place. But in an old building like that, the walls might
likely be shiplap and plaster instead of Sheetrock. Charlie should know."

Tru nodded, writing.

"If it's plaster, run your hand across it to see if it's
textured," he said. "Textured is easier to fix if you crack
it, but it can be a bi— It's, uh, it's sometimes difficult
to fit perfectly."

Tru gave a quick glance and continued writing, commenting sotto voce, "Can be a bitch to fit perfect."

Eli managed not to smile.

"You'll need to decide about the color. If Charlie can
remember the name of the paint, then it would be possible to match it. But contrast is always an option, as well.
I don't know what the cups look like, but you probably
don't want that color."

"They're kind of white," Tru said. "And they're really more mugs than cups, I guess. Mom found them
and figured out how to personalize them. That's one
thing pretty neat about my mom. She's, like, supercre-
ative about problem-solving stuff. No matter what kind
of hole she digs herself into, she always manages to put

together a ladder. Even if she has to use duct tape and toothpicks."

Tru laughed, but the sound had as much pride in it as humor.

"When we were in Wilmington, this psychologist thought that I should go to this teen support group. I only went a couple of sessions. It was way too hard-core for me. The other kids, a lot of them had parents who were, like, serious criminals. Some had been abused or abandoned on their own for days at a time. They'd be forced into state care and then suddenly back home, wherever home happened to be. I mean, wow. I realized Mom really hadn't done such a bad job. I always have food and clothes and a warm, safe place to stay. So, I mean, she's not perfect. But she's pretty cool."

"I think so, too," Eli answered, although his mind was whirling. He was trying to sort through the new information.

Mazy had sent her son to a strange teen support group? What could that be? Sons of Moms Who Love Guys Who Are Wrong for Them?

"Do you have everything in your notes?" he asked.

"Yeah, I think so."

Tru started to tear the pages out.

"No, leave them in," Eli said. "It's harder to lose the pad than little slips of paper. And then you have a record of everything you did and the how and why of doing it. At least, that's how my dad taught me."

Eli scooted his own notepad toward Tru and he opened it up.

"Wow, cool drawings," he said.

Eli shrugged. "I do bigger ones, of course, on the drafting table. But this is good both as a quick reference and a reminder of the different incarnations of any particular piece."

"What do you do when it gets full?"

"I have the start date on the front," Eli said. "When I get to the last page, I put that date underneath it and then I put it in a box. If I ever need it, I know it's there."

"Good idea," Tru said.

Eli watched as he turned to his own notepad and wrote the date on the top line of the cover.

27

Mazy had been delighted at dinner when Tru gave her his update on the shelf-building project.

"Eli had me take notes, just like in school. And tomorrow I'll go over and assess the sight and decide what design to use. We want to build a shelf that correctly fulfills the needs of the client."

"Listen to that," Beth Ann said. "He already sounds like he knows what he's doing."

Mazy's brain had gotten stuck on the word *we*.

"So, Eli is helping you with this," she clarified.

Tru nodded. "He's going to show me how to do things. But it's important for me to do, rather than watch. That's how he learned from his dad."

She had needed the shelf built. She'd asked her son to do it, worrying that it was beyond his abilities. Now Eli had agreed to help him. So the shelf would be built and her son would learn a useful skill. Mazy was very pleased how that turned out.

She hurried through her meal.

"Tru, would you do the dishes tonight?" she said. "I want to talk to Eli."

He agreed and Beth Ann insisted that she would help. Mazy slipped on her jacket and headed out the back door.

There was still a light on in the wood shop, so instead

of making her usual trek to Eli's basement apartment, she walked down the slope to his place of business.

A small bell tinkled overhead as she opened the door. She remembered it from her childhood as being as magical as any damselfly or woodland sprite. The interior was much as her memory recalled. Flashes of the past assailed her. She had been here so many times as a kid. Laughing and playing. Getting into mischief. She had been here with her father. And she had been here with Eli. Strangely it all seemed smaller than the image in her mind. But comparing was inaccurate, as Eli seemed much bigger.

"Well, hello," he said, looking up from the pieces at his workbench.

He rose to his feet and it felt like the most natural thing in the world to walk up and give him a kiss.

"Mmm," he said by way of compliment as he wrapped his arms around her waist and pulled her closer. He kissed her back with a little more than friendly intent. As they parted, he couldn't seem to resist one final peck on the lips.

"Did you come down here just to kiss me?" he asked.

"Isn't that a good enough reason?" she teased.

"I suppose it is."

"Actually, I came to say thank you."

"Oh, yeah?"

"For helping Tru with the shelf," she told him. "He's willing and he's enthusiastic, but I warn you—he doesn't actually know much about building anything."

"I know what I'm getting into," he said. "We all have to learn on something. And a shelf is a pretty good place to learn, especially a shelf for somebody else. If you make one for yourself, you'll have to look at your mistakes for the rest of your life."

He laughed and she laughed. He still had his hands at her waist.

"Well…as I said, thank you."

He released her and took a step back. "Nothing says 'thank you' like a well-timed blow job."

Mazy glanced around the very masculine, very memory-filled place from her childhood.

"Here?" she squeaked the question.

Eli glanced around and his expression changed. His narrow-eyed gaze widened and his hardened jaw appeared to relax.

"Probably not," he answered. "I remember hearing my dad joke once that my brother, Clark, was conceived in here. But I've always made it a point to keep my personal life and my work life separate."

Mazy was glad. She would not have told him no, but somehow such an act in this place seemed strangely irreverent.

She changed the subject.

"So, what are you making?" she asked him as she looked at the joined pieces of wood atop his workbench.

"I'm doing a sheet-music cabinet for the museum conservatory in Boone," he answered. "One of the donors is gifting it. It's a tax write-off probably, but it's needed. And I want to make something functional, beautiful and guaranteed to last a couple of hundred years."

"A couple of hundred years?" Mazy repeated incredulously.

Eli nodded, proudly.

"These are the doors," he said. "Inside there'll be a series of thin pullouts. They'll function like drawers, but take up less space and allow you to store more in less size."

He got out his notebook and showed her what he'd drawn up.

"It's really pretty." She ran her hand along the raw poplar.

"It's going to be more than pretty," he assured her. "I'm going to veneer the exterior in a cracked ice pattern."

"What does that mean?"

"Well, veneering is putting a very thin layer of another wood atop this sturdy poplar," he explained. "Typically you do this in a sheet. As if you're trying to pretend that the entire piece is actually the wood that you've put on top."

"Right."

"But what I'm going to do is cut the veneer wood in rectangles, one by two. And then attach them kind of crazy-quilt fashion. With the grain of the wood going every which way, what it ends up resembling is cracked ice."

"Wow. It sounds incredible. I can't wait to see it."

"Me, neither," he said. "Unfortunately, something really special takes a lot of time."

"And I'm interrupting you."

He grinned at her. "You are my favorite interruption," he told her. "Besides, I was about to quit for the night, anyway. I need to go up and see my dad."

She nodded and watched as he began putting away his tools.

"Would you mind if I went with you?" she asked. "I miss Jonah and I haven't seen him since his stroke. But I don't want to intrude."

"He would love to see you," Eli said.

"Good."

A few minutes later, Eli was turning off the lights and locking up the doors. He took Mazy's hand as they walked up the path. It was such a sweet gesture. It felt genial and familiar. He was still her best friend, even if he was also a very exciting lover.

On the porch he hesitated.

"You're going to be shocked at how much he's changed," Eli said. "He's more or less paralyzed except for his left arm. He can move his mouth and make noise, but he has no intelligible speech. And he's about half the size he was when he was still on his feet."

"Okay," Mazy said.

"I know he looks bad, but I don't want you to burst into tears and race out of the room."

"Eli, I am made of sterner stuff."

He smiled and kissed her on the forehead. "I know you are, Mazy."

Inside, Jonah sat in his recliner in front of the television. Ida was seated close by, feeding him from a plate on a tray table.

The woman jumped to her feet at the sight of Mazy and made hasty apologies about the way she was dressed and the presence of her apron.

Mazy greeted her with pleasure and waved away her concerns. "You look very comfortable. That's what we're all going for at home. And please forgive me for barging in on you two. I twisted Eli's arm to get him to invite me."

Ida insisted that her guest needed some refreshments and bustled off into the kitchen. Eli stood on the other side of his father.

"Dad, you remember Mazy, of course."

"Like he could ever forget!" she said, smiling down at him. "Hi, Jonah. Long time no see."

He was looking up at her. She could see all the life that was still in his eyes. She hadn't remembered that they were so much like Eli's eyes. Perhaps her younger self had been too busy to notice. Or her younger self hadn't spent enough time looking at Eli. Either way, she'd always liked him. He was a connection to her father. And reminding her of Eli didn't hurt anything, either.

Because Ida had gone into the kitchen, the chair next to him was empty. And the tray table with his dinner sat abandoned. Mazy sat down and twirled the spoon in the plate of shredded meat over rice.

"This looks good," she lied.

She offered a bite and he opened his mouth to accept it. To counter the silence, she began to talk. First about beef tips and gravy, which she was pretty sure this dish was supposed to represent. And then on to great meals she'd eaten in Wilmington and elsewhere.

"Sometimes how good I think the food is turns out to be directly proportional to how hungry I am," she told him, rattling on. "When I was on litter pickup, we would have a truck…" In midsentence she realized what she had revealed. Stutteringly she attempted to dial it back. "My…my employer enrolled the company in one of those adopt-a-highway things," she lied. "So we, uh, we all had to do some pickup. Like sort of a community service." Mazy knew she was making a mash of it. Determinedly she moved on. "I was totally not used to that kind of exercise. When the truck showed up with our meals. I didn't care what it was, it tasted great."

Ida returned to the room with some very weak and watery cups of tea. She was completely charmed that Mazy had chosen to feed Jonah.

"I don't think I've gotten him to eat that much in a week," she said.

After he'd finished, the four sat around chatting.

Actually, Ida did most of the talking. It was obvious to Mazy that any woman trapped in a house with a man who could no longer speak might seriously need some airtime. Mazy was happy to give it.

But when Eli got his father to bed and they were ready to leave, she was pleased about that, too.

"I can lift him," Ida told her. "I can move him around, get him to the bathroom or change him if need be. But it is a genuine blessing to have Eli coming twice a day to get him dressed and undressed."

"I'm sure he's grateful to be able to help," Mazy said.

Eli came back into the living room. "I think Dad wants to say good-night to you."

Mazy followed him back into the bedroom.

Jonah lay on his side. He was wearing blue flannel pajamas and covered by an expanse of eiderdown.

She got down on her knees on the floor next to him.

"It was really good seeing you again," she said. "I promise I won't stay away so long again."

He reached his arm out and laid a hand against her cheek. She covered his with her own.

When he removed his hand, he laid it across his heart.

"Thanks." Mazy leaned forward and planted a kiss on his cheek. "Good night."

Eli was waiting for her at the door to the room. Mazy offered one last wave before he turned off the lights.

Then, standing in the doorway, silhouetted in full view of his father, Eli pulled her into his arms. His mouth came down on hers, the warmth of it unexpected and evoking both sensitivity and sensuality.

"Let's go home, Mazy," he whispered. "I really want to make love to you."

28

⟶ ⟵

A couple of nights later, as Mazy was setting the table for dinner, Tru burst through the kitchen door. He was beaming with enthusiasm.

"Hey, Gram. Do you think we could get through dinner a little quicker tonight?"

"I suspect we could."

"I'm going to the basketball game."

"You're going to the basketball game?" Mazy repeated with surprise.

"Yeah, you, too," he answered. "And Gram if she wants to go."

The two women shared a speculative glance.

"Eli is taking us."

Mazy couldn't stop the smile that spread across her face. "Is he?" she asked. "And your gram and I are included in the invitation?"

"Absolutely. He asked me to ask you."

"I'll stay home and watch my shows, thank you," Beth Ann said. "But I think it's nice that you kids go out and have fun."

Tru chuckled at having Mazy included as one of the "kids."

After the meal, Beth Ann insisted that Mazy leave the cleanup and get ready for her outing.

It was an outing in more ways than one. It would be the first time that she and Eli had been seen together in public. Of course, Tru would be with them. She didn't know if that would make it seem more serious or less.

She didn't have any clothes that Eli hadn't already seen. She assured herself that it didn't make any difference. She also wished that she'd chosen to save just one pair of fashionable jeans over the "mom" ones. But it was way too late for that now.

Still, looking in her mirror, she thought she probably looked as good as any woman her age in town. She turned and peered over her shoulder, trying to get a better look at her backside.

Was her butt really big?

"No!" she admonished herself aloud. "You look fine."

All those years, all those guys, it had undermined her self-esteem. She was forgetting what the shrink had told her to do with negative talk.

Nobody can unhear what people say. But they can rephrase it and repurpose it. She'd forgotten to do that, because it was Eli. She knew he would never hurt her, so she'd let her guard down. She could never control other people's words, she could only control her reaction to them.

"Rephrase. Pardon me, I couldn't help but notice your ass." She laughed to herself as she recalled the old joke: "It's big and white and follows me everywhere."

"Okay, repurpose..." That took her a second. "If he's not averting his eyes from it, then he must like the way it looks. And he certainly can't keep his hands off it. So there."

She nodded at her reflection. "I can live with that."

"Who are you talking to?" her mother called out from the kitchen.

"The mirror," she answered.

Eli showed up a few minutes later, wearing striped black and gold.

"Oh, my God, you still have a Bee sweater!"

He laughed. "Everybody has a Bee sweater."

It was true. The home team section, known as the Swarm, was where all the black-and-gold-striped sweaters of the world went to die.

Eli had found one—once belonging to a younger, slimmer Clark—for Tru to wear. Amid the crowd, only Mazy stood out like a sore thumb. Or maybe like a thumb with a stinger in it.

Although she saw a number of people she knew, they weren't the people that would step up to say hello. A few greeted Eli like a long-lost friend. Apparently he did not attend that many community events.

"And who is this pretty lady you've brought with you?" came in several different versions of the question.

Eli would introduce her, and then the greeter's eyes would grow wary and, after minimal politeness, he'd scurry away.

If Eli noticed anything, he didn't comment.

The building was a new, larger version of what they'd had when Mazy was still in school. It was modern and well lit, with a very shiny, unscuffed floor. But the bleachers weren't any more comfortable than she remembered. The murals of Buzz on the walls weren't any more artistic. And the three championship banners from years gone by still fluttered slightly from the pull of the exhaust fan.

The place filled up fast. Even the first section on the other side of the court was beginning to have a splattering of Bee sweaters.

She was seated between Tru and Eli. The latter entertained her by pointing out people they both had known back in the day, and updating her on any foibles or fiascos she might have missed.

"Those are my nieces," he said. "There on the front row."

Mazy followed his gaze to see two little blonde girls, both dressed in tiny black-and-gold outfits that perfectly matched the uniforms of the current high school cheerleaders.

Mazy almost moaned aloud. "Uh, are they official mascots or something?"

"Nope," Eli said. "Sheila dresses them that way so that they'll always feel like they are part of the action until they are old enough to take their rightful place on the squad."

Mazy looked him straight in the eye. "You realize that your sister-in-law is a nutbar."

"More aware than you could ever know," he told her. "I love my brother, but his priorities are all screwed up, too. They truly are perfect for each other."

They shared a laugh. It felt so good to look at him. To talk to him. To laugh with him. Mazy thought that a woman could put up with a lot of grief in the world if she had this man to share a smile with her from time to time.

Once the game started, attention focused on the court. It was a conference game with a solid rival. The teams were so evenly matched that every play mattered.

But as Mazy watched, she got the distinct feeling that someone was staring at her. She shrugged it off. In her years in Brandt Mountain, she'd been more infamous than popular. And her position at the bank was not making her a town favorite.

Also, it was her first time in public with Eli. There were bound to be people who were more than a little interested. It might not even be about her. Eli had obviously not been a monk in the years she was gone. He might have jealous old girlfriends all over the gym.

She tried to shrug it off, but it persisted. It was almost as if she could feel the eyes boring into her. Finally, she couldn't stand it another minute and turned for a quick peek.

Across an expanse of cheering crowd, her eyes met Tad Driscoll. Her jaw dropped.

He quickly looked away and she did, too.

Tad? Why would Tad be staring?

She waited a minute, feigning total engrossment in the game, and then glanced back in that direction. Caught him again.

That was completely weird. What interest could Tad have in her? Why would he care if she was out with Eli?

Right then one of the Brandt Mountain players made a nice block and Tru nudged her.

"That guy is in my physics class."

Mazy nodded absently before the obvious dawned on her.

Tad is not looking at you, he's looking at Tru.

A wave of nostalgia swept over her that was so bitter her eyes filled with tears. A million times in her life, a million musings, she had hoped, dreamed, imagined, the moment when Tad saw his son for the first time. Never among those expectations did the scene include crowded bleachers at a basketball game.

From the days before Tru was even born, she'd fantasized about Tad seeing him, wanting him, loving him. And wanting *her,* loving *her,* by extension. She remembered secretly believing that he would show up at the hospital while she labored. When he'd not even acknowledged the birth, she'd phoned every day for months on end, begging, pleading, for a visit. She'd had friends and family try to talk him into meeting his child. She had threatened and cajoled to no avail.

Even then she hadn't given up. She'd plotted a hundred times to "accidentally" run into him. Every time she came home, she tried to show up where she thought he might be. She'd often taken Tru to the little playground near the Driscolls' home. They'd gone on toddler walks along Tad's favorite hiking trail in hopes of confronting him. But it had never happened. Tad had deliberately, determinedly steered clear.

At last the moment was here. It was now. And it no longer meant anything to her. It meant even less to Tru. Tears stung her eyes. It had been a terrible, stupid waste of her youth, of her heart.

Suddenly a hand clasped hers. She looked up to see Eli's face full of concern.

"What's wrong?"

"Nothing," she told him, shaking her head. "Just a sad moment."

The explanation didn't smooth the wrinkle in his brow. But they did turn back to the game. Eli never let go of her hand. And that kept the bleakness at bay. Yes, her past was full of mistakes. But she had taken a stand for herself and the present was better. With Eli at her side, even the future seemed to brighten.

At halftime Tru was invited to sit with a group of other classmates, most of them girls, Mazy noted. All around them people began heading down to the restrooms or the concession stand.

Eli stood up. "Would you like a Coke or something?" he asked.

"Sure, I could go for a soda."

Eli made a move and then hesitated. He glanced at

her again, made a big display of stretching, and then sat down. "Get me one, too, won't ya?"

"Oh, okay."

Mazy rattled through a moment of confusion before she grabbed her purse and headed down the steps.

By the time she was down the aisle she began to re-think what had just happened. Hadn't he offered her something? Or had she said something first? Maybe they had simply been chatting? But by the time she was in the line for drinks, she was clear that a giant mistake had been made. She didn't even have to open her wallet to know she was carrying $3.36. All the money that she had until payday on Friday. She had been hoarding that money like a miser, in case an emergency came up. Al-though she had to admit that it wouldn't be much of an emergency if three bucks could fix it.

Still, it went against her principles to spend her very last bit of cash for something as discretionary as soft drinks. But Eli had paid for their tickets to the game. It made perfect sense that she should buy the refreshments. Perfect sense if she were not as hard up for cash as she currently happened to be.

She was the next person up at the window. If she were going to walk away, now was the moment to do it.

"Hi."

She looked up to see Tad suddenly standing beside her. His blue eyes were bright and he was smiling at her in that way she remembered from her teens.

"Let me get this—what are you having?"

"Oh, I can't let you buy."

Tad leaned closer with a flirty whisper. "Hey, you're letting me cut in line. Now what will you have?"

"Two Cokes, please."

"Make that three," he told the volunteer at the window as he peeled a ten off the wad of bills in his hand.

Mazy stood there next to him feeling distinctly uncomfortable. Her presence here with Eli might cause a little swirl of gossip, being seen with Tad might reenergize a storm that had never truly blown over.

"Thanks," she said simply as she took her drinks. She had hoped to move away entirely, but Tad followed.

After a quick consideration, Mazy halted, believing it was better to be seen conversing with Tad in a crowd than standing alone with him in an open part of the floor.

He hesitated, as if his preference was more privacy rather than less. But he apparently decided to accept what was available.

"I saw Truman," he said. "He's…he's a good-looking kid."

Instead of an inconsequential "Thank you," Mazy rolled her eyes. "You mean, he looks like you."

Tad actually chuckled as if it were funny. "Yeah, that's what I was thinking, but it sounded pretty conceited to say it aloud."

His self-deprecating words were deliberately funny. He could be so charming when he wanted to be.

"If other people notice," she said. "That can't be helped and it can't be part of our agreement. Tru can't hide out just because his likeness to you might be inconvenient."

"No, of course not," Tad said. His brow was deeply furrowed and his expression suggested he was wounded by her words. "I want all good things for him, just like I do my girls. He's an innocent kid. Our mistakes only belong to us."

It was strange wording, but she nodded.

"Agreed."

"Mazy, I know you never expected to hear this from

me," Tad continued, "but I'm sorry that things worked out the way they did."

The shock must have shown on her face.

"I know that's not how I behaved when you showed up in my office," he said. "Honestly, you caught me off guard. And then I was so surprised about…about your recent problem. Your solution was unexpected. I reacted to what felt like a threat."

He shook his head. His eyes, those beautiful blue eyes that she loved in the face of her own son, gazed at her in a way that simply had to be sincere. "We just kind of got restarted on the wrong foot," he said.

"I think we must always have been on the wrong foot," Mazy replied.

Tad shrugged. "You're probably right about that. I know it's all ancient history, but I need to set the record straight. I cared a lot about you, but I was in love with Genna. I should never have allowed my feelings for you to go as far as they did."

Mazy was slightly stunned at his revelation. She'd been convinced for some time now that he'd never *had* any feelings for her. She'd been convinced, because that was what he'd told her. She'd been a convenience for him. She'd been a lonely, lovesick girl who would put out for him when his steady girlfriend wouldn't.

"I know that what happened was one hundred percent my fault," he said.

Mazy felt a sudden shock of guilt surge through her. "No, of course it wasn't one hundred percent your fault."

Mazy was fairly certain that it wasn't even fifty percent his fault. Her sessions with Dr. Reese had taught her to take responsibility for her own mistakes. There was no use in beating herself up about them. Only by owning them and living them would she succeed in not repeating them.

She *was* owning them, she was taking responsibility for them, but did that mean she should confess them? The secret that she'd kept so guarded, so close to the vest for so long, weighed on her. But she wasn't even tempted to share it.

"What happened between us simply happened," she lied. "We were young, stupid kids."

He smiled at her. It wasn't the toothy, confident smile that made women sigh and men eager to be his friend. It was a smaller, softer smile that seemed somehow infinitely more private.

"Thank you, Mazy," he said. "Thank you and don't worry about anything with me. It has never been, nor will it ever be, my intention to cause trouble for you or your son."

She was amazed at how freeing that statement made her feel. She hadn't even realized that the low-level worry had been there until it was removed. She took a deep breath because it was suddenly easier to breathe.

The safety of the crowd around them had disappeared. The game was about to start and most people had taken their seats. Tad and Mazy might as well have been in the middle of the court with a spotlight on them, everyone in the building saw everything.

"Look," he said. "Why don't we talk again, someplace a little more private? Maybe... Well, dinner is way too scary, right? Why don't we try to do lunch together? Do you think we could do that? Sometime?"

Lunch with Tad Driscoll?

Warning alerts went off all over Mazy's brain. Her frontal lobe kept repeating, *It's just lunch,* but deeper, less straightforward and logical recesses were flashing *Danger* in bright red lights.

"No," she said. "I don't think that would be a good idea."

He accepted her refusal amicably. "Perhaps you're right. It's a small town and we have a lot of history." He glanced up into the stands. "You're here with Latham. Are you two...?"

"We've started seeing each other," Mazy answered.

Tad nodded. "He's a good guy, Mazy."

"Yes, he is," she agreed.

The game had recommenced as she made her way up the steps to the seat where she'd left Eli.

She scooted in beside him and handed him his soda.

"Was Driscoll bothering you?"

"No," she answered. "Of course not. We were just talking."

"You shouldn't have to even acknowledge his existence," Eli said. "He has a lot of gall talking to you."

"Well, he thinks you're a nice guy," Mazy told him. "And these drinks, by the way, are on him."

29

With a big win, it was traditional to show up at Brandt Burger for a celebratory meal. Eli didn't ask Mazy if she wanted to go. The thought occurred to him, but he'd already passed his good-guy quota. This evening he was back into bad-boyfriend mode and bad boyfriends do what they want to do. Their girlfriends go along to get along. So, without so much as a "Why don't we..." he drove them directly from the school parking lot to the hive of school spirit "after-gloat" out on the highway.

Tru was obviously delighted, as well as hungry. Eli found an amazing parking spot very near the door, with a great vantage point on all the activity. He put down the tailgate to form their personal dining area and left Mazy there while he and Tru went for food.

Inside they ran into Clark, who had snagged a booth. Eli introduced Tru, who was very polite to Sheila and the girls.

"How was your first Brandt Mountain basketball game?" Clark asked.

"Fun. It was fun."

"You look tall enough to be on the team," Sheila pointed out.

"It's not really my game."

"Well, you look like a hometown boy in the sweater," Clark said.

"It's your sweater," Eli pointed out.

Clark laughed.

His daughter Ava was astounded. "Daddy used to be that size?"

A few minutes later, Clark privately buttonholed Eli for an aside conversation as Tru held a place in line.

"So Mazy came with you," Clark said. "But then she's practically throwing herself at Tad Driscoll."

"She didn't throw herself at anyone," Eli replied tightly.

Clark shrugged. "That's the way I saw it," he said. "Sheila thought exactly the same thing."

"They talked to each other in plain view of the entire community," Eli said. "It was probably about business."

"Business? Is that what she said?"

"I didn't ask her," Eli told him.

Clark shook his head. "I'm worried about you. I don't want you to get your hopes up again only to have Driscoll swoop in and get her two-timing you."

"Nobody is two-timing anyone."

Clark looked skeptical. "Driscoll doesn't chat up women for his health."

That was probably true, but it was also true that half the community, including his brother, wanted the entertainment of another juicy scandal rehash.

"You're going to need to up your game," Clark suggested.

Eli pretended to discount the words, but he couldn't quite shake them. The memory of Mazy in the gym calmly chatting with Driscoll left a very sour taste in Eli's mouth.

That was not helped by Mazy's acknowledgment

that the jerk had bought the sodas. Eli had deliberately foisted the refreshments on Mazy. Now he refused to be "cheaped out" again. When they finally reached the front of the line, he bought enough food to feed a small army.

Fortunately, he discovered when they got back to the tailgate that teenage boys eat like a small army.

The burgers were good. The activity around them was fun and upbeat. Mazy seemed to be actually enjoying herself. The reswarm of after-game revelers was not limited to high school teens. Although there were plenty of those, there were also families with young children and grandparents with memories of games long gone by. There was a warm feeling of community camaraderie and, surprisingly, Mazy seemed as comfortable easing into that as anyone else.

Eli was pretty sure that wasn't a good idea. As he slathered French fries with ketchup, he tried to come up with a bad-guy plan. A public scene would certainly fill the bill. But Eli had never done anything like that. He was not sure that he could pull it off. And all those who saw Mazy with Driscoll might see it as a jealous tantrum. No, he didn't want that.

With an extra burger in hand, Tru went running off with other kids. Mazy's conversation was casual, superficial, as if they were merely a couple of friends seated next to each other. Clark was right, he needed to up his game. Or, in line with his current plan, kick it down a notch.

He watched the goings-on around him and ruminated on the lovelorn woes of the internet lamenters. What would their boyfriends do out in a public place? He knew the answer immediately.

"Whoa, check out the rack on that one," he said as he gestured toward a young woman with a very nice figure.

Significantly more endowed than Mazy. "Yellow-and-black stripes have never looked so good."

Beside him, Mazy stiffened. Eli saw her brow furrow, but she said nothing.

Deliberately he kept his eyes on the young woman as he made a smacking sound with his lips. "Oh, I'd sure hit that."

A shocked sound emitted from Mazy's throat that she attempted to cover with a cough. Eli enthusiastically pounded her on the back.

"I'm okay," she assured him.

Eli got a better look at the face of "nice rack" girl and realized that she was little more than a teenager. He felt slightly sick. She was closer to Tru's age than his own. That was way too creepy. But it *had* gotten Mazy's attention. He decided to limit his attention to women who were obviously older.

A moment later a female deputy from the sheriff's department came out the door of the burger joint. Perfect, Eli thought to himself.

"I'd hit that."

In his peripheral vision he could see Mazy's wide-eyed expression evidencing disbelief. This was good. This was really working. He decided to go for the jugular.

A young mom with a preschooler in hand walked by. "I *have* hit that," he said to Mazy in a quiet, boastful aside.

Mazy was completely silent. Eli couldn't be sure if it was jealousy or hurt. Either would probably work.

Going into the restaurant door he spotted another woman with a short cropped hairdo and slightly wide backside covered in a black skirt.

"I've hit that, too," Eli bragged, stuffing a handful of fries in his mouth.

"What?" Mazy's voice was a squeak of disbelief before she dropped her tone to a furtive whisper. "You've had sex with Mrs. Markowski?"

Eli nearly choked as he immediately recognized the name as that of the pastor's wife at the Church of Christ. Clearly this was not a good strategy for a small town.

And it was not one that he shared with his dad during bath time the next day.

"I'm going to be helping Tru with a project," he told Jonah. "It's just a shelf, so it's weird that I'm so jazzed about it. Tru doesn't know anything about anything. And it remains to be seen if he even has an aptitude for this stuff. But it's fun to see his mind working. To see him enthused. I guess I get tired of being the only one who really loves what we do." Eli sighed heavily. "I miss working with you, Dad. Clark is…well, Clark is just Clark."

Clark had moseyed into work that day, late as usual. And when questioned about the storage it was clear that he hadn't actually bothered to even make the phone calls.

Eli refused to let that dampen his day. He was going to be working on a project with Tru. That was like doing something nice for Mazy without the consequences of doing something nice for her. He could hardly wait.

The teen showed up a little after four. Eli waved him over to the workbench.

Tru proudly opened up his notepad and showed Eli the dimensions that he'd measured. There was easily room for any number of shelf configurations. He'd gotten answers to all the questions except the one about paint.

"The wall isn't painted," he told Eli. "It's got wood on it."

"Wood? Like paneling."

"Yeah, I guess it would be paneling. It's tall, but it doesn't go all the way to the ceiling."

"Ah, so it's more of a wainscot."

"Okay."

"So we'll probably need to match that as best we can," Eli said. "What kind of wood is it?"

Tru screwed up his face uncomfortably. "Brown wood?"

They both laughed.

"When we put the wood shipment up the other day, did you see anything like it?"

"No, I don't think so."

Eli shrugged. "Well, wood looks different when it's finished. Lots of folks can't tell a mahogany from a maple and describe everything as oak."

"I guess that's me," Tru said.

"Don't worry, you'll learn," he told him. "Come on. Let's take a field trip."

As they headed to the coat hooks, Eli stopped at his brother's workbench. "You'll need to get those bench planes sharpened today. And the spray gun needs cleaning." Eli glanced around. "And sweep before you lock up. We're gone for the day."

Clark's shocked expression was priceless, but Eli hardly spared a moment to even notice.

On Main Street, there were several empty parking spaces in front of Local Grind. Inside there were only two tables with customers.

Charlie greeted them both warmly.

"So, you're back already," he said to Tru.

The teenager shrugged. "I didn't know what kind of wood is on the walls," he answered.

"Oh, it's some kind of oak, I think," Charlie responded. "I wanted to tear it out, it looks old-fashioned, but Alice liked it."

"Your wife has good taste," Eli said.

He was staring at the wall. His expression was totally calm, but his heart was beating faster.

He walked to the side of the room where the tables were empty and slowly, almost lovingly, ran his hand across the paneling. At the edge of one, where the tongue fit snuggly within the groove, he pressed a fingernail into the wood.

"I don't think this is oak, Charlie."

Eli glanced back to see both the building's owner and Tru standing behind him.

"It's not oak?"

Eli shook his head. "I think it's chestnut."

"Chestnut?"

"Uh-huh."

"You don't see much chestnut these days."

Eli glanced over at Tru. "American chestnut was one of the most abundant and useful native wood species in the country. It was strong, but relatively lightweight. It was durable, easy to work and it could be finished up to look beautiful. Best of all, there was a lot of it. One out of every four hardwoods in Appalachia was chestnut. And when a wood is abundant, it's inexpensive."

"So why don't we use it anymore?" the teenager asked.

"In the early twentieth century, commercial nurseries imported ornamental trees from the Far East. Unfortunately, along with the pretty mimosas and Japanese maples, they brought in a blight that virtually wiped out the entire American chestnut species in less than a decade."

"That can happen?"

"It can and it does," Eli said. "It keeps happening. It's happening right now. We were still staggering from chestnut loss when we were hit with Dutch elm disease. It's a fungal infection, just like the chestnut blight. We've done a little better with it and with oak wilt, but our trees are always at risk from plagues. These are all fungal infections. I think the pine problems out west are the same."

"Wow."

He turned to look at Tru. "So you are looking at a remnant of a type of wood that you and I will probably never work again. It's like a rare antique."

"Jeez," Charlie said. "I'm sure glad I didn't rip it out and dump it. I would have. I wanted the walls to be a muted green. It seemed like it would brighten the place up."

Eli glanced around. "It would," he said. "If you still want to do that, don't trash it. Take the chestnut down carefully. You can sell it."

"I can sell it?" Charlie repeated. "People will buy the wood off the walls."

"There's no other way to get this kind of wood," Eli answered. "There is a big market for reclaimed chestnut."

"Do you want to buy it?"

"Me? No," Eli assured him. "I could use a few pieces, but nobody should be making furniture from this. And it's too rich for my blood. Ten-foot lengths of chestnut lap and gap in excellent condition, somebody will pay some cash for that."

"Seriously? I could sure use some cash. And there is more of this stuff upstairs."

"Upstairs?"

"Yeah, the whole second floor used to be a ballroom," Charlie answered.

Eli and Tru took the dimensions of the downstairs wainscot and then repeated the action on the second level. The ballroom wainscot was significantly shorter, more of a chair-rail height. But it also had some decorative beams around the stage area.

Back in the coffee shop, Charlie was excited.

"Give me a day or two," Eli told him. "I'll make some calculations on how much chestnut there is, what kind of buyers are out there and how much you might get for it."

They drove home eager to get online. Tru wanted to start the search right away.

Eli shook his head. "Your mom and grandmother are going to be expecting you home for dinner," he said. "I've got to get something to eat myself and then go see my dad."

"Eat with us," Tru suggested. "Gram won't mind. And that way we can get started."

Routine refusal was his immediate inclination. It was incredibly rude to show up at somebody's house expecting dinner. And when that somebody is the woman you're sleeping with, it would look like an overreach expectation worthy of an insensitive misogynist. Which, he quickly reminded himself, was what he was going for.

Sometimes it was hard for Eli to remember why he was doing all this. Why he was cultivating his inner bad guy and jerking Mazy around in a way she never deserved. It would be so much easier when he could simply love her and she would love him back.

Not yet. They were not there yet.

"Dinner at your house sounds great!" he told Tru. "Let me grab my laptop and I'll meet you there in five minutes."

30

$\longrightarrow\!\!\longleftarrow$

She had been surprised when Tru had announced that Eli was coming for dinner. The basketball game had been unexpectedly fun. And being out in the open with Eli had felt wonderful. She was proud to be with him.

Well, at least most of the time. She hadn't remembered him as a guy who had such weird moods. And his openness about his conquests of other women, that was positively embarrassing. Of course, she knew that he'd slept with other people. But she sure didn't what to know who. And poor Reverend Markowski! She hoped that had happened before the couple married.

Feeling attraction was human nature. But to gawk at women while she was sitting right there. That just didn't seem like the Eli she knew.

But even with that strange episode, the sight of him sitting so relaxed and looking so at home in her mother's kitchen felt wonderful. The idea that he was there at the invitation of her son warmed her heart. She couldn't recall any guy that she'd dated that Tru had actually liked. But he liked Eli. He clearly respected him and the feeling appeared to be mutual.

If that wasn't enough to make her day, the news about what they'd found in the Local Grind building easily put her over the top.

"It's like the walls are lined with money," Tru told her.

"They're old boards. It can't be that much," Beth Ann said, looking toward Eli for confirmation.

"It very nearly is," he told her. "Narrowing it down to actual buyers will take some time. The going rate is twelve bucks a board foot. And that's ordinary lumber. This is gorgeous lap and gap, twelve inches wide and ten feet long."

"What does that mean in English?" Mazy asked.

"It means the wood in that building could be worth maybe forty thousand dollars."

"Good Lord!"

"That's more than he owes on the building," Mazy blurted out before she could stop herself. Fortunately, her gaff was effectively covered by her mother.

"For some old boards?"

Eli nodded. "They're chestnut."

Beth Ann quickly glanced around the room and then rose to her feet to slap the wall surface near the doorway. "What about this? What is it?"

"That's 1960s laminate paneling," he answered with a chuckle. "But it's good to keep your eyes open, Mrs. Gulliver."

The mood for most of the evening was lighthearted, optimistic. And Mazy felt that way, too.

After dinner, Beth Ann insisted that Mazy sit with "the men" in the living room while she cleaned up. Mazy agreed because she thought Eli was there to see her. But he hardly glanced in her direction. She sat in a chair across from him as he and Tru searched the internet, looking at what Eli jokingly described to Tru as "wood porn," photos of trees and cut lumber and furniture construction.

"'American chestnut trees grew to a diameter of ten

feet and heights up to one hundred feet until an airborne fungus killed up to three million trees in the early twentieth century,'" Tru read aloud.

"It's hard to even picture how the landscape must have looked with all those big trees."

Tru was nodding. "I have to do a paper in history this semester. Do you think something like this might count as history?"

Eli shrugged. "You'd have to ask your teacher, but it certainly counts as history to me."

"And it's for sure more interesting than what politician said what to whom at the time of the Louisiana Purchase."

Eli laughed. "Those things are important, too. A guy has got to know a little bit about everything in order to have credibility when he talks about anything."

He would have made such a good father, Mazy thought to herself. If she had married Eli back when they were first together, Tru would have never known anybody else as "Dad."

Even if she married him now, Tru would likely accept him as a father figure. That's what she should do, she decided as she watched them together on the couch. She should marry Eli.

But as the evening wore on, it seemed less and less obvious that she would have that option. Eli never directed a word at her. He didn't even make eye contact.

Mazy told herself it was because he was totally wrapped up with Tru and the wood research.

But when Beth Ann joined them from the kitchen, Eli changed the subject to one more general and pulled her into the conversation. Still, he never directed a word in Mazy's direction. And when, on two separate occasions, Mazy asked him a direct question, he managed to answer without ever looking at her.

Mazy caught herself sinking back, retreating within herself. She was surprised, both that she was doing it and that Eli had brought it on. The retreat was a warning signal that she and Dr. Reese had discovered. And she could not allow herself to give in to it.

Rephrase and repurpose.

Okay, she decided. Rephrasing the unhappy refrain in her head, she decided that Eli was not paying attention to her because he didn't see her mother and son as often as he did Mazy.

No wait, she could only rephrase things that were said. Rephrasing things that were done was the same as making excuses.

She needed to repurpose. Eli was devoting his time to Tru and Beth Ann. This gave her time to watch him and see what a good stepdad he would make.

No, no, that wasn't a good repurpose. The repurpose needed to be about Mazy, not about Eli. All right, his time with her family freed her up to do…something else.

She excused herself and went into the kitchen.

It was spick-and-span, of course. Her mother had already cleaned up. But there was nowhere else for her to go. She couldn't hang out in Tru's room, or her mother's. Her only other option was the bathroom. Sitting alone in a chair was better than sitting alone on the toilet. She opened her briefcase, but then closed it again. There was no real work for her to do. She never brought home files because they were all confidential.

Mazy got to her feet and began straightening cabinets that were already straight. Her mother's kitchen was as regimented and organized as an atomic lab. Even the area under the sink where she kept cleaning supplies was neat and tidy.

"I need a hobby," she mumbled to herself.

Unable to come up with one on short notice, she spent the evening reading warning labels on household cleaners. Lots of good information there and a woman never knows when she might need to know the poison control toll-free number by heart.

It was after ten when Tru called out a "Good night, Mom."

Mazy answered him as she rose to her feet. Suddenly Eli filled the doorway. He may have ignored her all evening, but he was looking at her now. He was looking at her as if he'd been starved for the sight. It made her heart beat faster.

"Hi."

"What are you up to?" he asked.

"Nothing," she answered. "I was just waiting on you. Do you want me to…to walk you home?"

"Dear God, Mazy, you are beautiful."

It wasn't the answer that she expected, but she liked it, anyway.

Eli stepped forward and drew her into his arms. Mazy relaxed against him. His ardor was unexpectedly rough and hungry. She teased his lips until the response she got from him was passionate. All of her senses reveled in the embrace. The taste of his mouth. The masculine scent of oil and sawdust. The stubble of his five-o'clock shadow against her skin. The sound of his breathing and her own heart pounding in her chest.

It was there. That feeling, that oneness, that she'd always sought, that she'd always longed for, that had always eluded her. It was right there in each other's arms. She had found it at last and she wanted to revel in it, expand it, prolong it. She wanted to make it theirs, forever. And keep it both secreted inside their hearts and shared with the entire human race.

He groaned against her mouth before he moved his attention down her throat. She felt him nip the skin near her collarbone. The feeling *zizzed* through her like an electrical current. Setting off sparks that she worried she couldn't control.

Reluctantly she managed to end the kiss, or at least in her own mind postpone the continuance of it. She was more than willing to lie in his arms, making out like someone half her age, until the need for sexual release became unbearable and inevitable. But they needed to be safe and secluded someplace private.

Their lips parted and she pulled back slightly.

"Nice," she said.

There was a strange change in his expression. A furrow appeared in his brow and the genuineness of his smile faltered. After a moment, he took a step toward her. Without even understanding why, she took a step back.

"I'll show you better than nice," he replied. He jerked her off her feet as if she weighed nothing and set her up on the edge of the table.

"Eli!"

His name was a whispered squeal.

His hands were at the button on her waistband.

"Let's get these jeans off you, babe," he said. "There is nothing I like better than getting some on the kitchen table."

"What?" she asked in a scandalized whisper. "Not here."

"Yes, here," he replied, undeterred.

"No."

"Come on, babe. I know you're hot for it. You've been waiting all night long."

"Eli, we can't."

"Of course we can."

"My son's bedroom is across the hall."

"He's probably got his earbuds in."

"Well, my mother certainly doesn't."

"She knows I'm screwing you. You know she knows."

"Yes, but not in *her* house. That's…that's…disrespect-ful."

"Respect has never been one of your things."

"It is," she insisted. "Please, we can't."

"Come on," he urged. "It's exciting. A little risk adds some spice to keep things from being so boring."

"Boring?"

Mazy left her pursuit of that question as Eli had managed to get her zipper undone. His left arm around her was lifting her from the table as the right hand attempted to skim the pants off her. Fortunately, even her mom jeans were too tight for that.

"Stop!"

He did, immediately. Dropping her abruptly onto the table. She went back to whispering.

"I am not having sex where my son or my mother might walk in any second. That is not happening."

He stepped back from the table.

"Fine," he said.

Mazy attempted to right her clothes. She glanced up at Eli. She felt as if she didn't even know him. He was her Eli, but somehow he was not.

"Look, we'll go over to your place," she said. "We'll do…whatever, something really kinky and unboring. But here, in my family's home with my son and my mom, I'm not doing anything."

He was looking at her. Intently looking at her. She couldn't tell what he was thinking, what he was feeling.

Eli was out of line. Risky sex was one thing if it was only about two consenting adults setting themselves up for potential humiliation. But repaying her mother's generosity with insolence was an unpleasant idea. And the possibility of embarrassing, maybe even traumatizing, her son was beyond the pale of motherhood. Eli shouldn't expect that and Mazy should never give in to it.

She knew Eli was way off base. She knew it was the only decision she could make. She knew she was totally right. She knew it even as she heard the words that came out of her own mouth. "I'm sorry."

Eli stared at her for a moment and then turned and walked toward the door.

"Let me get my jacket," she told him.

"Don't bother," Eli answered. "I'm out of the mood."

"But wait, I—"

"Seriously, no big deal," he said. "I'll call you."

Of course, she already knew that he wouldn't.

31

Mazy was sitting at her little desk next to the bank's copy machine gazing at Nina Garvey's loan file. There was something about it that bothered her, but she wasn't sure what it was.

Nina had been in early that morning. She'd brought Mazy a cute little cake. It was covered in yellow icing with a couple of slightly shaky-looking orange frosting leaves on top.

"It tastes better than it looks," Nina assured her. "And I wanted to say thank you for your help."

In truth, Mazy didn't have much help to offer. Nina's loan was a perfect one to bundle and sell. There was nothing to recoup and very little chance that the economics of her situation would improve. And there were no assets to go after. Not even sufficient wages to justify garnishing.

Mazy should have told her that it was hopeless. That the loan would be sold. Nina's credit would be seriously harmed. Creditors would hound her for years to come. It would impact her ability to get a job. Make it tough for her to rent a home, nearly impossible to buy a car. Rule her out for most insurance. Even impact what she'd be charged for cell phone service.

But Mazy wasn't ready to tell her that. She wasn't sure why she held back. Was it merely empathy or was it instinct? Something about the file bothered her. Something about it wasn't quite right. She kept looking at it, trying to figure out what it was.

This afternoon, however, looking had disintegrated into simply gazing. Her mind was completely elsewhere. Last night had been a strange mix of exuberant highs and gloomy lows and she was still reeling.

Her mother had always been a fan of Eli. She was delighted to have him in Mazy's life. And watching Eli with Tru convinced her that he would be a great family man and stepfather. He was a commitment guy. That's what she needed. She had begun to seriously consider marrying him the next time he asked. And she anticipated that he *would* ask her from all the times in the distant past when he already had.

He was Eli. Her Eli. The guy who had loved her all his life.

But, he wasn't.

She went over the events of the previous night in her mind. She began to see that they were not so different from the weeks that had preceded them. The sex was great. The friendship even better. Eli was honest and kind. He was funny, entertaining. She enjoyed being with him, laughing with him. And at times his love for her just oozed out like an aura that enveloped her in well-being.

But he could also be selfish and bossy and disinterested. He treated her disrespectfully and was careless of her feelings. At times he behaved like a first-class SOB.

There was something messed up about their relationship.

Mazy sat back in her chair and covered her mouth with her hand as if her silence could stop the questions that were forming in her brain.

"You are not blind to the defects in these men," Dr.

Reese had told her. "Subconsciously you have chosen them specifically for those qualities. The only way to change that dynamic is to consciously prefer different criteria."

She had thought that was what she was doing.

"A penny for your thoughts?"

Mazy glanced up to see Tad standing in her doorway, smiling at her.

"Mr. Driscoll, the bank is already paying for what my mind has to offer," she told him.

"Ah..." he replied with a little laugh.

He had papers in his hand. She thought he was bringing her more work to do until he stepped over to the copy maker and put them in the machine. In the weeks she'd worked here, she'd never seen him make his own copies before.

When he smiled like that, the years melted away and he looked much more like the teenage boy Mazy had fallen in love with, though the feeling was more nostalgia than anything else.

Still, she knew even nostalgia could be dangerous.

She turned back to the data on her computer screen.

"There's something about the Garvey file that doesn't feel right to me," she said. "I can't put my finger on it."

Tad made no response at all. After a moment she turned to look at him. He was carefully tapping the ends of his papers together as if they would somehow scatter if not held firmly.

"I understand that you want to help. She's a sad case," he said. "But we're a bank, not a social service agency."

"I know that," Mazy said.

"If you want me to jump in and play the bad guy with these people, I'm willing to do that," he said.

Mazy tried to cover her surprise. Wasn't that the whole

idea of giving her this job, to make *her* the bad guy? Maybe what he had said at the basketball game was true. Maybe he *had* overreacted and now regretted it.

"No, it's okay," she assured him. "I'm not afraid to tell people the worst. Most of them already know it."

"Well, better to do it sooner than later."

Mazy nodded. She knew he was right. Still, there was something that held her back. She glanced up at the little cake at the edge of her desk. Maybe it was simply soft-hearted empathy.

"I'm sure you're right," she told him.

After work she met Karly at Local Grind. Charlie moved around the room with a spring in his step that was almost as if he were walking on air. He was not saying much about the treasure he'd found on the walls, although the whole town had heard about it by now.

"I don't want my good luck to seem like bragging," he explained. "Besides, once I pay off the bank loan, I'll hardly be a dollop richer than I was before."

"It will be nice to own your building, free and clear," Mazy pointed out.

"It will," he agreed. "Especially when I see Brakeman and Driscoll, thinking they put one over on me by getting me to buy this white elephant that was actually stuffed with cash."

Mazy enjoyed his enthusiasm. Of course, he still wasn't out of the woods. He needed to get these empty rental spaces occupied. That was the best way to secure his business for the long run.

But making customers he could keep helped, too. And he was obviously doing that as he made his way around the room chatting with the people and insuring that they had everything they needed.

Mazy joined Karly at their usual table.

"Did you bake us something?" Karly asked, pointing to the plastic cake carrier that Mazy had with her.

"Me? You're kidding, right? Cookies are about the limit of my baking abilities. Nina Garvey made this."

"Well, that was nice of her."

"It's a thank-you," Mazy told her. "One I haven't yet earned and I'm not sure I'll be able to."

Karly shrugged. "Trying is the best you can do," she said. "I tell the kids at school that all the time. The only way to truly fail is not to try."

"Wise words," Mazy agreed. She looked down at the cake again. "Why don't we slice this," she said. "You and I need the sugar like a hole in the head. But if I take it home, Tru will eat the whole thing in one sitting."

Karly feigned horror. "You are evil to tempt me. My youngest just turned nine and I still haven't lost the baby weight."

Mazy got a knife and saucers from Charlie and ended up slicing the whole cake, saving only a couple of pieces for Beth Ann and Tru. She offered them to the other patrons at the coffeehouse.

By the time she returned to their table, Karly was well into her portion.

"This is the best cake ever," she said.

Mazy assumed the praise was hyperbole, until she bit into the dessert. The cake was incredibly light and moist, but without any hint of soggy.

"Mmm, this really is great," she told her.

"Nina may not have a clue about how to pick a husband, but she sure knows her way around a baking pan."

Mazy agreed.

Karly showed her the coffee mugs she'd decorated. The one she had done herself was Kandinskyesque, with colorful lines and circles barely revealing her husband's name. Her children had decorated the other mug with Karly's name. One side was festooned with smiley-face flowers. While the reverse revealed a black mess of something her son thought to be a zombie.

"I can hold it left- or right-hand, depending on my mood," Karly explained.

Mazy laughed as she demonstrated, utilizing a smile with the happy side and the curled lip of the undead for the face of gloom.

"People are going to love doing this," Mazy told her.

"Yeah, it was a great idea. When everybody in town has their own mug, I hope you'll remember to pat yourself on the back."

"If I hadn't thought of it, somebody else would have," Mazy said.

"I'm sure Thomas Edison said exactly the same thing."

"I hope there is no need for me to even point out the discrepancy in achievement," Mazy said.

Karly shrugged. "Small town, small successes. We'll take a breakthrough wherever we can get one."

Mazy shook her head as she scraped the very last of the cake's vanilla frosting from the edges of her saucer.

"So I saw you at the basketball game with Eli," Karly said. "You were looking good."

"We were looking like bees."

"Bees that spend a lot of time mating, I think. Kind of glowing with sexual satisfaction."

"What? I'll have you know I'm a Brandt Mountain church lady now. I have no idea what you're talking about."

"Brandt Mountain church ladies invented sex," Karly told her. "Spill the beans. I want to hear everything. And I swear on my mother's grave not to breathe a word."

"I thought your mother was still alive?"

Karly shrugged. "Whatever. Dish. I gotta know."

Mazy laughed at her enthusiasm. "We are seeing each other. You already knew that."

"And it's no longer a big sneaking-around-for-sex secret…." Karly allowed that statement to wander off with a suggestively raised eyebrow.

"No, it seems like it's not."

"And you really like him, don't you?"

Mazy allowed herself an instant of hesitation before she nodded. "Yeah, I do."

"I am so glad," Karly said. "He is such a wonderful guy, everything that you deserve."

The phrase *everything that you deserve* replayed in Mazy's head. She remembered the previous night in her mother's kitchen. Was that what she deserved? Eli had been rude and unreasonable. She knew him to be kind and thoughtful and generous. She knew him to be considerate, to show deference and to be responsible. But the man she was having a relationship with didn't show any of those qualities. At least, he didn't show them to her, not anymore.

"What?" Karly asked.

Mazy looked up realizing she'd been lost in her own thoughts.

"Sorry," she said, shaking her head. "True love never runs smooth."

"True love?"

Mazy felt herself blushing. "I don't know. Maybe. It's complicated."

"Anything worth having always is," Karly pointed out.

"At least things are going better at work."

"And you made that happen," Karly said. "Word is getting around how you are actively trying to help those in financial trouble. It takes folks longer to believe good things than it does bad things, but people do change their minds, even in Brandt Mountain."

"It would be nice not to feel like a pariah," Mazy admitted. "But work is going better because Tad has quit being mad at me."

Karly's jaw dropped. She closed her mouth, but her eyes continued to be wide with disbelief.

"Seriously?"

Mazy nodded. "Yeah, he's being very nice actually. Helpful. I never thought I'd say this, but I think we can have a perfectly reasonable working relationship."

"So, he's been angry, vengeful and lying about you for fourteen years," Karly pointed out, "but now after, like, fourteen days, everything is hunky-dory."

"I know it sounds a little crazy," Mazy admitted. "I talked to him at the basketball game. He said he'd forgiven me a long time ago."

"He didn't need to forgive you. You needed to forgive him."

"Well, yeah, of course," Mazy said. "But we know that I was to blame as much as he was. Maybe I was to blame more. He was dating someone else and I shouldn't have pursued him."

"Is that what your doctor told you?"

"No, not really."

"Then don't you dare believe it."

32

Watching Tru work out the details of the shelves was a lesson in patience that Eli shared with his dad.

"It's so tempting to jump in and do it myself," he admitted. "The kid has been working for three days on something that would take me less than a half hour." Eli chuckled. "I can't even imagine what it must have been like for you to have to watch both Clark and I muddle around until we figured things out. But it is the best way to learn. I only help him when he truly needs it. And that's pretty often. I swear, Dad, I don't think the kid held a chisel before Mazy brought him here. But he's interested and I think he's learning."

He's father gazed at him intently. It was the only indication that he understood what was being said.

"We're using French cleat for his shelves. When I called them that, Tru said it sounded like some kind of condom." Eli laughed aloud. "I told him that it works pretty much the same way. We seriously cover up the part that matters."

He shook his head, still chuckling.

"He's a real good kid, Dad," Eli continued. "I think you're going to like him. Mazy has made a lot of mistakes, but Tru isn't one of them. He's smart and thoughtful and funny. There is not one dollop of that Driscoll arrogance and guile. Tru is as straightforward as a hammer. It was probably a lucky break that Driscoll didn't snap Mazy up when he had the chance."

Eli was thoughtful for a long moment.

"Things are going good with Mazy, I think," he told his father. "Truth is, I thought it was going to be harder than it is. When I started, it just killed me to be mean to her. But now, I kind of like it. She's always available and I always get my way. It's not really a bad deal at all."

His dad couldn't comment.

"I'm thinking that maybe she was right all along. I *was* too soft, too nice. As it is now, when I do her the smallest kindness, it's like a gift. She's *so* grateful. A guy could really get used to that. I *am* getting used to that."

Eli laughed. His father's face was stoic, but the look in his eyes had changed. Eli simply discounted it as tiredness.

He was whistling by the time he got back to the shop. With a quick stop in the basement he'd retrieved his lovingly packed lunch. He had taken to inviting Mazy over earlier in the evening and then asking her to cook for him. She was nearly as good at it as her mother. And there was the added benefit of having her clean the kitchen while he watched TV. Last night he'd even had her do his laundry. She'd given him a shocked look, but she'd done it.

So he was getting cooking, cleaning, laundry and the best sex of his life. All the companionship he'd ever longed for with the one woman he had always wanted.

Who needs heaven? He'd found it here on earth. And all it took was a bad attitude and some nasty behavior. He was no longer worried about keeping it up—it was starting to be fun.

Maybe he wouldn't even marry her. Why should he? She'd try a lot harder to please him if she wasn't sure where she stood. Wives took things for granted. Everybody said so. And lots of them try to tell their husbands what to do—he just had to look at Sheila and Clark to see that. Eli had no idea how Mazy might be as a wife, but she was the kind of girlfriend who took orders.

Of course, he'd always wanted to be her husband. And he always thought it was wrong for her to take that crap from guys. Maybe it was even wrong for her to take it from him. Was it?

Hey, he reasoned, he was being the kind of jerk she liked. It wasn't what he had wanted for her, but it was what she wanted. He was doing this for her. She ought to be grateful.

"Yeah, grateful," he said aloud.

And he was grateful, too. Being a bad dude definitely had its benefits.

When he got back in the shop, Clark was talking on his cell phone as he worked on dovetail cuts. Eli didn't know which was worse, that his brother would try multitasking with something so easy to mess up or that he wasn't even ashamed enough of his sloppy practice to try to hide it from his brother.

"Who are you talking to?" Eli's question and snappy tone came straight from the bad-dude persona he'd recently cultivated.

Clark looked up, startled. "Uh, Jimmy Ray."

"Tell him you're on the clock and you'll call him later."

Eli walked past him toward his own workbench. He heard Clark making excuses to get off the phone. Eli was surprised. He hadn't raised his voice, he hadn't gotten angry or threatening. He'd simply said what he was thinking, what any boss would be thinking, and his brother had complied.

Eli could almost have laughed at how easy it had been.

But he did not. Instead, he returned to dry fitting the pieces of the music cabinet. He'd selected his veneer and was eager to get the cabinet pegged and glued so he could begin the process.

He worked silently across the room from his brother for several minutes before Clark spoke.

"Is Dad doing okay?" he asked.

Eli glanced up. "Yeah, he's the same."

Clark was nodding.

"How are things going with Mazy?"

"Good. Everything's going good."

It was quiet again, but it seemed less deliberately so.

"I was probably wrong about Driscoll," Clark told him after a minute. "And you're right. It's none of my business. I won't be sticking my nose in again."

"I believe you," Eli answered.

"Just so you're not mad about it."

"No, not at all."

"Great, great," Clark told him. "And the kid seems to be working out okay, too."

"Yeah," Eli said. "I like him a lot. He's not afraid to learn. He's pretty much putting together the shelves for the coffee shop on his own."

Clark nodded. "The kid's smart and he has you for a teacher."

Eli shrugged off that compliment.

"So, we're taking down that chestnut paneling this weekend," Eli said. "Do you want to show up to help us?"

"Me?" Clark chuckled humorlessly. "Why should I help? I don't even drink coffee. Charlie is just too lucky. He does absolutely nothing and you walk in and discover a fortune hanging on his walls. I wish something like that would happen to me."

It occurred to Eli that something very similar *had*

happened to Clark. He'd never worked anywhere except the family business. Although he and Eli had drawn the exact same salary, Clark had never managed to save a nickel. When he'd married Sheila and they started a family, it was Eli's savings that had bought Clark's half of their parents' house. It was Eli's loan that had purchased his brother's share of the business. A lot of people might have thought it a great stroke of good luck that Eli had not only been willing to buy Clark's share, but had the money to do it.

However, he didn't point that out.

"Well, if you're not down there helping, then you're free to pick up the slack for me."

"Pick up the slack? What slack?"

"You'll need to get Dad up and get him his shower," Eli said.

"What? Me? I don't know how to do that."

"What's to know? I wait until about ten, after he's rested from breakfast and morning meds. Then I put him in the shower. I scrub him up, rinse him down and get him dressed."

Clark was shaking his head.

"But Sheila and I always come over in the afternoon."

"Well, you'll have to come over by yourself in the morning," Eli said.

"I've got the girls' soccer team."

"One of the other dads will have to be the coach that day."

"Eli, I'm not really good with this kind of stuff," he said. "You're so much better at it."

"It's not a question of who is better or worse," Eli answered. "He's your father, too. I'm not asking you, I'm telling you. It's my day off and it's your turn."

Clark's brow came down. "Now wait just a minute."

His tone was threatening. "Where do you get off telling *me* what to do? You may think you're the boss around the shop, but nobody orders me around on my day off."

Eli felt the muscles in his back tighten all the way up to his neck. His teeth clenched. He had never "ordered" his brother around. More typically that was Clark's routine. But today, Eli was in exactly the mood to take him on.

"I don't *think* I'm the boss around here. This is my business. I *am* the boss. You work for me. And I don't keep you on here because you're my brother. You're a capable woodworker. If you weren't I'd let you go and hire somebody who is." Eli deliberately relaxed his jaw. "By the same token, if you're not happy working here, you can hand in your notice, like any guy anywhere, and walk away. That's one of the perks of working for somebody else."

Clark's eyes were wide with disbelief and shocked into silence.

"But job or no job," Eli continued, "Dad is the father of both of us. He's raised us, loved us and been responsible for us. These days, he needs us. We have to do right by him. Both of us have to do right by him."

Eli raised his chin determinedly. "The way it looks to me, you've not been doing your share. Every day, twice a day, you see me spending time with him, caring for him, while you're sitting on your butt pretending you're not obliged. Yes, I know you're married. Yes, I know you have a family. But that doesn't give you a pass. Dad is your family, too. And you are going to start acting like a son to him."

Eli exhaled a huge puff of air that somehow felt as if a great weight had disappeared from his shoulders. He no longer felt angry, simply resolute.

33

———◆————

When Saturday showed up it felt as festive as any holiday. Tru was excited about the role he was going to play in the renovation of Local Grind and Mazy found his enthusiasm irresistible. It had been barely two months since he'd sat sullen and silent in the passenger's seat as she'd driven away from the life that was familiar and all the friends he knew.

He was hardly recognizable as he explained with enthusiasm about the use of tools.

"It seems like the power saws would be the most fun," he told her. "'Cause they're loud and dangerous and stuff like that. But the planes…ah, Mom, you've just gotta feel it. You peel off that thin layer of wood like you're slicing through butter. It's so…so…well, it's really something."

Mazy nodded. Tru was eager to explain all the tools to her. Every gouge and rasp was an adventure. Every task and method prime for sharing. The explanation of the physics of cleat shelves had come, she was sure, directly from the words of Eli Latham. And she'd loved the sound of it on Tru's lips.

Eli himself arrived so early that Beth Ann insisted on feeding him hotcakes.

"Really, I've already had a big bowl of cereal," he told her.

Beth Ann waved away the refusal. "A working man needs a breakfast that will stick to his ribs."

Mazy was pretty sure that with all the syrup her mother poured over Eli's plate, his meal would be plenty sticky.

He eyed Mazy across the table as she lingered over a cup of coffee.

She couldn't resist grinning back at him. At moments like this she felt so intimate with him, so connected. As if their time together wasn't simply having sex, but sharing a life. She got these little glimpses of what they could be together. What they could have.

But then the reality of their relationship would come crashing back in. Everybody knew Eli was a nice, kind guy. He always had been. He always would be. But many times, when it came to her, he was neither nice nor kind. It was hard to avoid the fact that sometimes he treated her as thoughtlessly and as callously as any guy she'd ever been with. She didn't understand it. He had always loved her. But it seemed sure that he didn't love her anymore.

"Is something wrong with the coffee?" The question came from Beth Ann.

"No, it's fine."

"You had such a look on your face."

Mazy shrugged. "Just thinking."

"I'd hate to be what you were thinking about," Beth Ann teased.

"Everything's loaded," Tru announced as he tromped in through the back door. He looked impatiently at Eli. "Are you going to eat forever?"

Both Mazy and Beth Ann scolded him for his manners, but Eli laughed.

"Last bite," he said as he shoved nearly half a pancake in his mouth.

Mazy donned her jacket. The morning was surprisingly mild.

The truck was idling in the driveway. Tru let her in and she slid across the seat to sit next to Eli.

He smiled at her before turning his attention to the windshield. Then he hesitated.

"Tru, did you bring the measuring tape?"

"Measuring tape? Isn't there one in the toolbox?"

"I think I took it out," Eli said. "Could you run and grab one for me?"

"Sure."

The metal door creaked as he opened it. Then with a slam, Tru was gone.

Eli turned to Mazy and pulled her into an embrace. His lips came down on her own. It was a sweet and tender kiss. His mouth gently pulling at hers as if he wanted to draw her in more closely than human form allowed.

"Mmm," she responded when there was once more distance between them.

"I couldn't resist," he told her. "I like the look of you over breakfast. I could hardly wait to get you alone."

She laughed. "Are you telling me that this was a premeditated kiss? You sent my son off so you could get your lips on me?"

He smiled. "If only it had been a little more premeditated, I would have hidden every measuring tape in the shop."

Eli pulled her close one more time, as if he couldn't get enough.

"Thanks for doing this," Mazy said.

"Kissing you?"

"Helping Charlie and teaching stuff to Tru. He's pretty excited."

"I'm pretty excited, too," Eli told her. "But then I usually am when you're this close to me."

Mazy grinned at him. "Do you want me to sit farther away?"

"Want? I *want* you to sit on my lap, but it's probably difficult to drive that way."

She liked him like this. Funny and playful. She gave him another little peck on the mouth. He responded by resting his forehead against her own.

"I have one whole wonderful day stretching out in front of me and I'm spending it all with you," he said.

"Me and my son and half the population of Brandt Mountain," she pointed out.

"Details," he said dismissively. "When you're around everyone else fades into the background."

"Pretty words."

"And pretty much true," he said as he kissed her again.

Mazy understood the sentiment, even if she didn't believe him. She was the one who got so caught up in her infatuations that she couldn't think straight. Eli seemed to always know what he was doing.

The passenger's-side door creaked open.

"Got it!" Tru announced as he set a big red-and-black plastic measuring tape on the dashboard.

The two adults quickly moved apart.

"I saw you guys kissing," Tru told them. He leaned forward slightly and smiled very deliberately at Eli. "Don't make me have to get rough with you."

"Tru!"

Eli chuckled. "Message received," he answered.

Despite his threatening words, Tru's enthusiasm for the day had not diminished. When they arrived at the coffee shop, Charlie already had the place open. He and

Alice had moved all the tables to the center of the space and had set up a serve-yourself coffee urn.

"It's the only thank-you we know how to do," Charlie said. "All the coffee you can drink."

Mazy held off, but Eli drank some. And Tru, who as far as Mazy knew had never shown any interest in even tasting the stuff, fixed himself a cup, although he heavily laced it with cream and brown sugar.

They had expected help and they were not disappointed. Men with toolboxes began trailing in almost immediately. Some of them were guys that had been avoiding Mazy. She did not, however, take the opportunity to talk to them. She was off the clock. And besides, she hoped that as word got out that she was actually *trying* to help, the more wily debtors would seek her out.

Kite Bagby strolled in. And Jimmy Ray Esher was not far behind him. Pastor Blick arrived in "civilian" clothes, teasing that he was there to insure that the job got finished today.

"The weatherman says it's going to be gorgeous tomorrow. I want to make sure we get this done today, so that no one misses out on a beautiful Sunday in the Lord's service."

"Well, we're all hoping you'll turn out to be as good a carpenter as your boss," Charlie joked.

Mazy was surprised when Karly and Che showed up. She'd expected her friend to make an appearance later in the day, but she hadn't thought that Che, who had been out of town all week, would give up his day home with the family for community service.

"Oh, we just couldn't stand not to be a part of the biggest makeover the town has ever seen," she declared.

Mazy hadn't seen the legendary Indian motorcycle rider since her high school days. And had he not walked in with Karly, Mazy was not sure she would have recognized him. The long black hair was now cut short and flocked with silver highlights. And the silent, solemn face that she remembered was bright-eyed and smiling.

"I'm not sure we ever officially met," Mazy said as she shook his hand.

"People don't meet in high school," he agreed. "They simply become aware of each other. And I was already brooding along the highway when you girls were still going to pep rallies."

"Yeah, I wouldn't have met him myself if I hadn't gotten a job at Brandt Burger."

"I didn't know you worked at Brandt Burger."

She smiled. "It was after…after your retreat from school."

"Ah, the 'I'm invisible in my own hometown' era," Mazy said. "I guess I wasn't allowed to get a burger."

"They weren't any good, anyway," Karly said.

"What? I ate a million of them," Che said, feigning shock.

The loosely organized, or perhaps mostly unorganized, crew began removing the top cap on the wainscoting. Each piece of chestnut was being taken down with great care, hoping to limit any damage to the wood. Mazy was honestly surprised at how quickly the work went. Once the walls had been exposed, those who were less skilled with the removal, including Mazy and Tru, were relegated into plaster patching. The walls behind the wood were mostly in good shape and feathering in the quick repair material was straightforward. Mazy worked, steadily gaining confidence as she went along.

As the morning wore on, more people showed up. There was an almost social aspect to the work. Local Grind might belong to Charlie and Alice, but a lot of folks saw it, and the building where it was housed, as an asset to their little community. They wanted to help it thrive.

The expanding crew relieved many of the early-bird workers. Mazy's efforts were taken over by a faster, more experienced and generally better plaster repairer. She was happy to give over. Her arms were aching from the unaccustomed activity. And she'd been up and down the ladder so many times it practically qualified as a gym workout.

She got herself a cup of coffee and wandered around watching other people work for a while. On the second floor, removal of the paneling was still ongoing. They had managed, with the help of Pastor Blick, who had apparently worked a summer job once at Otis, to get the ancient freight elevator operational.

"The mechanism is all good," he assured everyone. "It just needs regular maintenance and inspection." Without certification, no one could actually ride on it, but it was very helpful in getting the stacked chestnut down to the alley to be loaded.

Mazy managed to surreptitiously watch Tru work for several minutes. He was happy and seemed to find a comfortable place in the company of these men. For much of the morning he was the only teenager at the site. Then Gerald Youst showed up with his two sons. The three high school kids were polite to one another, but the Youst boys were quiet and mostly kept to themselves.

From across the distance of the room, Mazy caught Eli's eye. He smiled at her so intimately, as if they were some old married couple who had been together long enough to read each other's thoughts. He was clearly pleased with how well things were going and showed genuine pride in her efforts to make a difference. For one long, wonderful moment she allowed herself to be completely caught up in it.

Here it was, at last—the love she'd searched for all her life.

As if she were on a thrill ride, the bottom dropped out of her stomach and the dizzy feeling it left was slightly nauseating.

Had she come back this way again? Where a handsome smile could make her forget everything she knew about relationships with men?

Mentally shaking her head, she went down the stairs and found an out-of-the-way place to sit, which luckily had already been scoped out and partially occupied by Karly.

"This is my favorite part of working," she said. "Finding a place to get off my feet while other people get it done."

Mazy laughed. "Okay, we'll give it ten minutes and then we'll figure out a way to be useful."

In fact, their break turned out to be even shorter than that. Alice arrived with a car full of groceries. Both women were recruited into sandwich making and, ultimately, lunch service.

The volunteers came down in shifts, found a place to eat at one of the tables. When they finished, they tagged someone else to take their place.

Eli and Che were among the last to load up, giving Mazy and Karly the opportunity to join them at a table for four. They had all worked up an appetite, which seemed to make the simple sandwiches surprisingly good.

"It's definitely the skill of the sandwich makers," Karly teased. "Constructive layering of the meat and cheese, with a generous helping of lettuce and a hint of mustard."

Everyone laughed.

"No, no," Che disagreed. "You've left out the special ingredient."

"Special ingredient?"

"Our ladies made them for us with love," he said.

Eli looked over at her, his eyebrow raised. "Is that what it is?" he asked.

Mazy felt herself blushing and hated it. She couldn't help herself from being in love with him. But until she had a better handle on whether he could reciprocate, having her feelings out in the open, as they obviously were, didn't help.

She decided to change the subject.

"So Karly has promised to tell me how you two got together," she said to Che. "But she hasn't gotten around to it yet. Maybe you could fill me in."

Che's eyes widened slightly. "Oh, it's one of those sordid tales that Brandt Mountain is famous for. I picked her up on the side of the road."

"Oh, yeah?"

"Would I lie to you?" Che asked. "She was walking down the side of the highway and, man, she was looking hot."

Karly shook her head and gave a rueful laugh. "It was the middle of summer and I was wearing a tulle skirt. And I wasn't walking, I was limping. The heel had broken off one of my shoes."

"There's got to be more to this story," Mazy teased.

Che gave a quick glance toward his wife. "Well, it's, uh, it's way too a long story for such a short break." He wiped his mouth on his napkin. "And I'd better get back to work if we intend to get this done today."

"I need to get Tru started on his shelves," Eli said.

"The poor kid has already been about as patient as any teenager can bear."

He rose to his feet and then bent forward to give her a quick peck on the lips. It was their first public kiss. It wasn't much, but her heart flew to her throat and her blood raced.

"Yes, it's official," Karly said the minute they were alone. "That man is totally in love with you."

Mazy shrugged. "Maybe, but sometimes love isn't what you hope it would be," she said.

"No," Karly said. "I think love is exactly what you hope it would be."

Mazy wasn't eager to argue the point.

"So now I'm really intrigued about how you and Che got together," she said. "When do I get this 'long story'?"

"Not right now," Karly answered as she scooted back her chair. "Too much stuff going on today that's *not* ancient history."

34

$\longrightarrow \longleftarrow$

By the time they were finished with the lunch break, all the wood had been removed from the main floor. The plaster patching was complete and being allowed to cure as the work continued on upstairs.

Primer and paint would need to go on the walls before the shelves could go up, so Eli and Tru got that started. He enjoyed working with the kid. Their personalities were well suited, he thought. Or maybe it was that Tru reminded him of Mazy. And being with Mazy, for better or worse, made him happy.

Happy.

That thought bounced around in his brain. Being the bad boyfriend made him feel powerful, but it didn't make him feel happy. Today he was simply Eli with no persona, no agenda. And it felt good. It felt right. It felt happy. He could use a lot more happy.

What he'd felt being dumped by Mazy had ranked high in his personal misery index. No, it wasn't as wrenchingly painful as his mother's death, nor as chronically sad as his father's failing health. But it had been real heartbreak. He wasn't sure he could go through it again.

Maybe he wouldn't have to. He'd seen that blush when Che had suggested that she was in love with him. He couldn't keep the grin from crossing his face. She was in love with him.

No, wait, he reminded himself. That wasn't true. She was in love with the jerk that he was pretending to be.

Eli wanted to growl out loud. He did enjoy being the jerk, he was willing to admit that. But he didn't want to be that guy forever, did he? He liked being himself. Couldn't he love her that way? And if he couldn't, was it really worth it?

"Is it too messy?" Tru asked beside him.

"Huh? No, it looks fine."

"You sure did get a grumpy look," he pointed out.

Eli shrugged. "Thinking about something else," he hedged.

"Something not good," Tru said.

"Definitely not," Eli agreed. "Old stuff, unpleasant crap from the past."

"Maybe you should try the spitwad cure."

"The what?"

"Something I learned in that support group," Tru said. "When something bothers you and you can't fix it, write it down on a piece of paper, crumple it into a spitwad and shoot it into the trash. That's the only thing negative thoughts are good for."

"Wise advice."

Tru nodded. "Although some days my trash basket can really fill up."

"For all of us," Eli agreed.

The day turned surprisingly mild and, one by one, jackets, sweaters and sweatshirts began piling up on every vacant chair. Eli opened all the doors, which somehow made the work more lighthearted and the paint dry more quickly. It was only slightly tacky when Tru and Eli brought in the completed pieces for the shelving.

They had chosen to do cleat-supported floaters, painted to match the walls. That would draw the eye more to what was set on them than to the shelves.

Eli watched as Tru did the measurements. He pulled out the notebook Eli had given him as a reference and he rechecked everything about a half dozen times before he finally predrilled the holes. Eli was pretty sure that nobody had ever drilled more slowly, but he got the job done and it was a perfect fit for the anchor.

Eli held up one end of the one-by-two cleat as Tru screwed it into place. Once it was secure, Tru dry fitted the shelf and the two stood back a moment and surveyed the work.

"Okay, everything's looking great," Eli told him. "Have you got this?"

It was a pivotal moment. Eli knew the power of being trusted.

Tru may have swallowed a bit more seriously, but he nodded. "Yeah, I think it's all good."

"If something comes up or you need a hand, come find me."

"I will."

Eli turned away, willing himself not to look back. The kid needed to know that it was all on him. A man had to be given responsibility before he could learn how to take it.

He went up the stairs to check out the progress on the second floor. Ultimately deciding that the best use of his skills was on the trailer. Some of the volunteers had piled up the chestnut as if it were merely the used paneling that it had pretended to be. He put on his gloves and sorted and restacked the flatbed in a way that *he* would have wanted to receive a forty-thousand-dollar investment in wood.

It was close to an hour before he decided to check on Tru. That was more than enough time to complete the project, even when using the drill as if it were the dentist's office.

He stuffed his gloves in his pocket and headed into the building. The smile on his face and the spring in his step wavered as he saw Tru still hard at it, and not alone. Tad Driscoll was holding one of the shelf blanks as Tru ran a bead of glue along the area that would attach to the cleat.

They both looked up as he approached.

"Hello, Termite," Driscoll said.

Eli didn't respond.

"This is my last one," Tru said.

Eli glanced up at the wall before forcing a smile to his lips. "It's looking good," he assured the teen.

The two men stood side by side, watching as Tru fitted the shelf in place. He carefully tacked it in with finishing nails.

"It looks really good," Eli repeated.

Driscoll folded his arms across his chest in a proud stance. "Tru's very clever," he said. "I don't know many kids his age who could do something like this."

Eli was fairly certain that most of them could put together a similar project if someone took the time to teach them how it was done. He didn't say that, however. Tru was glowing with the praise. And Eli knew his own feelings were heavily colored by the unwelcome proximity of Mazy's ex.

What in the hell is Driscoll doing here?

The downstairs area was mostly completed. The only people besides the three of them were pulling up the drop cloths and sweeping up the debris.

He was not leaving Tru alone with Driscoll. He didn't know what the guy was up to. For sure, he was no civic volunteer. He didn't do anything without an angle in mind. All Eli's protective instincts were on red alert. He would not leave Tru in Driscoll's sights.

The shelves had been put up so carefully that there was virtually no touch-up painting required. With his major task completed, Eli had planned to suggest that Tru get something to drink and spend the rest of the day lolling around and celebrating his accomplishment. But he was not about to allow him to loll around with Tad Driscoll.

"There's work to be done upstairs," Eli announced. "Let's go."

"Oh, sure," Tru answered. As they headed toward the back, the teenager turned and offered a little wave. "Thanks for the help, Mr. Driscoll."

"What did he want?" Eli asked when they were out of earshot.

Tru shrugged. "Nothing. Well, maybe basketball," he answered. "He's, like, the millionth person who's asked me about playing basketball."

"Hmm."

"Like I told everybody else, it's not my game. But you know how people are. They always think if they just say things a little bit differently you're going to suddenly slap your forehead and say, 'Wow! I should be playing basketball.'"

Upstairs, he made sure that Tru had a paint roller in his hand. He seriously doubted that Driscoll would follow him upstairs. But just in case, he decided to stay close.

He sidled up to Charlie, who was trying to work harder than anybody else. Eli deftly relieved him of his paintbrush and engaged him in conversation.

"Putting paint on the walls sure brightens this place up," he said.

Charlie agreed. "Getting the windows washed will

help, too," he said. "Then I'm getting that elevator serviced and putting the place up for rent. Somebody in town has got to have something that they need to put up here."

Eli was nodding agreement when suddenly he realized who that somebody might be.

"You know, Charlie, I've been looking for a place to store pieces for the winter. And it sure would be nice to be able to store them where I could bring people to see them."

If anybody were more surprised than Eli, it was Charlie. They discussed the idea and Eli had the distinct feeling that Charlie was trying to talk him out of it.

"I know you're a friend of Mazy's," he said. "And I so appreciate what you've done for us already. I can't let you do this. I can't accept…charity."

"Good Lord, Charlie. You can't accept it. I can't afford to give it. But I am seriously looking for heated inside space. I can't shake on it until I've talked to Clark. He may have found a site already. But I'm not acting to be *nice*. I'm not that nice."

Charlie chuckled. "You say that like it's a dirty word."

"For some of us, it is."

He was still smiling moments later as he used Charlie's paintbrush to do touch-ups next to the floor. Since they'd removed the shoe board with the wainscoting, the transition was tricky. Now that he was thinking that this place might be *his* place, he was keen on getting it exactly right.

Eli rose to his feet near one of the front windows and the sight outside froze him in place. It was almost like a scene from the past, but the characters were older now. Older and, he had hoped, wiser. But the sick feeling in his stomach belied that.

Driscoll stood totally relaxed in the afternoon sun, leaning against the light post. He still had that youthful confidence of a man whose physical abilities had never failed him. Calm and in control, he was looking down at Mazy as if she were his. As if he still owned her, heart and mind, the way he had in high school.

His expression was serious, almost somber, as he spoke. And just like in their teen years, *he* was doing most of the talking. Mazy was looking up at him, her dark hair blowing across her cheek. She was listening intently to him, as if his words, his ideas, his opinions, mattered to her. She was smiling up at Tad Driscoll. Then, inexplicably, it was more than that. They were laughing...together.

Eli tried to turn away from the sight, but he couldn't stop looking as each second ticked by and they continued to stand together like friends.

After all that Driscoll had done, she was still going back for more.

35

By the end of the workday, the chestnut was tied down and covered on a long-bed trailer and headed down the highway to its new home. The walls downstairs had been painted in a pale terra cotta that somehow seemed very chic and urban.

The team was exhausted, but when the day finally ended, nobody could let it go.

"It's Saturday night. Why don't we all go grab a beer somewhere," Jimmy Ray suggested.

Pastor Blick demurred, suggesting he had work to do on his sermon, although everyone understood that a preacher going out for a beer would be considered grounds for termination by many in his flock.

Fortunately, most everyone else was eager and available. It was decided to meet at the Horse Cove roadhouse.

Eli dropped Mazy and Tru off at home. Mazy wanted to shower and dress. Tru whined a bit about not being allowed to go, since he had worked as an equal all day. But his complaints were mostly perfunctory. He might be tall and he might have worked hard, but he was still only fourteen. Even if he could overcome his mother's scruples, his arguments would likely have little effect on the roadhouse's proprietor.

Mazy rushed through a shower and tried to put on

makeup in a steamed-up mirror. She was actually excited. It had been a great day. She had had fun and had felt accepted. And it was great to see Eli and Tru working together. Her heart caught in her throat at the image. Mazy didn't know if it was a natural affinity or having a great role model, but Eli had that blend of high expectations and genuine respect that helped children believe in themselves. The only other quality that was required was love. And Tru was, in her undoubtedly biased opinion, highly lovable.

He'd even seemed to win Tad over.

That had been, perhaps, the most surprising thing of the day. Tad had shown up to work. It had taken her a while to reason that out. Was he there because of the bank debt? Mazy knew for a fact that Charlie was not one of his "bros." While holding back on most of the other local businessmen, he'd thrown Charlie and his loan right in her lap, assuming that it would get sold off and foreclosed.

So if he wasn't there for friendship, then it must be that he felt a certain civic responsibility. That thought gave her pause. The Tad Driscoll that she remembered was no altruistic volunteer. Everything he did had some kind of payoff.

But if she had been able to change, maybe he had to. He certainly was talking a different game from their encounter that first day in the bank. He was talking about Tru as his son.

"He seems like a thoughtful, talented kid," Tad told her. "He's polite and well-spoken. That doesn't happen by accident."

"Well, maybe not completely by accident," she admitted. "But he's always been a reasonable, biddable kid. I've tried to be straight with him about stuff. I've had to trust him. And I think that's paid off by making him more trustworthy."

"I couldn't agree with you more," he said. "Genna has always tried to shelter the girls from our family problems. As if somehow the girls themselves were not actually a part of the family. I often think that, since they don't know the whole story on things, they fall back on ideas of black-and-white. One person is the good guy and the other is the bad. I'm sure you know, as the noncustodial parent, which side of that I typically end up on."

Mazy was sympathetic, but she actually thought he might be wrong. Kids, she believed, often romanticized the parent that was not there while vilifying the one who had to enforce rules on a daily basis. She didn't say that, however, because he was back on praise for Tru and she loved the sound of that.

"I was impressed with those shelves that he built. I've never put together anything like that in my life. Of course, I've never really *had* to, but it would be a nice skill to possess, anyway."

Mazy smiled. "Eli has been teaching him. He really enjoys the work. And I think it's good for him to hang out with the Lathams. They're decent men with salt-of-the-earth values."

"Well, sure they are," Tad agreed. "And I'm sure they like having Tru around. He's a very congenial kid. I'm sure it's great for the Termite to have a chance to lord over somebody. He's never had a 'gofer' to give orders to."

She felt a momentary urge to defend Eli from such a negative characterization, but then she reminded herself that they weren't talking about Eli, they were talking about Tru. And her prickliness on the subject of Eli Latham had more to do with her than with either Tad or her son.

"Tru is really enjoying himself," she commented instead. "I think he might even have an aptitude for it. You should hear him wax poetic over dados and rabbets."

"Sounds like some kind of critters from the hills," he pointed out.

They both laughed.

Tad nodded as if he understood Tru's enthusiasm. "Being clever with his hands," Tad continued. "Physically that's all about coordination. He gets that from me, I guess. He'd really make a fine athlete, if we could get him interested in that. I know if he would play he'd see how much fun it is. If I had been there for him when he was growing up, I'd have had him out on the court from the time he was a toddler."

Mazy nodded, but in a strange disconnected way. She'd always wanted that. She'd always imagined, dreamed, that it would be that way between Tru and Tad. But somehow, hearing it on his lips now, was strangely unwelcome. That was not how it had been, and today she couldn't seem to dredge up any regret about that.

She dressed in what she was now referring to as her "date night" clothes. Eli, of course, had seen the outfit and she didn't have time to shorten the skirt again. But she decided that date nights having actually been rare might have an upside, after all.

The evening had turned warm enough that she didn't bother with a coat. She'd be snug and warm in the truck and the roadhouse was guaranteed to be hot and close.

Eli was waiting for her outside. She wished he'd come to the door, but apparently his expectation was that she should go to him. So she did.

Mazy was very aware of how he watched her as she came toward him. He didn't blink. He didn't look away. As she got closer, she saw stark hunger in his eyes. For a moment she thought he might suggest that they stay in. That wouldn't be the worse offer she'd had.

"Do I look okay?" she asked him as she pirouetted to give him the full view. She had seen his expression and recognized it for what it was.

Her words, however, seemed to snap Eli out of his trance. Instantly his expression changed. "Well, babe," he said, giving her a long up and down, "I've told you before that your butt looks best in black. Have you ever thought about fake boobs? I think if you saved up some money and bought yourself a pair of really big ones, it might balance you out or something."

Mazy felt as if some evil villain had pricked her happy balloon.

"No," she answered firmly. "I have never considered cosmetic surgery. I don't think it's necessary for my happiness and it's expensive. I have a child to support. Any extra money I earn will be used to better provide for him. Shall we go?"

"Sure," he said calmly. It was as if he was so obtuse he didn't even know he'd insulted her.

He opened the driver's-side door. At first she thought that he expected her to slide across, no easy task in a skirt. But then he climbed in himself. As Mazy walked around to the passenger's side, she did a quick reevaluation. Eli might have great potential as a father, but as a boyfriend he definitely came up short on the social graces. Still, she reminded herself, sweet-talking guys with all the moves down pat were typically taking a woman down the expressway to Bad News Town. Maybe it was better that he wasn't the type to play those kinds of games.

He turned over the ignition as she climbed into the car, but he did hesitate for a moment.

"I hope I didn't hurt your feelings," he said. "I mean, your boobs are fine. Still perky, even after having a kid," he added.

Was that an apology? Mazy wasn't sure.

The roadhouse was located off the shoulder of one of the hairpin curves on the highway down Brandt Mountain. Parking at the site was at a premium and cars lined the edge of the road next to the mountain. Eli's option was to either park on the ledge side or a good distance away. He chose the latter.

Walking back up the steep slope in high heels was challenging. Eli never offered an arm. He kept his hands stuffed in his pockets. He was walking so quickly, she could hardly keep up. Finally, she grabbed his jacket, halting him. She threaded her arm through the crook of his elbow.

He glanced down at her. In the moonlight he still looked like her Eli. The best friend she'd ever had. The man who could hold her with such tenderness, make love to her so earnestly and stand beside her so stalwartly.

"Are you cold?" he asked.

Was he going to offer his jacket?

"No, I'm fine," she said. "Being close to you keeps me warm."

"Really? I'm pretty sure I can see your nipples through that shirt."

Mazy's jaw dropped in disbelief. Not exactly words of love.

36

The image of Tad and Mazy standing together on the sidewalk replayed over and over in Eli's brain. It made him slightly sick, like a sudden drop where the bottom of your stomach disappears. Driscoll didn't chat people up for nothing. He was busy every moment of his life pursuing whatever it was that he currently wanted. Eli was afraid that at this current moment, it might be Mazy. It might be Tru. It might be exactly the same things that Eli was pursuing for himself.

Eli didn't blame Mazy. She was a victim of her own trusting heart. But he did blame Driscoll. Hadn't he done enough? Shouldn't he have moved on to some other vulnerable young woman by now?

And Eli blamed himself.

He had started strong on dirt-bag highway. But lately it had gotten too easy. If his jerkiness no longer bothered him, then Mazy was probably getting used to it herself. He needed to raise the temperature some more. Remind her that he, Eli Latham, was as rotten and worthless a dude as any out there. They had to get to the edge of the cliff before there would be any chance of taking the leap.

He hadn't bothered to check the bad-boyfriend blogs lately and could only spare a minute while he was getting cleaned up, but he did happen on one that fit the bill perfectly. It was a combo jealousy/insensitivity play. If this didn't get her to sit up and pay attention, he didn't know what would.

He was excited to be out with her. Grateful that the workday at Local Grind had given him such a good excuse. He loved to dance. Mazy had taught him when they were in about third grade. He hadn't had the honor of standing up with her since then. He wanted to hold her in his arms and twirl her around the room. But he had to remember his larger purpose. He couldn't allow the pleasure of the moment to become a risk to their future together.

With that thought in mind, he deliberately offered a verbal slap almost the minute they were alone together.

He was slightly pleased that she'd pushed back on the boob job crack. She was gorgeous and surely she knew that. But the comment deflated her from all smiles to grim determination.

Eli kept up the less-than-stellar behavior until they got into the roadhouse. They were immediately pulled into the exuberance of the rest of the crew. Everybody was in a great mood, with the kind of exhaustion that was pure second wind and giddiness.

Eli got them a couple of beers from the bar, but Mazy was already gone by the time he got back to the table.

Kite Bagby, who had come straight from the coffee shop and was already on his third drink, urged her out to dance.

Eli took a seat in a booth next to Karly. It gave him a good vantage point of Mazy out on the floor.

The roadhouse was mostly country, but the DJ occasionally played Top 40 and old favorites. Mazy was actively two-stepping, keeping a wary gaze behind her as Kite seemed very likely to run over any other pair of partners who chanced to be in the way.

"She's a good sport," Che said from across the table. "Karly always tells the old guy that her feet hurt."

"If you dance with Kite, your feet are going to hurt," his wife defended. "That old coot runs roughshod over a woman's toes. And it's not as if I don't know how to follow, I just don't care to be dragged."

The music was so loud that any serious conversation had to be limited to the people immediately next to you. So Eli turned his attention to Karly. He asked her about her boys. He asked her about her job. He tried to listen to her answers and to keep his eyes from straying to the woman on the dance floor.

"So," Karly urged, apparently deciding it was her turn for questions. "Is it serious between you two?"

Eli froze as if sensing danger. "Who's asking?"

"Karly Farris," she answered. "I like Mazy a lot. I always have. She was good to me when nobody else was. I wouldn't want to see her hurt."

Eli nodded. "Fair enough," he said. "I'm serious. I'm serious as a heart attack. But I'm taking my time. I don't want to rush fences, scare her off."

Karly accepted that for a moment. "Well, don't bide your time overlong. Just saying. Tad Driscoll has been sniffing around and I don't trust that guy farther than I can throw him."

"You're a smart woman to feel that way."

"It was a lesson learned from experience."

"Ah…" Eli said. "So you're not allowing any 'fool me twice.'"

Karly shrugged. "In my case it was more like third time's a charm. I let that creep humiliate me twice before I smartened up. I know how he can be when he wants something. I don't want Mazy to even have a reason to be tempted."

"I'll do my best," Eli told her.

Kite finally brought Mazy back to the table and Eli scooted in enough to give her a seat. She was laughing, in a great mood, as she sipped her beer and shouted out conversation to those around her.

"It's been ages since I've been out," she confessed to Alice McDee. "I'd forgotten how much fun it is to simply do something different."

Alice agreed. "I can't remember the last time Charlie and I were on the town. Every day we come home, eat dinner, watch TV and go to bed."

Mazy smiled at her. "Well, when you're with the right person, that kind of life is a paradise on earth."

Alice laughed, but Eli could see she agreed. Mazy shot him a look, as if to see if he thought so, as well.

He wanted to wrap her in his arms and tell her he loved her. But that was what the old Eli would do. She had never fallen for the old Eli, but she was falling for this version of him, he could feel it.

He leaned closer and whispered snidely, "Well, I know how much you like getting in the sack."

His response clearly surprised her, but she managed a wan smile.

"Do you like to dance?" she asked him.

He picked up his bottle. "I need to finish my beer."

"Oh, okay."

She continued to try to talk with Alice and Che and Karly over the din of music while Eli deliberately nursed his beer. He listened and listened, waiting for his chance. Finally Mazy was telling a story about Tru's first swim team in Wilmington. She was delightedly sharing some funny observations about novice competitors when he abruptly interrupted her with a little slap on the knee.

"Okay, babe, let's dance."

"What? Oh."

He began physically scooting her out of the booth. He spared only one glance toward his friends, all of whom seemed relatively slack-jawed at his behavior. He couldn't be concerned with that now. He needed to get her out on the dance floor.

Luck was with him. Not a minute after they set foot on the expanse of sawdust-strewn hardwood, the enthusiastic "Cotton-Eyed Joe" concluded and the DJ followed it with a romantic, slow dance melody. He pulled her close in his arms. His chin nestled against the hair at her temple. If she couldn't look into his eyes, then he wouldn't accidentally betray his feelings. He closed his eyes, reveling in the feel of her, the scent of her. He moved to the music and she complemented him effortlessly. It was as if they had been dancing together for twenty years. In fact, the last time was that long ago. He remembered how it had been. He had felt stiff-legged and clumsy. Every time he'd made a mistake, she'd giggled. It was those giggles that had finally loosened him up, allowed him to take the risk and led him to this. It felt so perfect, so right. He opened his eyes enough to see her in the flash of shimmering blue-and-green lights.

Eli recalled the very first time he'd held her in his arms. That long-ago day that was memorable for their first kiss, the first time they'd made love. It had seemed so simple then. He loved her. She would love him back.

He had since learned that life was not at all simple, not if there were people in it. But the love he'd felt then coursed through him just as keenly now.

He bent his head forward and planted a little peck on the nape of her neck.

"Mmm." She made a sound that was almost purring.

Eli couldn't resist. He moved back just enough to capture her chin in his hand. And he brought his lips down upon hers. Their kisses had always been about passion, about heat. This one was about tenderness and reverence. His mouth conveyed the devotion that he dared not speak.

They moved apart only far enough for him to rest his forehead against hers. Within the pulsing rhythm of the music and the swaying of their bodies he could feel her breath as it touched his skin. Smoothly and in a unison unlikely for two so unpracticed, they moved across the floor, motions synchronized, hearts full.

Mazy raised her head and he looked into her eyes. She was as open, as honest and as vulnerable as any human he'd ever seen. When she spoke, her words were barely above a whisper.

"Oh, Eli, I…" She hesitated.

The song ended abruptly. There was only an instant of silence between them. Then a twangy guitar rift ushered in an upbeat Western swing.

Eli led Mazy back over to the booth where their friends were sitting. What had she been planning to say? The unfinished sentence could have been anything. Was she going to tell him that she loved him? Was she going to tell him that she was done? That she was sorry? That she and Driscoll were going to try again?

The kiss had been incredibly sweet. But it had been full of his emotion, his affection, his heart. Had she seen the truth in him and rejected it again?

He felt sick to his stomach and nervous enough to jump out of his own skin.

From the corner of his eye, he spotted a familiar face.

He had gone out with Enna Brakeman a few times. She was a beautiful, leggy blonde with a bubbly personality and a wry sense of humor. After her divorce, Eli had been interested. But they both quickly discovered that since she liked social life and parties and he liked private sunsets and home cooking, they'd had no future together.

That didn't mean that they couldn't share a dance for old times' sake.

"Mazy, do you need another beer?"

"No, I'm fine."

"Okay. I see somebody I know."

With that he turned and walked across the room. Deliberately he forced himself not to glance back in her direction.

He caught up to the blonde at the far end of the room. "Enna. How have you been?"

She looked up, surprised, and then gave him that gorgeous grin that charmed every man between eighteen and eighty-five.

"Eli, what a surprise. I never see you here."

"Yeah, I'm busy a lot," he said.

"You know Skeeter, of course."

The stocky, dark-haired man beside her was looking daggers at him.

"Sure, how you doing?"

"Do you want something, Termite?" he said. "We were just leaving."

Eli knew the guy was trying to warn him off, but he was thinking this might work out even better than he thought.

"If you're going to take home the best-looking woman in the building," Eli said, "at least you've got to let me have one dance with her. Otherwise, I'll have come all the way down here for nothing."

Skeeter didn't look happy, but Enna laughed out loud.

As it turned out, it was little more than half a dance. Eli swung and twirled her as they circled the dance floor. He made sure that he was in the line of vision for the booth that Mazy was in. But he made a point never to once look in her direction. He favored Enna with all his attention and all his smiles.

When the dance ended, he wrapped an arm possessively around her waist and walked her back toward Skeeter. The man looked even less happy than he had before. Fortunately, he was at the side door, which was not visible from where his friends were sitting.

"Okay, you've had your dance," the man said.

"Yes, thank you very much," he said to Enna. "Thank you both very much. I'll walk out with you."

Out in the parking lot, Eli didn't hesitate parting with the two. He walked to the road and turned to look back. The neon beer signs blinked in the darkened windows.

Was this the right thing to do? Everything about it felt callous, cruel, just plain wrong. Did he even want a relationship that flourished on behavior that he was ashamed of? He thought about holding Mazy close on the dance floor. He'd looked down into her eyes and saw everything he'd ever wanted.

He could go back in there right now. They could dance together, laugh with their friends, have a great time. Later, they could go home together and make love to each other, slow and lazy, fast and furious, all night long.

Just as that choice tugged so fiercely, the image of Mazy with Driscoll, laughing and chatting, sprung into his mind again. She'd smiled up at Tad the same way she smiled at Eli.

His jaw tightened. The chill around him was all anger. The risk he was taking *had* to pay off. He had to win

Mazy for himself. Even if he had to forfeit his own self-respect to make it happen. It was worth it to keep her from making a mistake again.

Eli turned his steps down the road to his truck.

37

──◆──

Mazy was having fun hanging out with friends. Laughing. Dancing. It had been so long since she'd done anything like that. The last time had to have been before her affair with Gable Sherland. Married men don't take their girlfriends out dancing. And with night school and parenthood, her evenings had not been her own for many years. It occurred to her that for a woman who had an iffy reputation, she certainly hadn't been having her share of nightlife.

Then again, her favorite flavor of nightlife involved a quiet basement apartment with a hunky, sweet guy who laughed at her jokes and wowed her in bed.

Eli was acting more than a little bit weird. Maybe he was tired. Or he hadn't really wanted to come out tonight, but had felt pressured into it. It could be that he resented all the time he'd had to spend with Tru today. People who weren't used to kids sometimes didn't appreciate large doses of them.

No, Mazy decided, most likely he was simply stating what he saw as the truth. He had always said that he valued honesty in a relationship over social niceties.

That phrase caught her up short. *Eli never said that.* Coby Dax had said that. Coby Dax was an A+, number-one, certified asshole. Coby Dax had treated Mazy like she was useless, worthless. It was a disservice to Eli to even be in the same brain wave as Coby Dax, let alone have a Dax quote attributed to him. She'd made a lot of excuses for Coby, but he'd been bad news from the beginning.

Maybe that's why she'd thought of him. Because she'd been making excuses.

When Eli took her out on the dance floor, no excuses were necessary. They had never danced together. In high school it would have been lowering for her to dance with a younger guy. And in two stints as her rebound guy, Mazy had kept their relationship close to the vest. At the time, she'd told herself, and Eli, as well, that she didn't want more scandal. The truth was less flattering. She hadn't wanted Tad to find out, in case he might be interested in her again.

It was embarrassing to be the woman she had been. But as Eli pulled her next to his chest, she edged her face against his smoothly shaved cheek and she was grateful. If all that awfulness in her past had brought her here, then it had been worth it.

She moved easily with him. He was both graceful and confident. Just like he was in bed. Just like he was in life. She'd inhaled the scent of him. This was what she wanted. This was the man she could build a future with. No, it wasn't going to be perfect or easy. There were still problems. He was going to be disappointed in the truth about Tru. He was going to be shocked by the revelations of her recent criminal behavior. He might not even be willing to get past either of those things. But she knew she wanted to try.

As they parted slightly, he rested his forehead against hers. It was a strangely intimate touch. Mazy wished that everything she was thinking, everything she was feeling, everything that she'd experienced, could just be transferred directly from her brain to his. And she wanted his hopes, his dreams and even his hurts to be in her head next to her own.

If only life were that easy. If only sharing minds were as easy as sharing bodies. She had never once, in all the miscued relationships and nameless one-night stands, been able to share the person she was, the interior of her life. If there was such a thing as a soul mate, then she was a soul virgin. At last, Eli was the man she wanted to open to.

Mazy looked up into his eyes. She saw the love she felt reflected there. All that was necessary was to say the words.

"Eli, I…"

At that moment the music stopped. As if a hypnotist had snapped his fingers, the look in Eli's eyes disappeared. Mazy was once again aware of their surroundings. A crowded dance floor in a rowdy roadhouse that smelled of beer and bodies and barbecued chicken wings was not the place to declare herself.

With a hand at the small of her back, Eli guided her back to the booth where their friends were waiting. Later tonight, when they were alone, she would tell him the truth, the whole truth. Including that she loved him. And they would see together what they could make of that.

She reached their table and scooted in to make room for him.

"Mazy, do you need another beer?" he asked.

She'd consumed less than half of the one she had.

"No, I'm fine."

"Okay. I see somebody I know."

"Oh, okay," she answered, but he had already moved away. In a place so close to home, it was certainly not amazing to see somebody that you know. It was probably more amazing to see somebody that you didn't.

Mazy turned her attention to Karly and Che, Alice and Charlie. Several of the others had either wandered off or were enjoying the dancing. The discussion evolved into more tales of parenting. With three different groups represented. The Farris kids were in elementary school. Tru was a teenager. And Charlie and Alice's children were young adults with starter jobs and college loans. The perspectives were interesting. Everybody seemed to think their particular stage might be the best of times, might be the worse of times.

Mazy wasn't sure what made her glance up, but she did. Eli danced past them. He had a huge grin on his face and a beautiful woman in his arms.

The sight jolted her so much that she blurted out, "Who is that?" before she could stop herself.

Everyone turned to look.

"Enna Brakeman," Alice told her.

"We didn't go to school with her," Karly said. "Paul married her and brought her to town."

Mazy nodded in what felt like relief. "Oh, she's married."

"Divorced," Che answered.

"She's very attractive," Mazy said.

"Don't be silly," Karly said, knowing exactly what Mazy was thinking without her having to say it. "She's not one whit better looking than you. And he's just dancing with her."

"Yeah," Charlie confirmed. "Those two were keeping company for a while, but that was a couple of years ago."

"I don't think they were keeping company," Karly clarified. "They only had a few dates, I think."

"Well, yeah, that's what I meant."

"It's not like they were a couple," Karly declared firmly.

Mazy gave her a reassuring wave and chuckled with deliberate lightness. "Everybody's got a past," she said. "Mine's even a little more bumpy than most folks'."

She turned the discussion back to their offspring and tried, without complete success, not to watch Eli with the blonde. Mazy almost sighed with relief when the dance was over. She was not typically a suspicious person. She had never been one to make unfounded accusations or fly off the handle in a rage. But what she did know about herself was that jealousy tended to exaggerate her self-esteem issues. Believing in herself was not always easy.

Mazy tried using her mentally repurposing tool.

Eli being comfortable dancing with another woman right in front of her certainly meant nothing was going on behind her back.

She could live with that.

As the minutes passed and the conversation moved on to concerns about county road grading, Mazy listened politely as she waited for Eli to return to the table. She watched the dancers come by, trying to see if he was still out on the floor. Finally she excused herself for a trip to the ladies' room. She was smiling as she traversed the building, but she had her eye out for Eli. He wasn't anywhere.

She took her time, combed her hair, fixed her makeup, assuring herself that he would be back at the table by the time she returned. He was not.

Mazy sat with the group for a few more minutes before deciding to get herself another beer. That allowed her the opportunity to stand up next to the bar and peruse the area.

Just as her bottle arrived, Kite Bagby stepped up beside her.

"Let me get that for you," he said, handing money to the bartender.

"Thank you."

"My pleasure. Thank you for the dance. I don't get to tear up the rug much with young women these days."

A flash of green shirt caught her eye and she quickly glanced in that direction, but it wasn't him.

"You looking for somebody?"

"I seem to have misplaced my date," she said, making a joke out of it. "Have you seen Eli?"

"Can't say as I have," Kite answered. "Lloyd," he called out to a man nearby. "Lloyd's the bouncer. He sees everything."

Introductions were made.

"You know Eli Latham?"

"Sure. He was here earlier, but he left."

"He left?" Mazy repeated.

"Yeah, maybe a half hour, forty-five minutes ago. I saw him head out the side door."

"Maybe he's outside," Mazy suggested.

The bouncer shrugged. "Possible, I guess. He was with some other people. Can't remember exactly who. Skeeter Moran, I think. And for sure Enna Brakeman. She's hard to miss."

Kite's expression became pained. With a meaningless mumble he allowed himself to be swallowed up by the crowd around him.

"Thanks," Mazy told Lloyd brightly.

She carried her beer back to the table just as Alice and Charlie were getting up.

"We're getting so old, we really need our beauty

sleep," Charlie said. "Well, at least I do. Alice still looks like she did as a girl."

"Oh, Lord, we have got to go," his wife teased. "When Charlie starts giving me compliments, you know he's had one drink too many."

Charlie didn't appear to have had any drinks at all. Still, everyone laughed and congratulated him again. He went around one last time, shaking hands and thanking them all for their help.

The exit of the guest of honor signaled the breakup of the party. Mazy said goodbyes, shook hands and sipped her beer. She checked her phone for texts or messages. Nothing.

"Where in the heck did Eli get off to?" Che finally asked.

"I'm not sure," Mazy said. "I think he must have gone outside for some air. Look, don't let me hold you up. If you need to leave…"

"The kids are spending the night with Che's mom," Karly assured her. "We're in no hurry."

Both were eager to offer assurance. Mazy was pretty sure that neither was telling the truth.

When Jimmy Ray came by to announce he was leaving, Mazy managed to slip out of the seat. Nonchalantly she walked across the room. She was still looking for Eli, still hoping to see him. A million unanswered questions swirled in her head.

Outside, the parking lot now had more empty spaces than full. The breeze was only cool, but Mazy wrapped her arms about herself.

Chin high, determinedly hopeful, she walked down the hill to where he had parked the truck. It was gone. She remembered exactly where it had been, but in case she was wrong, she walked on farther until there were no cars at all. He had definitely left her here without a word of explanation. It didn't make sense. Finally, she pulled the phone out of her purse. There was no signal. With a sigh of exasperation she turned and walked back up the hill.

By the time she reached the roadhouse parking lot, there was a tiny tower distinguishable on the phone face. She called his number. Without even a ring it went to voice mail.

She stood there trying to reason it out. Something must have come up. Maybe he'd gotten a call that his father was sick or his brother was in a wreck or the shop was on fire. Only an emergency would have necessitated such an abrupt departure.

If he left her here, that meant he'd be coming back. Eli didn't let people down. That was not the kind of man that he was.

She began to worry that she might not be convincing herself.

Instead, she decided to consider her options. She could walk home. As the crow flies, it was probably not more than three miles. Of course, she wouldn't be able to tear off across country. She'd have to follow the road, which was probably twice that long with twists and turns, as it wound itself up to a higher elevation.

She could call her mother to come get her. Beth Ann would probably be in bed already. And she made a point not to drive at night, but her daughter stuck at a roadhouse might be considered reason enough to break her own rules.

Or she could go back inside and wait. If Eli left her here, she could try to trust him to come back and get her. That's what love was supposed to be about, wasn't it? Believing beyond the time when belief seemed possible.

"I've got a foolish heart, but I'm not an idiot," she said aloud.

She chose option four—going back inside the roadhouse and throwing herself on the mercy of her friends.

She didn't have to reenter the building. They were coming outside as she reached the doorway.

"There you are!" Karly said. "We were wondering where you'd gotten off to."

"I went down to see if Eli's truck is still here," Mazy said. "It's not. He's apparently left me here. I'm hoping that you guys can give me a ride home."

"He left you?" Karly sounded incredulous.

Che's brow had come down in that fierce look that Mazy remembered from his motorcycle days. "That doesn't sound like Eli."

Mazy shrugged.

"Something must have happened," her friend said.

"Yeah," Che agreed. "There's a lot of guys I wouldn't put it past, but Eli's seriously decent. He wouldn't dump a woman at a roadhouse."

"She hasn't been *dumped*," Karly insisted. "He's just kind of disappeared, I guess."

"Yes," Mazy agreed. "I guess so."

"Did you two have an argument or something?"

"No, nothing," she answered. She considered mentioning Enna Brakeman but decided against it. If that wasn't what happened, it would just make her look jealous. If it were true…well, she'd deal with that when she knew for sure."

"Have you tried calling him?"

"It goes straight to voice mail," she answered. "I hate to ask, but…"

"Absolutely."

"No problem."

Mazy was very grateful, although they continued to keep up the defense of the *great guy,* the *straight arrow,* the *perfect gentleman,* all the way to their car. Once inside, they apparently noticed that Mazy was no longer nodding and they fell into silence. For which she was even more grateful.

As they turned on Sawmill Road, she'd visualized the house next door alive with activity, maybe even an ambulance in the driveway. But, no, it was closed up tight. Eli's truck was nowhere in sight. She tried not to speculate on where he was. She tried not to imagine him in the arms of the blonde. It was like trying not to see the elephant in the room.

Mazy couldn't think about it anymore, she couldn't repurpose it any further than she had. Eli had finally taken her out on a date and dumped her at a roadhouse. It was tough to find any positives in that.

She waved goodbye to her friends and let herself in through the back door.

Tears welled in her eyes. She bit her lip against them. She had vowed never to shed one more tear over a worthless man. But it went against all that she knew to imagine Eli as worthless. He had always been the one guy she could run to. The one guy she could believe in. The one guy who was living, breathing evidence that she was worthy of love and care.

Obviously, he no longer loved or cared.

"He wouldn't do this," she whispered aloud. "He wouldn't. He wouldn't."

But he had and he did.

38

Eli woke up to the sound of youthful laughter outside his window. For one sweet, thoughtless moment it was a happy sound. Then he remembered the night before.

He moaned aloud.

For most of the night he'd walked around in darkness. He had stashed his truck on Tinker Street, near where Enna Brakeman lived. Then he'd walked home in the darkness to watch for Mazy's return. The roadhouse typically stayed open on Saturday night until 1:00 a.m. He'd already decided that if she wasn't home by midnight, he'd drive back out there and get her.

Fortunately, a little after eleven, he saw Che's car pull up in the driveway next door. From his basement window he saw Mazy, looking perfectly fine, wave goodbye to her friends as she let herself in the back door.

He did catch her glancing in his direction. He knew exactly what she saw. His truck was not there and the entire house, including the basement, was dark.

When she closed the door behind her and switched off the porch light, Eli let out a sigh of relief. At least she was home and safe.

Let this be the last, he silently pleaded. *Let this be the worst.* This had to put her feelings over the top. It had to make her finally value him. She would plead for a commitment and he would give her one. It would keep her out of the clutches of Driscoll and in his arms forever.

Someone tapped excitedly at his door.

Eli ignored it. The need to sleep kept his eyes closed and his body horizontal. He'd walked back and forth across the dark apartment, thinking, planning and worrying until nearly daybreak. Then he'd sneaked out quietly, walked the eight blocks to where he'd left his truck and drove it home to park it in its place. Just in case she'd slept through the engine noise, he slammed the heavy metal driver's side door for good measure.

Left the roadhouse with another woman. Returned home at dawn. Let Mazy try to filter that through her Mr. Nice Guy stereotype.

The knocking at the door began again, this time louder.

Eli's eyes popped open with a surge of adrenaline. It might be Mazy. She might have come to have it out. It was like a trumpet call to battle stations.

Eli rolled off the couch, where he'd obviously crashed. He was in a T-shirt and pajama bottoms as he went to the door. He opened it wide, but it was not Mazy standing there.

With the excited giggles, his nieces, Ashley and Ava, greeted him. The two girls were rosy cheeked and literally bouncing with enthusiasm.

"Come out and play with us, Uncle Eli," Ava pleaded. "Come out and play!"

"We're kicking the ball around like soccer, but it's really more a game of Monkey in the Middle."

"We need you to be the monkey," the five-year-old pleaded.

He loved the little girls and enjoyed time spent with them. But today was…today he was incapable of having fun. The blood of the bad dude was still running in his veins. It was hard to recapture his nice-guy self.

"Can't play today, sweeties," he told them. "Get your dad to do it."

Ava shook her head. "Daddy's busy. He's taking care of Grandpa."

"What?"

"It's such a pretty day," Ashley said. "Mom and Dad decided to bring Grandpa out to sit in the yard."

Eli was pretty sure that his jaw must have dropped. He was stunned into inaction for a half minute. And then, without stopping to acquire more clothing, he stepped out the back door.

Ava clapped excitedly, as if he'd agreed to entertain them. But Eli walked disbelieving to the little semicircle of lawn chairs sitting in the afternoon sunshine. In the center, seated in the wheelchair that was typically used only for doctor visits, Jonah Latham was wrapped warmly in a red-plaid hunting jacket and breathing fresh mountain air.

His brother looked up and gave a hearty grin. "Hey, it looks like the girls have finally rousted the lazy slug-a-bed. One day working outside the shop and it takes him all the next morning to recover."

There was laughter. Eli looked at his father. The old man's expression was unchanged, but his eyes looked bright and he moved his arm as if in greeting.

"Ashley, bring Uncle Eli a chair," Sheila called out to her daughter.

"He's going to play with us."

"Let him wake up first."

The girls began dragging one of the ancient Adirondacks that had been part of their backyard for so long. Eli became aware of his state of undress.

"I need to get some clothes on."

"I wondered when you were going to notice that," Ida told him with a chuckle.

He hurried back into the basement. He went into the bathroom and splashed cold water on his face. His mind was a complete whirl. *His father was outside? His father was outside and the sun was shining on his face.* And it was Clark who'd brought him there. It was an image so far out of his current expectation that he could hardly grasp it.

Dressing in jeans, Eli pulled on his old-school Connies without socks and loped back outside.

An extra chair had been added to the group, but Beth Ann Gulliver was now sitting in it. Tru was out on the lawn in between the little girls, generously playing the part of monkey.

"Oh, I got your place," Beth Ann said.

Eli waved away her concern and seated himself cross-legged on the wheat-colored grass. The ground beneath him was colder than the air around, but it provided a better view of his dad's face, looking somehow happier than he had in months.

The conversation was light and ordinary. It was the kind of talk that might have happened years before. Eli noted that his father was not the only one who seemed happy to be outside. Ida's smiling face seemed to have dropped a decade of years as she sat next to her husband, laughing and joking.

Beth Ann told stories from long-ago days when she and her husband, Truman, first moved to town. And Ida added her own tales of sleepy life in Brandt Mountain when she was a girl. They spoke of old friends and old times. But their conversation wasn't totally about the past.

"So what are your plans for Thanksgiving?" Beth Ann questioned.

"Sheila usually brings us a plate by," Ida answered with a grateful smile toward her stepdaughter-in-law. "I've never cooked a turkey in my life and I don't think I can start now."

"Why don't you come over to our house," Beth Ann suggested. "It's not much of a holiday with only the three of us."

"Oh, we wouldn't want to be a bother," Ida said.

"There is no such thing as a bother on Thanksgiving," Beth Ann told her. "It would be a joy. And remind me of times gone by. Jonah and Daisy must have invited us over for holiday feeds with them a half-dozen times. I never really got to reciprocate. Though I'll admit it will be a lot quieter than when you boys were still at home."

"Why don't we come, too?" Clark suggested. "Eli's going to want to be with Mazy. And we're not going to Sheila's parents this year. So we could bring the kids with us for a big celebration."

Sheila laughed. "Sorry, Beth Ann," she said. "Normally, Clark doesn't invite himself to other people's houses."

Clark shrugged as if it were a joke. "We could serve it here at Dad's house. We could set up the dining room, just like we used to. Beth Ann cooks at her house and Eli and I carry it over here."

Beth Ann nodded thoughtfully. "What a wonderful idea, Clark. All of us together again for the holiday."

"Well, I can't let you do all the cooking," Sheila piped in. "I have a recipe for sweet potatoes that can't be missed. And I make a real green bean casserole, not the one with the canned mushroom soup."

The plans went on as if getting together were the most

normal thing in the world. The last time the Lathams and Gullivers had shared a dinner, Eli and Mazy must have been young teens. And the last time there had been any kind of celebration in his house was before his father's stroke.

As the discussion moved to pies, Clark gave a nod toward Eli, the head gesture urging him aside for a private discussion.

Getting up from the ground, he followed his brother to the area of the lawn where the path was worn between the shop and the house.

Clark stood scuffing the denuded ground with his foot.

Eli hoped this was not going to be a rematch of their argument on Friday. Still on pins and needles about the ongoing drama with Mazy, he really only wanted peace. He decided the best way to have it was to make it.

"Have you contracted for a winter storage unit?" he asked.

Clark looked momentarily guilty. "No, honestly I haven't put enough time into it," he answered. "I'll do what I can when I get home and try to have something lined up in the next few days."

"Would you go look at the second floor of Charlie's building?"

"The coffee shop building?"

Eli nodded. "I talked to him about it yesterday. It's big enough and probably cheap enough that we could keep it year-round."

"If that's what you want," Clark said. "You're the boss."

Eli did not detect any snideness or resentment in his words. That was a good sign.

"I think it's a doable idea," he told Clark. "But I'd value your opinion. We could interact with customers

there and keep them out of the shop where it's dangerous and they're kind of a nuisance."

Clark nodded thoughtfully. "I like the sound of that,"
he said. "It might actually be a smart move for the business to have a presence on Main Street. But I'm not that
keen on dragging some of these big pieces up to the second floor."

"There's a freight elevator," Eli said.

"Then that sounds even better," Clark said. "I'll run by
in the morning and see if Charlie will let me have a look."

Eli nodded.

Clark continued to rough up the ground underfoot.
"What do you think about this path?" he asked.

"The path?"

"Do you think it's smooth enough for the wheelchair
or would it be better to continue the ramp down the hill?"

"Continue the ramp?"

"I was thinking this morning," he said, "that maybe
we could bring Dad down to the shop during the day."

"Huh?"

Clark's brow furrowed. "Well, not every day, of
course. And not all day. But sometimes we could bring
him down to be in the shop with us. It would be good for
him to get out of the house. Probably good for Ida, too."

Eli stared at his brother, too stunned to speak.

"You don't like it?" Clark tone was worried.

"No, I do like it," Eli told him. "I think it's a great
idea."

"The weather is mostly going to be too cold this time
of year," Clark said. "But some days, like today, are going
to be nice. And if he's…if he's still with us in the spring,
that would be good, right?"

"Right," Eli agreed. "I'm sure Dad would love that."

"He went down to work almost every day of his life,"

Clark pointed out. "It seems kind of wrong for him to be kept out of there now."

Eli nodded. "Just being down there ought to make him feel more like himself."

"Yeah," Clark agreed. "It kind of makes his life seem more normal again."

Eli nodded. "Of course we should bring Dad to the shop. The only place he ever sees is home or the doctor's office. I should have thought of it myself. I should have thought of it long ago."

Clark shrugged. "I don't know why you should be expected to think of everything," he said. "If it is a good idea, I don't think it matters who comes up with it."

"No, it doesn't matter," Eli said. "And it *is* a really good idea."

Clark let out a long breath as if he'd been holding it. "I didn't want you to think that I was stepping into your territory, second-guessing all you've done for Dad. I know it's been mostly on you and, honestly, I kind of thought you wanted it that way."

"How could you think that?"

Clark shrugged. "Maybe I wanted to think that. It kind of let me off the hook, I guess."

It was more honesty and self-reproach than Clark was typically noted for.

"I'm…I'm sorry about going off on you the other day," Eli told him.

"You were right," Clark said. "I knew it when you said it. But it still pissed me off. I'm not used to this new, more ballsy kid brother. I went home and griped to Sheila about it. She helped me kind of talk myself through it. That's one of the advantages of having a wife, you know. They understand exactly how to help you take a long look at yourself."

Eli raised an eyebrow, but nodded.

Clark pulled the cap with the team logo off his head and ran a hand through his hair. "I feel so bad in so many ways," he said. "It's like I'm so glad that Dad's still with us. But then I feel guilty that he's so broken."

Eli nodded. He knew that feeling.

"The more Sheila and I talked about it, the more I realized that I just hate that room," Clark said.

"The room?"

"It was never Dad's room. It wasn't a room that he shared with Mom. It's a sickroom. And I hate being in there."

Eli could see that, but there were practical considerations. "If we move him upstairs…we can't move him up and down two or three times a day."

"I know," Clark said. "I'm not criticizing your decision on this. I'm saying what I feel."

Eli nodded.

"Anyway, Sheila said that I should come up with a new idea. And the idea I came up with was…well, to see him someplace else."

Clark motioned toward the semicircle of chairs. Their father was still seated there.

Eli felt an expansion in his heart. Seeing Dad someplace else was really about *seeing* him. He had gotten so accustomed to seeing his father as the invalid in the sickroom that perhaps he, too, had stopped looking at him as a person who had a life and interests not limited to his own health and well-being.

Jonah Latham definitely had physical limitations. But maybe it had been Eli's limited vision that had kept him trapped within his house for so long.

"Thanks, Clark," he said. "I'm sure getting down to the shop will mean a lot to Dad. And knowing it was your idea will be even better. I know you two have had your issues."

Clark shrugged. "We haven't always gotten along," he agreed. "But I love him as much as you do, Termite. He knows that, but still it's time that I showed it more, too."

Eli was amazed. He'd allowed the worthless-dude mentality to spill over into his relationship with Clark and it had acted like a wake-up call for his brother. This jerkish behavior stuff was powerful.

Clark gave Eli a brotherly shoulder punch. He reciprocated by wrapping Clark in a hasty bear hug.

As he wandered back down the lawn, Eli suddenly felt a lot better about the stunt he'd pulled last night. So far, Mazy seemed able to take whatever he dished out. But it would be impossible for her to pretend that his date desertion hadn't happened. A big, angry accusatory argument was inevitable. He hoped he was ready.

The internet was very clear about how bad boyfriends handle conflict. No matter what they've done, they turn it around to make it the woman's fault. At first glance, that appeared to be a challenge. How could Mazy be blamed for Eli's behavior? But he'd already figured out that if a guy threw veracity out the window, he could talk his way around anything with smoke and mirrors.

And really, when he got right down to it, running out on her *was* her fault. All of it was. If Mazy hadn't been a sucker for guys like Driscoll, Eli would have never had to do any of this scheming.

He nodded to himself, but the smug satisfaction was partially feigned. He had nothing to feel guilty about, but there wasn't a whole lot about his behavior that he wanted to celebrate, either.

"Uncle Eli! Uncle Eli! Come play with us," Ava called out to him.

The soccer match was still going on. Tru was a good sport to hang in there entertaining the little girls as long as he had. The teen truly deserved to be rescued, or at least offered assistance. Eli had not really grown up expending a lot of energy on the game. He'd been much more interested in hanging out in the wood shop than he had been in team sports. But he'd done his fair share of kicking a ball around at school recess and community picnics.

He quickly determined that Tru was a fairly formidable opponent for the two little girls. He thought the competition might be more evenly matched if he and Ava took up defense against Tru and Ashley.

It was only a few minutes into play that Eli realized he'd miscalculated. The two best players were on the same team. He and Ava were doomed to be creamed. So they improvised the rules to include tackling. Within minutes, the inevitable pile of laughing players was accomplished.

The girls finally ran off together when Ashley suggested searching for acorns.

Eli kicked the ball toward Tru. "You want some one-on-one?"

"Nah," the teen answered. "I'm done with it. They have a lot of energy for little girls."

Eli nodded. "Hey, when I was growing up, my best friend was a girl. Don't buy all that sugar-and-spice, pink-princess propaganda. The female of the species is plenty tough."

Tru shrugged. "I've never been around any little kids that much," he said. "They're kind of fun, really."

Eli agreed. He'd always imagined himself as a father. Maybe it wasn't too late. It definitely wasn't too late if a certain woman that he was in love with could get her head around marrying him and allowing him to share her teenage son.

"Listen," Tru began, his hands stuffed in his pockets. "Would you...would you introduce me to your dad?"

"Sure. I assumed somebody already had."

They walked back up the lawn. As they neared, Eli saw that his father was beginning to tire. He should take him in for a nap. But meeting Tru was important. It was important for all of them.

Beth Ann vacated the chair next to Jonah. Eli gestured for Tru to take a seat before squatting down in front of his father.

"Dad, this is Tru Gulliver, Mazy's son. He's the one I told you about. He's helping out in the shop after school."

The face of the boy looked anxious. The face of the man never changed its frozen grimace. But his eyes surveyed the teen beside him. After a moment, he reached out to Tru with his one good hand. The boy took it in his own. He smiled a bit shyly and began telling the old woodworker all the things that he liked about the shop and all that he had already learned.

Eli retreated to the edge of the semicircle and watched Tru interacting with the silent, shaky Jonah.

Mazy might be a mistake-prone person, but she had definitely done something right in raising this wonderful boy.

As if his thought had conjured her up, Mazy suddenly stepped up beside him. His heart caught in his throat and his fight-or-flight response engaged. She held a steaming cup of coffee in her hands and for an instant he thought she might fling it in his face.

She did not. She held it up to him.

"I thought you might need this," she said.

39

Mazy awoke groggy and hungry. She had tossed and turned miserably on the lumpy couch. Around her the house was completely silent. She figured that Beth Ann had taken her weekly trip to Walmart and Tru had gone with her.

Wandering listlessly into the kitchen, she found that her mom had left half of a tuna sandwich in the fridge. She ate it standing at the counter. As she watched the coffeepot fill, she tried to figure out how her life made sense.

Things had sort of gone off the rails for her when her father had died. By the time she'd hit puberty, she was looking for love in all the wrong places. Tru's birth had given her purpose and meaning, but it had also ramped up the longing for a man she could call her own.

Of course, Dr. Reese had called her on that.

She wanted a wonderful man, like her father. But the thought that had so burned itself in her subconscious was the fact that her father had left. All the bad-news guys she'd picked weren't supposed to change that narrative.

She'd thought she'd worked through that. She thought she'd finally gotten her head straight enough to own the qualities that she truly loved in her father, rather than the fatal accident that had taken him from her.

Her very genuine feelings for Eli had encouraged her

to believe that she'd finally made that transition. That she could finally love a man who wouldn't leave her.

But it seemed as if she'd been wrong. He *had* left her last night. Maybe mistaking Dax's words for Eli's wasn't so far off the mark, after all.

Mazy wished she could talk to Dr. Reese, though she knew that wasn't possible. It was often said that the poor person's therapist was a best friend. Of course, Mazy's best friend was Eli.

A sound outside caught her attention and she turned to see a small heap of laughing people in the backyard next door. As the pile began to untangle, she recognized Clark and Sheila's girls. And Tru and Eli.

Standing at the window, she watched the man she was in love with casually conversing with her son. A stab of pain and a jolt of fear hit her simultaneously. She had learned to protect Tru from the men that would leave her. She'd discouraged any camaraderie or attachment to her boyfriends. She hadn't wanted him to feel any of the abandonment issues that had scarred her life. But she had not taken that precaution with Eli. She had not felt one worry. Because she knew Eli. She knew him to be different from the kind of men she'd gotten caught up with before.

She poured her coffee and took a couple of sips as she leaned against the counter watching the two of them.

Mazy no longer knew what to think. She no longer knew what to feel. But she did know Eli Latham. She wasn't sure what was going on, but she was certain that your best friend didn't turn on you simply because you fell in love with him.

She poured a second cup of coffee and carried them both outside.

Her son was talking to Jonah Latham. How could that

not be a good thing? One of the sweetest, kindest, most honorable men in the world and her impressionable son was sharing a moment with him.

She stepped up beside Eli.

"I thought you might need this," she said.

"Mazy!" he breathed her name in a shocked whisper. Then he took the cup out of her hand with a polite thank-you.

He looked guilty—embarrassed and guilty.

They stood side by side, not speaking, as they listened to Tru talk about all the tools that he'd been allowed to use. He sounded so happy. He was so pleased about what he had done, some of it more or less on his own. And he was excited about what he was going to learn in the future. Jonah continued to hold his hand as if it were a lifeline.

Ida greeted her with delighted pleasure. Sheila gave her a little finger wave that was a little more than pseudo-friendly. Beth Ann was eyeing her approvingly. Clark had a big grin spread across his face. All in all, the mood was not suited for the giant blowup that she and Eli needed to have.

Mazy realized that she shouldn't have come. She didn't need normal, happy time with Eli. She needed a serious, down-to-brass-tacks talk about the night before. He needed to make some kind of explanation and she needed…she needed to decide if she could live with it.

But she couldn't do that here. She couldn't turn to him in front of his entire family and demand to know if he spent the night with another woman. He showed no outward evidence of having spent the night in the hospital or in jail, both of which somehow seemed to be preferable. His father looked better than the last time she'd seen him. No crisis, short of amnesia, was in any way evident. And alien abduction seemed unlikely.

If she had stayed in her house until he was alone, she could have immediately confronted him. She was not about to do so here.

"Can I get you a chair?" he asked politely.

Only if I can hit you over the head with it, she thought. Instead of speaking that aloud she replied, "No, thank you."

The longer she waited, the more normal their interaction together, the more difficult it would be to have it out with him, and the less likely she would get any straight answers. She already wanted to forgive him. She wanted to believe that the Eli she knew could never do what she suspected him of doing last night. She wanted to put it all behind them. But she couldn't do that by pretending that it hadn't happened.

She wandered away from the group, hoping that he would follow her down the lawn and give her the opportunity to ask questions. He didn't.

Instead, the two little girls came running up to her. She had never actually met them and they were excited for their opportunity.

"Are you Tru's mom?"

"Yes, that's me."

"Tru's my boyfriend," the littlest girl told her.

The big sister rolled her eyes. "She says that about everybody."

"Only the boys," Ava corrected her.

Mazy certainly understood the challenge of believing that every guy you like is your boyfriend.

The children had gathered up an impressive pile of acorns. They wanted Mazy to assess their collection. She appropriately oohed and aahed at the biggest, the small-est, the one with the best "hat" and the variety in general.

"Why do I feel like this trio of younger women may be plotting against me?" Sheila asked.

Mazy looked up and gave her a smile.

"We're not plotting, Mom. We're getting acorns," Ava assured her.

"If you gather up all the acorns, the squirrels will get lazy," Sheila suggested.

"Not if we throw them back."

That immediately commenced a new game of tossing them, one by one, back into the woods from which they came. Mazy threw one, but she left the rest of the pile for the girls as she rose to her feet.

She glanced toward the house. The lawn chairs were all empty.

"Where did everybody go?"

"The guys are taking Jonah back inside for a nap," she said. "Ida and Beth Ann are talking out the Thanksgiv-ing menu. I don't know where your son got off to, but for sure it's not far."

Mazy nodded.

The two began walking back up the lawn together. She knew that Sheila had never cared much for her. And she wasn't in a mood to try to change her mind. Truthfully, it didn't bother her. Nevertheless, she did make minimal effort to be civil.

"It's such a beautiful day today. Really unexpected this time of year."

Sheila agreed with the lovely weather. "I hope my girls haven't made a nuisance of themselves," she said.

"Your girls are lovely," Mazy answered. "Very bright and well behaved."

No parent ever minded hearing praise about their children.

"It seems like we're going to be spending Thanksgiving together," Sheila said.

"Are we?"

"It's what Ida and Beth Ann are planning."

"How nice."

"It's probably a good thing that we're not actual enemies."

"We definitely aren't," Mazy assured her. She knew that Sheila had undoubtedly said plenty of negative things about her. But she'd already learned that part of moving back to town meant relinquishing any grudges.

"Yes, that was all a very long time ago," Sheila agreed. "All of us have made some sort of screwup as teenagers. Maybe that's the best news about being over thirty. All those mistakes are part of a distant past."

That was not true for Mazy, of course. She was over thirty when the surprise audit revealed the crime she'd covered up. She'd turned thirty-one wearing an orange jumpsuit and picking up trash on the side of the highway. She was unwilling to share either of those facts with Sheila.

As they took adjacent seats in the lawn chairs, Mazy went back to the subject of weather and the likelihood of rain in their future.

The conversation dragged on interminably. She began to think that Eli was deliberately staying inside the house. She had waited all night on him, now she was waiting all day.

She was tempted to question Sheila about Enna Brakeman. It seemed fairly obvious that Eli's sister-in-law kept up with every snippet of gossip that was ever spoken in Brandt Mountain. She would undoubtedly know how long and how serious any relationship between the woman and Eli had been. That would give Mazy good insight to what last night might have been or meant.

But she resisted.

This was between Eli and herself. She would draw no one else in. She would give no further information out.

Finally Eli and Clark emerged from Jonah and Ida's house. Sheila was eager to go. She and Clark rounded up the girls and, after plenty of goodbyes, Mazy and Eli were left alone in the backyard.

They turned to face each other. He was stiff and unsmiling.

"We have to talk," she said.

With an extended arm, he invited her into his apartment.

Once inside, he walked behind the kitchen counter and began retrieving things from the shelves.

"What are you doing?"

"Fixing drinks."

"I don't want a drink."

"Hey, babe, when a woman is about to throw a tantrum, a guy needs a drink to get through it."

"Is that what you think of me? That I'm going to throw a tantrum?"

"Pretty much."

It *was* what she wanted to do, but it wouldn't get her the answers that she needed.

"Did you sleep with her?"

"Who?"

"Enna Brakeman."

He hesitated, as if trying to recall. "Ever?" he asked finally.

"Last night," she answered, a bit more loudly than she intended.

He took a sip of his drink.

She held herself together by sheer force of will.

"No."

The relief washed through her like a gasp. For an instant she thought she might burst into tears. She quickly turned her back on him so he wouldn't see the evidence if she did. Mazy had totally steeled herself against the worst. And the wait to hear his answer had made her brittle. She gazed slightly away from him, controlling her breathing. In…out…in…out. She tried to repurpose, but she couldn't manage it. The moment dragged on.

"So, I guess, if that's all you wanted to know, we're done here."

She turned on him. "Where were you?"

Eli shrugged and held up his hand. "Do you see a ring on this finger?" he asked. "I don't answer to you as to where I go or what I do."

"You left me stranded at the roadhouse."

"Looks like you made it home all right."

"Why?" she asked. "Why would you do that?"

He took another good slug of his drink. "I thought a dose of your own medicine might do you some good."

"What? What are you talking about?"

"Driscoll."

"Driscoll? Tad Driscoll?"

"Is there another one? I'm not sure that son of a bitch could be duplicated."

"What about Tad?"

"Yesterday, on the street in front of the coffee shop, I saw you two together."

For a moment she thought he must be lying. Yesterday seemed so long ago. But it had happened.

"Oh, that."

"Yeah, that," he said. "I saw you all cozied up with him."

"We weren't 'cozied up.'"

"Maybe that's not what you call it," Eli said. "But you and Driscoll, I guess that's back on."

"What? No."

Mazy could hardly believe it. Not in any of her wildest imaginings would she have thought that Eli's actions had been based in anger. There hadn't been even a hint of that at the roadhouse. But he was admitting it here. He had been angry and jealous. Jealous of her? Or maybe jealous of Tad. But somehow deliberately lashing out in jealousy seemed better than callously doing so.

She turned to face him again. "Tad and I were just talking."

"Talking?" He repeated the word in a fashion so snide it was as if it were a euphemism for some very sinful deed. "What on earth could you and that creep have to talk about?"

"Tru," she answered. That seemed inexplicably to make him angrier. "Yesterday was the first day he'd met Tru."

"Driscoll doesn't deserve to even speak to Tru," Eli said. "I hope you told him not to get near the kid again."

"Well, no, that's not what I told him," she answered. "He was curious. He wanted to meet him."

"He's a little late for that," Eli pointed out.

"I know. It's almost funny, really. After nearly fifteen years of insisting he's not the father, it only took fifteen minutes of getting to know Tru and Tad's kind of taking credit for all of his best qualities."

Eli's jaw hardened. "I doubt seriously if Tru's *worst* qualities even bare a resemblance to that creep. Why would you even talk to him after what he's done to you, to both of you?"

"He's my boss," Mazy answered. "And besides, it's not really his fault."

"What? His behavior is totally his fault. How can you let him off the hook like that?"

Mazy wasn't letting him off the hook, but she wasn't sure she was ready to explain. She should, but she hated to do it.

"Tad's changed," she told him instead. "I'm not going to hold the past against him."

The iciness in Eli's gaze chilled all the space around them. When he spoke softly and deliberately, his words were crushing. "He's got you on the hook again. He'll play the line for a while before he reels you in. Again."

"No," Mazy reassured him. "Nothing like that. He'd finally met Tru and he wanted to talk about it. Nothing else."

Eli snorted unattractively and shook his head. "Don't believe it," he said. "The guy wants what he wants. And when it comes to you, he's always wanted to keep you right under his thumb."

"I don't fit under his thumb anymore," she said. "I'm not saying I trust him, but I'm not afraid to give him the benefit of the doubt."

"After all that he did to you? After all he put you through? You're still defending him."

Mazy wasn't sure how much of her worst self she was ready to confess. But Tad had taken the brunt of the blame from her friends and family for way too long. She owed him some kind of defense.

"It wasn't his fault," she told Eli.

"I've heard all that," he answered. "It takes two to tango, and all that. But he was almost an adult and you were still mostly a child. And you took all the blame while he skated away with practically none."

"Because he shouldn't have had any," Mazy said. She only hesitated a moment more before blurting out, "I didn't accidentally get pregnant, Eli. I did it on purpose. I tried to win him away from Genna and couldn't. I believed that if I got pregnant, she would break up with him. And he'd want his child, so he'd take me."

There was a stunned silence between them.

"If he didn't want that to happen, he should have used protection," Eli said.

"Well, he thought we were protected," Mazy told him. "I…I 'forgot' to take my birth control pills. And I didn't tell him."

"Oh, Mazy…" Eli moaned aloud.

"I know you see me as a victim," she said. "I've seen myself that way for a lot of my life. But I've stopped that. That kind of thinking gets me right back to flailing for control. I have always made my own choices—maybe some of them were bad choices, but they were mine. I did everything I could to take Tad's choices away."

He stared at her and shook his head. "So now I'm supposed to feel sorry for poor old Tad?" he asked. "Okay, what you did—that was low. You tried to trap him. But if he was a good guy, a decent person, then it wouldn't have stopped him from being a part of Tru's life. He was still a father, whether he chose it or not. But poor old Tad, no matter what he does, no matter how he treats you, no matter what kind of a son of a bitch he continues to be, you still put him up on a pedestal."

"What? No," she said. "People change, Eli. That's all I'm saying, is that maybe he has changed."

"People don't change," he answered angrily. "The heart of people, the truth about who they are, that doesn't change. You can clean it up or gloss it over, but it's still there. We are what we are."

Mazy's breath caught in her throat. "I don't believe that," she said. "We can take our lives in our hands and be whoever we want."

It was true. It had to be.

Eli's eyes had narrowed. The expression on his face held nothing of the man she had fallen for.

"You can hardly wait to get back into bed with him."

She felt her jaw drop open. Where had that accusation come from? "No, no, Eli. I'm not interested in Tad."

"Of course you are. You always are. The guy just has to crook his little finger and you practically drop your panties at his feet."

"What a terrible thing to say!"

He shrugged. "Just speaking the truth. I've always known you were Driscoll's discard. But I've never been that interested in an actual time-share."

"I would never, I *have* never—"

"Whatever."

"That's the most horrible, cruel, disrespectful thing you've ever said to me."

"Yeah, probably gets you hot, doesn't it?"

"Excuse me?"

"That's the 4-1-1 on you, you know. Whether it's Driscoll or a dozen others, you like the guys who treat you like shit."

"I just…I just…" Mazy wanted to defend herself, but couldn't find the words.

"He kicks you to the curb and you come running back for more," Eli said. "Well, I can do that, too. I can be as shitty as any of them. You like being walked on? I'll stamp my muddy boot prints right on your ass."

"Eli?"

"Yeah, it's your dumb, devoted Eli. But you see, I've finally wised up. I'm not going to stand by while some other guy puts you on a leash."

"Why are you acting like this?"

"You've always thought you could pick me up, let me down, have sex with me until somebody better showed up," Eli said. "Well, I'm not the innocent heartsick sucker that I used to be. I call the shots in this relationship now. I'll call the shots and that's the way it's going to be."

"What about…what about love, Eli?"

"Love? You wouldn't recognize it if it dropped down right into your lap."

Was he right? Maybe he was.

Mazy felt the tears welling in her eyes. Was she incapable of recognizing love?

Or was she so flawed that she destroyed it? Without any intent, she'd managed to turn a wonderful, sweet guy like Eli into the same kind of creep she always ended up with. She'd thought she had changed. That she had grown. That falling for him was somehow evidence of that, but she had been wrong. It was exactly the same pattern. She had fallen in love with him and now he was going to treat her like crap.

40

Eli did not typically let himself get angry. But he'd found that once he started doing it, it became easier and a lot more dangerous. The thing about flying off the handle was that you really couldn't know where you might land.

He'd turned the tables in his argument with Mazy. Like any bad boyfriend might do, he'd made her the guilty party while he played the innocent victim.

That part went even better than he'd expected. She was completely thrown off by his attack. It was almost as if she'd forgotten what he had done to her, as she'd defended and explained what she had supposedly done to him.

And then it had all spiraled out of control. He had been jealous and scared. Mazy *was* interested in Driscoll again. Eli was certain of it. She had turned the tables herself in that "accidental pregnancy" revelation. Making it out that a creep like Driscoll, who had taken advantage of a young, vulnerable girl, had somehow been maltreated by a pregnancy he'd never acknowledged or supported.

Eli didn't doubt that Mazy had manipulated things exactly that way. It was a painful admission that said awful things about the person she had been. But it gave Driscoll a pass that he didn't deserve.

What happens between two people can never truly be seen from the outside. But Eli knew Driscoll and he knew Mazy. And if given the words *deceitful, lying* and *manipulator,* Eli would have been sure they described the former person much more than the latter.

That's what he should have said. That's what he had, on some level, wanted to tell her. But he'd slipped into his now-well-practiced bad-dude persona. It had gotten out of control. It had taken over and lashed out.

He'd wounded her. He knew that. Even as it was happening he'd wanted to take it all back. But he was afraid. He was afraid that it was all true. That she could only love a man who rejected her. So he'd rejected her as harshly, as completely, as utterly, as he could.

This was supposed to be the moment of his transformation. The plan required the inexplicable upending of the universe. He was to be outrageously the bad boy. He would blame Mazy. He would argue mercilessly. And then he would conveniently lose.

That was the key. In order to win the woman he loved, he would have to lose the argument. He had felt pretty confident about that part of it. He'd been losing to Mazy most of his life.

Then he would spout mea culpa, beg her forgiveness and ask her to marry him. She would say yes. He would pull her into his arms. They could enjoy some fantastic makeup sex and start shopping for diamonds. But somehow things didn't always play out as he'd intended.

Mazy's eyes glistened with tears. The pain behind them was stark. There was a ramrod stiffness to her back.

"Fine," she said. "I guess that's all I need to know. Goodbye, Eli."

His jaw dropped as she turned and walked to the door. They weren't finished. They hadn't got to the good part.

"Mazy, wait."

He hurried to get between her and the door.

"I think we've said all that we need to say," she told him.

"I haven't."

"What more could you possibly have to say?" she asked. "I'm incapable of recognizing love, unable to remain faithful and have no chance of ever being a better person tomorrow than I was yesterday. I may be immune to your insults, but I don't have to stand here and listen to them."

"Mazy, I want to marry you."

"What?"

"I was wrong. Leaving you at the roadhouse was... it was terrible. I'm sorry. I want to talk this out, make it right. I really care about you. I always have. And I promise I'll be a better husband than I've been a boyfriend."

Mazy stared at him in utter disbelief for an instant before some realization dawned in her eyes. "You think I should want to marry you?"

"Let me explain..."

"No further explanation required. I have plenty of experience with men who try to talk me out of the truth I can see with my own eyes. You don't want me under Tad's thumb, because you like having me under yours. I got involved with you again, Eli, because I believed that you were a nice, decent guy. But in the past few weeks you've shown yourself to be as big a selfish, boneheaded prick as Tad Driscoll ever was. I deserve better. Me, Mazy Gulliver, I deserve more!"

She clutched her hands to her heart as if safeguarding it.

"Yes, I've made some mistakes in my life. Yes, there are some things I've done where I would like to make amends. Even some things that I've done to you, Eli. But I refuse to pay the debts of the past with a future that looks just like it. I owe it to Tru and Beth Ann, but mostly I owe it to myself, to become the person that I was always meant to be. If you're not the person that can help me do that, then you are not the person I'm supposed to be with. Now get out of my way. I'm not wasting another minute with the wrong man."

Eli stepped aside. He was too stunned to stop her. This was not how it was supposed to work. She was supposed to be broken Mazy. Needy and crippled with low self-esteem, yearning for the bad boy who wouldn't give an inch and offered her nothing. This woman, this woman who had turned her back on him, was not that Mazy at all. But somehow he loved her even more.

41

It had been a long, lonely week for Mazy. She'd realized, almost too late, how easily it had been for her to be sucked into another bad relationship. Dr. Reese had once likened her dysfunctional love life to an addiction. She could see that now. She could see that sharing smiles with Eli, being in his arms, quaking beneath him in release, was truly akin to an alcoholic socially sipping martinis at a cocktail party. It was not going to end well.

So Mazy was determined to end it now. When she'd turned her back on him last Sunday, she'd called it quits.

She had thought that what they'd had together was maybe something more....

She sighed heavily. As usual, all the finer feelings involved had been her own. Mazy would never have believed it if she hadn't seen it herself. It was sad. She knew she should be grateful for such a close escape, but the sad feeling lingered.

Day by day, she would get better, stronger. Day by day, her feelings for Eli would fade. Once they were faded enough, she could toss them away.

With another sigh, Mazy scanned the spreadsheet on her computer. Concentrating on her work was what would get her through the day, the week, the future.

Tad had asked her to get together a bundle of nonperformers to be sold off. She had cringed a bit about doing it so close to Thanksgiving. But he'd pointed out that it had to be done by the end of the year. Was Christmas-time better? Not hardly.

The choices weren't truly *choices* at all. They were the accounts that wouldn't or couldn't be helped. She had her mouse cursor over Nina Garvey's name. She hesitated. There was still something....

As if she had conjured her by magic, Nina appeared at the door.

"Hi, may I come in?"

"Yes, yes, come in!"

Mazy rose to her feet and offered the young woman the chair next to her desk.

"I brought you a cupcake," Nina said, handing over a small piece of bakery art. The frosting looked like a deli-cate lace and was topped by a purple flower.

"Oh, how lovely!"

"It's Fay Jean Esher's birthday," Nina said. "They're giving her a little party at the Ladies' Auxiliary. I made extra in case some of them didn't turn out."

"You made this? It's beautiful."

"Oh, it's easy, really," Nina insisted. "You just press the lace onto the icing to make the pattern. The flowers are more time than they are trouble. You could do it if you practice a bit."

Mazy was pretty sure she could practice for a lifetime and never produce anything worth showing off.

"You can eat it on your coffee break or save it for des-sert after supper."

"I think it's too pretty to eat," Mazy said.

"It better not be," Nina said, laughing. "I pride myself on how good my cakes *taste*."

"Well, thank you," Mazy said. "I will enjoy looking at it this morning and eating it this afternoon."

After a moment Nina's expression sobered. "I brought you some money," she said.

"What?"

Nina opened her handbag and pulled out a plastic bag with a collection of bills and change.

"I've heard that you've been telling folks that even if they can't catch up their payments, if they put something on their account, it buys them more time."

"Well, yes," Mazy answered. "In many cases that's true."

"I want to put something on my account," she said. "I've been making cakes for people and putting all that money aside for the debt. This is my first payment. It's not much, but I've talked to some folks about pies for the holidays, so there'll be more."

Mazy felt sick. There was no way that Nina was ever going to qualify for an extension on the loan. She owed way too much and she had no dependable income. Taking this money from her would simply be taking it. It would be absorbed into accrued interest and make no difference to the bank's decision to sell the debt. And the cash could mean a lot more to Nina and her son.

"Wait. I think—"

"Excuse me, I didn't mean to interrupt."

The words came from Tad. He had come in through the open door, but paused at the sight of Nina in the side chair.

"Hello, Nina."

The young woman visibly stiffened. His unexpected appearance was a little startling. And she was obviously afraid of Tad, which probably made sense. She was in a precarious financial situation and as bank director he represented the bureaucracy that must have felt allied against her.

Tad could certainly recognize this. Mazy assumed that was why he'd used her given name instead of adhering to the policy of more formal address for clients during business hours. The familiar first-name basis was undoubtedly meant to reassure her. However, it didn't seem to work. The bright, cheerful woman who had come through the door disappeared into a pale, fearful woman who looked almost cornered.

"Mr. Driscoll," Nina responded without ever meeting his eyes. Bravely she raised her chin. "I've come to pay some on my account. I'm earning a little money—I want to put it toward the debt."

"Excellent idea," Tad said. "But you don't need to bother Ms. Gulliver with that. Take your money out to the teller and she'll take care of it for you."

Tad stepped slightly to the side of the door and held his arm out, as if inviting her to leave the room.

With only a quick, haunted glance toward Mazy, Nina gathered up her money and pretty much fled.

Tad hardly spared a glance at her. Instead, he seated himself in the chair she'd vacated. "I hope you've got a minute," he said.

As he had already made himself comfortable in her little office, she could hardly refuse.

"Oh, wow, did Nina make this?" he asked, picking up the beautiful cupcake from the desk. "Do you mind? I'm starving."

Mazy's heart sank as Tad's teeth sank into the top of the perfect little purple flower. The frosting stuck to his lips for a moment before disappearing forever.

Determinedly, Mazy looked at her spreadsheet. "I

don't have the delinquent loan bundle completed. But I'm working on it."

Tad shrugged without concern as he swallowed another bite. "Next week is fine," he said. "I wanted to talk to you about Tru."

"Tru?"

"Yeah, Paul and Bo and I are taking our kids to the App State game in Boone this weekend. I thought Tru might like to come with us."

Mazy looked at Tad in complete disbelief.

"I'm sure he knows the other boys from school. If he doesn't, then it's a good opportunity to get acquainted. He'll have a great time and it'll give you a night off. I'm sure Latham will appreciate that."

"We're broken up," Mazy said, although at that particular moment her love life seemed the least of her concerns.

"Are you? Can't say I'm surprised. The guy is way too much milquetoast for my Mazy."

The phrase *my Mazy* was one from high school, and hearing it aloud evoked a strange sense of unease. She pushed that back, too. Her relationship with Tad was not the important issue, either.

"You're thinking to take Tru somewhere with your daughters?"

"What? The girls? No, the girls won't be there. This is a guys thing."

"You said 'taking our kids.'"

"I meant Tru, of course."

"Tad, Tru doesn't know you're his father. You didn't want me to tell him and I haven't."

"Well, I'm rethinking that," Tad told her. "Not about you. It's probably good that he doesn't hear it from you. When I think the time is right, I'll tell him myself."

"I'm not sure that's the best idea," she told him. "He's actually said that he didn't want to know."

"He has to know," Tad said. "It's such a small town, it's bound to come out. Best to hear it from us."

Us wasn't a word Mazy was that sure about. And she was experiencing a certain amount of whiplash from Tad's previous position on the subject.

"He's not a little kid you need to protect anymore," Tad said. "He's practically grown."

"He's tall, not grown," Mazy protested. "He's only fourteen. And needs as much protection as any child."

Tad waved away her concern. "Moms always think that," he said. "I'll tell him myself. It would probably be better for him hearing it man-to-man, anyway."

"No!"

Mazy's response was a little louder than she'd intended. She immediately quieted to nearly a whisper. "Please don't say anything to him until I talk to him. Please."

"Okay, okay," Tad told her. He patted her knee as if to offer reassurance. "I won't say a thing. But I'd still like to take him to the game."

"I'm not sure that's a good idea."

"Ask him. I'll make sure he has a good time," Tad said. "He's practically a grown-up guy. And guys need to hang out with guys."

Picturing the scenario of Tru hanging out with a bunch of good old boys and their sons made Mazy kind of queasy. She remembered the guys Tad used to run with. She tried reassuring herself that Tad had changed. Maybe they all had changed.

She'd agreed to meet Karly for coffee after work, though she'd been thinking up several excuses to bow out and go home. Between concern for Tru and sadness about Eli, she knew she wouldn't be very good company. But when the time came, she showed up.

They sat at their usual window-side table and Charlie eagerly served them their beverages in their personal mugs. The scent of fresh paint was still noticeable when Mazy walked in the door, but it was easily overpowered by the aroma of coffee when it was under her nose.

"I like the color on the walls better than I thought I would," Karly told her.

Mazy nodded. "It lightens the place a lot. The wood was pretty, but it really made the room seem small and dark. This is nicer. It's more of a family feeling place."

Karly agreed.

When Mazy heaved a huge sigh, Karly looked at her questioningly. "What's up?"

"What? Oh, nothing. The idea of family. I guess it always makes me sigh."

Karly's brow wrinkled. "Why is that?" she asked. "When I think 'family' I want to pull my hair out, but then I've got two rambunctious boys."

Mazy smiled at her. "Enjoy it while you can. They'll be grown up and in high school before you know it."

"True, but still not a reason to sigh."

She looked over at Karly. She had been a good friend to her these past couple of months. Mazy was grateful.

"Eli and I broke up," she said.

Karly heaved a big sigh of her own. "I was afraid that was going to happen," she said. "Che and I were both blown away that a guy like Eli would treat you that way."

"I know. It's not what you'd expect," Mazy said. "It's not what I'd expect. And this is not the first jerk move he's made. I've come up with a lot of excuses for him lately. Deep down, he's a good guy. He's good to my mom. He's good to Tru. But he's not good to me. Not anymore."

"It is really about the strangest thing I've ever heard," Karly said.

Mazy nodded. "I'm not sure what happened," she said. "But maybe it's not all that strange. Remember my shrink back in Wilmington? She told me that I sought men who subconsciously I knew would reject me."

"Yeah."

"Well, maybe it's gotten worse than that," Mazy said. "Maybe I'm creating the behavior that I've been blaming men for."

"Creating it? How on earth could you do that?"

"I don't know, but look at the evidence," Mazy said. "Everybody in town would say that Eli is a great guy. But when he has a relationship with me, he turns into a creep. That can't be an accident. I'm somehow turning him into a man who rejects me."

Karly shook her head. "I'm not sure I buy this whole scenario that this psychologist came up with. My father was a mean, angry drunk who walked out on our family and never looked back," she pointed out. "And Che and I have managed to be pretty dadgum happy."

Mazy smiled at her. "Well, you are obviously a whole lot more emotionally healthy than I am," she said. "But I'm working on it. I'm trying to get better."

Karly reached across the table and squeezed Mazy's hand. "You are a good person, Mazy," she said. "You were good to me in high school when it would have been smarter, socially, to keep your distance. You've been good to the people of this town when it would have been easy to exact some payback. You deserve to be loved and you deserve to be happy."

"Thanks."

"I really thought that maybe Eli was Mr. Right. I can't understand how he got to be so Mr. Wrong."

"Yeah, it's been hard for me to get my head around, too," Mazy said. "I thought it could be different for me if I steered clear of the smooth-talking players who typically treat me like this. But Eli is not one of those men. So…so I must encourage this behavior somehow. It's like that question 'Which came first, the chicken or the egg?' But somehow I've got to break that pattern."

"Well, you don't break it by blaming yourself," Karly said.

"You're right," she agreed. "That's what the old Mazy would have done—believe that it had to be something *she* did wrong and go running to him with an apology."

"Oh, yeah," Karly said facetiously. "Like there is any way that his running out on you at the roadhouse could be your fault."

"Actually, that's exactly what he said."

"Really?"

"He said it was a deliberate payback."

"For what?"

"He's got some crazy idea that Tad and I are seeing each other or interested in each other or something."

Karly, who had been raising the coffee mug to her mouth, stopped abruptly and looked over at Mazy, her eyes wide with concern.

"You're not, are you?"

"No, of course not," Mazy said.

"Thank God," Karly said.

"But I don't want you or Eli or anyone to continue to blame him for what happened with me," Mazy said. "Having Tru was the best thing I did in my life."

"He's a great kid," Karly agreed. "And Driscoll keeping his distance probably turned out to be a blessing."

"We've all made mistakes," Mazy said. "Honestly, compared to how Eli is behaving, Tad's looking like the good guy lately."

Karly shook her head. "No. Don't even go there," she said. "Driscoll is dangerous. And he's had it in for you forever."

Mazy waved that away. "That's all so long ago," she said. "He's changed."

Karly shook her head. "The only thing that's changed about him is that he's more conniving than he used to be. I do believe that people can change. That we aren't defined forever by the mistakes we made in the past. But I'm not sure that our basic personality gets altered. You were the girl you were before your father died. I think it's not only possible but likely that you'll be more like that girl again. Driscoll has been a user all his life. He preys on vulnerable people. I don't know if he could change. And even if he could, would he?"

"Good grief, Karly. That's a hefty verdict based on some clothespins in elementary school." Mazy gave a slight chuckle. "It almost sounds like you had as much trouble with him as I did."

Mazy meant the statement as a joke, but the look in Karly's eyes said otherwise.

"Oh, my God."

Karly took a sip of her coffee. She set it down in a careful, deliberate motion and took a deep breath.

"After you left school," she said, "things were very strange for me. Nobody talked to me. Nobody noticed me. One day Tad did. He started coming to see me at work. He told me sad, sad tales of how he and Genna were for sure breaking up over the baby you were carrying. He assured me with such sincerity that it wasn't his. We started seeing each other on the sly."

Mazy felt strangely cognizant. As if she were watching the events take place right before her eyes.

"You remember the story about Che picking me up on the side of the road?"

"Yeah."

"He wasn't just picking me up. He was rescuing me. Tad had invited me to a party. We had never gone out in public before and I thought that it meant that he was completely done with Genna and I was his new girlfriend. I spent a month's worth of my Brandt Burger salary on that tulle dress. As it turned out, it wasn't really appropriate for the party happening down on a sandbar at Harkin Lake. There were about a dozen people there. I was the only girl."

"Oh, no."

"I knew what it was and I was scared. Tad just laughed at my fear. He asked me why I thought any guy would be interested in me for anything else."

"Oh, Karly, I'm so sorry."

"I ran away from them. He let me go. Or maybe he thought I'd come back when I realized I was on foot, at night, twenty miles from home. When Che stopped, I thought he was one of them. When he figured out what happened to me, and once I figured out that he wasn't a part of it…well, he turned out to be a knight in shining armor, although he was on an Indian motorcycle instead of a white horse."

"I liked him before," Mazy said. "I like him even better now."

Karly nodded. "I'm lucky," she said. "I know that. And I know how capable Driscoll is of winning people over, even those who have good reason not to trust him. Please, be careful."

42

<hr/>

Eli was getting a lot of work done. Attaching the small pieces of veneer was a slow, painstaking task. More important than the glue and razor knife was a sharp focus, an attention to detail and plenty of time. The first two Eli found himself struggling to achieve. The latter he managed to have in spades.

With his dad visiting with them in the shop most days and Clark helping out more and more, Eli suddenly found a glut of time on his hands. Hours and hours of alone time that he no longer knew how to fill. Hours and hours that he wanted to spend with Mazy but couldn't.

He should have had a backup plan. He'd been so sure that she had fallen in love with him. He had been so perfectly horrible, that she couldn't have helped herself. Yet, she had walked away. At the very last minute when it felt like it was too late, she had finally realized that she deserved better.

What was he supposed to do about that? As one week turned into two and there was nothing from next door but complete silence, he was at a loss as to what should be his next move.

At night he scoured the online blogs. His enthusiasm for reading the bad-boyfriend stories had completely vanished. It was no longer wild or crazy or even interesting. Eli wondered how he ever saw it as anything but pathetic. But now he needed answers about how to turn it all around.

Surely one of these couples made it. The gal stopped venting online and started making demands. The guy cleaned up his act and proved he could change. That's how he'd assumed it worked. But the more he read, he realized that either that never happened or, if it did, people simply stopped commenting.

Eli waited. He watched her house. He paced his floor.

"I don't understand it," he told his father. "It seemed like such a smart plan. But it's turned me into the biggest idiot on the planet."

His dad's expression never changed, but somehow Eli felt he was saying, "I told you so."

Finally, in desperation, he tried calling one night. Mazy didn't pick up on her cell, so he tried Beth Ann's house phone. As soon as she heard his voice she hung up.

The next day he went down to Peggy's Flowers and had a vase of peach roses and purple asters sent to her office. On the note he wrote simply, "I'm sorry."

There was no response. Not even a chilly "thank you."

He also noticed that Tru had gone quiet.

At first the teen had not seemed bothered.

"You and my mom are on the outs?"

It was more of a statement than a question.

Eli had shrugged. No matter how tempting it was, he was not about to drag Tru into the dysfunction of their love life. The kid had enough to deal with—new town, new school, new job. He sure didn't need the stress of two crazy people trying to find happiness together.

But a few days later the sudden silence settled in. One afternoon, out of the blue, he came to work and didn't really speak to anyone. He responded if someone spoke to him. He would chuckle at Clark's stupid jokes. They'd started bringing Jonah down to the shop. Tru made a point to always greet him. Tru swept the floor, put up the tools. He continued to fetch and carry, lend a hand whenever requested. He calmly and cooperatively did whatever was demanded. But there was a stillness, an almost secretiveness, that was new. And it was worrying.

At any other time, Eli would have asked him what was wrong. Now he feared the boy's answer. It was likely that Tru had realized that he and Mazy were done for. The kid had probably got his hopes up, just as Eli had. Now he was grieving.

Eli wanted to take him aside and assure him that it would all be fine. He wouldn't let Mazy go this time. He would do whatever it took to win her back. But "doing what it took" had been his whole strategy for the past two and a half months. He no longer knew what it would take. And it scared him to think that maybe there was nothing.

Clark had made the deal with Charlie McDee to rent the upper floor of his building for storage and showroom. The space was large enough to allow each piece to be shown to best advantage. Which made it a lot more likely to get sold.

They were in the middle of their final load when Tru showed up for work. He immediately put his back into helping to move furniture into the truck. When it was all carefully covered and strapped down, Eli motioned him into the truck.

"Let's go."

"Can I...can I talk to you for a minute?" Tru asked.

Eli couldn't avoid it any longer. The poor kid was hurting. He could have put him off. They needed to get this furniture down to Main Street and unloaded before dark. But some things were even more important than schedules.

"Clark, why don't you drive the truck," he said. "Go get yourself a cup of coffee or something. Tru and I will walk."

His brother glanced back, but didn't question him. He climbed into the driver's seat and started up the truck.

As it headed down the driveway, Eli and Tru followed on foot. The day was crisp and almost still. The bright sun overhead made it seem warmer than it felt.

Tru had his hands stuffed in his pockets and was staring straight ahead as they walked in the empty street up Sawmill Road.

Tru had asked to talk, but he now seemed hesitant. Eli wanted to get it started, get it over. He didn't know yet how much he could explain about what had gone wrong between Mazy and himself. There wasn't that much that a kid really needed to know about how grown-ups organized their private lives. The only thing Eli knew that he truly had to convey was that he cared about Tru. And that Tru could always trust him.

The trees along the street had dropped their leaves, the remnants bunched in piles here and there. The empty branches exposed every burl and wound. The oaks and maples, all beautifully adorned the rest of the year, were no more than naked wood in winter. That honesty somehow inspired candidness in humans within their meager shade.

"Okay, so you want to talk?" Eli asked.

For a second he thought the boy might stick with silence. Then after a hesitation, Tru heaved a huge sigh. The kid's shoulders slumped as if the weight of the world were upon them.

"I…I gotta talk to somebody," he told Eli. "I'm going

crazy. I go over it and over it in my brain and I…I don't know."

Clearly, this was going to be hard for both of them. Eli screwed up his own courage.

"I want to assure you," he said. "That no matter what's going on with me and Mazy, I am still your friend and you can talk to me."

Tru took a deep breath. "It's about my father."

Eli was so surprised that he momentarily stopped to stand still in the street.

"Your father?"

"Tad Driscoll. Did you know he's my father?"

After an instant of hesitation, Eli nodded and they began walking again.

"Yeah, of course you know," Tru said. "Everybody knows. That's what he told me."

"He?"

"Tad Driscoll. My father. He told me that he's my father."

Eli had to shut his mouth. He also had to bite his tongue. *What the devil was Driscoll up to?*

"He decided that I needed to know," Tru explained. "He said that Mom believed I'm too young to understand. But if I don't know, I look like a fool."

"Under no circumstances would anything not under your own control make you look like a fool," Eli told him.

"He says that Mom still thinks I'm her little baby," Tru said. "She thinks I can't own up to my own heritage, my own position in the town."

"Your position in the town?"

"Yeah, you know, being a part of the most prominent family in town. Being a Driscoll."

Eli felt slightly nauseated.

"If I'm going to live in Brandt Mountain, or really any

of the western North Carolina counties, I should start thinking of myself as a Driscoll."

Eli clenched his fists tightly and then released them as he got a grip on his initial reaction.

"Truman Gulliver is a fine name," he said with deliberate calm. "I remember your grandfather. Any fellow would be proud to be named for him."

Tru nodded. "Mom and Gram really loved him and I know they named me for him because they love me."

"Absolutely."

"He…my father said that if I wanted to pursue a name change, to be a Driscoll instead of a Gulliver, he would pay for it."

"He would, huh?"

"Yeah, he said that he would be proud." Tru smiled at that. "Imagine. My father. Being proud of me."

"Any father would be proud of you."

"Thanks." The smile faded as the confusion returned. "It's all so different from how I thought it would be," he said. "I always thought that if I met my father, I'd punch his lights out. How dare he desert my mother! How dare he refuse to claim me! What an asshole, right?"

"Right."

"But then I meet him and, you know, he's nice. He said that he'd always wanted a son and when he saw me, he realized that he had one."

"It's unfortunate that he didn't realize it earlier," Eli said stiffly.

Tru nodded. "He told me how it was back then. Back when it all went down. Before I was born. He had a girlfriend that he was in love with. And then there was my mom, who was so crazy and she was, like, putting out for guys."

"Putting out for *guys?*"

"He didn't say it that way, but that's what he meant. She liked him *that way* and she was available to him. Stuff happens."

"Yes, stuff does happen," Eli said. "But it doesn't always happen the way people remember it. Mazy was very young and naive and Driscoll was…he was a cad."

Tru shrugged. "Sometimes guys are like that," he said. "I heard about you dumping Mom at the roadhouse. Uh, wow. That was cold."

The truth caught Eli off guard. He could hardly argue against it.

They reached Main Street, stepped up onto the wide sidewalk and continued their uphill trek.

"So, anyway, I've been seeing him a little and we've been texting, but my mom doesn't know. And that feels weird."

"You don't feel comfortable telling her?"

"He asked me not to."

"Why would he do that?"

"He's afraid she'll get all freaked out and run away with me like she did before."

"She didn't run away with you," Eli said very carefully. "Mazy was getting on with her life. Driscoll didn't choose to be a part of that."

Tru nodded slowly. "I know that he's not seeing it quite the same way that Mom sees it. But it's not like both of them can't be a little bit right and a little bit wrong."

Eli wanted to state unequivocally that in this instance Mazy was one hundred percent right and Driscoll was totally wrong, but he could see that Tru was confused and trying really hard to make sense of the whole situation.

"You remember that support group I told you about?"

Eli nodded.

"One of the things that we talked most about was kind

of getting past the bad things that our parents had done," Tru said. "We all wish that things had been different. But they weren't and there's no fixing that. The future, though, doesn't have to look like the past. We've got to be willing to hope, even if our experience warns us that our parents may be hopeless."

What kind of teen support group was this? Eli wondered again.

"That's how I get my head around you and Mom," Tru continued. "Everything I know about Mom and men tells me that you're just the newest guy passing through. But I *choose* to hope that she's ready to be with somebody who's decent enough to love her back."

"And if that doesn't…doesn't happen?"

Tru shrugged. "Disappointment isn't easier just because you expected it all along."

The kid was right about that. But Eli was certain that Tru was wrong about Driscoll. There was too much past behavior for Eli to give him any benefit of the doubt.

He started to tell Tru exactly that. Then he remembered what Mazy had said to him. *A person deserves to believe that they were conceived in love, even if it was only love of the moment.* Eli was sure there had been love, at least on Mazy's side. She'd told him that children need to have a good opinion of both their parents, no matter what the two thought of each other. Each of us is half of two people. It's not fair to teach someone to hate half of himself.

Eli bit his tongue on the truth about Tad Driscoll, although he was absolutely certain that Driscoll would have no such compunction. The creep had never had a problem portraying Mazy as the villain. He had done it before, to basically the whole town. He wouldn't hesitate with Tru or with anyone to do it again to get whatever he wanted. But what on earth could he want?

Tru answered the question that Eli hadn't even asked. "He…my father…he wants to spend more time with me. He wants us to do things together." Tru eyes brightened at that. "I guess like it used to be with you and your dad, huh? He said that he asked Mom. That he really tried to persuade her to let him be a part of my life. She wouldn't go for it. He thinks she might still be holding a grudge."

"You know your mother, Tru. Does she hold grudges?"

The teenager hardly hesitated. "No, she really doesn't," he admitted. "But I'm certain she would never grant my father any custody or visitation rights."

"Custody? Visitation? Driscoll talked about that?"

"Yeah. He says that Mom has already controlled the situation long enough. We can go to a judge and I can ask for time with him."

Eli didn't like the sound of that at all.

"He says he knows the county judge. They were friends in high school and he knows the whole story already."

Eli knew the county judge, as well. Bo Spalding had been one of Driscoll's crew back in the day, and one of several who had spread lies suggesting Mazy's promiscuity.

"There is still a lot more to it than a couple of old buddies making a deal in court."

Tru's brow furrowed. "I kind of wondered about that myself," he said. "And I feel bad talking about something so big, making plans for stuff we're going to do and keeping it a secret. Mom would definitely want to know. And he…my father shouldn't ask me to keep it from her. Mom and I, we've always been a team. And she's always shared…she's shared some really bad stuff with me, even when she didn't want to. Some of those talks were really hard for her. And I didn't always make it easy. If feels wrong to be going behind her back."

"It feels wrong because it is wrong," Eli said. "You've got to tell her."

"Do you think she'll be mad at me? I mean, I should have told her right away. Will she be mad about that?"

"I don't know," Eli said. "I don't think so, but she might. That doesn't mean that you don't do it. It's a big part of being a man to own up to your mistakes even when you know it's going to bring trouble down on your head."

Tru took a deep breath before nodding agreement. "Thanks, Eli, I knew I could count on you."

43

Mazy had been successfully avoiding Eli. As long as she kept her distance, she reassured herself, her feelings for him would lessen. That's what always happened. The breakup would be intense and painful and the world would feel cold and hollow. Then slowly, slowly, one foot in front of the other, she would move on. Life would begin to shine once more. She would recognize that the man was wrong for her. She would take heart that someday she could, she would, love again.

Seated in her tiny office, the copy machine droned behind her providing welcome white noise that couldn't quite obscure the thoughts in her own head.

Mazy had ignored Eli's existence. She'd refused to take his calls. She'd given the flowers he'd sent to the Mountain View Nursing Home. But she couldn't stop thinking about him. She'd gotten used to talking to him, sharing with him.

He was just a habit, she assured herself. One that would be broken.

Typically when a romance went sour, she would move across town or to another town. She'd start her life over someplace where she would never run into the guy again. That wouldn't happen this time. The same reasons that had brought her home kept her here. She had to put in the time to reestablish herself. And her son deserved to get through high school without another move.

The thought of Tru had her determination melting into sadness. She regretted allowing him to get so close to Eli. She knew he was hurting. In all the ins and outs of the relationships she'd had, Tru had stayed disconnected. He'd been, at best, neutral when it came to the men in his mom's life. But she knew he liked Eli. And she surmised that his personal relationship with him was the cause of his current silence. He was appropriately responsive, agreeable and obedient. But an unfamiliar silence had settled in on him. He was holding something back. She feared that it was an attachment to Eli and a disappointment in her latest romantic failure.

Mazy hated that for Tru. But it couldn't be helped. No one was going to drive her away, force her to abandon her goals or make her feel uncomfortable. She had done nothing wrong. Except to be lured in by the same dysfunctional pattern that had kept her from being her best self thus far.

She knew, of course, that in a small place like Brandt Mountain, they would at times be thrown together. But she hadn't really expected that a family occasion like Thanksgiving would be one of those times. She couldn't really see any way to get out of it. Her mother was planning the meal.

She tried to rephrase and repurpose. Eventually she would have to face Eli again. What better time to do that than amid friendly faces and family.

That made her feel a bit better. She tried to hang on to it.

Mazy stared determinedly at the file on her screen as she leafed through the paperwork on her desk. With the holiday only days away, Mazy knew she had to finalize the list of uncollectable debt being bundled and sold. She was, for all intents and purposes, finished. She had gone over the particulars again and again. She had spoken with all the parties involved. The action would not be a surprise to any of them, although bad news was always jarring no matter how expected it happened to be.

The only thing left was to add Nina Garvey's loan to the list.

Something about the paperwork continued to nag her. Something about the file felt wrong, but she couldn't put her finger on it.

Mentally she scolded herself. Shame on her for allowing herself to get too involved. Banking, especially this kind of banking, required impartiality. No one should get a break just because she liked them or worried about them. That wasn't merely bank policy, it was basic fairness.

Of course, she thought unkindly, Tad had made some allowances for *his* friends. But that was his decision that he had to live with. Mazy lived with her own decisions and this one was clear-cut—favoritism was wrong. She liked Nina. She felt sorry for the raw deal her crappy husband had left her. And she wished that she could help. That's what kept her, day after day, checking and rechecking numbers that she already knew were accurate.

It was time to bite the bullet and turn in the list.

Mazy sighed heavily.

Behind her came a chuckle as Deandra came in to unload her collated copies from the machine.

"You sound like me viewing the kitchen after my hubby decided to cook dinner as my anniversary gift."

"Sorry," Mazy apologized.

"I was, too," she teased.

Mazy smiled.

"Hey, we all have those days," Deandra said. "In your job, there may be more of them than for the rest of us. Tomorrow we start over and do it all again."

Mazy nodded stoically as she scooted the mouse until the cursor was at the edge of the file. She clicked to shrink it and then dragged it across to add to the debt bundle folder.

There, it was done.

She leaned back in her chair. She didn't feel one bit better. There was something, *something,* that was a little bit off.

"Deandra," she said. "You handled the Garvey file, right?"

"Sure did."

"Did it ever feel like to you that something was missing there?"

"Missing?" The woman was thoughtful for a long moment. "No, I think everything always seemed okay. Except for having to deal with Wesley Garvey. He was such a slimeball."

Mazy couldn't speak to that, but she'd heard a lot about the guy, and none of it was good.

"Nina's nice, though."

"Yeah, I don't really know her," Deandra said. "I've seen her around town, though. She's looks real sweet, but I've never talked to her."

Mazy was surprised at that. "You never discussed the loan?"

"No, actually, I never did," she answered. "I always dealt with Wesley Garvey. And the day after he died Mr. Driscoll took the account from me. He said he would handle it personally."

"Tad handled it?"

Deandra cleared her throat before giving a warning

nod toward the empty doorway. "Yes, *Mr. Driscoll* handled that loan."

"His initials aren't on it anywhere," Mazy said, thumbing back through the pages in case she'd missed it.

Deandra shrugged. "I don't know about that," she said. "I haven't seen it since the morning that Garvey wrecked."

The woman gathered up the last of her copies and left the room. Mazy sat staring at her computer screen. In the back of her mind, snippets of past conversations played in her head.

He showed up at my house the day of the funeral.

I've been scared to come to the bank.

I'm so glad that it's you handling my loan and nobody else.

Ordinary statements that had gone unnoticed when they were spoken.

Karly's words came back to her, as well. *Driscoll has been a user all his life. He preys on vulnerable people. I don't know if he could change. And even if he could, would he?*

Mazy clicked open the debt bundle folder. She dragged Nina's file out once again and opened it up. There was something…something. She knew it. She just had to find it.

44

They got the last of the furniture to the second floor with not so much as a scratch on any of it. It was an accomplishment, but Eli's upbeat, cheerful mood was completely fake. Inside his head, he was mad enough to spit. The image of Tad Driscoll cozying up to Tru like a father made him sick to his stomach.

He kept up the calm demeanor through the unloading, the trip home, the closing of the shop. Once Clark had driven off and Tru was walking home, the pleasant mask he'd been wearing slipped into a steel-jawed anger. He was in love with Mazy. And Tru was a terrifically decent kid. It was like watching a traffic accident happen and being powerless to do anything about it.

He went up to see his dad. As soon as Ida stepped out of the room, it all poured out of him like a flood of fury, incredulity and despair. "I've got to do something," he told Jonah. "But I don't have any idea what."

Eli felt like moaning aloud. He hated feeling so powerless. A glance toward his dad put that in perspective. His father had physical use of only one arm and somehow he still managed to make a positive impact on people's lives.

"I should get you to bed," Eli told him.

He got Jonah to his feet and, with his good arm around his shoulder, walked him to the makeshift bedroom.

"I can't say anything to Mazy. That's something Tru has to do himself," Eli said. "Of course, I probably couldn't tell her, anyway, since she's not exactly talking to me right now."

He sighed heavily at that thought. "She needs to hear it from Tru. And once Mazy knows what's going on, she'll straighten out Driscoll once and for all."

He lowered Jonah to a sitting position on the side of the bed.

"At least I hope she'd be as mad about it as I am. I could be wrong about that." He hesitated a moment, considering it. "She always wanted Driscoll to acknowledge Tru," he said. "And she'd thought that by having his child, Tad would take her, as well. Maybe she still wants that. She says no. But on some level…"

Eli retrieved his father's pajamas as he considered that thought. "She does, after all, continue to work for the guy. Everybody says he's the worst boss in town. And she's told me herself that he's treated her like a jerk. But she won't even consider looking for anything else. That should tell me something, right? She says she deserves better. She tells me that she's changed. But can I trust that? Can I believe that she's not tempted when she's thrown into his path every day of the week?"

Eli growled like an old bear before he began undoing the buttons on his father's shirt.

"Driscoll won't marry her," Eli said. "I'd bet my life on that. Why else would he be talking custody and visitation? No, he's going to want to do what he's always done. Get the best of Mazy and leave her with a big heartbreak. And she'll let him."

Eli knelt at his father's feet and began removing his shoes.

"No, I've got to have more faith in her than that," Eli

said. "Believing that I knew what she was like and how she would react has not paid off big for me. Maybe I was simply doomed to unrequited love. Maybe it could never be anything on her side more than good laughs and great sex." Eli sighed. "It's a shame that I was too greedy to settle for that."

He wrapped his arms around Jonah's waist, raising him to his feet so he could finish dressing him for bed.

"But you know, Dad, if she kicked *me* to the curb for being a jerk, then she can do the same to Driscoll. I have to trust her to do that."

He eased his father back onto the bed, lifting his legs to lay them against the sheet.

"But none of that logic makes me one bit less mad," he admitted. "When I think of Tru 'taking his place in the community as a Driscoll,' I want to choke somebody. Jeez! Truman Gulliver would come barreling out of his grave in retribution."

Eli pulled the covers up on his father and knelt at the bedside, but there was nothing prayerful about his thoughts.

"Back in high school when everybody found out that Mazy was pregnant and Driscoll and his buddies were spreading all those lies about her, I wanted to beat him to a pulp. Do you remember that? You told me that the two of them needed the chance to work it out on their own. You were right, but I still wanted a fight. He was probably twice my size, but I didn't care. I needed a pound of flesh, even if it was my own." Eli looked over at his dad's face. Jonah's eyes were watching him intently. "I feel exactly the same way now. I know that letting Mazy handle it is the right thing to do. It's the civilized thing to do. It's what she would want me to do. But I'd still like to the wipe the floor with that son of a bitch."

Eli rubbed his eyes with his hands as if he could rub out the images in his own mind. When he felt his father clasp his wrist, he didn't resist. His father was undoubtedly tired. Eli had been talking forever. The old man needed his rest. And this was, Eli assumed, his father's usual gesture of love. Jonah would take Eli's hand and carry it to his own heart.

His father surprised him. Instead of bringing Eli's hand to his heart, he set it palm up on his chest. Jonah put his own hand on top and then slowly drew it into a tight fist.

Eli looked from the fist to his father's eyes, shining with cold, stark anger.

Slowly Eli smiled. "Absolutely," he said. "At least one punch will be for you."

45

Mazy found it a few minutes after four. Or rather she *didn't* find it. She finally realized that amid the giant stack of papers, the original agreement, the payment record, the insurance coverage and cancellation, the past-due notices, the death certificate, the adjuster's declaration of total loss, one important slip of paper was not there.

At first, she couldn't quite believe it.

She went through everything, page by page, making sure it wasn't stuck to another sheet or tucked behind something else. Then she went through the scenarios where perhaps it could have been lost. Mazy read through page after page after page, but there was no evidence of its existence at any time, ever.

Lyda McKirk stopped at her doorway. "Hey, you know your shift ended a half hour ago, right?"

Mazy smiled. "I'm almost done."

Finally she picked up the phone and called Nina. They talked for several minutes. Mazy mostly asked questions and took notes on the answers.

"All right, Mrs. Garvey. Thank you for this information," she said in her most professional tone. "I believe that's all I need right now. May I call you later on this evening? Will you be at home?"

Nina was a bit disconcerted by the tone, but agreed that Mazy could phone her later.

She leaned back in her chair and closed her eyes. Slowly a smile came across her face. "Do I have the best job in the world?" she said aloud. And then she laughed at her own skewed view of the career that she had once described to herself as *the worst, most depressing job in banking*.

Some people might say that the hard part was still ahead of her, but in fact, she thought she might actually relish this task.

Mazy got up from her desk and walked out of her tiny, closed-off little room and across the brightly polished floor of the lobby.

Tad was coming out of his office. He was wearing his coat and carrying his briefcase.

Mazy pointed to the door that he had just walked through.

"I'll see you in your office for a moment, Mr. Driscoll."

He looked wary. "I was on my way out. Can it wait until tomorrow?"

"No. It cannot."

She led him back into his own lair. He angrily set his briefcase on the desk and tossed his coat in the chair. He turned to glare at her.

Mazy was not intimidated. She looked at him as the worm that she had already known him to be.

His face fell and he cursed vividly. "You found out, didn't you," he said.

"You knew that I would," Mazy answered calmly. "You only hoped it would be too late for me to do anything about it."

Tad shook his head. "I worried that I couldn't trust the kid, but I hoped that I was wrong."

Mazy thought it was very strange that Tad would call Nina Garvey a kid. She was younger than they were, but she was a grown woman with a child.

Tad had begun to pace the room. His expression was grim as he strode back and forth "I don't know what you think you can do about it," he told her. "You seem to forget that I have the upper hand here."

"You mean, by being my boss?" she asked incredulously.

"Oh, that." He waved off the question. "I'll tell the judge I didn't know about your past when I hired you. It's your word against mine and *you* are the convicted thief and liar."

"The judge? You're thinking of taking this in front of a judge?"

"You're damn right, I am," he answered.

"What do you think that will get you?" she asked. "The rules are very straightforward about this kind of thing."

"The rules? You think there are *rules* in child custody? It's strictly dog-eat-dog."

"Child custody?"

The bottom went out of Mazy's stomach. She tried to keep the shock from showing on her face.

"I've already talked to Bo," he said snidely. "You remember Bo Spalding? He's now a county judge and he says that I've got you right where I want you."

"What?"

"You're a convicted felon," Tad pointed out. "I'm a pillar of the community. And you have no idea how a good lawyer can twist your whole life into something awful. You're halfway there already. I'd say you'll be lucky if you don't get a ride out of town on a rail."

Mazy concentrated on controlling her breathing. Fight-

or-flight hormones were flooding through her nervous system, but she knew she had to resist the urge to panic.

"The kid likes me," he said, like a bragger's boast. "After you probably spent the past fifteen years poisoning his mind against me, I was able to turn him in one short conversation."

Tad had been talking to Tru. A wave of nausea was added to the almost overpowering fear that was dogging her.

"He's too soft, of course," Tad complained. "Pussy-raised boys always are. But I can get that out of him. Once he spends some time around some real guys. Guys who are not being nice to him because they're screwing his mother. Ones who recognize and have respect for a winner when they see one. He's got that blood in him. A natural superiority to the run-of-the-mill losers around here. He's a Driscoll. Tru Driscoll. Did he tell you that? We're having his name changed."

For one terrible, horrified moment, Mazy visualized her smart, funny, interesting son becoming the snarling, vindictive, egotist in front of her. Then, as quickly as the image came, it went.

Her son, Tru *Gulliver,* would never be this man. It was too early to say what he would make of his life, or what effects circumstance or tragedy might throw his way, but his character was already formed. He could improve on it or he could struggle against it, but it was already there, the foundation that everything else was built upon.

Tru's life with Mazy had been chaotic and riddled with his mother's mistakes, but she had loved him unconditionally. And she'd instilled in him the same sense of kindness, justice and fairness that Beth Ann and Truman Gulliver had taught her.

Poor Tad Driscoll could never know that or understand it.

Mazy raised her chin and kept her voice steady. "So this is why you've suddenly decided to be nice to me, to get to Tru."

"I thought it might be easier than an all-out war," Tad answered. "Although I have to admit pushing your face in the dirt has always been more fun than kissing up."

Mazy didn't doubt that at all.

"I was willing to pork you again, too, if it came to that." Tad gave a nasty chuckle. "I guess you'd have to do the humping while I held my nose."

Mazy ignored the crudeness of his words.

"Did you think I was interested in you?" he asked. "I wasn't even interested in you back in the day. You were easy and convenient. You were worthless trash back then. Now I guess you've upgraded to used garbage."

He apparently found his quip amusing, but his obvious anger somehow gave Mazy a better toehold on her own control.

Rephrase: Tad Driscoll has zero respect for you and never will.

Repurpose: If he wants to have a relationship with Tru, he'll have to swallow that disdain every day for the rest of his life. Otherwise, Tru will toss him out on his ear.

"What the hell are you smiling about?" Tad suddenly demanded.

Mazy hadn't realized that her feelings were showing in her face.

"Tad, honestly, you didn't need to go to all this trouble," she said softly. "I've always wanted you to have a relationship with Tru. Remember, I'm the one who begged and pleaded for you to see him." She gave what she hoped sounded like a contented sigh. "It's wonderful, really," she said. "After all this time and all the lies you spread about me, I'll be vindicated. I mean, anybody with eyes could see that you're his father, but changing his name to Driscoll. Finally, everyone in town will know—Mazy was right and Tad was lying."

The look on the man's face was priceless. Mazy could have laughed out loud, but she didn't.

"And, of course, there are all the practical aspects of Tru acquiring another parent with another income," she said. "I've been stuck living at my mother's house so that he doesn't have to move to another high school. From what you've said before, I know you're not keen on paying back child support, but even support going forward will be a big help toward moving to our own place. Though, if you're not thinking joint custody but full custody, then I'm free as a bird. With all my financial troubles, no judge will expect me to contribute to your bottom line. And I've been so worried about how I'll afford to send him to college. Tru's a good student. I'm sure he'll be able to get into an excellent university. Unfortunately, he's not quite good enough to get a ton of scholarships. So I guess you'll have to cough up those expenses. That or take out loans for whatever money he needs."

Driscoll's expression would have sat well on a cartoon character just hit on the head with an anvil.

"Really, Tad," she added. "There is no need for all this drama and clandestine scheming. I'm delighted with how things are working out. Welcome to the family."

Mazy walked toward the door and then turned back. "By the way, I discovered that Nina Garvey was never a cosigner on that loan for her husband's car. Not when the note was issued or afterward, when it got into trouble. She wasn't even listed on the insurance when he had it. So she's not liable for a dead man's debt. We'll be writing off the total amount to her deceased husband. And I sincerely hope that she won't be filing a complaint with the comptroller's office about our bank illegally harassing her for six months."

She stepped outside and quietly closed the door behind her.

46

$\blacktriangleright$ — $\blacktriangleleft$

Eli arrived at Driscoll's home before he did. He parked his truck at the curb and got out to walk around. There was a big moon, nearly full, that lit up the landscape. The air had turned very cold in the clear night. If he had any sense, Eli thought unkindly, he'd get back in the truck and turn on the heater. But he didn't want to be comfortable. The edginess was empowering and he wasn't willing to give it up.

He looked around Driscoll's place critically. The house had been in the family since pre–Civil War days. A structure that old required plenty of maintenance. Old Mrs. Driscoll had always kept the place up. She had used it for rounds and rounds of social occasions and the annual, grandiose Founder's Ball. Those lavish events had not survived her demise and the house had quickly ceased to be a showplace. But even Tad's ex-wife, Genna, had been willing to call a handyman or a gardener. Tad had allowed the place to fall into genuine neglect since she'd left him. The paint was peeling so badly, Eli could notice it in the dark. And the wide, elegant porch now listed slightly to one side. There were only dead weeds in the flower beds and they were at least three feet tall.

Eli wondered if Driscoll didn't notice how it looked. Or had he become so accustomed to having other people take care of things, it never occurred to him that no one else would.

As Eli leaned against the front fender, his hands in his pockets, he tried not to think about Mazy. That was impossible, he decided. It was like telling himself not to breathe. No, he corrected himself, it was worse than that. He could hold his breath. But he couldn't make his heart stop or his brain quit firing. Mazy was that elemental to him.

He thought about how Driscoll was manipulating her. Using psychological tricks to control another person was despicable.

Of course, Eli reminded himself, Driscoll was a despicable kind of guy. No one should expect anything else. Eli was not that kind of person, yet he'd used the same kind of emotionally underhanded deceit to get Mazy for himself. Even worse—unlike Driscoll, Eli actually loved Mazy. To do that to somebody that you *love* had to be the definition of vile. He was disgusted with his behavior. Even more so because, in all honesty, he'd kind of enjoyed it. Having the upper hand with Mazy had been a new experience. It had been fun. It had allowed him to strut around in smug arrogance at her expense. And there was, he was ashamed to admit, a bit of a revenge element to it, as well.

For the first time in weeks of sadness and desperation, Eli was glad that his plan hadn't worked. He was grateful that ultimately she walked out on his deplorable conduct. She didn't deserve to be treated that way. It was progress that she'd refused to accept it. And it gave him hope that in the future, she'd be strong enough to turn her back on other worthless, no-account men, as well.

Down the street a pair of headlights were coming in his direction. The car slowed as it passed Eli's truck.

Then the late-model Mercedes pulled into the driveway next to the house.

Eli pushed away from the truck and slowly, casually, walked toward the vehicle. The light in the car came on as it opened. Driscoll stepped out looking dapper and businesslike in a well-tailored overcoat.

"What are you doing here?" he demanded.

"Looking for you."

Driscoll held his arms out. "I guess you found me."

"I've been talking to Tru Gulliver," Eli said. "And I don't like what I'm hearing."

"You don't, huh?" Driscoll said. "Seems to me like it's none of your business."

"It is if I say it is."

Driscoll shook his head. "Nope. Doesn't work that way. The kid is my flesh and blood. You're just his mom's boyfriend. Oh, wait, didn't Mazy already dump you? I guess that means you're just…nothing."

"I'm Tru's friend," Eli told him. "And I have his best interests at heart. You don't qualify on either of those counts."

"You don't know anything about it," Driscoll said.

"I know you're going behind Mazy's back to talk to him. And I know that you're lying to him, that you're trying to prey on his youth and his trust. It's an amazingly crap thing to do to your own child, but it's your standard operating procedure, isn't it? First you fill them full of praise and affection. Then, when they're puffed up like that, you shade the truth. Not a lot, just a little. Hook them into believing something they know they shouldn't. Then you praise again, not quite as much as before. The lie that comes after, though, is bigger. Fondness and lying, admiration and deceit, jerking back and forth until they don't know if they're coming or going. It's a good game, Driscoll, but not one I intend to let you play with Tru."

Driscoll waved away his words. "I don't have time for this," he said, stepping past Eli as if he were not there.

"Well, you'd better take time," Eli said.

Driscoll turned and stared at him in jaw-dropped disbelief. "Or else what? You gonna teach me a lesson, Mr. Nice Guy?" He laughed. "Now that's rich. You probably think that she'll take you back if you try and grow a pair. But it ain't happening, bro. Mazy's already said okay."

"What?"

"She told me less than an hour ago. I can contact Tru anytime I want. See him whenever he's available."

"She would never do that."

"The woman does what I tell her. Always has, always will."

"I don't believe it," Eli said.

"That's because you don't know what I have on her," Driscoll answered. "I could ruin this town for her today, just like I did fifteen years ago."

Eli shook his head. "If you think I'm going to buy the sob story of you as the victim in her planned pregnancy…" Eli rolled his eyes. "I've got no sympathy for a guy who seduces vulnerable innocents. All of that crap went down a hundred years ago. Mazy is a different person. She's an honest, honorable person. The people in this town know that now."

"Honest? Honorable?" Driscoll said. "You'd better rethink that. Not all the crap she's involved in happened a hundred years ago. In fact, do you know why she left Wilmington? You don't, do you?"

"She lost her job."

"She lost her job, all right. That kind of thing happens

when you're not only screwing your married boss, but helping him embezzle from the company."

"No way."

"It's public record, Latham. Look it up. She pleaded guilty to fraud and conspiracy. She's on probation right now—not exactly ancient history. How do you think the folks in Brandt Mountain will go for that? There's not a judge or a jury anywhere in this town who won't side with me when they hear the truth."

Eli's first thought was that it couldn't be true. Driscoll hated Mazy and he was a known liar. This was another example. But even as he tried to rationalize it away, Eli suspected that it might fit with the facts. She never talked about what had happened in Wilmington. She never mentioned friends there or said anything about the place where she had lived so long. And then there was Tru's support group. Why would he be in a support group with teens whose parents were in jail or facing criminal charges if Tru weren't dealing with exactly the same issues?

"The yokels in this town, they don't go for cheats," Driscoll said. "If you're going to break the rules, you've got to cover it up a lot better than Mazy was ever able to." He gave a nasty chuckle. "Those ignorant hicks are going to be on my side. I'll be the hero for stepping in to sweep up my son and keep him from going down the drain with his trashy jailbird mother."

The image caused a snap of realization in Eli's mind. Nowhere in the scenario that Driscoll pictured was the very smart, very sensitive, very astute son that Mazy had raised. Tru would never stand idly by in some kind of war of words perpetrated against his mother. Tru already knew what she had done. And he had obviously forgiven her.

"You ought to thank me, Latham. I'm saving your biscuits here," Driscoll continued. "You're wasting your time chasing after her. Now you know the truth, so you can move on. Mazy Gulliver is a pathetic loser. She was born a loser and she will die a loser. Nothing about her is ever going to change."

"Oh, I don't know," Eli said. "Change is hard. But it's not impossible. By the way, I consider this my last official act as a complete jerk. It's called a sucker punch."

"What?"

The word had barely left Driscoll's mouth when Eli's balled fist connected with the side of his face. He staggered, nearly dropping to his knees. Eli would have left it at that. Driscoll, however, screeched in fury and came charging back. He threw two wild rights. The first caught Eli's collarbone. The second missed completely.

Eli buried the next blow in the middle of the banker's soft solar plexus. A woof of air escaped his lips and he doubled over. A swift upper cut caught Driscoll squarely in the nose and laid him out on the dead grass in his front yard.

Calmly, confidently, Eli walked back to his truck. His knuckles hurt but his spirits were high. He slid behind the steering wheel and glanced back toward the house in time to see Driscoll, on his hands and knees, crawling up the steps to his house.

Eli laughed out loud. Not being the nice guy had its moments. He would miss it.

47

⊶ ⊷

Snow began falling on the morning of Thanksgiving, although there was little chance that it would pile up enough to hide the rugged edges of winter in the mountains.

Beth Ann had been up since dawn, bustling around the kitchen with enthusiasm and energy and joy.

Yes, Mazy decided, her mother was joyful. As if the opportunity to prepare a giant holiday dinner was something that she'd been longing to do.

Mazy had been drafted as her mother's assistant. She'd chopped and stirred and kneaded as directed. The kitchen was hot and steamy. The aroma of roast turkey blended with the scent of orange zest collards and yeast bread. The pies were cooling, the gravy bubbling.

"Okay, I think the rolls are all we have left," Beth Ann announced. "Tru!" she called out toward the hallway. "We're ready for you to start carrying the food."

The teenager was already dressed in hat, coat and gloves. Beth Ann quickly sent him bounding out the door with a huge casserole dish of corn-bread dressing, and he seemed as happy as his grandmother.

Perhaps her mother's cheerfulness was contagious, Mazy thought. She was, herself, feeling very much that all was right with the world. And there was absolutely no explanation for that.

She was still a single parent on criminal probation, living with her mother, barely able to eke out a living while paying off court-ordered restitution. She might not even be able to do that if she lost her job, which was a genuine possibility. Tad hadn't spoken one word to her since that night in his office. But on Wednesday he'd held an impromptu office meeting where he had unexpectedly handed out one-hundred-dollar gift cards as "Thanksgiving bonuses." Mazy had been the only employee not to receive one. She'd almost laughed aloud. If that was the best he could do in retaliation, she'd scored even better than she'd thought.

Of course, there were still her personal demons to contend with, the threat of a custody challenge and facing the holiday season with another broken romance. Worse yet, she would be celebrating this particular holiday with her recent ex and his entire family. That should have given any reasonable woman a serious case of indigestion. But of course, Mazy thought to herself, she had never been a very reasonable woman.

She opened the oven and slid in the first tray of light bread.

Eli was a great guy. Everybody said so and she believed them. That said, he was a bad-news boyfriend and she was done with that. If they could get back to being casual friends, that would be wonderful. If they couldn't… then so be it. When she had come from Wilmington, that first day in her mother's house, she remembered thinking that she wanted Tru to have the experience of living in a happy home. He deserved that kind of life. She realized that she wanted that for herself, as well. And more than that—she deserved it.

Dr. Reese had once told her that grief can get a lot of people off track. And that children and teens dealing with loss are especially vulnerable to drugs and cutting and other self-destructive behaviors. She'd explained that longing for the lost loved one can lead youth into the camaraderie of gangs or the insatiable search for closeness that is promiscuity. Looking back on her life, Mazy was not as critical of herself as she once had been. She had made mistakes. And the worst of them long after she should have known better. But it was never too late for a new beginning. And she was thankful today that she still had that opportunity.

The back door opened. Tru stomped in, followed by Clark and Eli.

"Come in, come in," Beth Ann said. "Happy Thanksgiving."

The two men replied with greetings of their own.

Mazy's heart caught in her throat as she caught sight of Eli. It had been seventeen days. Not that she was counting. She'd almost convinced herself that he couldn't be half as gorgeous as she remembered. But he still looked very good to her.

Deliberately, she kept her demeanor calm and her nod polite. If there was ever to be any chance of friendship between them, she simply could not go weak in the knees just because he looked in her direction.

The next few minutes were a flurry of activity while turkey, cranberries, corn, collard greens, gravy and pies were transferred from Beth Ann's house to the one next door.

Finally Beth Ann herself pulled on her coat and headed out carrying a big bowl of turnips au gratin.

"That's it," Mazy said. "I'll be there as soon as these last rolls come out of the oven."

Alone with the silence remaining in the kitchen, Mazy bucked up her courage. Yes, Eli was gorgeous and sexy and she was still in love with him. That made her vulnerable. But being vulnerable was not the same as being defenseless. She was learning to be strong, she was learning not to settle for less than the kind of love she knew was out there, somewhere.

She was up on her toes attempting to retrieve the breadbasket from the top cabinet. Behind her the door opened with burst of cold air.

"Can I help?"

She turned to look at him, but didn't actually have to answer. Eli stepped up next to her and reached to grab the basket.

"Thanks."

They stood looking at each other for a long moment.

"How are you?" he asked finally.

"I'm good," she answered. "I'm very good."

Another uncomfortable moment lingered between them. If there was any chance that they might be friends again, Mazy knew this was probably it.

"I wanted to thank you," she said. "For advising Tru to talk to me about seeing Tad."

Eli let out a breath. "Oh, so he did talk to you. I'm glad."

"I appreciate that you encouraged him not to keep the secret," Mazy said. "He trusts you a lot. If you'd agreed with Tad that it was best to keep me in the dark, he would have gone with that. I'm grateful that you didn't. And I know that right now I'm probably not one of your favorite people...so—"

"You are," Eli interrupted. "You are always one of my favorite people."

They stood staring at each other. Mazy wasn't sure what to do with his words.

"Oh, the bread!" She rushed to the oven.

The private moment was completely absorbed by getting the rolls snug in their basket and safely next door to Thanksgiving dinner, where the atmosphere was all festive and family.

Sheila had outdone herself with setup and decoration. Mazy remembered the Latham china from when she was a girl. The dining room seemed completely transformed with the table sporting two extra leaves, making ample space for food and drink and ten people.

Jonah was seated at the head looking so much as he had in his days of vigor. Ida at the other end, clearly delighted to be sharing the feast. Clark and Shelia were in good spirits, and their girls were both bright-eyed and well behaved. Mazy saw her mother beaming with pride at the beautiful meal she'd created. And there was her son, Tru, at last in the bosom of a family, a real family, who loved him.

Mazy blinked back the sentimentality.

As the eldest son, Clark took it upon himself to say grace and his prayer was simple. Gratitude for all those seated together around the table. That was miracle enough.

It was easier to pass the plates than the serving dishes. So Mazy ended up being the one to spoon up green beans. When her own plate finally returned, it was heaped up with more food than she even thought possible to consume. But somehow, one bite at a time, she and everyone else ate their share. Eli and Clark took turns feeding their father. The old man seemed more interested in the people surrounding him than the food on the spoon. The conversation was lively and full of optimism.

If Mazy's gaze tended to return to where Eli was sitting, it was force of habit. If their eyes met again and again, it was lingering effects of a lost love affair. And if the sight of his smile still filled her with butterflies, it was an understandable reaction based on that desperately needy facet of her personality and lifetime of happily-ever-after hopes.

She was working on it. Baby steps. Day by day.

She still wanted to be loved. But she deserved a relationship based on honesty, respect and consideration. Mazy was no longer willing to accept any romance that was not a pairing of equals.

Ida had been past her prime when the right man with the right heart had finally arrived. Beth Ann had suffered having her other half ripped out of her life at a young age.

But both were luckier than Mazy to have known the real love of a true life partner. And now Mazy was determined never to settle for anything less.

Dessert was put off due to full bellies and lack of interest around the table. Since the major cleanup was still in Beth Ann's kitchen, getting the dishes scraped and in the dishwasher went pretty quickly. The dining room table was defrocked from its formal attire and turned into a giant setup for dominoes. Multiple boxes of the rectangular blocks were retrieved from the bottom drawer of the sideboard and spread out so any number could have a turn.

Tru was unfamiliar with the game, so he was given the honor of teaming up with Jonah. Mazy watched as the old man would signal which tile to play. His body might be weak, but his mind was quick enough to keep up the scoring pace.

Mazy felt a hand on her shoulder. She glanced up and her heart went thump.

"I've finished that piece I was working on," Eli said. "The music cabinet. I'd like to show it to you."

She glanced around the table. Everyone seemed intent upon the game. She wasn't sure if it was cowardice or self-preservation that urged her to refuse. Mazy pushed back against both. They were going to be neighbors. She wanted them to be friends.

"Sure," she said, turning her dominoes facedown and scooting them into the "boneyard."

The outside air was crisp and cold and the snow was still swirling. It caught on Eli's hair, giving Mazy a presumed glimpse of an older, wiser man decades in the future. Somehow that soothed the nerves that being alone with him seemed to encourage.

The wood shop was welcomingly warm. Mazy shrugged out of her jacket, which Eli hung on one of the hooks by the door. The windows to the outside were fogged up, giving a strange sense of privacy and isolation.

Only a few steps inside, Mazy saw the piece near the back of the building and gasped with appreciation. As she got closer, she felt almost a reverence for the work.

With obvious pride, Eli showed the details to her. On one level it was all practicality, with wide doors and drawers. It was sturdy, well made, useful. But the visual impact of it was pure art. The wood veneer was put together in a way that wood did not exist in nature, the grain scattering across the front in lines that were both seemingly random and beautifully part of a complete pattern.

Mazy ran her hand along the slick surface.

"It's amazing," she told Eli. "Wonderfully, wonderfully amazing."

He nodded, but his expression was almost melancholy. "I'm never doing anything like this again."

"I'm sure it was a lot of work, it must have taken a lot of time."

"It's not the time or the work," he said. "It's you."

"Me?"

"I told you, I don't do veneers. I make things out of plain wood. I make beautiful things out of plain wood."

"Yeah."

"I'm a plain-wood kind of guy."

Eli was looking at her as if he expected her to say something, do something, understand something. Mazy was at a loss.

"Underneath this veneer," Eli said, "there is a piece of furniture that is solid poplar."

"Okay."

"Poplar is a very good wood. It's strong and sturdy. It's durable and easy to fashion into whatever you need. It's easily available. It grows in a wide area, making it very sustainable. But it's not a flashy wood. It doesn't catch the eye the way this fancy veneer will."

He continued to look at her intently.

"This is what I've been doing," he said. "I've been veneering."

It was as if he was waiting for a response from her.

"It's a beautiful job," Mazy told him, running her hand across the front of the music cabinet again. "Very beautiful."

"I'm not talking about the furniture," he said. "I'm talking about myself."

"Yourself?"

"Mazy, I'm a really ordinary, dependable, responsible, boring guy," Eli said. "Twice you ran out on me for some…some flashy something that caught your eye. I wanted… I guess I wanted you to notice me, to care for me, to fall for me. So I acquired some showy veneer."

"What are you talking about?"

"It seemed to me that what attracted you, generally, and what attracted you away from me, specifically, was the type of selfish jerk of a guy who would treat you like he didn't give a damn."

Mazy could hardly deny her past history.

"So I decided to be that guy," Eli explained. "I got on the internet and read all these complaints about these bad boys that women always fall for, and then I set out to emulate them."

Mazy couldn't quite take it in.

"I thought if I was the same nice guy who treated you kindly, you would throw me away like you did before," he said. "So all of the things I said, all of the things I did, were meant to be mean and hurtful and unkind, by design. I was playing so hard-to-get that I was sure you would *have* to get me."

"I can't believe this."

"It's true," Eli said. "I love sleeping with you in my bed. I don't ever want you to go home. I don't expect you to cook for me or clean my own house. I love having sex with you. But I love talking to you, too. And dancing with you. And watching old movies. And just being together. I'm not interested in other women. And I wouldn't walk out on a stray possum at a roadhouse. All of those mean, nasty things—I did them on purpose. It was all part of the flashy veneer that was supposed to make you desperate to be with me. I thought that if I could be the jerk you fell for, that I could keep you from falling in love with some *real* jerk. And finally make my own dreams of being with you come true."

Mazy was stunned. Before she could even think about how to respond, she reached out and slapped his face.

The bright red mark that blossomed on his cheek shocked her.

"Oh, wow," she said. She stepped back, stumbling into a work stool and sitting down quickly, as if she thought she might not be able to stand.

Eli put a hand on his cheek and gave a strange chuckle. "I've been secretly wishing that you would deck me for a couple of months now. The reality turns out not to be nearly as pleasant as the fantasy."

"I didn't know I was going to hit you," she said.

"It's okay. I earned it."

They stared at each other across an expanse of floor in a very long minute of silence.

"So you really haven't turned into…into a creep?"

"No. Or at least not completely," Eli answered. "I have to admit that I've learned some important lessons. I think I've learned that it is possible to be too nice. And that sometimes a guy has to stand up for himself."

He sat down on the stool opposite her.

"I blamed you, Mazy, for those times that you left me," Eli said. "I thought it was all about you and your…your defects that kept us apart. You didn't respect me and I thought that was a mistake in you."

"It was," she told him.

Eli shook his head. "You didn't respect me because I didn't demand respect. I wanted to be with you. I wanted you to love me. But I didn't respect myself enough to believe that you could do that. So I always let you call the shots, decide what we would do and when. I let you be the senior partner in our relationship."

"Wait! That's my M.O.," Mazy said. "That's what I always do."

"It looks like we have more in common than we thought."

"But not now," Mazy said. "I've changed. And I am changing. I told you that, but you didn't believe people could change."

Eli was silent for a moment. "I said that in the heat of an argument," he clarified. "And that wasn't about you, Mazy. It was about Driscoll."

"Driscoll?"

"I was afraid that you thought that *he* had changed."

"I hoped that he had," Mazy said. "But I haven't seen any evidence of it."

"I was afraid of you two working together every day. You told me that you didn't come back here to get back with him. But I was afraid that you might."

"No, that's not going to happen."

"Not even if he and Tru…work out their situation?"

"You're thinking we might end up as some kind of happy family?"

"Well, I did worry about that until Driscoll told me about the trouble you got into in Wilmington. He said he was going to use it against you in court. That didn't sound like happy family material."

"It's not," she said. "I guess I shouldn't be surprised that he told you. I think he sees you as some kind of a threat."

"It turns out I am," Eli said. "Part of my newfound bad-boy status allowed me a couple of very satisfying punches to that guy's face."

Mazy's jaw dropped open. "Are you telling me that *you* are the door he ran into?"

"Solid hardwood," he answered.

Mazy laughed. "I love it."

Eli smiled, as well, but his tone was still serious.

"Are you worried about what might come out in court?"

"It will never go to court," she said. "I've already told him he and Tru can be together as often as they like."

"You don't care?"

"My feelings don't enter into it," Mazy said. "It's about Tru and his biological father. Tru has to decide what that means to him. I've raised him and I love him. Now I have to trust him."

"You're a pretty amazing mom," Eli said.

Mazy shrugged. "I've had a pretty spectacular example."

Eli nodded. "We were very lucky," he said.

"We still are." She got up from the stool and walked the three paces that separated her from Eli. She wrapped her arms around his neck and said, "I feel lucky to be all alone here with what I believe to be a very nice guy. It could be totally perfect if he would kiss me."

48

Confessing to Mazy was like a weight off his shoulders. Eli was done with being the bad boyfriend. He had learned from the experience that he needed to be accepted on his own terms.

Having her walk into his embrace was the sort of terms he could get his arms around. He'd told himself when he'd decided to bring her to the shop that he was telling the truth with no hope or agenda. He was out of the manipulation business. If she could forgive him, that was good. If she couldn't, then so be it.

Slapping his face was of the so-be-it variety.

"It could be totally perfect if you would kiss me."

Even the nicest guy in the world couldn't resist an invitation like that.

Eli turned his head slightly and lowered his mouth on hers. Her lips were so soft and the taste of her was both familiar and sweet. The warmth of those curves he knew so well pressed against him. And the scent that was uniquely her essence enveloped him.

He both heard and felt the murmur of pleasure at the back of her throat.

"I've missed this," she confessed in the instant their lips parted.

Eli had missed it, too. So much so that at the moment

he was unwilling to waste his lips and his tongue on anything as unneeded as speech. He deepened the kiss. Spreading his knees he pulled her closer to him, wrapping one arm around her shoulders and the other on her waist as he drew her to his chest.

She felt so perfect in his arms. She was not perfect. He was not perfect. But together, they were perfection.

He heard a moan of pleasure. Eli wasn't sure if it came from her or from him.

With all the layers of clothes that separated them, there was nothing sexual about their touch, but the rightness of it, the real genuine oneness, made it seem far more intimate.

When their mouths parted, he ran little pecks along the line of her jaw and down her throat. He loved the sound of how her breath caught. He reached her collarbone, but was unwilling to give up his journey.

"Let's get this sweater off," he suggested.

Eli didn't have to ask twice. She stepped back and jerked the offending knit over her head, casting it off on the floor.

"The blouse, too?" she asked.

Worrying his voice might fail him, Eli nodded. He watched her hurriedly releasing the buttons. The last one resisted. He reached forward, thinking he would help her fumbling fingers. Instead, he ripped it open. The button went flying and the blouse slipped off her shoulders onto the floor.

"Pretty," he said of the lacy bra that hinted at what was beneath it.

Mazy reached behind her in one fluid motion and released the hooks and discarded it.

"Prettier," he told her.

She came back to his arms, but he stood and carried

her to sit on the edge of his workbench. He seated himself on the stool, which meant her breasts were exactly at the level of his mouth. Such an opportunity should never be passed up.

Eli tried to take his time. It had been a long three weeks, but they were gorgeous breasts and deserved all the attention he wanted to lavish upon them.

Mazy, however, was squirming. He knew exactly what she was feeling.

He rose to his feet and with two hands slid her skirt up to her waist. When he brought his hands back down, he hooked his thumbs into the elastic waistband of her panties.

"Lay back, Mazy," he told her. "I know what I want for dessert."

He spread her wide before him and ran his tongue from her knee along the inside of her thigh before indulging his sweet tooth. The sounds she made were like music to his ears, even when she got so loud he had to cover her mouth with his hand.

When she was still quivering with release, he climbed up on the workbench himself. He was nearly hard enough to hammer nails, but when he slid inside her hot, throbbing womanness, he knew he was home.

It was the last conscious thought he had before sheer mindless sexual need took precedence over all other natural inclinations, and their movements, both effortlessly timed and increasing frantic, drove them both to a peak of physical pleasure.

There was an instant that was both relief and joy, almost painful and almost enough to laugh aloud, before Eli momentarily collapsed against her.

He was heavy and she was small. He tried to roll his weight off her. But she held him fast.

"Don't go yet," she whispered. "It feels so good to have you inside me."

It took him a minute to capture his breath before he answered. "If you'll let me, Mazy, I will be inside you every day for the rest of our lives."

She gave a murmur of satisfaction. "I like the sound of that," she said.

He liked the sound of it, too.

They lay there stretched out across his workbench, connected.

Eli was still mostly dressed. Mazy was wearing her skirt and her shoes. They were both grinning like idiots. It was a crazy, imperfect, romantic fantasy. And they both reveled in it.

Finally he eased over to his side, but pulled her with him to keep them close. They couldn't stop looking into each other's eyes. They couldn't stop smiling.

"I thought you didn't have sex in this workshop," she said.

"I don't," he assured her. "I only make love."

"You indicated before that thank-you blow jobs were not allowed, but what you did comes pretty close to qualifying."

"I'm getting flexible on that rule," he said.

"Very flexible," she agreed.

"And what happened to the very nice guy who would never forget to use a condom?"

"Oh, crap," he said.

"Oh, crap indeed."

"I swear, Mazy, I didn't do it on purpose. I guess even nice guys can make mistakes."

"I'd say this particular nice guy has been making a lot of mistakes lately."

"Will you forgive me?"

"I do forgive you," Mazy said. "Because I believe that you can change."

"Will you marry me?" As soon as he'd said it, he knew it was crazy. But it was honest and it was in his heart. And he'd promised to give that to her always.

The smile that had so pleased him faltered. A moment passed in such total silence, Eli could hear their hearts beating.

"Maybe," she told him finally.

"Maybe?"

"The thing about change," she said, "is that it's not instant. It's not *poof!* I'm all different now. It takes time to achieve and time to believe. I love you, Eli. If you love me, I need you to give me that time."

Five Years Later

The little office on Main Street got a lot of foot traffic. Perhaps because it was next door to Local Grind, the most popular meeting place in town. The glass on the window announced it to be the Brandt Mountain Credit Counseling Service. Inside, Mazy sat at her desk facing Mildred Taylor and a mess of freshly cleaned brook trout in a giant plastic bag.

"Thank you so much. This will make a lovely dinner for us. But you don't owe me anything, Mrs. Taylor," Mazy explained, not for the first time. "The credit card companies pay me to help people get back on track financially. It's my job."

Mrs. Taylor shook her head. "You just don't know what you've done for us," she said. "I swear, Gus and I were at our wit's end. Couldn't sleep, fighting all the time. We couldn't see a way out. We want to show you how much it means to us."

"Well, the best way to do that," Mazy said, "is to stick to the budget. If something comes up—and it will, emergencies happen—don't try to keep it a secret. Come see me and we'll figure out a way. Time and determination. That's what it takes."

Mrs. Taylor nodded. "Every time we make a payment, we feel a little stronger," she said.

Mazy was very glad to hear it.

The business was not exactly what she had thought she wanted for her life. But she'd discovered that she had a real talent for helping people out of trouble. And in a town where her reputation had always been up for discussion, she had earned for herself an ample measure of respect and success.

After Mrs. Taylor left, Mazy was pulling up the stats on the credit report of a new client when a familiar truck parked in front of her door.

She clicked off her screen and waited as a pair of very short legs came running across the sidewalk and a pair of very small hands turned the knob on her door. Like a surge of energy, Jonah Latham burst into the room.

"Mom, Twoo is coming home!"

"He is?"

The curly head nodded excitedly. "He phoned Daddy and he'll be here in nine sleeps. *Only nine sleeps!*"

"Inside voice," Mazy cautioned.

"Nine sleeps," he repeated only slightly above a whisper.

"That's really good news," she agreed.

The door opened again and Eli came inside. "I take it you've been notified," he said. "He's like our personal town crier."

"I talked to him, too," Jonah continued. "He misses me."

"I'm sure he does."

"What's this?"

"It's a fish."

"Is it dead?"

"Well, actually, yes. We're going to eat it for dinner."

"Oh, okay. Can I go to Miss Nina's? She might have a cookie for me if I go there? Can I?"

Nina Garvey's bakery next door was very likely to have a cookie and Nina was even more likely to give one to Jonah.

"Just one," Mazy said, holding up her index finger in illustration. "One."

"One," Jonah repeated before racing around his father and tearing out the front.

Eli stepped back out onto the sidewalk to watch the little boy safely go inside the shop next door. Then he came back in to join Mazy, taking one of the client seats.

"Nice fish," he said.

"So why does Jonah get to talk to Tru, and Eli get to talk to Tru, but Mom, the actual woman who went through hours of labor to bring him into the world, doesn't get to talk to Tru?" she asked.

Eli shrugged. "It wasn't a social call. Jonah only got to talk because he begged."

"Not a social call? What kind of call was it?"

"Business."

"Business?"

"Yeah," Eli answered. "He got offered a summer job up in Maine. Before he agreed, he wanted to find out if maybe there was some work closer to home."

"What did you tell him?"

"I said good woodworkers are always in demand. Now Latham Furniture probably can't pay him as well as they could in New England, but that we'd let him live for free."

"That sounds good."

"Of course, he still got some negotiating in."

"What kind?"

"He wants to open the basement apartment and live there over the summer."

"And you agreed to that?"

"Are you worried about wild parties and loose women? This is Tru we're talking about. Such a nice guy. Everybody says so."

"Yeah, well, we know where that can lead."

Eli raised his eyebrows in a comical attempt at leering.

"I told him his mom would be giving the final answer on living arrangements," he said. "I brought you something." Eli pulled an envelope out of his pocket. "It came in today's mail."

Mazy took it curiously from his hand. When she saw the return address her eyes widened.

She picked up her letter opener from the desk and carefully sliced it open. She took at deep breath and slowly let it out before reading it aloud.

"'Notice from the State of North Carolina General Court of Justice Restitution. Enclosed the fulfilled Disposition of Deferred Prosecution/Dismissal.'"

She looked over at Eli and he smiled. "Mazy, you have paid your debt to society…literally."

She laughed.

"It's been a long time and a lot of payments," he said.

"Making things right isn't supposed to be easy."

Eli nodded. "So, what should we do with this?" he asked. "Do you want to crumple it into a spitwad and shoot it into the trash?"

She was looking down at the paperwork. "You know, I'm thinking I might frame this and hang it on the wall."

"You're kidding."

"Nope. I'm thinking it might be good for my clients.

Good to know that no matter how deep you get into trouble, you can change. You can turn the situation around. It doesn't have to define who you are. What do you think?"

"I think you are amazing," he said.

"Oh, well, you're in love with me, so that probably doesn't count," she said. "Now that I'm no longer a criminal on probation, how should I define myself?"

Eli was thoughtful. "Well, you are a small-business woman."

"Yes, I am that."

"And you're the mom of two great boys, a college student and a preschooler."

Mazy laughed. "Not particularly good planning on my part."

Eli shrugged. "It takes two to make that kind of mistake," he pointed out. "You are a valued member of the Brandt Mountain community, a regular churchgoer, unbeatable domino player and you are the love of my life."

"Hmm, I like all of those things, especially the last one."

"But you know, there is one thing that you are not."

"Which is?"

"You are not Mrs. Eli Latham," he pointed out. "What do you think, Mazy? After all this time and all we've been through, have we proven to each other that we are the people we hoped we would be? Do you think that being my wife is something you might take a chance on?"

She hesitated, more for effect than consideration.

"I do," she answered.

* * * * *

REQUEST YOUR FREE BOOKS!

2 FREE NOVELS
FROM THE ROMANCE COLLECTION
PLUS 2 FREE GIFTS!

YES! Please send me 2 FREE novels from the Romance Collection and my 2 FREE gifts (gifts are worth about $10). After receiving them, if I don't wish to receive any more books, I can return the shipping statement marked "cancel." If I don't cancel, I will receive 4 brand-new novels every month and be billed just $6.24 per book in the U.S. or $6.74 per book in Canada. That's a savings of at least 22% off the cover price. It's quite a bargain! Shipping and handling is just 50¢ per book in the U.S. and 75¢ per book in Canada.* I understand that accepting the 2 free books and gifts places me under no obligation to buy anything. I can always return a shipment and cancel at any time. Even if I never buy another book, the two free books and gifts are mine to keep forever.

194/394 MDN F4XY

Name	(PLEASE PRINT)	
Address		Apt. #
City	State/Prov.	Zip/Postal Code

Signature (if under 18, a parent or guardian must sign)

Mail to the Harlequin® Reader Service:
IN U.S.A.: P.O. Box 1867, Buffalo, NY 14240-1867
IN CANADA: P.O. Box 609, Fort Erie, Ontario L2A 5X3

Want to try two free books from another line?
Call 1-800-873-8635 or visit www.ReaderService.com.

* Terms and prices subject to change without notice. Prices do not include applicable taxes. Sales tax applicable in N.Y. Canadian residents will be charged applicable taxes. Offer not valid in Quebec. This offer is limited to one order per household. Not valid for current subscribers to the Romance Collection or the Romance/Suspense Collection. All orders subject to credit approval. Credit or debit balances in a customer's account(s) may be offset by any other outstanding balance owed by or to the customer. Please allow 4 to 6 weeks for delivery. Offer available while quantities last.

Your Privacy—The Harlequin® Reader Service is committed to protecting your privacy. Our Privacy Policy is available online at www.ReaderService.com or upon request from the Harlequin Reader Service.

We make a portion of our mailing list available to reputable third parties that offer products we believe may interest you. If you prefer that we not exchange your name with third parties, or if you wish to clarify or modify your communication preferences, please visit us at www.ReaderService.com/consumerschoice or write to us at Harlequin Reader Service Preference Service, P.O. Box 9062, Buffalo, NY 14269. Include your complete name and address.

ROM13R

PAMELA MORSI

31537	LOVE OVERDUE	___ $7.99 U.S.	___ $8.99 CAN.
31541	BITSY'S BAIT & BBQ	___ $7.99 U.S.	___ $9.99 CAN.
31540	THE COTTON QUEEN	___ $7.99 U.S.	___ $9.99 CAN.
31376	THE LOVESICK CURE	___ $7.99 U.S.	___ $9.99 CAN.

(limited quantities available)

TOTAL AMOUNT	$ _____
POSTAGE & HANDLING	$ _____
($1.00 for 1 book, 50¢ for each additional)	
APPLICABLE TAXES*	$ _____
TOTAL PAYABLE	$ _____

(check or money order—please do not send cash)

To order, complete this form and send it, along with a check or money order for the total above, payable to Harlequin MIRA, to: **In the U.S.:** 3010 Walden Avenue, P.O. Box 9077, Buffalo, NY 14269-9077; **In Canada:** P.O. Box 636, Fort Erie, Ontario, L2A 5X3.

Name: _____
Address: _____ City: _____
State/Prov.: _____ Zip/Postal Code: _____
Account Number (if applicable): _____
075 CSAS

*New York residents remit applicable sales taxes.
*Canadian residents remit applicable GST and provincial taxes.

HARLEQUIN® MIRA®
www.Harlequin.com